I pulled my taser ~~and stepped back into~~
the shadows of the darkened flat.
It's always better when you
can make an entrance.

They came in already half undressed. His shirt unbuttoned, her skirt hiked to the waist. Hands roaming everywhere. From the outfit I figured out pretty quick that she was a working girl, and not one of the registered ladies from the red light. I waited until she had his pants down around his ankles.

"Mr. Smythe," I said calmly, separating from the shadows. "I'm from the Credit Union."

That got his eyes open real quick. He stumbled to the side, tripping over his pants, barely staying upright. The hooker stayed on her knees, shuffling backward, keeping low. Smart girl.

"W-wait," Smythe stammered. "I can pay."

"Sorry," I said. "That's not my department." I raised the taser and took steady aim. "I'm legally bound to ask you if you'd like an ambulance on standby, though you will be unable to secure another artiforg from the Credit Union in replacement."

"Wait," he said again, "don't—"

That's as far as he got before my taser darts slammed into his chest and released their electricity. He went down twitching, and I stayed clear until he was down for the count. Back then, I was always careful about safety.

Other Titles by Eric Garcia

CASSANDRA FRENCH'S FINISHING SCHOOL FOR BOYS
MATCHSTICK MEN
HOT & SWEATY REX
CASUAL REX
ANONYMOUS REX

REPOMEN

ERIC GARCIA

(Originally published as *The Repossession Mambo*)

HARPER

An Imprint of HarperCollins*Publishers*

Orginally published as *The Repossession Mambo* in April 2009 by Harper.

This is a work of fiction. Names, characters, places, and incidents are products of the author's imagination or are used fictitiously and are not to be construed as real. Any resemblance to actual events, locales, organizations, or persons, living or dead, is entirely coincidental.

HARPER

An Imprint of HarperCollins*Publishers*
10 East 53rd Street
New York, New York 10022-5299

Copyright © 2009 by Eric Garcia
ISBN 978-0-06-171304-0

First Harper paperback printing: March 2010

HarperCollins ® and Harper ® are registered trademarks of Harper-Collins Publishers.

Printed in the United States of America

Visit Harper paperbacks on the World Wide Web at
www.harpercollins.com

10 9 8 7 6 5 4 3 2 1

For Garrett and Miguel.

You are weird, twisted people,
and for that you have my eternal friendship.

CHAPTER 1

The first time I ever held a pancreas in my hands, I got an erection. I think it was the adrenaline more than the mass of tissue and metal between my fingers, but the medical nature of what I was doing did little to deter the jolt of energy that hit me down below. Prior to that day, my main source of excitement had been sexual, just like any young man, and somewhere along the line, the wires must have gotten crossed. Arousal equals erection, so there I was, pancreas in hand, stiffy in the pants.

Surrounded as I was by four other trainees, there was little I could do but hunch over and pretend it wasn't happening. Jake, standing to my right and examining the clacking valves inside a fresh new heart unit, was positively glowing like a mother holding her newborn child. Even if I'd been able to tell him what was going on, he probably would have just laughed and told me to take care of it in the bathroom. He wouldn't have understood that I didn't want to feel attracted to this job, didn't want any kind of rush associated with what we were being trained to do. Yet at the same time, I knew, deep down, that I never wanted to do anything else.

And now I know, like it or not, that I was probably right. My future career options, as seen from my current vantage point on the fourth floor of an abandoned hotel, surrounded by scalpels, extractors, and a single shotgun, are limited at best.

But maybe I'm getting ahead of myself. Context, perhaps. I've never been good at context, but I recognize it's something that's valued. Peter likes it, it must be worth something. So here goes; I'll give it my best try. Bear with me if I get distracted. If I wander. Consistency has never been my strong suit.

———

When I was on top, I worked in the shadows. I knew how to get in, and when to get out. I was feared, respected, villified. The story's as old as the gig: Men wanted to be or beat me, women wanted to screw or slap me, and most days it didn't much matter which—the jobs went on like they always did, one night blending into the next and into the next.

Don't get me wrong—I remember every receipt I ever wrote, every 'forg I ever hauled back into the Credit Union. Those memories weigh on me now, each of them, like small leaden balls strung around my neck, pressing against my chest. Back then, though, when I was in the thick of it, I didn't take much note. Job's a job. That's how you get through the night.

Typical gig, just for shits and giggles:

———

I'd swung into the Credit Union after a long weekend, eager to pick up a few extra pink sheets. I'd made a few bad bets on sure-thing college football games and wanted to cover my losses before Carol noticed the hit on our bank account. She could be awful fussy when it came to that sort of thing.

It was a good time for the Credit Union and for those of us who worked in repossessions—the economy was booming and the credit rates kept creeping up, so while folks continued to buy, there was no shortage of those who defaulted and returned their merchandise back to the lender. No worries all around. For most of us, at least.

"You see this?" I asked Frank. "Says this guy lives north of Braddock." The pink sheet gave us address, phone, credit ratings, registered firearms, the works.

"If it's on the sheet, it's on the street," Frank said. "Why do you have to question it? Just go."

"That's a pricey area," I said. "I'm just making sure we didn't miss a payment in the mail." It had happened before; it will happen again.

Frank opened the door to his office, inviting me to leave and get on with it already. "He's eight months over—that's no missed payment. Hell, maybe he's got millions stored under his mattress, I don't give a shit. He's not paying *us*, so that's the end of that."

Frank was right, and I didn't argue the point. I'd seen it enough times—clients with cash who didn't feel the need to meet their obligations. Their fiscal choices were not my concern. So be it. I charged up my Taser, grabbed my scalpel case, and headed out into the night.

―――――

High-rise apartment, nearly fifty stories scraping the sky, and my client, Henry Lombard Smythe, lived on the thirty-eighth. The doorman gave me a nod as I entered and was smart enough not to hassle me—the tattoo on my neck usually takes care of that. A quick high-speed elevator ride and one ridiculously easy to pick deadbolt later, I was inside. No one around, so I made myself at home. High-end furniture, abstract art, views of the city out giant plate-glass windows from damn near every side of the apartment.

The photographs told the story; they usually do. I could check it all out on the pink sheet—date of birth, marital status, kids—but I've always gotten the most complete profile of my clients from the things they choose to put in frames.

There's Smythe—middle-aged, hair receding, a good set of teeth—next to a bottle blonde with great curves, both in scuba gear down in Fiji. Another of him on a ski slope somewhere in the Alps, next to a slim brunette who's holding on to his elbow like it's the last thing keeping her from falling off the mountain. Mixed throughout, photos of Smythe and a little girl, aging randomly. In one picture, she's in pigtails and they're at the circus; in another she's dealing with her first bout of acne and the look in her eyes says *hurry up and take the damn picture already*. These, combined with the swinging bachelor pad, made it clear: A divorcé with disposable income, choosing to spend his newfound single lifestyle traveling the world and making a general fool of himself with women way too young for him.

I would have made myself more comfortable—put my feet up, checked to see what kind of video setup he had going—when I heard the elevator bell *ding ding*, followed by a pair of footsteps stumbling down the hall. The uncontrolled laughter of the inebriated rang out as the lock began to turn, so I pulled my Taser and stepped back into the shadows of the darkened flat. It's always better when you can make an entrance.

———

They came in already half undressed. His shirt unbuttoned, her skirt hiked to the waist. Hands roaming everywhere. From the outfit I figured out pretty quick that she was a working girl, and not one of the registered ladies from the red light. I waited until she had his pants down around his ankles—I know, not much of a fair fight there—and nearly started her business. His eyelids fluttered as he leaned against the wall, expecting a wash of pleasure.

"Mr. Smythe," I said calmly, separating from the shadows. "I'm from the Credit Union."

That got his eyes open real quick. He stumbled to the side, tripping over his pants, barely staying upright. The hooker stayed on her knees, shuffling backwards, keeping low. Smart girl.

"Fuck. Holy fuck —" Smythe stammered. "Wait, I can pay."

"Sorry," I said. "That's not my department." I raised the Taser and took steady aim. "I'm legally bound to ask you if you'd like an ambulance on standby, though you will be unable to secure another artiforg from the Credit Union in replacement."

"Wait," he said again, "don't —"

That's as far as he got before my Taser darts slammed into his chest and released their electricity. He went down twitching, and I stayed clear until he was down for the count. Back then, I was always careful about safety.

It didn't take long to pull out the extractors and scalpels I needed for the job, and I'd barely made my first incision when something soft yet heavy whacked me upside the head. I turned to find the hooker, legs wobbly and eyes red with drink, standing over me, swinging her purse in my direction. "Don't you fucking touch me," she slurred.

"Jesus, lady," I said, fending off her feeble blows, "Why you gotta bust my balls? I'm not here for you. Let a guy do his job."

She was all of nineteen, twenty years old, I could see that now, not much older than Smythe's own daughter, and she was scared. All she had to do was walk out. Hell, she probably already had her cash—it would be the easiest job she'd see all week. But sometimes people do stupid things when the see the Tasers and the scalpels and the tattoo. Sometimes they get in the way. Kind of a shame, really.

She hit me with the purse again. Wasting my time, more than anything else. I hopped to my feet and grabbed her by the shoulders, pressing her firmly up against the nearest wall. I could smell the alcohol on her breath, mixed with the stench of way too much perfume, sweat, and sex.

"Look," I said, trying to keep myself as calm as possible. Remembering that I was talking to a child, more or less. "I'm here to do a job, that's all. Just like you. I've got paperwork and a boss and mouths to feed at home. That man on the floor is your client, I get that, but he's my client, too, and it's not my fault if he decided to start paying for blow jobs and stop paying his bills. So let's all be adults about this and let everyone get on with his business, yeah?"

She nodded—I expect she would have agreed to nearly anything I suggested at that point—and I let her go, kneeling back down by Smythe to continue my work. I wanted to get the job done before the effects of the Taser wore off; it's always such a mess to zap someone once they've already been opened up. The blood splatter is hell on a good cotton shirt.

I was wrist-deep in viscera when the hooker came at me again. I don't know if she'd already forgotten our little chat or chosen to ignore it, but she screamed and ran straight for me, purse swinging over her head like some crazed Viking in drag. With my free hand I pulled the Taser and shot my remaining dart; it hit her in the leg, giving her just enough time to glance down at it in confusion before 50,000 volts took over.

She dropped, I finished up, and dropped the Kenton LS–400 liver I came for into the stainless-steel sink in Henry Smythe's kitchen. His high-pressure faucet nozzle did just the trick washing off the blood and attached tissue, and before long the metallic organ was gleaming in the glow from the overhead halogens.

I filled out a yellow receipt, signed it in triplicate, and left a copy on Mr. Smythe's body. If his next of kin had any issues with the repo or its aftermath, there were numbers they could call. Funny enough, no one ever bothered. Just goes to show, I guess, that the system works, in its own way.

———

Ran out two more jobs that same night, then hightailed it back to the Mall and the Credit Union offices, where Frank was waiting for me. I'm sure he's got a lovely home, and occasionally I'll hear stories of vacations he's been on, but somehow Frank's always at the office. Like he's got a double taking his place when he goes home for a nap.

"Easy jobs?" he asked.

"Same as ever," I replied. We headed to the back room, where he took the artiforgs—the liver from Smythe, a set of kidneys from a bookkeeper, and a pancreatic unit that was only three months away from payment in full—and punched them into the system. From there, they'd be shipped back to the refurbishment plants of their respective manufacturers, where they'd be checked out for defects, spit-shined to a like-new gleam, and put back out on the showroom floor for the salesmen to hawk to new, hopefully more solvent, clients. For a small percentage, of course, there would come the inevitable delayed payments, the late-payment penalties, the increased interest rates, and finally default. Then they'd call me in and the circle of life would start all over again.

As I got ready to leave and go back home to Carol, flush with cash and the dwindling rush from the jobs themselves, Frank held another pink sheet up. "Priority job," he said. "Over a year past due."

"I'm tired," I told him. "The sun's coming up. I'll do it tomorrow."

"Double commission you get it done today," he said. "It's just a couple miles from here. Come on. It'll take, what, an hour?"

I took the gig. I nearly always took the gig. That's one of the things that made me so good at what I did—I didn't have much of a social life. When you're pulling out artificial organs for a living, dinner plans can really get in the way.

———

But all of that—the nights of work, the days asleep, the position of power and the bravado—it's a million years from where I am now. It's a past life, one that bears as much resemblance to my current state as would a career playing polo or managing stock portfolios.

Let it be known: Once, I owned the night. The right to go to the front of the line. To tell policemen to fuck off and get a smile in return. The streets were mine, to do as I pleased.

Today, I'm Mr. Smythe. I'm the one with his pants around his ankles, stumbling backward, hands raised, hoping and praying that the first shot will miss and give me a chance, however slim, to see tomorrow.

Hi-fucking-larious.

CHAPTER 2

All proper jobs—at least, every job I've ever had—begin and end with a full accounting of the materials at hand. Though my current daily activities amount to little more than huddling in the corner of this abandoned hotel and peeking furtively out the boarded-up windows every two minutes, I figure I might as well keep to the routine. It's sustained me so far.

My possessions:

One typewriter: an Underwood. Pale blue paint scraped down to the metal, worn from years of neglect and disuse. Found in the rear office of the hotel lobby, atop a file cabinet sporting a rats' nest made from decades-old newspapers. The ink strip is fading but otherwise in working order, which is more than I can say for the keyboard itself. The shift key is missing, and every time I hit it, the rough shaft of exposed metal spears my finger. Any run-on sentences are unlikely to be accidental; I'm simply wary of capitalization.

Alternately, the typewriter could be drawing blood on purpose. An autonomic machine, testing for my type, preparing for the inevitable surgery to come. For all I know, it's been stashed here by the Credit Union people as a sick joke. It's the kind of thing they'd do. It's the kind of thing I might have done. Perhaps there's a camera inside. A homing beacon.

The typewriter clacks, that's for sure, which is enough of a homing beacon in and of itself. Makes an awful racket, *rat-a-tat-tat*-ting away like a failing machine gun. What I wouldn't give for the soft strokes of a keyboard and the glow from a plasma screen to brighten my lonely nights. *Clack-clack, clack-clack*. It's sure to give me away, but I'm feeling saucy just now. How long this outlook will last, I can't say. It's not exactly up to me.

————

These sounds, these pages, are my sacrifice. For three months I've been holding down my breath, suppressing my sneezes, inhaling every cough. I move only at night, only in short, shuffling steps. This is what you do when you're hiding. The floorboards creak. Noise is a no-no, an amateur slipup. All noises. Any noises. *Call up the Appropriate Government Officials*, these noises say. *There's a man hiding out in the abandoned hotel on Fourth and Tyler*, these noises say. Can't have that, no sir. The last thing I need is to have to change apartments again. What with the housing crunch, it's getting tough to find abandoned buildings that adequately suit my elevated tastes.

This will be my typing regimen: One hour on, two hours off. This gives me a one-third chance of being detected, but I'm confident that anyone who truly cares to find me will do so without the help of the old Underwood here. They have radar, infrared, scanners beyond compare. Perhaps, if I'm lucky, those gadgets will be their undoing. No one thinks lo-tech anymore.

————

Let's keep going.

Paper: Half of a rodent-chewed ream of three-hole punch, found near aforementioned filing cabinet. Gum wrappers, tossed in a pile beneath the desk. Bottles of cleaning solution, long since emptied, but the labels are easy enough to peel off and feed into the cylinder of my trusty Underwood. The varying length of pages may pose a problem, but I'll attempt to fit my words to the medium at hand. I am nothing if not flexible.

Body: Eyes locked and loaded, full wide open. At night I have learned to sleep as the sharks in the ocean, lids propped up and attached to the top of my forehead with pilfered Scotch tape. I am ever-vigilant, the ultimate watchdog, protector of my domain, and I owe it all to the 3M Company.

Ears straining at every silent moment, so finely tuned they can pick up the cry of a dormouse amid the tide of midmorning traffic. Nostrils in a permanent state of flare, sucking up the available air, inspecting it for the slightest whiff of ether, and expelling it out again unscathed. Clean. Nothing. So far.

I need to reload my shotgun.

————

Weaponry, orthodox or otherwise:

Shotgun (1), double barreled, 23 shells remaining
Mauser (1), hand pistol, 16 shots remaining
Bowie knife (1), stolen from tent at Bear Scout
    campground
Scalpel (2), perfectly balanced to fit my hands and
    joint tension
Bone saw (1), worn from use
Rib spreader (1), little tactical purpose
Ether canister (2), 800-square-meter fill, give or take
Garrote (1), with two wooden handles ripped from

the legs of a chair, strung together with an
E-above-high-E wire from the busted piano in the
burned-out lounge downstairs.

A pitiful stash, I know, but it'll have to do me. Self-defense is an expensive proposition, and my pension ran out two months ago. Even if it hadn't, I'm sure the Credit Union has staked out my P.O. box by now—retrieving my monthly check would surely become one of my final acts, and my life, even at this stage, is worth a little more than six hundred bucks.

———

When I worked for the Union, I was one of the top-ranked Bio-Repo guys around. Level Five, and this is not idle bragging. This is fact. I made the jump in rank from Level Two to Level Four in just under two years, alongside my best friend and colleague Jake Freivald. It wasn't like there was a competition—not an official one, anyway—but Jake and I kept a close eye on each others' progress and made sure we locked our steps all the way to the top. I made Level Five two months before he did. Was I better at my job? Slightly more focused? Even a bit more talented? Let's sure as hell hope so. My life depends on it.

———

Everyone's got their favorite organs; it's the nature of the gig. Sure, you took the pink sheets that came across your desk and worked the clients that were given to you—job's a job, after all—but the liver was my specialty, specifically the Kenton and Taihitsu models, and I admit I took a singular delight in repossessing from the chronically inebriated. Let's face it: Anyone who keeps knocking back the booze even after they've been fitted with an artiforg doesn't deserve a whole lot of dignity in death.

One guy was so drunk when I broke into his place at

three in the morning, I didn't need to waste a milliliter of gas. He lay there, squirming around, legs kicking slightly, twisting his fleshy body in a slow horizontal mambo—nothing I couldn't handle—and didn't leak a peep when I started in on my business. "You havin' fun?" I asked him halfway through. My scalpel was buried deep within his viscera. The flow of blood onto the hardwood floor was steady, but lighter than I'd expected.

"Ohhhyyyaaaaaa."

"You ain't gonna be drinking much anymore, are you, buddy?"

"Ohhheee hee hee hee."

"Keep laughing," I told him. The sensor beacon blinked away behind a tangle of tissue, and I hacked for it like an adventurer scything his way through the jungle underbrush. "You just keep laughing."

The bloated bastard lasted a few minutes after I had his KL–418 in my hot little hands, and damned if he didn't giggle his way to the great beyond. Thank you, Jack Daniels, you saved me a pint of ether.

———

I'd rather do a liver job than any other organ, though I had many good nights running out that splenetic system from Marshodyne. The latest model—the one they've been displaying at trade shows for a year now—supposedly comes with a built-in detaching system that actually cuts the spleen off from the host body as soon as the nonpayment sixty-day grace period is up. Jesus H. Sure, it eases up the hack work on the repo job, but it makes you wonder when the day will come when we Bio-Repo men aren't needed anymore, when the organs will find a way to extract themselves from the deadbeats, squirm out of their host bodies, and waddle on down to the nearest supply house by themselves. I'll be long gone by then. Probably for the best.

Thing is, the liver's a beaut, easiest extraction in the body. Very little in the way, a clean path with remarkably little adjoining tissue. Everything else comes with problems. Jarviks are buried beneath all that bone and muscle mass, and the commission isn't worth the grunt work and ether release. 'Course, back in the good ol' days, I'd take any Jarvik job you could throw at me if the payoff was high enough, which is how I landed myself in this pretty mess in the first place.

Neuro-nets are—well, don't get me started on neuronets. I don't do 'em anymore, not if I can help it. I can't extract what I can't see, and no Ghost's gonna tell me different. Yeah, I took the required courses during repo training, but didn't fork over a lot of my attention. Ghost work may have the aura of respectability, and everybody's always up for a good story about your latest Ghost trip down some poor sap's brainstem, which makes it a lot more likely that you'll get invited to dinner parties. But livers . . . livers are real, solid, tangible. I can see them, I can yank them, I can hold them. I've got more important things to worry about than "phantom nerves" and "virtual sensory pathways."

Eyes and ears have too many bits and bytes and chips and things, and though I'm all for micro-extractions, I gotta admit to having been something of a slacker when it came to studying up on my nanoparts. Let's see, what's left . . . ? Thyroids are ugly, stomachs are messy, bladders are puny, kidneys are child's play. Slice down the back, a grab, a pull, and knock off for the night with a bottle of vodka for your pillow.

Basic limb prostheses are hack work, a real bore. No real nitty and only a margin of gritty. Hands, arms, fingers, legs, yawn yawn yawn. In the industry, we call 'em chain jobs. Short for chainsaw. Thing is, most of the extraction is done out-body, so you don't even need a full repo license to work the limbs. I used to send my nephew for limb work—he's fifteen, but the kid's got to learn a trade somewhere, and he's not the type for higher education. Hell, he's not the type for lower education, either, but he's a good little pisser and I thought it might be nice to make the repo trade sort of a family business. I couldn't ask my son to join up. Even if I knew where he was, I couldn't ask my son. He'd spit in my face, and I'd deserve it.

———

I haven't seen him in six years. Peter, I mean. My son. The last time I saw him, we were at a Snack Shack on the west side of the city, standing near a line of customers waiting to buy potato chips and beer, and he was beating away at my chest with his frail fists. Gotta admit, it didn't hurt, not physically, but I made a show of crying out in pain. For effect. Peter was always daunted by my physicality—dry weight I'm a good 95 kilos, nearly all muscle, whereas he's more like his mother—delicate bones, radiant features. He's a porcelain doll and I'm the gorilla running amok in the store. Peter looks an aristocrat in a time when aristocracy is crumbling under the weight of its own excesses. That's Peter, I tell everyone, that's my boy—beautiful and lonely and hopelessly out of his time.

———

Peter is my only son. He's my only child at all, the offspring of my third wife, Melinda, though for the most part he grew up around my fourth and fifth wives, Carol and Wendy, who were warm enough and kind enough to treat him as if he were their own. Good kid. Don't know how it happened, but he turned out to be a good kid. Melinda was gone from my life by Peter's second birthday, and I've only seen her once since then. Once was enough, for any of us.

We shared joint custody, that's true, but arranged the weekly transfer of our son through wholly impersonal means. Phone texts did the trick nicely for the first few years—I'd jot off a little note telling Melinda where she could pick Peter up at the end of the day, and she'd reciprocate. We'd leave the boy with friends, co-workers, anyone who'd take on the responsibility of temporary guardian and way station before one parent or the other could retrieve him.

This wasn't my fault. At least, not at first. I would have been more than happy for Melinda to come into my home, to sit down, have some coffee, talk about our week, but Melinda wanted nothing to do with me. She preferred to have our son passed around from contact to contact as if he were a piece of microfilm in a cold war spy movie than have to converse with her ex-husband.

––––––––

When Melinda filed for divorce, she wrote down only two words as her reason for seeking a dissolution of our two-year marriage: *Incontrovertibly self-absorbed.* Or is that three words? No matter. The question I have is: Did she mean me or her?

––––––––

Here are the reasons given by my wives for each of my five divorces:

Wife #1, Beth: *Interferes with my career.*
Uncommonly jealous.
Wife #2, Mary-Ellen: *Inattentive. Absent. Sexually non-performing.*
Wife #3, Melinda: *Incontrovertibly self-absorbed.*
Wife #4, Carol: *Adultery.*
Wife #5, Wendy: *Irreconcilable differences.*

Wendy was the only tactful one among them. She could have written down any reason she chose and I wouldn't have complained, because the truth is that I left her while our marriage was strong and steady, the greatest relationship I'd ever been in. Wendy could have taken me for everything I had left (not much), but she chose to dissolve our marriage in a no-fault state, placing the burden of blame on neither— or both—of us.

The rest of it is either lie or exaggerated truth, especially that bit about sexual non-performance. Now, there was a time . . . well, let's us say that there was a point in my life when the old badger wouldn't rise up out of his hole so quick, but *non-performance* is a strong word. And I never once cheated on Carol. I never once cheated on any of my wives. Carol needed a reason to divorce me from within her home state of Alabama, and adultery must have been the first thing to pop into her mind. She was always impulsive like that.

If there's a saving grace to most of my divorces, it's that there weren't any kids involved. No messy custody cases, no fiery late-night battles while the boy's in the other room with the pillow over his head wondering when Mom and Dad will finally kiss and make up.

Melinda and I, though, had Peter, and the stress of deal- ing with that aspect of the divorce took its toll on both of us. No doubt about it, we did a number on that kid. All we wanted to do was find a way to end something that never should have been started in the first place, but we never expected so much collateral damage.

———

Still, as far as I know, Peter doesn't blame me for our treatment of him. Peter doesn't blame me for any of his childhood traumas. Peter doesn't blame me for avoiding his mother. Peter doesn't blame me for our divorce. Peter doesn't blame me for any of my trespasses against Melinda save the very last one. And I don't blame him for blaming me.

———————

Jake and I liked to talk about blame. About trust. About everything, I guess. We had a lot of time on our hands. We'd theorize over whether or not there was a God, and if so, what He/She might have thought of artiforgs, of addictive anti-rejection drugs like Q, of people ascribing major sports teams wins and losses to His/Her divine intervention. I can't even claim that we were all that intellectually or spiritually curious; we were just hanging out and looking for something to chat about.

Most days, we'd roll out of bed and into work around 6 or 7 P.M., maybe catch a light dinner in the break room with some of the other guys. The back room of the Credit Union wasn't much more than a couple of poker tables and some rickety folding chairs, bad wallpaper from ten years back that no one cared to change, and a giant chalkboard divided into a chart that detailed clients, artiforg, time overdue, and the repo man or men assigned. It was good for coffee, light conversation, and the occasional stripper party, but little else.

But it was our space, and we used it whenever we wanted. Most of the other repo guys, they didn't have a whole lot of other choices when it came to socializing. It's hard to make friends when everyone thinks you're only waiting 'em out. Long-term commitment is tough, too. Out of the hundred or so repossession specialists I've known in my day, I'd wager that fewer than half were married, and less than a tenth of those stayed married for any length of time. I feel like I worked overtime in that department just to even the score for my comrades.

For me and Jake, being Level Five status had its perks—

we got first dibs at the best jobs, respect from our fellow repo men worldwide, and a pay grade commensurate with our abilities. But it also meant we had to deal with a lot of whining and petty shit from our inferiors.

Bobby Romain, a perpetual Level Two, was good at his job and looked the part—six-two, whippet thin, never said much and always sprung for the first round—but was continually misplacing his scanner during jobs and begging us to score him a new one before the bosses found out.

Vicente Salazar somehow made it to Level Four despite the fact that he turned down more work than the rest of us could accept. He wouldn't go into certain areas of town, refused to take jobs that required ether release. If the client's last name started with a K or W, that was the end of that—Vicente wasn't interested. The only reason he made it all the way up to Level Four was that when he deigned to actually work, he did it with a speed and accuracy seen in no one else except for me and Jake. Frank was supposedly thinking about promoting him to L5, but Jake and I put the kibosh on that one, quick. The guy can slack off all he wants, but you don't get five bolts kicking back every weekend.

Then there was Tony Park, perpetual splinter under my fingernail. Tony Park was a beast of a man, 110 kilos of muscle and sinew. He had the forehead of a man twenty thousand years his senior, a wide expanse of bone and skin that seemed to climb for miles before reaching a shock of thick buzz-cut hair, shot through with dyed streaks of green. Against all Credit Union guidelines and the mores imposed by society, he'd chosen to have his Union tattoo engraved not on his neck like the rest of us, but smack in the middle of that mammoth noggin. Just above and between the eyes, blasting out a warning front and center to

any and all unfortunate enough to see him coming. He'd
seen something like it in a comic book and decided that
if it was good enough for the funny pages, it was good
enough for him.

In addition to questionable fashion sense, Tony had an
unfortunately delicate temper. Despite what you might
think, this is not an admirable quality amongst repo men. In
this job, you're bound to get yelled at, goaded, sometimes
shot at and stabbed, and flying off the handle is rarely the
best option. Tony must have missed this part of the training
seminar.

As a result, Tony found himself in perpetual orbit, spin-
ning around the L2 and L3 marks, repeatedly promoted
and demoted as the years sped on. He'd pull down some
big job, take down a nest or high-profile debtor, and
just like that, he'd be flavor of the month, the next big
thing, easy bump up to Level Three. A week later, he'd
rip out some old lady's spleen in the middle of her 110th
birthday party at Denny's, splattering blood and guts all
over someone's French Toast Slam, and hello Level Two,
my old friend.

He was always on me about some favor or another. "Hey,
my nephew wants in," he'd say. "Give him a recommenda-
tion, get him in the program."

"Get him in yourself, Tony."

"I could, yeah," he'd respond, "but I figure the word
comes down from you, a Level Five . . . might mean a little
something to the assholes upstairs."

When I'd say no, he'd invariably slink away and
hit Jake up for the same thing an hour later, like a kid
trying to get his parents to let him go to the mall with his
friends. Tony never stopped—it was his best asset and
worst enemy.

As a result, Jake and I didn't hang out in the back room

as much as we used to. By eight, when most folks were just putting the kids to bed, we'd head into Frank's office to grab pink sheets. Sometimes we'd still be working off the same assignment from the night before, but more often than not, there was new work waiting for us.

Frank is old school, through and through, and doesn't waste time jabbering about the gig or the nature of what we do. He's got a business to run, and he doesn't understand why everyone has to *talk* about it so goddamned much. "You take all those chat shows and news reports and moralists jabbering on about the Union and put that energy into something important? Shit, we'd have jet packs and world peace by now." That's Frank—always thinking of his fellow man.

For whatever reason, Frank didn't love that Jake and I hung out together as much as we did. "I respect your little friendship and all," he'd tell us repeatedly, "but you're my two best guys. Working the streets as a team keeps you in one place. Split up, you can cover twice the territory, get a lot more accomplished."

"We split up all the time," I'd tell him. "I work alone seventy, seventy-five percent of the jobs."

"But when you partner up, it's always the two of you. Like you're married or something."

Jake would scoff, "If we were married, you think we'd want to hang out with each other so much?"

———

Jake and my wives never got along. He always harbored resentment toward my first wife, Beth, mainly because our long-distance relationship juiced up my paranoia something fierce. The other ones were either openly antagonistic toward him, either because of the nature of our job or the nature of our relationship.

Carol (wife number four) in particular couldn't stand the guy, and I'm pretty sure that one reason we stayed out of state was to keep me away from my best pal. Out of all of them, Wendy and Jake got along the best, even though she was the one who got me thinking about transferring over from repo to sales.

"Sales?" Jake asked when I told him one evening that I'd been considering the move. "You gotta be shitting me."

"Wendy's idea," I said, "but it's not a terrible one. I'm not getting any younger, and these fucking clients keep taking their shots. Last week I had a guy pull a goddamn bazooka on me—"

"But sales? You really think you see yourself sitting in a cubicle out in the front room?" He dropped into a clipped, high-pitched voice that he liked to do when making fun of the few salesmen we had contact with. "Mr. Johnson, we can give you this spleen at a rate that far surpasses every other corporation. You owe this to your family. You owe it to yourself." Jake shook his head. "You might choke on your own vomit."

"Still," I said, "a job's a job."

"Fuck that. Go dig ditches, if you're looking to get out. Go make license plates. You can't go from repo to sales. That's evolution in reverse. It just doesn't work that way."

He was right, of course. At heart, the job I was doing was the only job I was qualified for or happy to do, even if it was something that was bound to get me killed or disabled or, worse, hooked up to an artiforg. Not that *that* was ever going to happen.

By the time we hit the streets, Jake and I were usually two or three hours into a shift, having used up all of the remaining daylight hours with banter and the occasional beer. We'd roll through the streets, me driving and Jake shotgun, his scanner out, pinging the pedestrians and scaring the fuck out of most of them. There's nothing like the sharp ping of a scanner to strike panic into the heart of a crowd, and it delighted Jake to no end.

"Ooh, check out Fatty," he said, pointing to an obese man waddling down the street just in front of us. "You know his organs gave out a long time ago."

"Wager?"

"Drinks," he suggested. "Loser buys a round."

The bet settled, Jake fingered the trigger on his scanner and the digital readout came back almost instantly: *Kenton PK–5 kidney unit, 172 days Past Due.*

"Eight days left," Jake said, disappointed. "We should take him anyway."

"Settle down, Hoss." I steered the car up to the corpulent client and stuck my head out the window. "Nice night for a waddle, huh?"

The guy didn't even look back "Fuck off."

Rude, no? "How's that kidney holding up?" I asked, and made sure my Union tattoo was in full view.

The guy got one look and blanched, his face draining of blood as he stumbled backward. "I—I sent the check in yesterday," he stammered.

"You better hope you did," I said. "Eight days, and that kidney is ours."

It only took three seconds for the guy to spin around and hustle down the nearest alley, putting as much distance between himself and us as he could physically muster.

"Look at him go." Jake laughed.

We pressed thumbs, as we'd done for the last ten years. "Gonna need a new heart soon as he rounds the corner."

Jake looked at me, this strange glimmer in his eye, and for a moment, I wasn't sure if he was going to hit me or kiss me or both.

"What?" I asked.

"Brother," he said, "you'll always be repo."

There are three little girls playing in the street five stories below me. They are jumping rope and chanting this song:

> *There was a man from Troubadour*
> *Who got blown up during the war*
> *He would not die, would not concede*
> *How many artiforgs did he need?*
> *Stomach, heart, liver, pancreas, anus, eyes,*
>   *bladder, nostrils . . .*

If they go on, I think I will smother them.

This is the 115th day of my fugitive status. My house, my car, my belongings have all been confiscated due to mounting interest and nonpayment penalties. Fine. The house was falling apart, the car was a death trap on long-bald tires, and my belongings were of the knickknack variety, useless to all but the most ardent of flea-market bargainers. My assets, seized from all accounts, had long since dwindled to an asymptote—five alimony checks a month will see to that in a hurry. But that's okay. I don't need those things anymore. All I need is my trusty shotgun and cache of assorted weaponry. And maybe a few spare wits to get me through another day.

My case number, or "client designation," as the Credit Union so gingerly puts it, is K029J66VL. I have never seen my file, despite the so-called open credit law passed more than a decade ago. Every review application I submitted to the records clerk at the Credit Union was summarily lost, destroyed, misplaced, or mishandled, and I carry around with me the stack of crocodile-tear apologies the Union passed along in lieu of the actual documents. They are beautiful works of literature which promise that the information, though temporarily waylaid, is forthcoming. So, I am told by the man shouting outside on the street corner, is Armageddon.

Note to the custodians of my nonexistent estate: On the very strong chance that I should die at the hands of a Union Repo man, and on the equally strong chance that my body has been too mangled for proper viewing and subsequent burial, I wish to be cremated along with those official Union letters. I can think of no more fitting eternity than to merge ashes with the skillful lies of those who both gave me life and hastened my death.

————

No one is a Bio-Repo man by birth, no matter what the commercials and billboards say. And that slogan—"Help The World Help Themselves." Ecch. They make it sound like everyone's born to play the part of a killer, but that's not so. Like any other artistic endeavor, it can be learned. Some have a natural talent, of course, and some, like Tony Park, take to it a bit too easily, but there are nuances and techniques to the job that could fill the largest of instruction manuals.

But the Union persists with the "Born To Repossess" mythos. Just yesterday I caught a glimpse of a newspaper ad that read: "Learn a Trade. Join the Union. Fulfill Your Destiny!" It actually said that: Fulfill Your Destiny. They're always preaching halfway between the spiritual and technological, a precision religion bowing at the shrine of engineering and credit. Cheesy way to snatch recruits, but it works. Caught me. Caught Jake. Caught a lot of our pals, too. Of course, the usual codicils applied: We were young, we were foolish, we were bored after a long and overproduced war effort. We needed something different. Little did we know, we'd just be getting more of the same.

CHAPTER 3

A short quiz on the nature of battle:
   Soldiers are . . .

A) Prepared to die
B) Willing to die
C) Eager to die
D) All of the above
E) None of the above

The teacher's edition they use in today's Corps gives the answer as choice E. A soldier is nothing but an overgrown ragamuffin conscripted into a duty his adolescent brain can neither fully comprehend nor appreciate, and as such cannot be prepared, willing, or eager to do anything regarding his insignificant life. A soldier, they say, has nothing more than the knowledge that he will, potentially, be killed, and, more important, the belief that it will never happen to him. This is the Holy Grail of the military. Preparedness, willingness, and eagerness will always pale next to the mighty force of an irrational and unsupported faith.

The war was a bitch.

I'd love to type that without cracking a smile, but I can't. The war wasn't a bitch, despite what you might have heard; it was a bore at worst, a momentary diversion from real life at best. Two years of my life spent in near darkness, my body yoga-twisted into all sorts of unnatural positions, eyes glued to an infrared screen that rarely showed signs of life, movement, or anything out of the goddamned ordinary. No wonder my eyesight has dropped through the bottom of the statistical average. Had I known then where I'd be today, I would have taken on some artiforg eyeballs—the new ones from Marshodyne have zoom capability of 200× and near-perfect color enhancement. Sweet little babies.

Of course, had I known then where I'd be today, I'd have taken on artiforgs for damn near every part of my failing body. What's another twelve mil in debt when you're already running from the Union? They can't leave you any more dead.

Mother didn't want me to sign up for the war. Father thought it was a grand idea. Thanks, Father. Mother said it was dangerous. Father said it would build character. Thanks, Father. Mother based her opinions on neighborhood gossip and rumor. Father based his on his own stubborn ideology. Both were wrong.

Example: The Kashekians were a Persian family that lived across the street. Persians are what Iranians living in America called themselves after the first Middle Eastern war. Since the end of those first little skirmishes, Middle Easterners found themselves being subjected to snide remarks and sidelong glances from librarians and grocery-store baggers who thought they were doing their patriotic duty by snubbing the foreign infidels. It was grassroots prejudice, by golly, and it sure divided the "us's" from the "thems," easy as pie. So some bright Iranian came up with the idea of retrofitting their name to their language, and after a while, people up and forgot that Persians were Iranian and Iranians were Persians and the shopping-mall persecution came to a close.

This was a blessing for all Persians, but particularly so for the Kashekians, who wanted nothing more than to blend in with their adopted culture. The elder Kashekian was the spitting image of George Washington, only swarthier, and he passed his overflowing enthusiasm onto his family, perhaps genetically. When they took patriotic craps on their patriotic bowls, there's no doubt in my mind, their shit came out red, white, and blue. On national holidays, when my family would sit on our faded sleeper sofa, eat Italian takeout, and stare mindlessly at the end-less parades on the television, the Kashekians waved flags, held barbecues, and sang the national anthem ad nauseam. Father had to physically restrain them from erecting a miniature Mount Rushmore in the middle of our block one particularly fervent Presidents' Day. America was still the great melting pot, and they wanted nothing more than to be the representative feta.

Their son, Greg Kashekian, was two years ahead of me in school, and was as all-American as any Persian could hope to be. Football star, straight-A student, homecoming king, prom king, and president of the senior class. I thought he was something of a prick, but the rest of the student body obviously disagreed with my assessment. He kicked my dog once. No matter. Greg Kashekian graduated from high school with honors and only one illegitimate child and, in an effort to complete his patriotic duty, joined the military.

It was through Mrs. Kashekian that my mother obtained the majority of her information about the war. Hers was not a dispassionate viewpoint.

———

Greg Kashekian died on his eighteenth day in the desert, one of the seventy-five hundred and some odd deaths during the entire nine-year African war. His passing was a fluke, an accident, a needle-in-the-haystack coincidence that nevertheless convinced my mother that the deserts of Africa were a killing field, sand stained red with the blood of young American boys such as myself.

Mrs. Kashekian did nothing to alleviate the situation. "My boy was a war hero," she told my mother. "He died in battle, saving the other boys in his platoon. He took a bullet for America."

Beautiful. Not true, but beautiful. I saw the official report, the condolence letter sent to the Kashekians. They kept it locked in a hidden safe behind a staircase, beneath a chair, under a pull-away section of carpet. Why they kept it at all is beyond me; a good paper shredder would have done the trick.

The autumn that Greg died, I had the good fortune of going steady with his younger sister Tilly, a knockout in a summer sundress, and she showed me the letter one afternoon in a state of post-coital candor.

It went something like this:

Dear Mr. and Mrs. Kashekian,

I regret to inform you that your son Gregory was killed in a friendly-fire accident during routine peaceful military maneuvers near the coast of Namibia. I can assure you that his death was instant, that there was no pain involved, and that Greg died in service to his

*country. I knew your son well, and had the highest
respect for him as a person and as a private in the
United States Marine Corps. If you have any questions, please don't hesitate to write the Corps at the
address provided below.*

Sincerely,
Sergeant Tyrell Ignakowski,
M Platoon, 4th Division

A year later, Tig—Sergeant Tyrell Ignakowski—would
tell me in the privacy of a desert tent that Greg Kashekian
died because "the Iranian imbecile didn't know his dick
from an ejection lever." Sarge never was one to mince
words.

———

I remember the day they tweaked me.

They came to my high school in full military dress,
shining knights all gussied up for the next crusade. I was
in the back row of the lecture hall, cracking jokes with
Jake and a sixth-year senior we all called Turtle, but those
dress whites shut me up right away—the glitter of the brass
buttons, the crisp folds of the lapels, the blazing insignia
on the left breast. This was power. Authority incarnate.
Suddenly, they had as much of my undivided attention as
my raging hormones would allow. Stacey Greenberg was
sitting two rows down, and watching her cross and recross
her legs took up at least a fifth of my brain, but otherwise,
I was rapt.

"The military is not for everyone," they told us. "It's a
special job, for special people." I swelled with anticipatory
pride. Only later did I learn that the students who had been
called to the assembly had been culled from a list of the
decidedly average—no failing grades, no honors classes.

Lucky me, I fit the bill perfectly. Aside from a few B+ grades in my sophomore and junior English classes—hey, a boy's got to excel at something—I was Johnny Normal all the way. Cannon fodder, so to speak. But at the time I smiled inwardly, for I was going to be given the option of holding a *special* job and becoming a *special* person. Keen.

I excused myself from the back row and took a seat down in front.

Someone once said that it's the special people who are first up against the wall when the shit hits the fan. This is as good a reason as I can think of for keeping your butt firmly planted in the back row of any lecture hall.

———

The recruiter's name was Lieutenant Medieros, and he was the proud owner of one arm and one stump. The good lieutenant, it seems, had lost his left arm at some point during his esteemed military career. He didn't say how. He didn't say when. We accepted it. It wasn't so strange back then to see someone walking around with an empty sleeve hanging off his shirt like a garment worker's error—some war or another was always raging in some godforsaken part of the world, and only the wealthy could afford prostheses. The Credit Union, still in its infancy, had not yet opened wide the jeweled gates of mechanical rejuvenation to the poor and downtrodden working classes.

But the lieutenant had a voice like a bazooka and a knack for manipulation, and within ten minutes we were eating out of his remaining hand. He held us, rapt and wide-eyed, for a full half-hour, longer than any of our instructors had been capable of for the entire school year.

———

I took notes.

Places we would travel: Seven continents, seven seas.

People we would meet: First world, third world, developing cultures, savages, heads of state.

Things we would do: Train, exercise, hike, fight, play.

How we would do it: To the best of our abilities—further than we ever knew we could.

Why we would do it: For the love of America. For the love of democracy. For the love of freedom.

I believed every word.

———

After the assembly, Lieutenant Medeiros and his officers sat at a rickety card table outside the auditorium to answer any questions we might have concerning a career in the military. A husky boy with acne scars pocking his fleshy cheeks had cornered a command sergeant and edged him into a one-sided debate about current military policy in Southeast Asia. The second lieutenant, the only female in the group, was taking her time with three or four others of her ilk; I noticed Stacey Greenberg speaking quickly, earnestly within the small group, and wondered for a brief moment if she was talking about me.

But Lieutenant Medeiros was free. Rushing up to his table, startling the man with my sudden presence, I spat out, "Do you think I'd make a good soldier?" I made a show of flexing my puny muscles, though I doubt they gave the slightest ripple through my cotton shirt sleeves.

The lieutenant leaned back in his chair and gave me the once-over, clucking softly to himself. He cocked an eye, sizing me up like a prize hog at the county fair.

"You play a sport, son?"

"A sport, sir?"

"You got sports in this school, don't you?" He glanced meaningfully toward the gym entrance across the hall.

"Oh, yes, sir. Lacrosse. I play lacrosse."

"You any good?"

I shrugged. "We came in fourth in interstate competition."

"Fourth, eh? That good enough to get you a college scholarship?" he asked me.

"I don't . . . I don't know. I don't think so, sir." This was the first time the word *scholarship* had ever been mentioned in my presence. It sent chills through me.

"Your family got enough money to send you to college on their own?"

"No, sir, we don't." Same old story—father working hard to keep our family in the middle of middle class, grip slipping on that rung with every passing day. "Doesn't the military pay for your college education, sir?"

He ignored me. "You must have some other skills. You want to go into a trade, don't you? Computers? Mechanic? There's some awful good jobs for mechanics nowadays, if you have the right training."

"I—I don't know," I stammered, trying to force a grin to my lips. "I think I might like something like that, but . . . I don't really know. I think maybe first I'd like to see the world, like you were saying. Travel. With the Corps. I think I want to join the Corps." *That'll make him happy*, I thought. For those few minutes outside the auditorium, I wanted nothing more than to please this man, this magnificent creature of warfare wounded so nobly in the heat of battle.

It took some seconds to retrieve my answer, and in that time I imagined all of the possible ways in which I could be rejected from the position, right there and then. Every possible fear welled up inside, and my stomach did a loop-de-loop that threatened to take the next available turn up my throat and out of my mouth; I stifled a burp as I tried to keep from drenching these soldiers in partially digested school-grade lasagna.

Finally, Lieutenant Medeiros shook his head as a sentence formed about the corners of his mouth—then disappeared just as quickly. "Take these papers home and talk it over with your parents." He sighed, pushing a sheaf of letters toward me with his good arm. "You'll make as fine a soldier as any."

———

Lieutenant Medeiros tried to talk me out of it. I can see that now. It was a half-assed attempt, but he'd probably been trying and failing to talk boys out of joining the service for years, and after a while even the most passing effort can become a tremendous drain. But at the time I was blinded to all motives, hidden or otherwise, by those dress whites, those buttons, those lapels, and that beautiful shimmering insignia.

I signed up for the sake of a uniform. I was not the first, and I will not be the last.

———

Three years later, after my tour of duty had come to a close, I would once again join a profession with something less than the clearest of intentions, and I would once again have my judgment clouded by the accoutrements of office. Camouflage, knives, gas, guns—these were the privileged tools of the Bio-Repo man, and after two years of the military doldrums, I was ready to put myself to good use in the battlegrounds of America's medical establishment. Not coincidentally, these are the same weapons I am using to defend myself now that I am on the run from my previous employers. The war hasn't ended; it's just changed venue.

———

Jake never seemed particularly taken by the soldiers who came in to talk to us that day. He called them knobs and jarheads and a bunch of other things I'm pretty sure he'd gotten from the movies, but he took his papers home just like me and had 'em signed and ready to go by the next morning.

When I asked him why he was signing up, he just shrugged and said, "Free food. A man's gotta eat." It was easily the best reason any of us had.

———

The first time I met Jake Freivald, he kicked my ass. Third grade, Mrs. Tone's class, and we'd each been called upon to write a poem about our favorite time of year. I chose fall, partially because I liked the cool, crisp air of the season, but mostly because it was the first thing that came to mind and I didn't want to spend too much time thinking about it.

When the time came to read my poem, I approached the front of the class and read my words aloud. It went something like:

In the field of early autumn
I can see the cotton blossom.

Before I could get to the next line, I was interrupted by a voice ringing out from the open doorway leading to the hall. "That's not a rhyme, idiot."

The kid was bigger than me by at least a foot, and the heavy ridge of bone and flesh above his eyes gave him a distinctly Neolithic scowl, but there was something so plain about the way he'd said it that I thought at first he was joking. I continued with my poem, moving on to the next line:

Walking through the meadow still —

"It's not even close to a rhyme. I'm gonna kick your ass."

He walked down the hall, my teacher's only response a resigned sigh. "Go on," she told me. "Finish it up and sit down."

Three hours later, Jake caught me out by the bike racks and proceeded to lay down an ass-whomping of serious proportions. I got in a few blows here and there, and toward the end, I'm not proud to admit, I scored a glancing kick to the groin, but it only served to spur him on.

At some point, we were both grabbed by the lapels of our shirts and dragged down to the principal's office, where we were forced to wait for hours, side by side, wondering what our punishment was going to be. After a while, we got bored of waiting and started shooting spitballs at the school secretaries, aiming mainly for the ones with big hair. After that, there was nothing to do but laugh and realize we weren't all that different. By the time the administrator got to us, we were best friends for life.

———————

I imagine if Jake hadn't been walking by my classroom that day, or if the door to the hallway hadn't been open, or if I'd chosen two words that actually rhymed, I wouldn't be where I am today, and Jake wouldn't be where he is. But he was and it was and I did, and our fates have been intertwined ever since. Beginning to end. One way or another.

———————

Mother and Father threw me a going-away party the day before I was to report to Camp Pendleton for basic training, and it was a shindig for the record books. Not so much for the streamers and confetti and goofy party hats, but for the sheer number of girls who wanted to sleep with me before I went off to fight the enemy. There was something about my impending passage between civilian and military life that threw a flush into every girl's heart and drew a blush on every girl's breast. I didn't encourage it. I didn't resist it, either.

Father made a toast midway through the party, just as Sharon Cosgrove and I were emerging from the spare bedroom. "To my son," he said, glass of vodka-spiked bug juice held high above his head, "who will learn what it is to be a man." I smiled wanly, noticing with horror that the buttons on Sharon's dress were misaligned, a slipup made in haste by my faltering fingers. The party-goers cheered, and Father continued. "May he fight valiantly for his country, may he bring distinction upon himself and his family, and may he rid us of the scourge of evil." Drinks were tossed back, sucked down. Glasses were smashed in the fireplace. Father was always melo-dramatic when he drank.

But it was Mother who thought to add, in a soft, near whisper, "And may he come back to us in one piece." She really knew how to bring down a party.

———

Basic training was basic training. No need to go into it, just a lot of yelling and grunting and yessir-ing and nosir-ing and push-up-ing and pull-up-ing and running and stumbling and panting and wheezing and falling and crying and get-ting back up and doing it all again the next day and the next and the next. It was a chore, a strain on the muscles, but it wasn't earth-shattering. Not to me, and not in any meaning-ful sense.

Jake, perhaps predictably, was the star of the show. He had an indefatigable energy in whatever he did, whether it was playing sports or scoring chicks or staying up all night to talk about video games. I never heard him complain during basic, even when the rest of us grunts would carry on like housewives about our various aches and pains, and I only saw him flinch once, when a rifle misfired and he took a metal shard through-and-through to the flesh between his pinkie and ring fingers.

The fellow who slept on the bunk above mine was an affable guy from somewhere in Brooklyn named Harold Hennenson. For Harold, basic training was the be-all and end-all of the military experience. "You see how hard my muscles are getting?" he'd ask me. "Here, feel my triceps."

What the hell, I felt his triceps. "Hard," I said.

"As a rock."

"As a rock."

He'd drop and give the platoon fifty push-ups when no one asked him to. He'd clean the latrines. He'd take on extra KP duty. He was the gungiest of gung-ho, and he took the heat off the rest of us knobs who were just trying to make it through another day of backbreaking effort.

"See what I can do with my stomach muscles?" he asked me once, rippling his midsection in a tidal wave of abdominal strength. "See how strong they are?"

"They're strong," I told him, quite honestly.

"As a rock."

"As a rock."

Harold Hennenson would be killed when the tank he was riding in fell off the edge of the highest sand dune in Africa and burst into a fireball. He would represent another of those bizarre accidents that befell our servicemen during the War. He would receive a ten-gun salute. His ashes would be sent back home to his parents' crumbling brownstone somewhere in Brooklyn.

What Harold didn't know back then—what Harold couldn't have known—was that solid stomach muscles— even those as hard as rocks—don't do you a whiff of good when the tank you're riding in falls off a sand dune and explodes.

———

Had a repo job back about ten years ago with the Kenton supply house—direct contract, not through the Union. Outside gig, a little moonlighting, not uncommon among those in my profession. Frank, our Union shop manager, didn't care if we took on extra work, so long as it didn't affect the pink sheets we'd been assigned by the Union. Frank was a straight shooter, a fair guy—I once saw him knock off 3 percent for a low-credit applicant, completely on a whim—and I still feel a bit bad about going dark on him the way I did.

Not that bad, though.

I'd signed on with Kenton on a limited basis to bring in three artiforgs that had gone past their in-house grace period by a good ninety days because their in-house Bio-Repo men were all busy on other high-profile jobs. Kenton's been known to finance their own products outside of the Credit Union guidelines, and it's well known that they're more lenient with their clients. In fact, I've even heard of them requiring that the client be transported to a hospital, of all things, for some major extracts. That's above and beyond federal regulations, and shows a real sense of empathy for their clients' needs. Of course, you've got to have some serious equity in your home to even get into the Kenton credit office in the first place, but that's neither here nor there. Ninety days is grace beyond grace, and I didn't hold pity for anyone who welshed on a loan with straight arrows like Kenton.

The first two extractions were both livers, and they went smooth as, well, livers. The work was quick, cleanup unnecessary. But the third one was a stomach extraction, and I knew how messy they could get, so I brought along a few extra buckets, just in case: Two for the blood, one for the food remnants that were sure to be stuck inside the machine.

The last thing I wanted was to muck up my nice repo apron with partially-digested cauliflower.

According to the pink sheet given to me a day before the extraction, the guy had opted for a new Kenton ES/19, a moderate-size stomach artiforg with an expansion/contraction option which would regulate the food intake and, in so doing, the overall obesity of the client. The device could be easily recalibrated to a new volume setting by means of an external remote control which the ES/19 owner's manual suggests be kept out of the reach of children and small pets at all times. It's a swell little machine, top-notch all the way, and worth every penny. Still, it's a lot of pennies.

Pink sheet didn't say whether or not the client's natural stomach gave out or if it was an elective upgrade—usually it's cancer with a stomach job, but the rumor mill is always abuzz with new tales of organ expiration, everything from solar radiation to overgrown Szechwan ulcers. Whatever the case, this guy had the Kenton ES/19 installed in January of the previous year, and then settled into a predictable pattern: Regular payment for one, maybe two months, dropping soon into sporadic bi-monthly cycles, quickly degenerating into check's-in-the-mail promises. Calls were made, calls were not answered. Letters were sent, letters were returned unopened. Kenton gave him four months past grace 'cause he was some big muckety-muck over at the Tourism Ministry, but enough finally became enough and they called me in.

"You do stomachs?" asked the field rep, a slim blonde with a slight body who had dressed down to make her repo calls. She had obviously done her work, and knew how the average Bio-Repo man liked his women: Tight shirt, flared pants, hair teased to the sky. "We got you on our liver sheets, but there's one outstanding stomach job, might be tricky. I mean, if you do that sort of thing."

I gave my usual answer: "Everything but Ghost work. If the pay's right."

The pay was right.

Job started out as usual—scoped it, mapped it, gassed down the house, prepped the client—but here's the thing: My scalpel wouldn't dig. I planted, I swiped, I ripped into that flesh, but I couldn't get much further than a centimeter or two down before I scraped against what felt like a solid plate of steel protecting his midsection. Impossible. I cut some more, taking no heed of the blood that had already soaked through the mattress beneath the client.

After fifteen minutes, I had worked that body like a side of beef, flaying away nearly every ounce of flesh on that man's torso, and still I couldn't figure out how to reach that mechanical belly of his. Time was running out. But as my portable suction pump cleared away the pooling blood, I saw that my first guess, improbable as it was, had been correct: A metal plate barred my way, bolted into his body via attachments to his lower ribs and pelvis.

Now, why would a man go through the hassle of having a lead sheet implanted across his torso? To protect his precious artiforg from repossession, I suppose. But, try as I may, I can't see the purpose in this—the artiforg prolongs life, plain and simple. When your friendly neighborhood Bio-Repo man shows up on a doorstep to take an artiforg back to the supply house and suddenly finds himself stymied by a metal plate, he's not going to put Humpty Dumpty back together again once he's found he can't get what he's come for. He's going to leave the donor dead or dying, with nary a look over the shoulder. Heck, we're only trained in very basic paramedic techniques, and most of us play dice in the back row during the mandatory seminars.

Even if I'd known how to resuscitate the guy and sew

him back together, I sure as hell wouldn't have done it. The
bastard could drown in his own blood for all I cared. He
made me waste two pints of ether.

I broke his ribs, his hips, and his sternum, tossed the
metal plate out an open window, and walked out of that
bloody bedroom with his precious Kenton ES/19 artificial
stomach tucked beneath my arm. Appalling.

Harold Hennenson never would have accepted a lead plate
in lieu of strong, natural stomach muscles. And even if he
had, it wouldn't have helped him to be any less dead.

We went out on forty-eight hours' leave one Labor Day
weekend, me and Jake and Harold Hennenson, and had
ourselves one rip-roaring hell of a good time. San Diego
was the nearest big city, and we lit it up with the fervor of
religious missionaries, intent on bringing our message of
inebriation to all of the unsullied masses. I knew of two bars
with closing hours well past the city curfews, and through
conversations with regular patrons we found some after-
after-hours clubs as well.

Sometime during that blurry bender, I up and got myself
a tattoo on my right biceps, as anyone who is good and
properly drunk must at some point do. It says WHEN THE
BOUGH BREAKS in bright blue letters, and I still have it to
this day, even though removal would take only ten minutes
and twenty-five bucks at the nearest chop-doc shop. I don't
know what *When the Bough Breaks* means exactly, or why
I would choose to have it indelibly inscribed upon my flesh,
and I doubt I knew it even back in the tattoo parlor. But it
scares small children and entices large women. I like it. It
has style.

I have another tattoo now, of course—my Bio-Repo insignia, a small circle of black shot through by five golden

arrows inscribed upon the left side of my neck. That one will never come off, no matter how many times a doctor takes his lasers to my skin. Long after I die and my flesh and bones have crumbled into dust, I imagine that it will remain, floating ethereally above my ashes, a message to future generations that I was a member of the most feared profession on the planet.

Plus, chicks dig it.

CHAPTER 4

I met my first wife, Beth, on that trip into San Diego. She was a prostitute, and she was incredibly beautiful. She would divorce me six months later while I was sweating it out in the steaming heat of a desert tank. Our marriage had put a strain on her career.

––––––––

"I know a place," said Jake, leering at me and Harold through his half-empty beer glass. We had been in the bar for more hours than I could count on the blurry wall clock.

"We got a place," I drawled. "Look around, good as any." Our waitress came over, a pleasant college student who had been pushed too far that night by three soldiers with alcohol running wild laps through their addled brains.

She asked, "Anything else?" and amid some sloppy compliments and mishandled passes, we managed to order up yet another round of beers for ourselves. The waitress trotted away from us as quickly as she could, and we resumed our present business of moving from stone drunk to dead drunk.

After a few minutes, Harold remembered where the conversation had left off. "Jake said he knows a place," he mumbled.

"You said that already. You're repeating yourself."

"No," he insisted, building his voice into a whine, "a place. You know, a *place*."

Jake winked as best he could. "That's right. A *place*."

"Oh, a *place*."

"Yeah, a *place*."

I shook my head. The room spun. I resolved to speak to the manager about that. "We don't need a place. We got willing girls right here."

Right on cue, the waitress appeared with our drinks, plopping the mugs onto our table with practiced ease. Before she could read off our tab, I grabbed at her hand and somehow connected. Holding her delicate fingers between my meaty paws, I turned my bloodshot eyes up into her baby blues and asked, "Darling, sugar, honey—would you sleep with me?"

"Only if you were the last guy on earth," she said.

"But then you would?"

"Of course," she said. "A girl's got to have sex, too."

Given the right situation, I think I could have loved that woman.

———

I have only loved six women in my life, including my mother, and I married five of them, excluding my mother. But I could have loved many more. The cashier at the Downtown Deli, that co-ed who walks her Saint Bernard past the building every morning at 9 A.M., that sexy anchorwoman on channel 18 with the bob hairdo and pouty lips. I have a great capacity for love. I know this because that's what my therapist told me the two times I agreed to attend marriage counseling with my fourth wife, Carol.

"We got your tests back from the lab," said the man with a degree on his wall and the *cojones* to charge me three hundred dollars an hour for butting in on me and my wife as we fought and bickered, "and I would say that you have a great capacity for love."

I beamed. "So that's the end of it? Are we done here?" I had work to do, organs to remove.

"No, we're not done here," said Carol, agitated.

"Then what's the problem? You heard the man—I have a great capacity for love."

"The problem," Carol answered, "is that you're not living up to your potential."

————

By the time we found the "place" in downtown San Diego, we were sober, a real bummer. Dawn was fast approaching, and sex with strangers for money didn't seem so exciting without the rush of alcohol to smooth over the moral potholes. We searched in vain for a liquor store, but the squares had all closed up hours earlier; we were unfortunately under our own control for the rest of the morning.

Harold went first. I was nervous, I guess, for my first time with a professional. I mean, I'd done it all over the state of New York—even some in Pennsylvania and Jersey—even some while in a moving vehicle—but never with anyone older than me and never with someone as . . . knowledgeable as a prostitute was sure to be. What if my technique was wrong? What if I'd been doing it backwards all these years?

So I waited outside and read a *Vanity Fair* someone had left in the lobby. The operation was set up as a massage parlor, an old trick that I thought had lived out its usefulness long ago. Seemed odd to me that they'd still have a front like this inside the city limits, as San Diego had just instituted their Red Light District less than a year before—all bets off, sexually speaking—but I guess old habits die hard. The décor was strictly economy-class: fluorescent lighting, pressed wood, quarter-inch-depth industrial carpet.

The johns were streaming in and out of the place like horny worker ants coming to visit their queen. Doors opened and closed every few minutes, muffled moans echoing down the halls and about the small waiting room. This was a place for soldiers, from what I gathered, mostly Navy boys, but not exclusively—the clientele obviously ranged all over the armed services. I even caught a glimpse of a few familiar holographic insignias, but didn't say anything for fear that the Marine Corps soldiers would make me do push-ups or lick their boots right there in the lobby. A whorehouse is not the ideal location for emasculation.

Harold wobbled out through a sliding door twenty-five minutes after he went in, and I congratulated him on his stamina. "Didn't happen," he said, a little frown creasing his lips.

"She didn't go for you?" I asked.

"I didn't go for me."

Harold had encountered his first experience with the world of "sexual non-performance" long before I ever would, and I couldn't help thinking him less of a man for it. I know now that was foolish, but to the hormone-ravaged brain of a boy in his late teens, it seemed there was nothing in the world that could deter a real man from a toss in the sack once it was offered to him.

"You can try again," I offered. "Take my turn."

He told me to forget it, that he was done, and slumped into a nearby chair. "I've got fifty bucks," I said.

"It's not the money. Just . . . go on. Have a good time for me."

What could I do? I went inside.

Years after Beth divorced me—it was during my marriage to Carol, I believe—I received a particularly acerbic letter from her which read, in part, that I was a no-goodnik, a welsher on my debts and obligations, and that I should look into evolution classes in the hopes that it would help me to rejoin the dominant species. But tucked away inside the squiggles of vitriol was one sentiment which I'm sure it pained her to admit:

> *The moment I saw you walk into that massage room, your face flushed, your hands trembling, so excited that you had to cover your erection with that silly magazine, I knew you would fall in love with me, and I didn't mind it so much.*

Understand that from Beth, this miserable sentence was the equivalent of the most lovelorn Shakespearean sonnet. An admission, practically, that she might have cared for me at some point in her life.

So I wrote her back:

Dear Beth,

Thanks for the letter. It sure crystallized your perspective on me, though you know full well that my parents were married when I was conceived. Regarding your thoughts upon first meeting me: I was not covering an erection with that copy of Vanity Fair. I was covering a coffee stain.

> *Yours truly,*
> *Blah blah blah*

Nyah nyah nyah.

———

The sliding door led to a small foyer abutting the main "massage room," which lay just beyond a cheap bedsheet hung up to act as a curtain. A small Mister Coffee dripped a steady stream into its glass pot, and I helped myself to a cup. A little caffeine never hurt. I had another cup. And another. Minutes ticked by. I found to my surprise that I was still grasping the *Vanity Fair* magazine—I wasn't able to let it go. My fingers had clenched tightly around the spine.

A sugary voice called to me from behind the curtain— "You there, lover?"

No control—my hands trembled. I spilled the coffee. It stained my slacks. I suppressed a scream, dabbed at the stain with a nearby napkin, and held the *Vanity Fair* in front of my groin as I pressed myself through the opening in the gauzy curtains.

———

The prostitute—Beth—was naked. Just like that, splayed out atop the mattress. Blonde hair spread out across the pillows, breasts heading toward the ceiling, nipples pointing the way. She barely turned her head as I walked in.

"You're naked," I said. My mouth moved by itself.

Beth sat upright, her breasts drooping only slightly, dropping to either side. Natural, full, but still firm. "You new at this?"

"No, no," I answered hastily, fumbling with my own zipper. "I just—I didn't expect—I thought maybe you'd be wearing a nightie, and . . ."

"And you could take it off me," she finished. I nodded. Beth rose to her knees, yawned, tucked a seductive finger into her seductive mouth. She bounced playfully on the bed. "Weekends are tough for me, what with all the military bases nearby. And Labor Day—forget about it. I'm swamped. Dressing and undressing tends to clog up the line."

I told her that I understood, and we spent a few minutes chatting about the weather, the weekend, as I nervously removed my own clothing. The months of basic training had hardened my muscles, firmed up the contours of my body—perhaps not as much as Harold Hennenson, but I still felt myself to be an impressive specimen of manhood. This was not the first time that Beth had seen a young man flush with pride in his own body, but at the time I was bull-moose confident in my physique.

"Very impressive," she said, and I thanked her. To this day I don't know if she was humoring me.

"You want to lie down over here?" she asked, pulling the bedsheet to one side. There was a recent stain just below the pillows, and I tried to look away.

Her hands were all over me the second I sat on the bed, and I began to harden instantly. I wanted this to last. I *needed* this to last—my money was running low, and I couldn't afford another shot. "Shouldn't we talk first?"

"Oh Christ," she sighed. "You're one of those psych students, aren't you?"

I didn't understand. "The psych group from UCSD," she explained. "They come down, pay their money, and all they do is ask questions. How does it feel to do this, to do that, what do I think about the Red Light, that sort of thing. Am I demoralized? Am I victimized? Jesus . . . Tell you the truth, I'd rather screw than talk."

So we did. Screw, I mean. And then some. And as a member of the U.S. Marine Corps, I felt an obligation to prove myself more of a man than any psych student could ever be, so I made sure to keep damn silent during the act.

———

Peter—my son—went in for a few psych classes in school. I paid for that tuition—thought it would be a good way to screw his head on tight without having to fork over a wad of dough to the local shrink. But all it ever got me was six hundred dinner-table questions, a disapproving eye, and one full-scale intervention.

"Do you understand how your career is hurting this family?" the designated counselor asked me, hands folded, tone calm. Asshole was sitting on *my* couch.

"My career puts food in their mouths," I explained. "Puts this roof over their heads. That couch under your rear end."

"But do you know how much it *hurts* them?"

I didn't know if he was looking for something quantifiable or not, but Bio-Repo men don't deal with the abstract. It's here and it's physical or it's not our concern. "No," I said finally. "No, I don't. You wanna give me a number?"

That shut him up nice and quick. Man mighta had a doctorate in head shrinking, but he's shit outta luck when it comes to higher math.

———

After Beth and I came to a satisfactory end of our business transaction, we talked. I couldn't help it. "Was that good?" I asked, searching more for a grade than anything else.

"Mmmm . . . it was wonderful. You didn't have to—"

"I wanted to."

Beth smiled, held me closer. "Johns don't usually go for that sort of thing. Most of the time they just want in and out and then they're gone."

"'Cause my name's not John," I said, and she was kind enough to giggle. "You spend time with most of your clients afterwards?"

"Only the cute ones," she replied, and my chest puffed a little farther. The fact that she was being paid for her time had left my mind, and I took everything she said as the unvarnished words of a casual lover.

"I'm in the Marines," I said. I thought she should know.

Beth shrugged. "I probably coulda guessed," she admitted, "but I was a little wrapped up." Suddenly, she grabbed my hand—held it—squeezed it tightly—

"Aftershock," she whimpered, and rolled into my arms, grinding her groin into my leg as she moaned softly. It was easily one of the most entrancing things I'd seen in my young life. I could have watched it go on for days.

An hour later we had made love two more times, and the waiting room was quickly filling with paying customers. Beth gave me these last two sessions as a gift, and I couldn't believe my good luck—I'd been planning to lay some heavy bets in the weekly crap game back at the base in order to cover the expense of my weekend rendezvous, but now I'd be able to save my cash for another time.

"Maybe next weekend . . ." I began, and Beth, who had begun to prepare the bed for her next client, shook her head.

"Next weekend's no good—there's a convention in town, and I'll be working the hotels."

"Oh," I said dejectedly, surprised to find myself put out at the idea of Beth sleeping with other men. Sometime during our sexual congress, it seemed that a jealousy virus had infected me and planted its tendrils in my brain. Forget about your AIDS and Molié—already I could feel this new deadly disease throbbing away. This should have been a tip-off to drop any notion of a future relationship then and there, that my concerns, however prudish they might be, would ruin any chance we had at anything meaningful. But my intuition only whispers at me—it never shouts when it should.

"The weekend after next is open," said Beth, and planted a peck on my cheek that was more gratifying than any of the tantric positions we had occupied in the last hour.

And that was how our first date came to a close: I went to my home, she stayed in hers, and it ended with a peck on the cheek. Proper.

————

Basic training continued, an endless series of repetitive actions that our drill sergeant assured us would come in handy saving our skinny hides. I couldn't see how swinging over a pit of water could help any when we were going to be fighting the enemy in the desert, but after the first three stints of KP duty, I made a habit of keeping my mouth shut.

Got down San Diego way about twice a month, which was as often as I could wrangle a forty-eight-hour pass. I took on so many extra duty shifts—patrol, orderly, clerk—in order to clear my weekends, I soon found myself subsisting on less than three hours of sleep a night. But Beth and I had a swell time, mostly holed up in the back room of the massage parlor, testing out the tensile strength of her mattress and bed frame, though we managed to get to a few nightclubs now and again. Beth had been thoughtful enough of my feelings to clear out her weekends, business-wise, and only once did we have to rush out of a bar because she'd forgotten about a client's appointment she'd been unable to cancel. I waited in the lobby. I could hear the mattress springs creak. It lasted one hour and six minutes.

————

During the last few weeks of basic training, our instructors began to shift the focus away from basic military preparedness toward the practical and tactical. We engaged in mock military maneuvers, operations, whatever you want to call them. Our marching fields were transformed into great plains of faux warfare, littered with fake tanks and fake buildings and fake sniper nests sporting real soldiers writhing in real pain. Low-velocity rubber bullets were used. They stung like a bitch. One guy in E Squadron lost an eye when he took off his goggles to wipe off the fog.

On the last day—it was their mistake in the first place for telling us that these would be our last twenty-four hours of basic training—we cut loose. Red Team, ho!

We raided the Blue Fort, me and Harold Hennenson, and brought down three snipers in the process. Three-hour mission. Two-hours and twenty-five minutes of waiting, waiting, waiting, and thirty-five minutes of adrenal overload. Details: We shot up a flimsy plaster facade with a clip-full of red paint, smeared it across our foreheads, and wrote our names in the dripping excess while whooping up the sorriest of battle cries. We took prisoners, hostages, and bound them with ropes we pretended were thick sheets of eucalyptus. We interrogated them. We asked them for their names, their serial numbers, the women they'd slept with and their precise addresses. We were the RAF, the doughboys, and the yellow-ribbon brigade, taking our cues from every old war film we'd ever seen. We were Mongols making good, and we won the day.

Our instructors were furious. Each of us was given two hours of lecture, threats, push-ups, bunk and meal restriction, and one hundred hours' KP and trash-hauling duty. We would never see a minute of that time. They shipped us out the very next day.

———

The prior week, just before the Corps shipped our squadron off to fun and sun and gun in the desert, Beth and I did the deed and got ourselves married. A half-drunk preacher culled from a local bar near Beth's apartment,

Jake Freivald standing by my side as best man, and Harold Hennenson, who was often found scrubbing toilets with his toothbrush—not because he was forced to, but out of a fanatic zeal for order—signing all the witness papers in triplicate.

———

Unlike Harold Hennenson, Jake Freivald would live through the war. Like me, he would return to America feeling lost, without purpose, and without the necessary training to compete in what was already a staggeringly technological job market, where computer programmers were cast onto the street with the morning's refuse when they couldn't learn the latest version of C-Triple-Plus quicker than their counterparts. And, like me, he would turn to the one thing that had always sustained him through difficult times, the one piece of hide-saving equipment with which the military way of life had vested us:

We could kill people and not care all that much.

———

But during the wedding we knew none of this. Harold was alive, and Jake and I were just a couple of knob kids trying to get our business done before jumping onto a transport plane heading into the heart of darkness.

"Somebody here to swear?" gurgled the preacher. During the short ceremony, he kept turning his back to us, ostensibly to cough, but it was pretty clear from his breath that he was belting down a new slug of rotgut with every spin. "Swearing, anybody?"

Harold glanced at me, shrugging his shoulders, wondering what to do. I shrugged back, so Jake took the reins and stepped up. "I stand up for this man," he improvised. "I swear for him."

"And . . . who gives . . . who gives the lady?"

We hadn't discussed this. I turned to Beth, afraid that

our lack of foresight was about to put a kibosh on the whole deal, when she whispered in my ear, "Harold can do it."

"You sure?" I whispered back. "We can wait, I guess . . . Find someone else."

"Harold will do fine."

And he did. Stepped up, gave me my lovely bride—hair up; no veil; gown long, rented, slightly frayed at the hem—and backed away just as quickly. The preacher mumbled through a few benedictions, pronounced us husband and wife, and split to go find himself an after-hours club that didn't bounce men of the slightly stained cloth.

We made love in a motel room I rented for two hours, sweating fantastically in the San Diego summer heat. When it was over, when our time was up, I put on my military fatigues, bundled up my belongings, kissed my wife good-bye, promised to write her every day, and headed up to base and out to the battlefield with a new, purposeful stride in my step.

She took off work for the rest of the night. At least, that's what she told me.

In a letter she sent me while I was ensconced in one metal monstrosity or another during the war, Beth explained why Harold was the best choice to give her away. "He was the only man who had the chance to screw me and didn't," she scribbled, "and that makes him chaste enough in my book."

Stupidly—thoughtlessly—naively—I wrote back, "We could have waited and called your father."

I knew it was coming even before I got the reply letter, this one three days later than her usual response, the hurt and pain after all those years of good, healthy psychological burial resurfacing in every angry scrawl. "You're such a sweet kid," she wrote in part, "but sometimes you can be a complete asshole."

No argument.

————

Enough reminiscing. I'm going outside today. Here's hoping I make it back.

CHAPTER 5

Present day, present time, and my heart rate is back to normal—the audible series of beeps from the remote control welded onto my hip tells me I've reentered acceptable ranges—and I imagine my adrenaline levels have cooled from their nuclear-reactor fury. Hard night tonight. Hard night every night, but this is one for the books.

I went out this afternoon, a little reconnaissance mission into the heart of enemy territory. To be fair, pretty much any place outside of this stinking twenty-by-twenty room is enemy territory, but this time we're talking the big HQ, the see-and-don't-be-seen, the pigeon-in-the-hole:

I went to the Mall. Dangerous digs, no doubt, but it's a necessary evil predicated by my own seclusion. When it comes to staying alive for any length of time, playing badger is no way to survive. In order to run from the Union, a nearly impossible feat to sustain for any length of time, you have to know where they're looking, how they're looking, who they're using to look. Every Bio-Repo man has his own style, his own way of smoking out the bees, and if you know who's on your tail, there's that much more of a chance that you can blow the fumes right back in his face.

The "non-collection" rate for the Credit Union runs about .2 percent. That's one "escape" for every five hundred welshers, and those odds are regularly stated in big, bold ink at the bottom of every page of every artiforg contract. They must be initialed and signed in duplicate after a trained Credit Union reading clerk has dictated them aloud and ascertained that the client has, indeed, understood the nature of his debt to the Union, as well as the odds of his escaping the Union's clutches should he decide to flee with his as-yet-unpaid-for organ into some far-flung territory.

During my time with the Union, my personal non-collection rate was 0.0. That's a doughnut followed by a bullet hole, and it's a number that won me acclaim in the department as well as with the national Union reps. No one got off free and clear, and even those who evaded me for a year, two years, three at most, eventually wound up flopping around on a floor somewhere, wondering with their last thoughts how I'd finally tracked them down.

That's until the end, of course, but I don't think that one slipup counted. Then again, I hope it did. I'd hate to have ended my career as a Bio-Repo man without even one blemish on my record. No one should be too good at this job.

———

Some years ago, the Mall used to be a sprawling pedestrian marketplace in the heart of the city's west side, a mecca for trinkets and overpriced semi-designer clothes, much like any other consumer factory in any other town. Mothers scooted their children from store to store in bright red strollers provided by the management, girlfriends searched for gifts for their boyfriends, boyfriends searched for edible panties to force on their girlfriends, a lot of cash was transferred from hand to grimy hand, and all was right in suburbia.

The Credit Union was still in its infancy when the Kurtzman supply house bought out a doublewide store-front previously owned by The Gap and, two months later, opened the doors to the first artificial organ walk-in service station. E-Z Credit, open to the public, no qualified customer turned away. Atop the *Kurtzman Walk-In* sign, a bright neon heart—not the cartoonish Valentine's symbol, but an accurate representation of the bulbous, vein-ridden organ—pulsed in crimson and pink, the tubing flashing in a steady, even rhythm. And in time, as if to match the cadence, a singsong chant emanated from hidden speakers, the tune wafting its way through the Mall, luring customers like cartoon dogs inexorably drawn to the smell of fresh-baked pies. *Let's all go to Kurztman's, let's all go to Kurtzman's, let's all go to Kurtzman's, where a lifetime can be yours. . .*

The lines were out the door within an hour.

————

Arnold Kurtzman, who made his initial fortune recycling old NBA basketballs into cut-rate inner tubes before shifting his assets to the artiforg business, was a short, plump, balding man who never failed to attract the most dizzying array of young, beautiful women to his side. He was also a liar, a thief, a bad karaoke singer with a worse temper, and an absolute devotee of the French cinema. But despite these voluminous negatives, the man had a checkbook the size of the Eiffel Tower, and the cash he spread around kept him groin-deep in female flesh for nearly all of his life.

Frank, my boss at the Credit Union, had a genetic dis-

like of Arnold Kurtzman that went far beyond professional
envy, and he passed the hatred down to me. It didn't help
that we all attended the same conferences, were forced to
sit through his endless, patronizing speeches during inter-
minable seminars. There were few creatures on Earth I dis-
liked more than that foul-tempered, spittle-lipped old man,
which is probably why I lobbied for the job of ripping out
Kurtzman's artificial lungs two years after his business and
bank accounts went belly-up.

I was tickled to no end when I found him in a ramshackle
motel, roaches crawling over his bloated, sweaty body, his
brain partially eaten away by whatever syphilitic diseases
had taken hold, his only belongings scattered in a pathetic
pile on the stained carpet next to the bed. There wasn't a
woman in sight.

———————

Kurtzman's walk-in supply house was an instant hit
with the public, his *A Lifetime Can Be Yours* motto
the buzzwords on everyone's tongue—both real and
polyplastic—and it wasn't long before the other artiforg
manufacturers were angling for their own little piece of the
Mall. Gabelman, Kenton, Taihitsu—they lay in wait like
snipers in the underbrush, biding their time until a retail
space came up for lease; then, at one minute past midnight
on the day in question, they would descend upon the Mall
leasing office like storm troopers in blitzkrieg and throw
wads of cash at the rental agents until they cracked beneath
the green, green pressure and informed Banana Republic
or Pottery Barn that their time together, though fruitful,
had drawn to a close.

The unions and artiforg manufacturers swept like a tidal
wave through the Mall, demolishing everything in their
path. Soon the entire third floor of the place was filled with
supply houses, with the exception of one holdout company,

The Greatest Cookie Ever. This was a rocking little bakery that served a regular clientele with custom-baked erotic dessert treats, and—go figure—they somehow had the cash to match the supply houses when it came to lease-renewal time.

Nowadays, they're The Greatest Cookies and Organs Ever, and they do a brisk business in artificial taste buds.

————

Earlier this afternoon, the Mall (recapitalized some years back by overwhelming vote of the aggregate supply houses leasing office space) was an anthill of activity, medically challenged petitioners scurrying this way and that among the storefronts, trying to get someone, anyone, to give them a line of credit. There are no more holdouts inside the Mall, no last-ditch efforts to sell clothing or shoes or pastries of any sort. It's all artiforgs now, and it's the place to get up and go when your body won't.

The Credit Union sports the largest of the storefronts, a big gleaming portal practically slapping you across the face as soon as you walk in from the parking structure. Technicolor lights stream about the entryway, drawing customers inside, leading them down the path to a new, improved way of life. Ponce de León be damned—the new Fountain of Youth is inside a shopping mall.

Harry the Heart and Larry the Lung, two of the more popular Credit Union mascots, were out in force this afternoon, dancing in the way that only overstuffed, underpaid teenagers dressed up as artificial organs can dance. There's no sound box on these things—it's not like the ones they have down at the Union theme park (motto: *Where Entertainment and Rejuvenation Meet*)—so the two cartoon characters spent most of their time waving at the customers, tapping their shoes against the mall's tiled floor. At one point, Harry entertained a group of cancer patients by launching into a jump-roping act using a prop aorta while Larry the Lung clapped in time to the music.

I dated the girl who played Patty Pancreas once, but the relationship didn't take. Every time she climbed into that costume I had to fight back the urge to rip her right out again.

———

I left most of my weapons in the hotel this afternoon; it's hard enough to get through the weapons detectors without worrying about loose scalpels falling out of my pockets. Even in the city, it's the kind of thing that might attract suspicion.

I chose the Mauser, one of my smaller handguns, and loaded it with enough ammunition to get me out of a moderate jam. *Should I find myself up against a Bio-Repo man, I told myself this morning—even two—three, if they're fresh meat newly culled from the short training program—I will not hesitate to blast my way to safety. Should I find myself up against more than that, or even a single Level Five Bio-Repo, I will run like a roach with the lights turned on.*

Turns out I was being optimistic. Go figure.

———

The weapons-detection device at the Mall was easy enough to beat, though it's a sad state of affairs when you can sneak through any object as metallic as a semi-automatic German handgun. I followed my plan, culled from years of collected tricks and treats:

On the way downtown, I jumped into a china store and pilfered a leaded-crystal vase, along with an attending box from the trash Dumpster outside. My movements were swift and assured, but it didn't preclude me from taking momentary glances over my shoulder or executing 180-degree spins to check for tails. For all I knew, a team of

Bio-Repo men could have been waiting for me just beyond the next corner, ready to snatch me up in their arms, throw me into the back of a waiting van, and end it all right there and then. I didn't think I'd been spotted or followed, but that's the lure of many a talented repossessor. Silence is bait.

A quick ride on public transport—here the odds of being recognized dropped considerably, as the hangdog faces inside the bus didn't even look up as I entered, more concerned with their own misery than that of a fellow sad sack—and soon I was a block away from the Mall, a massive structure faced in beige travertine sprawling across 200,000 square feet of prime real estate. Word was they knocked down a V.A. hospital for this place, memorial stones and all. A steady stream of customers poured in and out of electric sliding doors set into the three-story structure; those entering did so with looks of determination and not a little anxiety, while those leaving were broken into two camps: smiles and tears. Hey, that's the breaks— sometimes you get a loan, sometimes you don't. But thanks to today's no-equity credit application, it's the rare down-on-his-luck sap who doesn't qualify for at least a bladder at semi-usurious rates.

Stooping by a small hedge, I unearthed the Mauser from within the folds of my jacket and buried it beneath an outcropping of leaves, digging the barrel into the dirt, using the gun like a miniature shovel. Standing up again, I strode purposefully toward the Mall, making sure to place the proper look of pain, degradation, and anticipatory humiliation on my face. The fake mustache and beard I wore were affixed with a strong resin that I had fished out of the trash behind a costume shop, and I hoped that it wouldn't give way to a firm tug by a security guard, let alone a strong burst of wind.

"All packages on the belt," droned the X-ray tech. I was twelve back in line, the lone metal detector able to accommodate only one customer at a time. Behind me, a young man held a small shih tzu dog to his chest; the fluffy thing panted heavily, its fur undulating with each breath.

"He's not feeling well," said the guy, noticing my stare. People rarely brought their animals with them into the Mall; it was very low class and generally frowned upon to drag a pet into any credit department. Loan officers were not impressed with man's best friend. "He needs a lung."

"Who does?" I asked.

"Muffin." He nodded down to the dog, and the thing stared up at me pathetically, big brown eyes rolled back in its head. "Yes, that's right," the man cooed to his ball of fur. "We're gonna get you a biddie widdle lung."

"What's that cost?" I asked. I'd heard of people getting artiforgs for their pets, but that was mostly celebrities who could afford to fund in cold, hard cash.

The man shook his head, saying, "I don't know yet. The vet told me he could set up a payment plan at eighteen hundred a month, but I thought I'd get a second bid."

"Good luck," I told him, then turned back to my place in line. Good luck, indeed. No union or supply house is going to extend credit to a guy who's only got his goddamned dog to lose.

The linchpin of the artiforg credit system is that all equity rides within the body itself. That way, when it comes time to foreclose, there's no way for the client to cut and run.

———

"Box on the belt, sir." The X-ray tech motioned for me to drop my package on the conveyor, and I gladly did so. Taking a step through the metal detector—the Mauser still hidden beneath that shrub outside—I came up clean and reached for my package on the other side.

My hand was grabbed, held. "What's in the box, sir?" A new guard, this one outfitted with a gun of his own. There were no external markings on his uniform to distinguish him from the woman still sitting on her butt five feet away, but I had a feeling he'd been trained to use that revolver with some degree of competence.

"A birthday gift," I explained. "For my credit advisor." This was commonplace, in fact, and not in the least out of the ordinary. In order to secure a line of credit or more favorable interest rates, customers often brought lavish bribes to their advisors, disguising them as birthday and holiday presents so as not to alarm the higher-ups. Of course, everyone knew it was going on, and everyone tolerated it, because the advisors would throw some of that booty up to their supervisors, who would, in turn, toss a few crumbs to their own managers. The series of kickbacks was endless, a thick layer of grease facilitating the slide up and down the pyramid. It was like Amway, only not quite as cutthroat.

"It's not showing up on the screen," he said, frowning at the display. "You'll have to open the box."

"It's leaded crystal," I patiently explained. "That's why you can't see through it. Look, it's very tightly wrapped, and if I try to —"

"Open the box, sir, or we'll do it for you."

I made a big show out of snatching the box from the guard's hands—the proper amount of insolence for a potential customer who feels he's getting the shaft— then set to opening the thing, carefully untying the very complicated knots I myself had made not thirty minutes before.

A minute passed, two, and the line of sycophants behind me, still stopped up, waiting for me to be given the go-ahead or be dragged out screaming bloody murder, began to murmur and mumble among themselves. Three minutes, four, and now there was audible dissent, snippets of criticism being hurled at me, at the guards, at the Mall in general.

"Get it open already," threatened the guard, one hand already moving toward that gun.

"You gonna shoot me over a box?" I asked incredulously. Behind me, the other customers were shying away, wishing to remain clear of blood and shattered crystal.

But he bypassed the weapon and came up with a pocketknife. Snatching the "gift" back from me, he tore into the ribbon with a vengeance.

The empty vase tumbled out and onto the stopped conveyor belt with a heavy *thunk*, setting off a palpable release of tension within the line. The guard stared down at the hunk of crystal for but a moment—long enough to decide on his next course of action—then walked away without even so much as a hint of apology.

"I'm gonna have to get more ribbon now!" I called out, but by that time he was already past me and eagerly abusing the next withering supplicant.

———

Thirty minutes later, I showed up again. Same line, same tech, same box under my arm, this time wrapped up in even more strands of ribbon. And once again, as I tried to pass through, the guard approached.

"You again."

"I needed to get it rewrapped. You cut up the ribbon last time."

He gazed at the display monitor, at the gray opaque shape clouding the screen, a grimace forming about the corners of his mouth. "The vase."

"The vase."

Impasse. As I stared at the guard, he stared at the display, and no one was going anywhere while we waited for a decision on the matter. The guard knew that if he asked me to open it again, it would take a good five, ten minutes to work out the knots, and that cutting the ribbon with the knife would only bring me back a third time with yet another layer of gift-wrapping.

I could wait all day.

The guard could not; even as we stared at each other and the package between us, the other X-ray techs were calling for his assistance in some matter or another, as if they were personally physically unable to badger customers into opening their bags for inspection.

Despite the tension—despite the very real possibility that I would be found out right here, right now, and shot on sight, my heart ripped from my rib cage and thrown into a chemical de-sanitizer somewhere behind the Credit Union walls—not a single drop of giveaway perspiration came from my brow. Bio-Repo men—the good ones, anyway—do not sweat. It felt like an hour, but the final decision must have come in less than ten seconds:

"Move along," said the guard, and stormed away, turning his back on me for the second and—as far as he hoped—final time.

I grabbed my box, shot a sheepish grin at the X-ray technician, and shuffled into the heart of the Mall, ensuring that my shoulders were slumped and my stride properly devoid of any victory or cock-of-the-walk strut.

Inside the closest bathroom, I entered and locked the farthest stall, tore open the ribbon with my teeth, pulled out the leaded-crystal vase, and extracted the .9 mm Mauser revolver from within.

———

My fourth wife, Carol, had a store the in the mall before it became the Mall, but she'd sold out her space to the Credit Union long before we'd ever met. Wise decision. Those

few holdouts who clung to their family-run businesses were
quickly expunged from every credit file in the known uni-
verse, and faster than it takes to say *Equifax*, their means of
doing business on any financial level was nullified. It was
those who sold out for gobs of cash who prospered. This is
the way it always works.

Carol's store was called All Things Good, and I remember going into it once, long before I knew Carol and longer
still before she would throw me out of the house and divorce
me on trumped-up charges of adultery. I'd gone in, if I remember correctly, during one of my few off-hours from the
job to find a six-month anniversary present for Mary-Ellen,
the second of my lovely brides. It would be our only anniversary together, but that's nothing I could have known at
the time, unless you count the weekly threats of divorce as
some type of precognition.

All Things Good was decked out in a frilly red-and-white
checkerboard pattern with stuffed bears of all shapes and
sizes peeking out of the window displays. Hand-knit sweat-
ers and hooked rugs lined the walls, and big wooden bins
filled with down-home goodies sat heavily on the floor. It
was country mouse meets city mouse, and I remember wondering how it made any money.

It didn't, I later found out.

But it was in the back of the store, behind the jars of pre-
serves and fresh-baked bread, beyond the stacks of home-
made glycerin soaps from which you could slice your own
chunk and pay by the pound, past the hand-carved jig-cut
wooden puzzles interlocking in a thousand different directions, where I found the items of most interest to me. Tucked
beneath an unassuming canopy was a small glass counter
displaying ten different types of long, rectangular plastic
boxes, each sporting two stubby metallic prongs at the far
end. They looked familiar, somehow, but the juxtaposition

among all this rural paraphernalia had my recognition center twisted and bent.

I called over the shopkeep—can't remember now if it was Carol, her sister, or one of the high-school kids they hired during the summer—and inquired about the boxes.

"They're Tasers," she said plainly.

"Tasers."

"To stun people."

I knew what they did—I used them nearly every week, in fact. If my client wasn't in a controlled, closed environment like a car or an apartment, ether release wouldn't do the job I needed it to, making the Taser the next best method of inducing immobility. What I couldn't understand is how the electrical devices had found their way into this otherwise homey store.

"I thought this was a crafts shop," I said.

The clerk shook her head. "It's called All Things Good."

"Tasers are good?"

"Safety," she told me, placing a hand over mine. "Safety is good."

———

I could have loved that woman, too. If it was Carol, I did.

———

The Credit Union queues were short this afternoon; the line stretched out the door, of course, but only by thirty feet or so. On a busy day, one of those Tuesdays just after a long holiday weekend when middle-aged beer-gut warriors burst themselves silly playing sports twenty years too young for their bodies, the lines could run a hundred yards or more, snaking around and about the mall, twisting through one another in a monstrous human braid. Once upon a time, the Mall management called in a famous theme-park designer to regulate the line movement, but even he was unable to tame the haphazard twists and turns of misery.

But earlier today, there were no more than fifteen or twenty folks poking out of the gleaming alabaster double doors of the Credit Union, not enough people to lose myself in the crowd. Even with the fake beard and mustache, there were too many people who knew me here; I couldn't take the chance of getting noticed.

I walked past the Credit Union and toward the back bathrooms, where I knew of an emergency exit that led out to the loading dock. Years ago, smokers who weren't allowed to do their business indoors had figured out how to jam open the exit without tripping the alarm, and no one had ever bothered to fix it. My plan was to sneak in through the back door of the Union and do my business that way.

Fortunately, I saw an even better option. Sitting on the edge of the loading dock, his two blue furry legs dangling off the side, was Larry the Lung—or at least the bottom half of him. The top of the mascot costume sat, lifeless, on the ground, while the teenager who the Union had hired to play the organ dragged on a cigarette. He took long, slow puffs, releasing his stress into his own cardiovascular system.

I approached from behind, tapping the gangly kid on the shoulder. He must have been six-one, six-two, and couldn't have weighed more than a buck fifty. As he turned, I plucked the cigarette from the Lung's mouth. "Aren't you setting a bad example?"

"Hey, pal, what the fuck," he started, "I'm on a break."

That's about when he got a look at me, and probably—no, definitely—wet himself. Even with the fake beard and mustache, he knew exactly who I was, and his bladder didn't like it. "What's the waist size in that thing?" I demanded.

"What?"

"Your waist size. What is it?"

"Twenty-eight," he said.

Fucking metabolism. I knocked him out with a quick elbow to the head and dragged him out of the suit. His urine had already stained the lower capillaries, but this wasn't a time to be picky.

———

I wasn't 30 feet from the Credit Union doors when a pudgy man and his similarly chubby wife jogged up to me, breasts flopping. "Hi, Larry," they chimed. "Can we take a picture?"

The last thing I wanted to do was get involved in any Kodak moments, but I had to play the part to keep up the charade. I gave a little thumbs-up with my lung fingers, and the two of them crowded around me while they got another potential client to snap the photo.

After it was over, the husband kept talking. "Third try today," he said, a bit sadly. People tend to talk to each other in these lines, I've noticed. Sharing their suffering as a way to defeat it. Spread the wealth around. All I could do was shake back and forth in a gesture of lung-sadness. Pantomime's a rough art.

As he nodded furiously, the second and third chin beneath his mouth jiggled back and forth. "It's her pancreas. Cancer's what they say. We stood in line for two hours at Kenton this morning, but they turned us down. Gabelman, too."

There are other suppliers, I wanted to say. They didn't have to go to the Union just yet. The supply houses, direct-lenders of their goods, tend to be more lax in their percentage rates and, should it come down to it, nonpayment grace periods, so it's always a good choice to try them before outsourcing to the Union.

As if reading my mind, the woman piped up, "We got ourselves too many negative checks already. One more and they'll never take us."

On that, they were right. Every time a supply or credit house turns down a prospective customer, the black mark of rejection gets instantly applied to their file and sent out into the informational ether for any and all to enjoy. I had no doubt that the Credit Union counselor would take one look at their file, shake his head softly, and promptly press the UNAPPROVED button on his keyboard. They could try other houses, other private loan options, but more likely than not, it's all over for Ma and Pa Kettle. She'll be dead within months.

A Lifetime Can Be Yours!

———

I shouldn't mock the marketing departments; they're what makes the entire industry tick in the first place. That's what people don't understand about the artiforg business—the marketing folks are the ones driving the car; the technology isn't doing much more than mindlessly stomping on the gas.

Let's say the Taihitsu Corporation decides that it's going to roll out a brand-new line of artiforg spleens. This is a top-level decision, often the brainchild of a new VP who wants to make his mark on the company before his almost certain ouster from the corporation eight months later. Hollywood studio chiefs have nothing on artiforg management when it comes to preparing resumes.

So spleens it is, and the idea is sent first to the marketing department; those folks neither bother with nor care about the medical components of the system—what a spleen does, how it works, why it works, how this spleen can do it even better—because they're workaday concepts and, in a marketing sense, boring. So they brainstorm up some extras first, like which color options the client will have, or whether the new spleen should also be able to detect police radar. There's a lot of one-upmanship in the artiforg business; if one supply house tacks on a new feature, the rest are sure to follow and raise the hand. From what I understand, the competition is fierce and incredibly draining, so the marketing people tend to take a lot of lunches and attend a lot of seaside conferences.

The ad campaign is created next, most often revolving around the new design features. A spleen, for example, might get a full television workup, with maybe some film product placement, especially if they can work in the radar detection during a chase scene. Print ads are distributed, billboards are erected, TV commercials are blasted, and the publicity machine gears up.

Orders are taken. No one wants the old Spleen-O-Matic anymore; sure, it still helps the body fight off infection, but what's the point of a spleen if it won't help you do ninety-five on the freeway? The frenzy takes over, and soon there are thousands of potential clients forking over reserve deposits and down payments, and the VP who thought it all up in the first place goes on a two-month vacation to Fiji.

Finally, they go to the company medical engineers, who are told they actually have to build the damned thing, using five-color ads from fashion magazines as their blueprints. The important thing, the engineers are told, is to work in the radar detection. If that fails, so does the business.

Somehow, the engineers are able to reverse-design this thing so it actually works, and in enough time to beat the Christmas rush. Now Grandma can conquer that nagging cough and drag down the boulevard without fear of police reprisal thanks to the Taihitsu Corporation and their miraculous splenetic efforts.

But before the artiforg is delivered to and implanted inside Grandma, it takes a run through the Taihitsu security offices. Here, a crew of specially trained Bio-Repo assistants being paid just over minimum wage weld a passive transmitter into the framework of the device, a rectangular chip no larger than a hair on their knuckles. It is placed in an inconspicuous, nearly invisible spot, so that even if the client were somehow able to access his own artiforg's interior, he would be unable to detect and remove the chip.

And there it sits, dormant, quiet, happy, and content in Grandma's new spleen, until a Bio-Repo man walks by with a scanner and pings it into life. Instantly, the scanner's readout displays the artiforg's manufacturer, date of construction, and leasing supply house. If the Bio-Repo man in question is not looking to repossess a spleen, or if the client to which he's been assigned is not an elderly woman, he strolls by with a tip of his hat and continues to scan the rest of the neighborhood, confident that he will soon smoke out the deadbeat.

If, on the other hand, Grandma hasn't been paying her bills . . .

This is why I rarely venture outside.

———

After twelve more photo opportunities and a couple of babies I was somehow supposed to kiss through two inches of fur and Lycra, I was through the double doors and inside the belly of the beast, the Credit Union itself. Here is where things could have gone terribly wrong, and nearly did, so listen up:

I was looking for a wanted poster. *My* wanted poster. It might have been sheer folly on my part, overextended megalomania, to believe that I'd be important enough to make the Union's Hundred Most Wanted List, but I had a feeling that they'd want to rein in their former employee as soon as possible. As it was, I'd stayed out of their clutches for three months now, slipped like water through their fists and remained alive longer than 99 percent of the non-pay cases, and the bare numbers alone had to rankle the higher-ups.

Heavy iron railings snaked their way through the Union lobby, directing traffic in a manner they were never able to establish and maintain outside the sliding doors. It reminded me of a trip I took to the Middle East once when I was tracking down a deadbeat sheikh who skipped town with six-hundred grand worth of Union-financed intestine. The guy bribed me in the end, offered to pay off his debts and give me a little extra on the side, but he caught me between marriages and in a rotten mood, so I took what I came for and left him on the floor of a brushed marble ballroom in the middle of his desert palace.

Point is, on the way into the country, I was routed through a series of concrete bunkers set up in a serpentine path at a distance from one another that made it impossible to drive straight through the border at any speed over 16 kilometers an hour. And, to make matters crystal clear to any vacationing tourist no matter how obtuse, loyalist soldiers were stationed atop these bunkers wielding automatic weapons of indeterminate origin. All I knew was that one pull of the trigger would make Swiss cheese out of my rental car, so I took it slow and easy on the drive, little old lady from Pasadena all the way.

That's a bit how I felt this morning, trapped between these waist-high rails, a cadre of Union security goons strutting up and down, barking at us to have our papers ready and in order once we reached the front of the line. I tried to worm past the riffraff, waving and dancing a lung-ish dance as I went, aping the moves I'd seen the real Larry make countless times in the past. Had I not been acutely aware of the Tasers and pistols all around me, I would have felt like a complete idiot. As it stood, I was glad for the anonymity, however pathetic.

If I ever see that kid again, the one who usually inhabits the lung costume, I'll cut him a little more slack. The peripheral vision in that thing is nearly nonexistent, and I probably knocked over a few ailing clients along the way. At one point, I bounced off the railing and into what felt like a wall—albeit one with thickly muscled arms.

"The fuck outta my way," growled a voice, and even before I got the mesh eyeholes turned around to see, I knew I'd made a big mistake.

Tony Park's beady little eyes and gigantic forehead pressed hard against the fabric of the costume, as if he was trying to climb inside with me. "Sorry, sir," I mumbled, trying to disguise my voice with a post-adolescent break.

Tony didn't give up. If anything, he only leaned in farther. A rank odor came off his body, like seaweed gone bad. "Keep your fucking eyes on the road or I'll pluck 'em out of your goddamned head."

I gave the best thumbs-up I could with the big white mittens I was wearing and shuffled away as best as possible. I could feel Tony's eyes boring into the back of my head—lung head—but didn't stop and turn. No need to give him any more reasons to bother me. It's not that I'd mind throwing down with the guy; he deserves to be taken down a peg. I just didn't want to waste bullets when they might be needed elsewhere.

Halfway up the line, the railing joined up with a wall, and I was able to peruse the abundant literature lining the gleaming marble. Most of it was come-on advertisements, hot talk designed to get a customer to part with more of his organs in favor of higher-grade, longer-lasting goods. *Can't belt it back like you could in grade school?* asked one ad in bright beer-colored yellow. *Try a new Taihitsu Liver today!*

But farther ahead, past the ads and the veiled threats, was

the meat-and-potatoes of this wall, the frowning faces of
the Hundred Most Wanted. Each poster measured a robust
eleven by sixteen, and aside from a full-color photo and
basic statistics on the debtor, the attached info sheets went
so far as to list last known address, phone numbers, credit
card statements, health records, hygiene habits, and shoe
size of the wanted individual, as well as similar information
about close friends and relatives. There is no privacy where
the Union is concerned; the forms they make you sign in
triplicate make that abundantly clear.

Sad sacks, all in a row. Ten by ten, a collage of
mug shots. Faces of lawyers, of carpenters, of dentists.
Fathers, brothers, it didn't matter. I was a bit surprised to
see that a woman rode the top of the list, that some blonde
lady had gotten herself in bad enough with the Union to
make that dreaded spot, but soon another grimace stole
my attention:

Second row from the left, two posters down, a familiar
face, a familiar half-worn grin, a fuck-the-world-and-its-
mother-too stare to the eyes that was mine and only mine lo
those many years ago. This was a shot culled from my original Union identification card, and something in me burned
at the knowledge that the bastards had used an element of
my previous identity against me.

I am the twelfth most wanted Union fugitive. Makes a
man feel important.

———————

I've been on Union lists before, of course, but only on the
other side of the oozing red line. During my marriage to
Melinda, I was awarded National Employee of the Month on
two separate occasions, each during a radically productive
period of Union growth that saw profits triple and expenses
cut in half.

During most average weeks, I brought in two, maybe

three artiforgs; during those cash-soaked heydays, I turned over at least twice that, spending every night on the prowl, caught up in the hunt. My ether consumption had skyrocketed so much that the dealer thought I'd gotten myself hooked on the stuff. But it was just a good month or two for business, and I worked the incoming cases like a pro, sometimes turning over as many as four artiforgs in a single evening. As a result, I was given my own parking space.

Melinda didn't come to either one of my award ceremonies. She didn't even cook me dinner when I got home. Jealousy is an ugly thing.

———

Seen my face, gotten the skinny, and without even having to read the fine print on the bottom of the poster, I knew instantly, just from my position on the list, that I was going to be assigned a Level Five. Not too long ago, it's a job I would have gladly taken on myself. The Union was sparing no expense to bring me in; I realized in that moment that I'd been lucky to stay alive this long, and that if I wanted to continue the breathing process for any significant length of time, I'd better stop taking foolish chances like this one.

But now that I was inside the Union, I was *inside* the Union. You don't make waves inside the Credit Union, not if you don't want to draw attention. Jumping the line is like leaping off the *Titanic*: You're gonna die one way or the other, but you might as well give yourself a fighting chance. Most folks who are in need of a little body replenishment don't reconsider midstream, so they tend to stick around to the bitter end, and even though I was dressed up as a lung, that's just what I was going to do. Get up to the front, wave to the guards and salesmen and any repo guys I saw along the way, then hustle out the back door and head on home to the grand ol' dump.

I think I was ten slobs from the front when the alarms sounded and the large men with rifles streamed into the lobby. Coulda been twelve; I wasn't really counting.

———

Due to the nature of my profession, I've been around death quite a lot, and while I'm not exactly on a first-name basis with the Reaper, we've exchanged business cards enough times to give each other a friendly nod when we pass by on the job. So it wasn't the sight of sixteen carbine rifle barrels pointed in my direction that sent my blood racing into high-G turns around my veins, nor the spectacle of sweaty, overgrown guards leaping the railings and barriers like world-class hurdlers. More than anything else, it was the way the crowd reacted, the way that my supposedly fellow comrades responded to what was essentially a small army descending upon the helpless and downtrodden masses stacked fifty deep here in the lobby:

They did nothing. There was no covering of heads, no fingers flayed in front of faces, no cowering and pleading for mercy. I expected maybe a few gasps, a mother covering up her infant child, something on the order of your basic peasants-in-the-square kind of mentality. But the only screaming or crying noises were those that had already been going on since I got into the joint, most of them emanating from the main credit room in back. Otherwise, there was little but silence, submission, and sadness—and that's what scared me most of all. Even sheep run for cover when wolves jump the fence.

———

The Mauser was tucked into the waistband of my pants, wedged between my sorely empty belly and a fourth-hand belt I had pinched from a nearby garage sale. As soon as the guards made their first grunts, launching themselves up and over the rails, rifles held high, fingers glued to the triggers, my right hand pulled itself out of the latex sleeve and grabbed the butt of my gun tightly, with speed, precision, and a comforting familiarity. I shoved the gun back into the dangling lung-arm, using the barrel as a makeshift fingertip. From the outside, it probably just looked like Larry the Lung was pointing his finger at someone, *j'accuse* style. But by the time the second Credit Union stooge had landed on our side of the bar, my finger was on the joy button and I was ready to play.

Odds calculation took a millisecond longer. Sixteen guards, eleven already over the rail, five on the move, another squadron of five in the distance, streaming into the lobby, each one sporting a weapon with approximately three times the firepower of my own pathetic piece. Grouping the folks around me into bunches of twenty-five, I counted one, two, three and a half—maybe ninety civilians in the way, each one a potential shield. No natural forms of cover, and the few metallic objects around were too small to hide behind. I might be thinning out from my back-alley diet, but no matter how much I get into this anorexia, no handrail is gonna cover up the more critical parts of my sorry ass.

Possible plan of attack: Fire a single shot at the fire alarm 15 feet away. Short out the circuit, send the sprinklers raining down. Next, grab the sap in front of me, tuck into a somersault, using his back to absorb the bullets that are aimed at mine. On the way up, kick out and throw his suddenly limp, probably bloody body into the nearest phalanx of attackers, then rinse and repeat. Duck and run through that lobby like a kid practicing his fire drills, blanketing my exposed surfaces with civilian flesh, taking whatever potshots I can at the walking body armor advancing my way, hoping to get in a lucky between-the-eyes shot. Flip out into the Mall proper and start a riot with a few well-placed bursts from the Mauser. Mass confusion, rip off the costume, sink into the crowd, run screaming out of the Mall with the rest of the stampede and disappear into the anonymous streets and alleys of the city on my way back to the safety of my abandoned hotel.

Odds on the plan working: A million to one against.

Odds on winding up in a body bag within the next ten minutes: The proverbial sure thing.

———

Here's what Sergeant Ignakowski used to say about the Sure Thing:

A big gambler has a dream one night: He's walking through the woods, minding his own business, thinking about the ponies, when a fuzzy little bunny rabbit bursts out of the brush, wrinkles his cute pink nose, and says "Five!" A few feet later, a chipmunk scurries up his arm, leans into his ear, and whispers, "Five!" Guy walks a little farther, and soon comes across a tree bending back over itself, the trunk deformed, mutated. But on closer inspection, it's simply twisted to look like a number 5. The clouds above are puffing in and out, forming *5*s and *55*s and *555*s, and soon enough the birds are singing and the animals are chanting and every living thing around him is pulsing *five, five, five, five, five.*

Poof, the guy wakes up. First thing he thinks is *I gotta get to the track.* So he takes a leak, shoves on some clothes, hops in the car, and takes five minutes making the five-mile drive to the horse races. Grabs a racing sheet as he goes inside, and opens it up to race number five. There it is, running in the fifth race, in the fifth slot, a five-year-old horse that comes from five generations of racers and that happens to be named Five Alive. Without another moment's thought, he goes to the fifth bank of windows, approaches the fifth teller, and bets most of his life savings, $55,555, on Five Alive to win in the fifth race.

Sure enough, the horse comes in fifth.

•

———

That's why I never bet the sure thing and always play the long shot: There's no room for depression. If you're going to lose anyway, you might as well rage against the odds.

———

But just as I was in the middle of pulling out the Mauser—just as the barrel had cleared my waistband and prepared for takeoff—just as my finger had already begun to depress the trigger and my reflexes had already trained themselves on the perfect shot to set off the overhead sprinklers—a guy in the next row over decided it was his turn to hog the insanity stage.

"Is this the return line?" he asked, his voice shaking with fear. "Somebody tell me, where's the return line?"

He was middle aged, graying around the temples and had a slight rasp to his voice, but otherwise seemed in perfect health. The man wandered through the line, stumbling against the other penitents, his limbs flapping against flesh, trying to clear a path. The Credit Union patrons were more than happy to oblige, and they did a Red Sea for the bozo, dropping away to either side in order to avoid getting caught by what was bound to be stray shrapnel.

"Please, just tell me where to find the return line. I'm trying to be helpful here."

As my hand casually slid the Mauser back into its waistband sheath, I followed the rest of the crowd as we backed up against the walls, allowing the guards a clear path to their target. No matter his age, he was about to reach the end of what was once a somewhat natural life span.

"I—I want to return it," he stammered, feet tripping over each other as the spiral of guards began to close around him. "I'm here to—I mean, I missed a few payments, and I thought, rather than make you guys come out, we could—we could make a plan or something—"

But the guards, who have been trained to expressly ignore any and all wheeling and dealing on the Credit Union floor, continued their march, guns at the ready. One was already on his phone, calling for the necessary backup and reinforcement. "We found him," he said. "He's right down here, in the lobby. Tracer worked fine. Send down a Level Three."

By the time I'd looked back to the soon-to-be-ex-customer, he'd already begun to disrobe, his dark navy sport coat splayed across the floor, hands working furiously at his pants, his starched-collar shirt buttons. "I didn't want to make it difficult," he was saying. "I know how hard it is, all these deadbeats—I know how hard it is to keep a profit margin these days—"

The lead guard approached, keeping his gun barrel aimed at the customer as a free hand reached out to provide an aura of support and understanding. "Please calm down, sir," he said. "No one here wants to hurt you."

But even if the guard hadn't been lying through his ceramic dentures, even if he had indeed been sworn not to lay a finger on the clients, the man in front of him had taken the A-train way past the sanity station. "I know how much you have to pay the—the Bio-Repo men," he choked out, "so I figured I'd help you guys—you know, maybe you could cut me a break—"

"Sir, please stop—"

"Maybe, maybe if I did it for you . . ." And as he whipped off his pants, nearly falling over backward as the last cotton leg pulled free, something silver and shiny in his hand glinted with the reflection of the overhead halogens. "Maybe you'd give me a break."

Before the guns sounded, before the crowd screamed and scattered, before the blood really started flying, I got enough of a glimpse to make sense of the whole three-ring circus:

A knife, flashing through the air, turned out, in, and sliding into flesh, as the customer whipped the weapon into his own body, slicing a ragged incision just below his stomach. The blood flow was instantaneous, a thick river of it pouring to the ground below in a crimson waterfall. The guards, who had been ready to shoot first and ask no questions later, stepped back to watch the first act.

Soft grunts choked out from the man's mouth as he dug the knife deeper into his own viscera, slicing up his stomach with little regard for skill or precision. Now the crowd was beginning to murmur, but more out of morbid curiosity than disgust; I saw a few parents covering their children's eyes, but for the most part, all attention was focused on the floor show.

A step backward, a drunken stagger, and the man raised his left hand—devoid of any weapons—high into the air. With a dramatic lurch, that arm swept down, axe-like, as his free hand plunged into the new, bloody body cavity. Another groan escaped his lips, followed by a gush of fluid, but he didn't pause for a moment. As his body lurched about the Credit Union floor, torso heaving, legs shaking in a herky-jerky dance of death, the deadbeat grabbed hold, and grabbed hold tight. And then, with what must have been his last remnants of strength and will, he yanked.

And as he stumbled forward—his mechanical PK–14 Marshodyne fully functional pancreas with Auto-Insulin release clicking away in his bloody, outstretched hands, the titanium receptacle catheters still attached to the frayed ends of torn veins and arteries—the guards, who had not been at all put off when this man was wielding an 8-inch-long hunting knife, got spooked enough by the sight of a fellow offering up his own artiforg for repossession to launch into a full-scale assault, even though the man was, by all rights, only seconds from death.

All sixteen rifles fired at once.

By the time the attack was complete, the crowd was in an all-out panic, running for the doors, trampling each other in their effort to escape the onslaught. The Credit Union doesn't have any policies in place for curtailing stampedes in their own offices; in fact, staff members are encouraged to let events play themselves out. At the very least, a few customers are bound to get stepped on in all the wrong places, creating a whole new profit base for the company on the next go-round. It's no coincidence that Union money spearheaded the effort to get the "fire in a crowded theater" exception stricken from the First Amendment some years back.

That's when I chose to make my exit along with the rest of the sheep, but I was pinned in long enough to see Frank arrive from upstairs with a Bio-Repo man in tow. He was a Level Three, just like they'd requested, his black tank top and bare neck displaying the Union tattoo belying his rank and profession. Hair cut short, military style, muscles firm and toned, a practiced scowl on a hardened face. Thin, wide-set eyes, blunt nose. In olden days, he'd have been a common street thug. In today's marketplace, a Level Three was good as gold, nearly as close to Midas as a mortal could get. I'd been a Level Five, of course, but this wasn't exactly the time to pull rank.

The Bio-Repo man flashed a scanner, pinging the already-quite-dead client, and confirmed that the artiforg was, indeed, Union property. Frank just stood there and stared at the bullet-riddled body on the ground, the outstretched arm holding the still-clicking Marshodyne PK–14. He spun on the contingent of guards, anger twisting his face into a scowl. "Who reclaimed that organ?" he bellowed, his voice carrying over the din of rioting customers. "Who reclaimed this goddamned organ?"

"The customer, sir," replied the guard. "He did it himself, sir."

"Customers don't reclaim their own organs," said Frank.

"This one did, sir." He pointed to the hunting knife in the dead man's hand with the barrel of his gun, as if to let the picture speak for itself.

I was halfway through the Credit Union door by that point, but as I hustled myself out, I could hear Frank spit in disgust. "Customers. Don't know their goddamned place anymore."

CHAPTER 6

A few more words about my current abode: It ain't quite the Ritz.

To be more specific, I am staying in the burned-out remains of the Tyler Street Hotel, a formerly low-to-lower-class establishment that, when it was a functioning place of lodging, boasted no celebrity clientele and a complete lack of standard facilities. There is a lobby with the customary broken chandelier, a shaky staircase leading up to rickety hallways, and six bathrooms for every twenty-four so-called "suites," two of which are currently functional. This would have been considered a "European style" hotel, which means, on top of everything else, that it was dirt cheap. None of the actual Europeans I know would have ever stayed in this place longer than the time it took them to don a respirator and haul their ass back out to the cracked parking lot.

On the ground floor, a long, narrow room with ash-covered walls and crumbling support beams represents what may have once been a coffee shop, but it's hard to tell in its current charred, decrepit state. There were fourteen floors to the Tyler Street Hotel once upon a time, but they called the thirteenth floor the fourteenth and the fourteenth floor the penthouse, so the fact that I'm living on the sixth floor means little, except that I'm about halfway up the place, with a stellar view of the brickwork on the high-rise next door.

My room is a good 4 meters square, and I've got ample space to walk around, squat, do my morning regimen of push-ups, crunches, and lunges, as well as a cozy corner in which to bed down for the night. The walls, formerly orange and beige, have been tarnished with the ash of some long-forgotten blaze, but the original color peeks through in spots now and again, so that the whole wall resembles one side of a monstrous cheetah.

My weapons are stashed in what remains of the hallway closet, haphazardly hidden beneath a rotting tarpaulin I found in the trash heap of a sporting goods store down on Savoie Street. The guns are tucked within a double fold, as if that were enough to buy them any type of added protection, but I make do with what I've got.

The same tarp that covers my only means of self-defense also serves as protection against the elements. It is my mattress, my quilt, and my pillow, and sometimes, late at night, I can almost pretend that I'm not sleeping on the hard, cold floor of an abandoned hotel, but instead resting the night away in an uncomfortable but well-kept bed-and-breakfast. My security blanket is the crossbow; some nights, I'll grasp it between my arms, cradling the wooden stock like a child.

And this typewriter is kept as near to the middle of the room as I can get it. A nearby portion of the floor has rotted away, and I take great pains to keep the typewriter away from that spot, in fear that I will come back to the hotel one day to find it, smashed, three floors down, a gaping rabbit hole leading the way. But it's close enough to the center that the relative distance from all walls should afford me some type of auditory block from the rest of the world while I jot down these notes.

But here's the point of all of this: As I've said, the Tyler Street Hotel is burned out, abandoned, an empty husk of a building that now serves no purpose other than to shelter me and my sins. The lobby is empty, the rooms unoccupied, the elevator long since crashed to the bottom of the shaft. The Tyler Street Hotel is mine and mine alone.

Or so I thought until this evening.

————

I returned from the Mall via a serpentine route, making sure to drop any and all tails that I may have picked up on my rapid departure from the Credit Union. Odds were slim that I'd been followed—most repo men don't wait until their client returns to the relative safety of their home to finish the job; an alley will usually do just fine. So the very fact that all of my major organs—artiforgs and regulars— were inside and intact a hundred yards down the road was a good sign.

But it didn't stop me from traversing the town, dropping in and out of parking garages, hot-wiring cars as a matter of course, slipping through culverts and washouts every time I got even the slightest glimpse of the law. The boys in blue aren't aligned with the Credit Union, but, like the rest of the public, they get kickbacks when they snitch on an artiforg deadbeat, so it always pays to steer clear.

By the time I got back to Tyler Street, it was nearing midnight and I was too tired to use the entrance I'd become accustomed to. My muscles were limp noodles, too weak to scale the back wall, leap for the fire-escape ladder, and climb in through the third-story window before beginning the rest of the ascent to Room 618. So I did what any careless on-the-run Bio-Repo man would do: I went in through the front.

So, what with the worry between being followed and the lack of security in making a front-door entrance, it's not too surprising that it took me ten minutes before I noticed that there was a sheet of paper sticking out of my typewriter, a sheet of paper that I had definitely not placed into the machine myself.

As I approached, my mechanical heart getting the signal from the rest of my body to speed up pumping action, I noticed that this was no ordinary sheet of paper, blank and begging to be typed upon. There was a message, not typed in the heavily inked letters of the Underwood, but scrawled in a tight, furious scribble of red ballpoint. I spun around, legs suddenly leaden, the world slipping into a slow-motion crawl, the camera inside my head panning around in a dramatic lurch as my vision settled on the paper and its freshly written sentence.

For ease of use, I will simply include the two-word note, original sheet and all, right here, right now. This is what it said:

SHUT UP.

———

The reality that I have been found out, that I am no longer alone, does not bother me as much as I thought it would; perhaps the concept of companionship, invisible or otherwise, is enough to blunt the dull fear of having been located and asked to silence myself. Odds are it's not a Bio-Repo man; they rarely leave notes, and when they do, they tend to be short explanations addressed to next of kin. Certainly, I'm not worried enough about it to follow the letter's rudely phrased advice and silence myself for any length of time. If the clacking of this typewriter is bothering my fellow hotel dweller, then he or she will simply have to find another abandoned building in which to bunk. Even if I were inclined to give up, that two-word order has lit a new fire under my ass, so now I'll type all through the night, pounding on that keyboard with every stroke until my knuckles lock up and my wrists are shot through with carpal tunnel lightning. I have never taken well to direct instruction.

————

The first night overseas, Harold Hennenson and I climbed off the cargo plane in Italy, leaden duffel bags slung over our shoulders, and made our way through the throng of fellow soldiers to the nearest ground transport. I'd been laboring under the impression that a throng of women would be crowding the tarmac when we landed, bearing flowers and kisses and keys to hotel rooms. But whatever pop-star fantasies I had cultivated dissipated as soon as the plane doors opened to allow a rush of angry male voices to filter into the open cabin. Orders flew by at top speed, and I didn't know which were directed at me, at Harold, at the rest of the grunts who were running around in circles. By the time I figured out where I was supposed to be, I'd already marched in time with three separate platoons and belted out two rum-tum choruses of "The Battle Hymn of the Republic."

The lieutenant in command had ordered me to get the hell out of the airport and not stop running until I found the platoon to which I'd been assigned. But as I sped out of the airport's double doors, my designated compatriots already having neatly boarded a series of open-bed trucks, a young, raven-haired Italian beauty stepped into my path, forcing me to skitter to a stop. Her breasts were not large, but swelled against her tube top in a way that instantly stopped my feet and made me forget about the United States, its military forces, and any traces of sexual morality.

"Soldier," she said, carefully forming each syllable with a pair of thick, pouting lips. "You go off to die for me." And with that, she fell into my body, wrapped her arms into a tight belt about my waist, and treated my tonsils to a long, slow, sensuous tongue bath.

I don't know if it was because I'd been expecting to see a parade of adoring women at the airport, if I'd been missing Beth, if I wanted to impress the woman with my sense of duty, or if I was just a horny young kid who wanted to get some action, but I leaned into that mouth and that body for all I was worth, working my lips and tongue into a mandibular cha-cha that would have gotten my ass a permanent restraining order from any county-fair kissing booth.

I do know this: The bitch stole my wallet.

————

"Gypsies," huffed Harold later that night as we unpacked our duffels. "Gotta watch out for 'em. They'll steal anything that ain't nailed down."

"She seemed nice enough," I said.

"Nicer still with another fifty bucks in her pocket."

Most of Harold's possessions seemed to be of the food-supplement variety. He had cans of protein powder, jars of specialized enzymes, and energy bars in six different flavors, each one of which managed to taste exactly like sawdust. As we spoke, he removed these supplements one by one, laying them in precise little rows at the foot of his bunk.

"Marines are gonna serve you food," I told him. "You don't have to eat those."

His answer was typical Harold. "Marine food is good," he explained. "If all you wanna be is a Marine."

"And you want to be more?" I asked.

"I don't want to be *a* Marine," he replied. "I want to be *the* Marine."

What he would finally be, of course, was nothing more than a splotch of red on an otherwise dun-colored desert. Poor Harold—at the very least, he would have liked his corpse to provide nourishment for a cactus or two, but the tank explosion pretty much took care of all the surrounding foliage.

———

The picture made the papers, though—THREE KILLED IN AFRICAN MANEUVERS, read the caption, and I'm pretty sure the *Stars and Stripes* photo caught my left sleeve as I was mourning my good buddy's loss. Snapshot of the charred earth, a wrecked heap of indistinguishable metal center stage. A few soldiers gathered around, staring mutely at the crash, impotent to do anything but look at one another and shrug.

———

But back in Italy, Jake and I were finishing up unpacking our gear, while Harold was downing his first powdered meal of the day. It was getting on past three, and we hadn't met up with our senior officer yet—he was away in the veldt, we were told, and wouldn't be back until nightfall.

As a result of our sergeant's non-appearance, the entire platoon had loosened up a notch from our usual basic-training shell shock. Jokes flew and barbs hit home as we spent a few hours meeting a bunch of other knobs who were just turning loose into the early war effort:

Ron Toomey was nineteen, from Wyoming, and had a sister who looked like she belonged on Mount Rushmore. Wasn't so much the granite features as it was the facial hair.

Bill Braxton's father owned a used car dealership back in Albuquerque and had told his son that he'd turn over the keys to the business as soon as he graduated from high school. Then his father said he'd get the job when he finished four years in college. Then it was a graduate degree.

Then a Ph.D. And still Bill Braxton's father clung tight to the reins of his successful dealership. When the suggestion of going to business school came up at a family dinner, Bill calmly stood, left the table, the dining room, the house, drove his father's prized 1964 Mustang down Main Street, ran it headlong into a telephone pole, stepped confidently out of the smoking wreckage, walked down to the local Marines recruiting office, and signed on up. He was thirty-four, nearly twice as old as the rest of us, and the Marines was his first paying gig.

Ben Rosner was slight of stature, short on words, but his girl had been featured in the December issue of last year's *Hootenanny Hooter Review*, and caused quite a controversy when she wore her department-store-issued Santa's Little Helper cap and absolutely nothing else in a two-page centerfold. The department store in question dismissed the poor girl and promptly threatened to sue *Hootenanny*, but the ensuing hubbub got her a gig as a full-time model for phone-sex ads. She was the girl you looked at when the sixty-three-year-old hag on the other end of the line was trying to get you off. Ben proudly passed out photos to each of us like a grandfather handing out pictures of the new baby, and we scarfed them up and hid them away for future enjoyment. We knew that once we hit Africa, it would be a long time before we saw any women.

———

Every once in a while I think about Bill Braxton, the Ph.D. Marine—Doctor Jarhead, as we affectionately called him—and something he said one night after lights-out. He had the bunk two down from mine, and over the snores of Elian Ortiz, a Colombian with some serious apnea issues, we discussed the nature of the cosmos and the breast sizes of various female celebrities. Mostly the nature of the cosmos, though.

To be fair, Bill did a lot more talking than I did; he was pretty damned well educated, and though I only understood half of what he said, and retained far less, occasionally he'd blow my mind.

"There's a scientist," he told me one night, "back in Germany, or Holland, I can't remember, and he proposed this experiment with a cat."

"So, what," I asked, "he'd give 'em drugs or do autopsies on 'em?"

"No," Bill explained, "it wasn't like that. It was a physics experiment, sort of. And he never really did the experiment; he just thought it up."

"What's the use of that?" I asked.

"It's theoretical physics. It's doesn't have to have a use."

I was impressed and disgusted at the same time. "And people get paid for this?"

"Pretty damned well. Anyway, he said to imagine that you took a cat and put it in a box, along with a radioactive device that randomly decayed and released a deadly poison gas. Half the time, the material would decay and release the gas, and the other half it wouldn't. But the thing is random, and since the box is closed, there is no way for the scientist to know when the poison is released, and when it isn't. That means there is no way for the scientist to know if the cat, inside that box, is still alive, or if it's dead."

"What about the screaming? Wouldn't it scream?"

"Soundproofed. Thick walls. No way to know. And since there is no way to know if the cat is alive or dead, then until he opens the box, the cat has to be both."

I said, "Both what?"

"Alive and dead."

"At the same time?" I asked incredulously.

"Exactly."

I processed it for a minute, maybe more, trying to wrap

my head around the answer. But it didn't make sense. How can anything be alive and dead at the same time?

"That's gotta be the most fucked-up thing I ever heard," I told him.

"Yep," said Bill Braxton, and then we were silent, for a good five minutes. I couldn't shake it, though. Something was bothering me.

"What happened to the cat?" I finally asked, breaking the stillness of the bunks.

Bill sighed, and I could see him turning over in his bunk, his back to me. He was done educating those who refused to learn. "There is no cat," he said. "There never was. Forget it. Go to sleep."

It was years ago, but some days I still think about Bill. About that story. About the cat and the box. And I wonder, where did I fit into that equation? Sometimes I like to think I was the poison—dealing out justice as I saw fit, handing out death on engraved invitations. Other days, I think I was the box. Holding it all together, keeping the experiment in place.

But most days—these days—I know I'm the cat. Scratching and clawing and screaming to get out, even as I lick my paws, curl up into a ball, and drift off to a nice, comfortable nap.

———

Jake Freivald was with us in that bunk, and he told some stories we hadn't heard during boot camp. "Back in New York," he said—which is always how he started his sentences, leading one to believe that he was from Manhattan as opposed to the upstate two-outhouse town where his family owned one of the last remaining private dairy farms in the Northeast—"I took two bullets in the back trying to steal a pumpkin off some old guy's front stoop. Right 'round Halloween, I ran up, snatched the big ol' thing, and took off running, and soon there's screaming and yelling and I'm still running, and I hear this bang, but I'm okay, only there's this powerful itch running up and down my back, and soon the itch is a sting . . . Next thing I know, I wake up in a hospital, the cops are all around me, and I'm answering questions for the next ten hours."

"What'd you do?" asked Harold. "What'd you tell 'em?"

"I lied," Jake said plainly. "If I said that I'd taken the pumpkin, they woulda given him a slap on the wrist, protecting his property and all that. So I told 'em I was doing trick or treat, house to house for candy, and that he just freaked out on me." He laughed then, like a child remembering his first trip to a theme park. "Guy got six years."

For the two months I was stationed in Italy, I rarely heard any actual Italian. As far as I could tell, they were just as happy speaking English as we were, and I didn't give the matter a moment's thought. Of course, the fact that I never left the warm, comforting bosom of the U.S. military might have helped in that regard.

Even when I managed to get off base, the Marines were there. It was as if we'd already invaded the southern half of the country, knocking off all the spaghetti eaters and installing ourselves in their place. Instead of Guiseppe the chef, we just threw in Tony from the Bronx and called it six of one, half a dozen of the other. Somehow, the military had managed to Americanize the entirety of Italy before I'd gotten there, so whatever cultural lessons I might have learned during my stay were prematurely obliterated by a government eager to make its fighting men feel at home.

I did come across one Italian fellow, though, who had managed to remain native on native soil. There was a convenience store, sort of a smalltown grocer, just a few clicks outside of town, and they were the only place for miles to carry anything other than American cigarettes. On the base, you could feel free to choke yourself on all the Winstons and Camels you could buy at the canteen, but Jake wouldn't light up anything other than a brand produced in the country in which he was stationed. "If I'm going all the way around the world," he used to say, "then my lungs are taking the trip with me."

Harold couldn't understand why anyone would want to inhale noxious gases into his lungs, but he didn't understand a lot of what Jake did. Unlike Jake and myself, Harold Hennenson would not have made a good Bio-Repo man— you have to lose respect for your own body long before you can lose respect for everyone else's.

The store wasn't large—six aisles at most, with nary a slushie machine in sight—but each shelf was packed with sundries, shoved in at any and all angles, fighting for space like rockers in the front row of a concert. A single cash register sat on a rickety desk out in front, complete with push-button NO SALE signs and a drawer that got stuck on its tracks three times out of ten.

The fellow who owned the joint was an ex-Navy boy named Sketch who was at least six-five, no more than a hundred and eighty pounds, and sported three tufts of red hair sprouting out of his otherwise bald head. He looked like one of those birds you see in nature specials, the ones where you call your stoned buddies into the room and laugh for hours at God's fucked-up sense of humor. Sketch had served four years with the military, most of it stationed in the Mediterranean, and was the only survivor of a submarine accident that had claimed the lives of ninety-eight comrades. Someone had left a torpedo tube open and flooded, a strict no-no when trolling through shallow depths, even during practice maneuvers. Two hours later, when a practice target had come into range, there was no way to know that a porpoise had somehow managed to get itself stuck inside the tube, and no way to know that the active-fire torpedo warhead would explode upon impact, sending bits of dolphin and human alike floating through the open sea.

Sketch doesn't even *drink* water anymore.

————

Despite his parental approach to the matter of cigarettes, Harold joined Jake and me on our weekly sojourns to the store, mostly to hear Sketch tell stories of his days with the Navy. The submarine accident wasn't the tall man's only brush with death, not by a long shot. He'd nearly been decapitated once when a rigging line had snapped and swung a two-ton mast directly at his noggin, escaping from that only because he had lost his footing on the slippery deck and gone down a second before he was to meet his·maker. Back at basic training in Maryland, he'd been shot at by a jealous husband who didn't understand that his wife needed more loving than his bimonthly drunken lovefests could provide, and three months after *that*, he was attacked by the knife-wielding *new* lover of the wife who didn't want any competition hanging around his conquest.

"You ever see any combat, Sketch?" asked Jake one time.

"You don't call that combat?"

"No, no," said Jake, "I mean *real* combat."

Sketch just laughed and rung up the pack of cigarettes on the old German register.

————

But about that Italian guy: He used to own the store. It was called Sputini, and Sketch was cool enough to keep the name after he bought the place. He was also cool enough to let the guy hang out on the property, day in and day out, rocking back and forth on an old hammock he'd set up on the front porch. Every time we went into Sputini for some cigarettes, we'd give a curt nod to the little old man swinging on his hammock, eyeing us up and down, like we were his entertainment for the day.

The third or fourth time we went, he finally perked up. "Your head is too big for that hat," he said as I walked by, his body practically creaking as he rose to a seated position.

"Excuse me?"

He spoke carefully, enunciating every English syllable with remarkable clarity. "Your head . . . is too big . . . for that hat."

Without another thought, I reached up, pulled my standard-issue Marine cap off my head, smoothed out the hair beneath, and threw it in his lap. He inspected it for a moment, his dark fingers running across the olive fabric, then popped the hat open and placed it atop his own head. It fit quite nicely, and without another word, he lay back down in his hammock and went to sleep.

———

I caught hell for losing that cap, but it didn't matter. From then on, Antonio—that was the Italian guy's name—was my best pal, and he repeatedly informed me when my uniform was too tight, too loose, or would simply fit him better. I tried to engage him in conversation a few times to get a sense of who he was, of why he would hang around a place that was no longer his and presumably no longer held any meaning for him, but I never got any further than hello before he started in on his fashion criticisms. Sketch told me he'd bought Antonio out for fifty thousand dollars American plus an old analog color television that only pulled in religious programming from the Vatican. Antonio blew the fifty grand in a month on failed jai-alai wagers in northern Spain, then came back to Italy and set up shop outside his old place of business. Now he just swings, watches the Pope on TV, and talks folks out of their clothing.

That's the kind of retirement a man can envy.

———

The Union has a pension plan, though I have stopped trying to receive my checks. It's a fair plan, from what I remember, with a number of benefits thrown in that are clearly over and above the usual accountant-and-janitor-type pensions. New skin grafts, for example, should liver spots become a problem, are available at very reasonable rates from the Union supply house, as are most major artiforg implantations. The loan percentages, I hear, are quite competitive, very few reaching into the thirties, almost none into the forties. They probably would have had a nice deal on a heart for me had I gotten myself into cardiac trouble *after* retiring, but since my ticker fizzled out while I was on the job, the post-retirement medical benefits of my profession hadn't yet fully kicked in. I understand this is somewhat backward in relation to the rest of the world, but the Union cadre never cared much about social standards.

The Marines were supposed to have a nice pension plan, too, but I signed away any benefits that might have been coming my way when I hooked up with the Union. It seems they only let you play the part of retired killer once.

———

Let me tell you about our sergeant: Tyrell Ignakowski, informally known as Tig, a short, squat, beefy rock of a man who kept his hair cropped, his reach long, and his sense

of tact someplace even bloodhounds would have difficulty
finding. If you were doing something wrong, Tig would
let you know it at six hundred decibels—that instant, that
moment, even if your mother, your best girl, and a photog-
rapher from *Stars and Stripes* were standing next to you.
Especially if they were standing next to you.

Tig wasn't afraid to humiliate his soldiers in order to
break them into shape. In fact, that was the linchpin of
his theory, that the concept of "molding" a soldier was an
anachronism and didn't hold in today's military. "Maybe
back in the day, when we were fightin' the Krauts," he told
me, "maybe then you could take a soldier and push him
gently this way and push him gently that way, press him
into the proper mold." Form him into military Play-Doh, as
it were.

"Kids these days," he continued, "can't be molded. By
the time they hit fifteen, sixteen, they ain't a piece of clay
no more. They've set, they've hardened, and pushing and
pulling don't help any more than it would on a vase that's
already been through the kiln for ten hours. Whatever
they are, they are. Only way to work 'em into a team is to
shatter whatever it is they've become, mix them hardened
fragments all around, then crazy glue the whole mess back
together however you see fit. You break 'em into small
enough pieces, you can make 'em into damn near anything
you want."

———

This is all you need to know about my relationship with
Tig:

One day in the desert, long after training and long before
they'd send me home again, I was in a foul mood, tossing
rocks out into the open sand. I hadn't heard from Beth in
weeks, and the last few letters I'd sent down to San Diego
came back with RETURN TO SENDER stamped on the front.

Just like the fucking song, which somehow made it even worse.

So there I was, tossing stones, not trying to hit anything, just skimming the sand, as if I were back in San Diego, standing next to my girl, staring out over the wide Pacific.

Tig approached from behind; I could feel him there. Despite his height disadvantage, he had a definite presence, a way of asserting himself without physicality. Some of the guys called him Sergeant Limburger, because you knew he was coming from a mile off. But it wasn't a smell; it was a feel.

After watching me for a while, he said, "You're not trying to hit anything."

"Nossir," I replied. "I'm just throwing rocks, sir."

He gingerly pulled the last stone from my hand and sat me down on the warm ground below. Kneeling into a crouch, his face came close to mine. "Son, throwing rocks at nothing is like humping the air. If you want to masturbate, set up a target. If you really want to get with it, set your sights on the bad men."

I nodded, not fully appreciating his advice at the time. Yet I understood that he was trying to assist me in something or other. "Thank you, sir," I said. "Thank you for helping me."

But Tig shook his head, insistent on this last point: "I'm not helping you a whiff," he said. "Before you got here, I was nothing to you. Once you leave, I'll be nothing to you. But while you're here, you're my boy, and it's my duty as your pop to tell you things you can't possibly understand." He paused for a moment, and added, "You understand?"

"No?" I tried.

Tig laughed and walked away. A few minutes later, I started throwing rocks again.

He was right about all of it. I never saw him after the war, and despite my fond feelings for him in retrospect, it wouldn't be right to see him now. Tig was a military man in a military place, and that was how he lived; to bring him into any other situation would be like putting a snowman in Tijuana.

———————

Second day in Italy, we were marched across the main field, into a low-slung building, and down three flights of stairs, descending the aluminum staircase in lockstep, the contraption vibrating roughly with the combined weight of forty-five men. Once we reached the bottom, they separated us into three seemingly random groups of fifteen, splitting us off single file and marching us down one of three hallways.

"Today," Tig had told us that morning at breakfast, "you will each be tested to see how you can best assist us in the African campaign. You will be poked, you will be prodded, and you will be assessed. Some of you may even like it. At the end of the day, you will be assigned to a training facility here on the base, and that facility will become your home for the next eight weeks. You may not like your assignment. You may not agree with your assignment. You may not understand your assignment. But just like here in the mess hall, gentlemen, there will be no substitutions."

———————

As an assistant led us down a series of labyrinthine hallways and corridors, each exactly like the one that preceded it, I was thinking that the test would be to find our way back out into the real world; those who made it would get to go home, and those who didn't would be sent to Africa. But after some time, we came to a pair of metal double doors set back into the wall, and a petite young female doctor awaiting our arrival. Strawberry blonde hair pulled back in a ponytail, rimless glasses perched on a jellybean nose, smiling at us as we approached, just on the safe side of beautiful. I considered getting a number, making a play for her after Taps had run its course, but it turned out that once she was done with me, I was in no position to play the springtime courtier.

"We'll take you one at a time," she told my group. "The rest will wait out here."

Numbers were assigned at random. Jake was sixth; I was last. We stood in the hallway, ramrod straight, eager to impress the chick every time she stuck her head out from between the doors and called the next soldier in. I thought of Beth; she hadn't written in a month.

Meanwhile, muffled bangs filtered their way in through the walls, patterned, well-timed beats growing in intensity, as if a giant had made his way down the beanstalk and was slowly tromping toward town. But after a minute or two, just when it seemed that on the next *thump* we'd be able to figure out what the heck all the fuss was about, the noises would come to an end, the doctor would call another of us in, and the cycle would start all over again.

It wasn't until Jake stepped through the double doors and I was left all alone in the hallway that I realized that none of the soldiers who walked inside that room had yet to come back out again.

———

If you look hard enough around the back alleys and hidden crannies of your workaday underworld, you'll find plenty of places that operate under that Roach Motel principle: Folks go in, but they don't come out. The Credit Union had one, in fact—the Pink Door, they called it, thanks to the Pepto-Bismol shade that some bright social psychologist had painted it back in the day when they still bothered to lull folks into a false sense of security.

The Pink Door was often used as a means of last resort with deadbeats who were public figures, clients you didn't want to drag back into the world of solvency by their dangling entrails. So rather than call out the Bio-Repo men and leave a messy Beverly Hills scene for the paparazzi, they'd send an embossed invitation, delivered by courier from the Credit Union offices, a tactfully worded letter that requested the louse's presence for a so-called arbitration meeting. Soon after, obituaries were released along with letters of credit reinstatement, and everyone went on with their merry lives.

Still, a Bio-Repo man usually was dispatched to accompany the creditor down to the offices, just in case things got messy. One time, I had the good fortune to escort Nicolette Huffington, software heiress and erstwhile actress, into the Los Angeles branch of the Union. Head held high, her gait confident and secure, she strolled past all the common riffraff begging for their lives and straight into the Pink Door waiting room. She was no longer the breathtaking beauty she had been back in her teenage years, and the ravages of time and excess plastic surgery had exacted their revenge upon her sagging flesh, but a Huffington was a Huffington—unpaid-for liver or no—and I couldn't resist snagging a signature for Melinda, my wife at the time.

"Just a quick autograph," I asked her, grabbing a pen from my pocket, flipping over the Credit Union invitation to use as a pad.

She huffed a little in that famous way of hers, eyeing me up and down. "Won't this keep till afterward, darling?" she sighed, tossing her carefully coifed hair to one side.

"No," I replied as I led her up to the ever-so-pink welcome mat, "I don't think it will."

———

Melinda showed that autograph to *everyone*.

———

The lady doctor asked me if I was seated comfortably, and I replied that under the circumstances, I certainly was. Surrounded by padded cushions, head resting on a thick pillow, body propped up into a frog crouch, legs flexed beneath my hips, elbows flared out to the side, everything strapped to a metal framework that kept me erect and balanced in this improbable position, I felt like I should be riding one of those old American motorcycles they outlawed years ago—knees splayed, back straight, arms spread wide to grip the handlebars—only there was no hog beneath me.

"What do I do?" I asked as she tightened the last of the belts.

"Nothing," she replied. "Concentrate on the wall."

"Where'd the other guys go?"

"The wall, please. Look at the wall."

The doctor returned to her lab, a small cubicle separated from the main testing area by what looked to be six full inches of lead-lined glass. This see-through wall was so thick that the room beyond took on strange, curved proportions at the edges, twisting and bending in on itself, like looking through a teardrop.

"You're not concentrating," the doctor told me, her voice crackling over a speaker set into the headrest just behind my left ear. "I'm getting the data in here. Please, Private. The wall."

So I decided to be a good little soldier and follow orders, but when I took a glance, the far wall wasn't there anymore. Instead, an endless desert stretched out in front of me, spreading to the horizon in an expansive wash of beige. The rest of the testing area was still extant—I was keenly aware of the doctor in the other room, her eyes roving along my body, across the digital readouts that were giving away all my physical secrets—but it was as if that far wall had been knocked down by a team of expert demolitionists, neatly, quietly.

"There we go," I heard her say, the voice at the edges of my consciousness. "Just like that."

A flare in the distance, an explosion just over the horizon. The blue sky above lit up with a splash of orange, and a very distinct *ka-boom*—crisp, not muffled like the sounds from the hallway—echoed through the room. Intrigued, I leaned against my restraints, trying to get a better look at the desert before me.

Another flash of light, this one closer, and a second explosion following milliseconds later, the sound waves shoving through my body, tickling me from the inside. Before I could pinpoint exactly what was going on, there was another crash, this one to my right, and I was barely able to flick my eyes in that direction before the next wall of bass was upon me, rattling my limbs inside their confines, my bladder going weak from the force.

"Wait," I tried to yell, but my voice was drowned out by the next wave of bombs—I was sure now this is what they were, that the enemy had somehow infiltrated our base camp, knocked down a portion of the training facility, and were coming back to finish the job. Lights flashed in rapid succession, popping off left and right, the shockwaves coming closer, stronger with every burst, my head compressing and expanding, a balloon in the hands of a child.

And that's when I saw the final missile, the one headed home and locked on to target. It was beautiful, really, a thin pencil line of light arcing through the sky, the tail of fire growing larger as it sped toward me, and even if I hadn't been strapped into six hundred pounds of metal framework, I might not have been able to move from the sheer magnitude of it all. Impending destruction, in its own way, has a kind of beauty that only small children and deer can appreciate.

I saw the light, but I did not hear the explosion. Not that time, I didn't.

CHAPTER 7

I have been knocked unconscious on four occasions. The first we'll come to presently; the second and fourth, I'm not ready to talk about yet. The third time was many years after I was discharged from the Marines, while I was still in training at the Credit Union. They'd hooked me up with one of the Level Threes, an old codger who'd joined up when it was all just Jarviks and some chain jobs, but he'd paid his dues, and as a result, he got a little assistance in the form of an apprentice. Only problem was, he wasn't too keen on actually making the runs that were assigned to him, and as a result, I got a lot of single-handed on-the-job training, and fast.

One night, we'd been given the job of retrieving a set of kidneys from a deadbeat who owned a plumbing supply company down in the warehouse district. Easy enough job, fair pay, nothing good on TV that night to sap our interest. Standard commission, to be split 70 percent for the senior Bio-Repo man, 30 percent for me; I was fine with the division of the proceeds. I was between marriages that month, and it wasn't hard to support myself on a steady diet of pasta and pretzels.

But when the time came to scooch our rumps down to the scene, my mentor gave out on me. Went to the movies, drank himself into a stupor, pulled a no-show. I could have waited until he was off the sauce, I suppose, petitioned the Union to push back the repossession appointment by a day or two, but back in those days the competition for jobs was fierce, and had I made any kind of fuss, odds were the case would have been reassigned. I knew the time would eventually come when I'd have to strike out on my own and make my bones, as it were, and this was as good as any. So I shut my trap and decided to go it alone.

The first step to any repo job is to map out the area. You've got to know where the client is, and you've got to know what else is nearby. How big is the house/office/hut in which he's staying? Any other people inside? Are they on the phone? Are they armed? Are they on the phone with someone who is armed? That sort of thing.

I went through the motions. From the maps I'd obtained from a bribed county clerk, I figured the warehouse to be around 800 to 900 cubic meters, quite the sizable hideout. He was inside and alone; I could hear him fumbling around in there even without the aid of a powered listening device, but I knew it would be hard to pinpoint his location. For a moment I considered using alternate tactics to detain the client—I was in possession of a dart gun at the time, as well as a long-distance Taser—but those methods were less reliable and more dependent on my ability—or inability—to properly aim and fire. My first solo job, I decided, would have to be a smooth one. I broke out the ether.

Using my Union-issued pencil laser—a signing bonus they gave to new recruits, ours to keep even if we chose not to make a career in repossessions—I sliced open a small circle in a pane of glass just above the warehouse floor. A hose, a knob, a twist, and a flip. Three full canisters of ether slowly hissed their way into the structure, and I patiently sat there in the dark, pressing myself against the shadows, waiting for the drug to take effect. My training in dosage and doping was nearly as complete as any board-certified anesthesiologist, but you never find any country-club society matrons begging their daughters to marry the likes of me.

Fifteen-minute wait after the last canister had run its course, and then I decided it was time to go in and finish the job. I'd heard the telltale *thunk* of a falling body by the second tank of gas, so I knew the client was down for the count and prepped for the only surgery I knew how to perform. I had a gas mask on me, just in case the ether hadn't yet completely evaporated, but I figured with a warehouse that size, there wasn't any harm of overexposure.

I figured wrong. As soon as I stormed in the front door, I had only enough time to realize that the warehouse, while looking quite massive from the outside, had been segmented into a number of different offices on the inside, each of which was no more than 300 cubic meters. I tried to turn, I think, to realign my body in hopes of making a dash for the door, but the thick air, oversaturated in triplicate with great clouds of ether, shot up through my nose and hit my brain with a stunning one-two punch. My knees buckled; my shoulders sagged, and I fell hard on my knees as I sank to the floor. I had a bruise for two weeks.

———

I woke up that time to the enraged, puffy face of my mentor, his breath reeking of sour milk and rotten rum, screaming about how I'd almost let a client get away, and how he'd had to chase down the bum in the warehouse alley and pull out the guy's kidneys with his bare hands.

In Italy, on the other hand, I woke up to a serene, porcelain vision of beauty leaning over me, her lab coat hanging open just a bit, the white cotton bra beneath barely visible against her skin, hand caressing my sweaty brow. She was waving a leather pouch beneath my nose that would have sent skunks reeling for cover, but all I could smell was the soft perfume caressing her neck.

"Take it easy," she said as I tried to sit up. I was in a cot of some sort, no longer strapped down. Harold Hennenson was on the bed next to me, and the other soldiers from my platoon were milling about the room, shaking their heads, blinking their eyes, each in his own separate, special state of confusion. Only Jake was on top of his game, already laughing it up with the nurses and making fun of the rest of us.

"Did we get bombed?" I asked the doctor.

"No one was bombed. Lie back down."

"That was the exam?"

"That was the exam."

Harold sat up then, squirming onto the edge of his bed, leaning over toward mine. "Concussion test," he said plainly. I could see his eyes floating around in their sockets, fluttering this way and that. "Wanted to see if we could take a hit."

"You pass out, too?" I asked.

Harold nodded, dropped his head. Ashamed, perhaps. "Yeah," he said, "I didn't take it too well."

"Maybe if they'd have hit you in the stomach . . ." I suggested.

This perked him up a little, and we spent the next twenty minutes drinking juice and clearing our heads, until we, too, were given clearance to pace the room in a half stupor, struggling to remain upright and dignified.

———

They gave us other tests, of course—vision tests, hearing tests, memory tests, reflex tests, tests of our sense of smell and our sense of taste, tests that seemed to go on forever, and tests that took no more than fifteen seconds. At the end of each, we were given a sheet of paper with a series of numbers on it, digits that were incomprehensible to us but caused our superiors to ooh and aah to no end.

A week later, we were ordered to line up and accept our new assignments, the posts at which we would train before heading out to Africa. Harold was two men down from me; Jake was a row back.

Sergeant Ignakowski ran through the names and assignments rapid fire. "Burns, Engineering. Carlton, Infantry. Dubrow, Infantry . . ."

As for me, Jake, and Harold, we got to drive a tank.

———

Six months later, I finally got up the nerve to ask Tig why I was placed on tank duty as opposed to some less colorful and more relaxation-intensive job. We were sitting inside a makeshift tent in the middle of the African desert, waiting for the orders that would send us back out into the field. We drank water from small foil pouches that never seemed to go dry, and recently I'd been sucking down as much moisture as possible, trying to reconstitute myself after fifteen days in the 110 degree heat. The fighting machines used by the Marines in those days might have been fierce, but they were not well air-conditioned.

"You got tanks because that's what the brass decided," Sarge told me. He'd just come back from HQ, and was still done up in his dress whites, the pits and back shining through with perspiration, dripping to the floor in a Niagara of sweat.

"From those tests?"

"Some of 'em."

"Which ones?"

Sarge didn't even try to fudge the answer. He always let you know the truth, and didn't care much of what the response would be. "Remember the concussion blast?" he said. I nodded. "That was the one. You, Freivald, Hennenson, scored in the top range, so they put you in tanks."

I still didn't quite understand. "So we . . . we didn't get concussions?"

"No," said Tig. "You all got concussions, pretty damn bad. But you came out of it sooner'n the rest of 'em, got control of your bodies. Guess you boys have bigger skulls than the others, so the pressure came off faster. That, or you've got smaller brains. Either way, tanks is tanks. Time to ship back out."

Bigger skulls and smaller brains. This was the kind of military precision with which we won the war in Africa.

———

I slept just now. Thirty minutes, maybe more. I hope it's more a sign that my body is adapting to the circumstances, and less a sign that I'm becoming complacent, that somewhere in my mind I've decided that rest is more important than vigilance.

My lack of restlessness may also be due to that note I found in my typewriter yesterday. The more I try not to think about it, the more I'm drawn back:

Shut up.

So curt. So final. I can't help but wonder who wrote it, and where they might be. And why they might be. The Tyler Street Hotel might be a great place to hide out, but it's my place to hide out; if there are other residents, I'd like to make their acquaintance. I may consider charging rent.

I have heard sounds at night, come to think of it. A bang or two from one of the lower floors, a creaking strut here or there. But these are the noises that come with any burned-out twentieth-century hotel, and although my stomach bottoms out with every thump and click, although my hands leap for their scalpels at every creak, I never before considered the possibility that these sounds could eventually bring me comfort. But I have been alone for months, and though isolation is very much the common thread that runs through any Bio-Repo man's life, it's one I'm always keen to cut.

I don't have any delusions about my ability to stay sane on my own: I'm a five-time winner, nuptially speaking, and there's got to be a reason for my inability to stay single for any protracted length of time.

———

Second trip to the psychiatrist with Carol, and the same shrink who told me I had a great capacity for love proceeded to tell me that I had a number of unresolved fears.

"You know what I do for a living, right?" I asked.

He nodded. Knew full well. "But that doesn't preclude the very real notion that you've got a lot of deep-set fear."

"Like what?" I asked.

"Death."

"Who doesn't? What else?"

"Failure."

"And you don't?"

"Loneliness," he said with a sly wink toward my wife.

I shook it off. "You know how many people there are in this world, Doc? Eight billion of us on this planet. A two-toed leper can't even find himself an isolated space without another six lepers coming by to say howdy. I can't be scared of loneliness—there's no such thing anymore."

———

That's not entirely true, I know now. Ninth year as a full Repo man, and I had just taken on a case to run out a Ghost system from James "T-Bone" Bonasera, a one-time music producer out in the suburbs. This guy had engineered some of my favorite songs back in the day, tunes me and the boys piped through the tank intercom system when the battle signs were down—this was the fellow who produced the Sammy Brand Trio's recording of "Baby in My Sleeve," of all things—and despite my reluctance to get involved with Ghost work, I felt like I owed it to the guy to tell him how much I appreciated his music before I ripped out his central nervous system.

I don't enjoy Ghost work. I'm not technically licensed for it, in fact, though every Bio-Repo man has done his fair share, authorization or not. I can understand a man needing a better pancreas or a spanking-new set of aluminum lungs, but when it comes to replacing and augmenting something as abstract as sense and memory, I tend to bow out and let the spooks do their job. Don't get me wrong—some of my best friends do a little pimping for the Ghost. But you've got to have a certain amount of empathy to get it done right, and that's where I come up short.

But the money was fantastic, the opportunity to meet a personal champion too great to pass up, and so I headed out to the suburbs. The back alleys and mangy street dogs soon gave way to paved sidewalks and scampering children, and the smells took on a decided twist of pine and oak. The leaves had just begun to change, and though we had reds and yellows in the city, they seemed so much more *proper* out there, in the same way a bottle of red wine tastes better in Venice, Italy, than it does in Venice, California.

The home was a mansion, 20,000 square feet, easy, but I was glad for its size. Any smaller, and I'd have been tempted to gas it out first, thus losing my opportunity to speak with the man. As it was, I'd never have enough ether to fill a house that size in any prudent amount of time, so I'd have to resort to more personal measures.

Gates, a half-mile driveway, topiary bushes gone to seed. T-Bone was still living in the mansion, I'd been told, but the IRS had turned the full power of their spotlight on his financial records and come up with more than a few question marks. As a result, they had attached his residuals from the last ten albums, and then added in the proceeds from the next ten as well, just to be on the safe side. The bankruptcy auction was set for a week from that Wednesday. House, furnishings, cars—he was broke beyond broke, and they were taking it all back. Unfortunately for him, so were we.

I found him down in the music studio he'd built in the east wing of the house, headphones wrapped around his ears, eyes closed, grooving intently to whatever was playing over the forty-track system. I stood there for a good ten minutes, watching him as he fiddled with the mixing board, fine-tuning whatever this newest piece might be.

Eventually, T-Bone sat upright and removed his headphones, placing them carefully atop the board. Without turning around, he said, "Good evening." His voice was low, gravelly, as if he needed to replace his own woofers. "You're from the IRS?"

"No."

"Good," he said. "Soul-suckers are taking everything back."

"So am I," I said.

He nodded. Took this new info in, and quickly made his peace with whatever gods he saw fit. "I see. Could I please finish this song?"

I looked at my watch. There was another outstanding job that day, but I remember thinking that it was just as easily done later that night or the next morning. "Of course," I told him, stepping back to wait my turn. "I'm a big fan. 'Baby in My Sleeve' . . . fantastic." I stopped before going whole-hog fanatic on him; it wouldn't have been the professional thing to do.

But he turned then, got up and came toward me—he was a wiry fellow, tics of energy flipping his limbs into spastic jerks—grabbing my arm, leading me toward the board. "You can help," he said. "I haven't had an assistant for months."

I protested that I wasn't trained, that I'd never even touched a mixing board before, but he claimed it was no matter. "Song's just a mess of little parts," he said, "all working together. All you need to do is listen for the parts inside the whole. If you can isolate the parts, pull 'em out and mix 'em around, we can improve the overall effect."

I told him I thought I might be qualified for the job.

———

The song I helped him mix that day—"Tailor Made Five" by Susan Lundi's Orchestra—became a posthumous platinum hit, and though I didn't get any credit on the inside jacket, I told everyone down at the Union that I'd helped out a little on the trumpets and vibes.

After two and a half hours, we were done with the mix, the sound was hopping, and the producer had already sucked up enough Q to kill a Clydesdale. He offered me the sparkling red powder on six or seven occasions, each time forgetting that I had flatly refused it not ten minutes before. I wasn't surprised to find, when I finally got the neuro-net out of him, that the central processor was crusted over, filthy with crystallized cerebrospinal fluid. That's the kind of thing that happens when you're hooked on the Q, and it's a shame that even after the most expensive of artiforg implantations, he wasn't able to reprogram himself to beat the habit.

He'd been on his own for nine months, he told me, after his wife had taken their twin baby girls and fled to their second home in Jamaica, and since then hadn't seen another soul until I broke in to steal his brain. He'd somehow been operating via the U.S. Postal service, connecting with the music companies, the bands, and the rest of the outside world solely by the slowest means of modern communication. As a result, his conversations were impossibly stunted, gaps of understanding and intent inherent within three-week-long mail deliveries, and it was this, more than anything else, that had contributed to his final detachment from reality. True loneliness, I learned that day, isn't the lack of others. It's the lack of others quickly.

———

Good news:

I went out for Thai food tonight, which is to say that I broke into the back room of a local restaurant, stole some cooking smocks, and snuck into the kitchen of my favorite eatery dressed as one of their own. I had two orders of pad kee mao and one of panang chicken curry stuck beneath my jacket before any of the regular kitchen staff noticed that I was neither Thai nor anything remotely resembling Thai, and I was out the door seconds later. Took the long way back to the hotel, slurping up one container of noodles as I went, staring up at the surrounding high-rises as I walked. If I stared hard enough, I could make out shadows even in those apartments and offices without lights, dull silhouettes moving back and forth in the darkness.

Rather than zip up to my room as usual, I stood outside the Tyler Street Hotel, grabbing a seat on the sidewalk across the street. The concrete was cold, but soon warmed up as I set to eating the chicken, the fiery spices of the curry sending beads of sweat up to my brow. I kept my eyes trained on the building above, not staring at any one spot too long. The trick to seeing in darkness—without an infrared scope, of course—is to keep the pupils moving back and forth, scanning horizontally for movement before locking in on a location. This was one of the tricks they taught us during tank training. Then again, they also taught us how to defecate in place without squatting, making a sound, or removing our pants, so not everything that came out of my military experience translated completely into civilian life.

After forty-five minutes of scanning and sucking noo-dles, I was prepared to tuck in for the night. But as I flipped onto my haunches, preparing to sneak back inside the hotel, a burst of shadowy movement up on the top floor caught my attention. I looked, glanced away, then looked back again, and sure enough, there it was, a vaguely human-shaped silhouette that had not been there before. It had stopped moving as soon as I spotted it, but I got the distinct impression that as I was staring up, it was staring down.

I bolted into the hotel lobby.

―――――――

Thirteen floors later, I was still running strong, and I slammed open the stairwell door with a mighty crash. No use being quiet now; it was too late at night for any nearby residents to care about the noise, and I was more than happy to spook out whoever was sharing the hotel with me.

The penthouse was empty. Floor-to-ceiling windows— some intact, others not so much—afforded a view of the downtown slums and the bright possibilities of the city beyond, but the room itself was abandoned. The walls were coated in the same dull ash as mine downstairs, only these looked like they may have had some semblance of a normal color beneath the char.

The floor, though, was curiously devoid of dust, and the one other flat surface, a rusted-out metal table in the center of the room, was clean enough for even the most ardent of germaphobes to eat off.

For a moment, I considered jogging back downstairs and grabbing one of the few scopes I had, maybe an infrared to pick up on lagging heat signals, but I realized that in the time it would take me to go down and back up, I'd lose whatever traces might be lingering around, waiting to die off.

So I ran a check the old-fashioned way. Fingers along the floorboards, eye to the walls. Searching for hairs, for nails . . .

For clothing fibers. On an inside doorway, one foot above

the ground, a broken rusty nail poked its way out of the wall. I squatted down and took a gander, focusing my eyes as best I could on that minuscule shard of metal.

Beige. See-through. Stretchy. It was a smidgen of nylon. Someone had run through here in a hurry, and someone had torn her pantyhose.

So, as I said, good news:

I'm living with a woman again.

CHAPTER 8

The tank training facility was ten miles away from base, set on what used to be a vineyard near the Amalfi coast. The Marines, I'd been told, had offered the owner a fair settlement for his land, but had been refused on three separate occasions, even after they repeatedly raised their price. The vintner held firm, and though he was always polite with the emissaries who were sent with cases of cash, he stuck to his guns and sent them away every time.

The next season, this elderly gentleman with three children, eight grandkids, and a great-grandson on the way found his crops overrun by a ravenous grape bug never before seen on Italian soil, a particular strain of beetle that was surprisingly resistant to any and all mass-market pesticides. When the harvest came around and it was time to pick the fruits of his labor, there was only enough to make a hundred cases of wine, as opposed to the three thousand cases the vineyard usually produced.

He sold the land two months later for half of the government's initial offer.

———

But it made for a great place to train; wide, flat land that could be built up by artificial means into any terrain desired, ringed by mountains to deflect the horrendous sound of heavy artillery, nearly impossible to spy upon, except by satellite. We were ten hours out in the field at a time, except when we trained combat style, in which case the training exercises could run into days.

When we first arrived at the facility, Tig showed me, Jake, Harold, and the rest of the tank crew to our bunks. Bill Braxton, the guy whose father owned the car dealership, was with us—his unusually large cranium was evident from the outside, so maybe we were the ones with the small brains—as was a smattering of other knobs I'd seen around base from time to time.

Rather than give us standard-issue military cots, the boys in Tank Group A were assigned "control chairs" for all our sleeping needs. These were replicas of the seats inside the Marine tanks, padded contraptions almost exactly like those in which we'd taken the dreaded concussion test.

"You will sleep in these," Tig told us, cutting off any comments we may have had, "and you will get to like it. I promise you that after a month of sleeping inside your control chair here on base and two more years of living in it out in the field, you will find that any other bed just won't do. When your time is done and you flip back to the real world, you will want to bring your control chair with you. You will lie on your back and wish you were curled into a ball. Your limbs will contract of their own volition, and you will find yourself spending nights at the dining-room table, tucked into a chair, elbows to the wall, knees into your chest. Your wife will not understand why it is that you will not sleep in the bed with her. There will be fights, and there will be confusion, and still you will resist. It may look funny now, but your control chair, gentlemen, will become your blue blanket."

I hated the sonofabitch for telling us these things.

I hated him again two years later because he was right.

———

Speaking of my wife and the bed that we would never again share:

Beth's letters arrived with less frequency. I told myself this was because I'd switched training facilities, because the Italian mail systems were notoriously faulty, because I hadn't exactly been writing up a storm myself. But there were suspicions, and there was doubt.

I didn't have any illusions about being married to a hooker. I knew she'd meet up with strange men, that said strange men would pay her for the privilege of doing unspeakable things to her body, and that it was all just a day at the office, no different from running accountancy spreadsheets. Sometimes the thought of it made me ill, literally queasy to the point of gagging, but most of the time I convinced myself it was nothing more than spreading a leg to this side and a leg to that side and letting the rest of the body go numb. She needed the cash, and I wasn't pulling down enough in the military to keep her in the style to which she'd become accustomed, which included such luxuries like eating on a regular basis.

But the longer I sat in that control chair—my body contorted into a suspended fetal position, unable to squirm, turn over, or scratch my ass—the more my mind wandered and filled itself with fascinating scenarios. Beth taking off with another client. Giving up the life altogether and running away to the Arctic. Holding a free-for-all session with the Green Berets, no extra charges, no money down.

After a week-long interval, I received a short letter from her, the usual news about her parents, about San Diego, about how she went to a street fair and bought an elephant ear and remembered the time a few days before we married when I burned my tongue on the hot oil from a stick of fried dough, which was pretty much like an elephant ear only without all the powdered sugar, and how it made her laugh, only I wasn't there to see it and she hoped I'd be able to come home soon.

And there was a perfume on the letter, like usual, but this time it didn't smell like Beth. It didn't even smell like anything Beth would, in theory, ever deign to wear. It was rougher than her usual ten-dollar bottles, muskier. Men's cologne? Why would there be men's cologne on her letter? Was another man, not just a client but a *lover*, standing behind her as she wrote it, caressing her breasts, sucking on her neck, letting his fingers drop between her legs, into her, making her moan even as she wrote false words to her husband halfway around the world?

In this manner, the nights passed.

———

The mornings, on the other hand, left me no time for my torturous little fantasies, filled as they were with the thrill one can only get from sitting in a tank and watching blips on a radar screen. Sounds like primetime for daydreaming, of course, but the blips could turn into bleeps within milliseconds, and if you didn't lock on target and fire, you were dead where you sat.

Not actually dead, per se, not during the drills in Italy, but come Africa, we were told, it would be shoot or be shot. Killer or victim, everyone got to play his part. Another hastily constructed military lie, I later found out. In Africa, you could choose to shoot, or you could choose to sit still and watch the enemy bungle themselves out of a victory, but the only folks who were going home in body bags were those who pissed off Fate.

We got a quick lesson in this on the third day of tank training. The first two days had been out-of-uniform classes, boring lectures during which we took notes and tried to absorb the more interesting parts of what our instructors had to say. Paper airplanes shot about the room. One kid had a spitball contest going with Bill Braxton, who wasn't too keen on returning the salvos. It was like grammar school, but they couldn't have expected any different; they tried to cram everything from fluid mechanics to weapons ballistics into our noggins, and I'd be surprised if more than two or three bits of information were still there an hour later.

But the third day they let us at the tanks, splitting us up into teams of three, and we ran to them like kids let out for recess. This was strictly a hands-off session; we were there solely to familiarize ourselves with the equipment inside the machine, not the manner in which everything worked. That, we were told, would come later.

I climbed into the tank from the rear, as our commanders had ordered, crawling past instrumentation and tubing on my belly before reaching the front control chair. The previous three nights of aborted sleep had, at least, introduced me to the inner workings of the seat, so I was able to get myself righted and in place before all the commotion started.

There was a bang, there was screaming, and there was the distinct smell of smoke, and when it was all over, a twenty-year-old private I never knew was dead.

———

Come to think of it, he was the spitballer, so maybe while he was supposed to be learning what buttons not to push, he was instead launching a gummed-up wad of tissue at Bill Braxton's hairy forearm. I don't know why he yanked the lever he did, or why he would have yanked any levers at all, but even if I knew the reason, it wouldn't bring him back. Nothing brings you back when you launch an ejection seat without first opening the hatch above your head.

———

The penthouse is still empty; I've just been up there, snooping around. Two days since I found that clue. Two days for me to wonder who this woman is, what she's like. Questions naturally arise. For instance: Is she a hider? Is she a seeker? And what sort of woman wears pantyhose in an abandoned hotel?

The penthouse floors are still devoid of dust, but I believe I may have detected a scuff mark on the floorboards, and from the size of it, I would venture to say it's been left by the mystery woman. She's been back, undetected. Not for long.

One of the few nonsurgical tools the Credit Union supplied us with was a motion detector, truly the device of a thousand and one uses. I've done everything from trap animals to snare dates using this thing, and though I was reluctant to use it before in preserving my own life—my chief worry that the reliance on technology would sap me of my inherent skills—I'm more than happy to put it to a field test and see if we can't scare up a loose critter.

The device is half an inch square, with a mostly invisible ray of light beaming out from one side. I say *mostly invisible* because it can be detected by a few means, one of which happens to be suffusing the surrounding area with smoke. I had a friend in the Union who died when the client he was tracking got wise to the motion detector, thanks to a nasty cigar habit; the deadbeat saw the beam, got a gas mask out, tripped the sensor, and when the Repo man gassed down the house and came strolling in, he got whacked on the back of the head with a 1959 Fender electric guitar, made way back in the day when they didn't know from lightweight rock 'n' roll.

But I doubt the interloper upstairs smokes, and even if she does, it won't help her to notice the motion detector; I've got it set low, knee level, so unless she's a leprechaun or does a mean limbo, the remote sensor in my back left pocket is bound to go off sometime soon.

Meantime, I'm sleeping with a gun in each hand.

———————

Mary-Ellen, my second wife, hated guns. Hated all weapons, in fact, and although her father was a decorated Army colonel, we were forbidden to talk about the military during cocktails, at the dinner table, and all the way through dessert. If we wanted to discuss "the science of hate," as my loving wife put it, her father and I were forced to stand outside in the chilly winter air—our marriage didn't make it through to the summer months—and huddle in the warmth of a pipe and cheap tobacco.

When we met, I was a third-year Bio-Repo man still coming hard off a four-year-old divorce. I'd been bedding every woman I met, taking into them with a vengeance, trying to make a hooker out of every one, but never finding my Beth. It was after a job, actually, when Mary-Ellen and I ran into each other, though if she knew then where I'd been an hour earlier, she not only wouldn't have married me, she would have run from the diner screaming like a chimp.

———————

Sonny DePrimo was the son of Harry DePrimo, who was cousin to Sonny Abate, who was underboss to the second-largest crime family in Chicago, and none of this would have ever concerned me, except for the fact that Sonny DePrimo was enough of a screwup with the mob that they pulled some strings and got him into the Credit Union training program. Only problem was, he was more of a screwup as a Bio-Repo man than he ever was as a bag man, but with more serious consequences. He was mired in the old ways, I guess, unable to understand that needless bloodshed and splatter only made the job more difficult than it already was, and brought a lot of bad publicity to a company that needed all the good will it could get. Gas, grab, go, that's all there is to it.

It didn't help that his mentor was none other than Tony Park, who'd already made a life out of gleefully taking others'. All of Sonny's worst tendencies were only amplified under Tony's tutelage, and soon Sonny was making a habit out of beating the clients before taking what he'd come for, often dragging them into a public spectacle that helped neither the Union's image nor his own. The final straw came when he was given the delicate assignment of retrieving a Klondike P–14 pancreatic unit from the ailing daughter of one of Chicago's former mayors, a man loved throughout the state of Illinois and beyond. She was already on death's doorstep, no more than three or four weeks away from ringing the bell and stepping inside; her debt to the Union was large, certainly, and unpaid, but was due to other mounting medical costs and a series of legal actions she'd undertaken against the wolves in the media who would have otherwise fed on her father's good name. Clearly, a simple, quiet repossession would have been the wisest option, but Sonny was the Bio-Repo man on call that evening.

He dragged her out of the hospital, onto a thirty-minute ride on the El—shouting obscenities all the way—and down to the Union offices, where he ripped out her Klondike with an unapproved bowie knife and left her to die six feet away from the lobby doors and a host of shocked, would-be customers.

The Union was displeased with Sonny. They sent me to talk sense into him.

An hour later, I walked into the Federal Way Diner, clothes beneath my jacket still sopping with blood, and met the gal who would soon become my second ex-wife.

———————

"You gonna eat the rest of that?" I asked her. She hadn't touched the second half of her tuna sandwich, and the effort I'd just exerted on the job had me starving. A patch of skin that used to belong on Sonny DePrimo's neck was folded up neatly into fourths, sitting in my jacket pocket. The Union had wanted their tattoo back. "Never seen anyone nurse a sandwich like that."

"Never had a stranger ask for my food before."

"Firsts for both of us, then," I concluded, already sizing her up as an easy catch. Different from my usual type. More of an Earth-mother feel she had going, as opposed to the trashy things I'd been bringing back home, though perhaps I'm confusing what I know of her personality now with what I expected from her body then. In either case, she would most certainly do for a night of entertainment.

Without waiting, I snatched the tuna sandwich from her plate, ate it while maintaining perfect eye contact, and didn't flinch a bit when she slapped me, full bore, across the face. That's how our life together began: something stolen, someone slapped.

Perhaps I should have taken it as a sign.

———

Most nights I'd come home at two, three in the morning, and she'd be up, sitting cross-legged in the middle of our bed, a grotesque four-poster that she'd so kindly brought into the relationship, like her lamps and her armoire and her little soap holders with the brass feet. My life was never *my* life with Mary-Ellen, at least not in the way I ever expected it to be, but I was willing to take a backseat to antiquities in order to make my second marriage work better than my first.

The fights didn't begin automatically. By the time I arrived at the front door, wiped out from a hard night, I wanted one of two things: sleep or sex. Sometimes both, sometimes

in varying order. Mary-Ellen, for all of her professed dislike
of my career, wanted to ask questions.

"Who was he?" she'd ask. "Where'd he live? What organ
was it? Did he struggle? Did you cry?"

She always asked this last one, and I always answered it
in the negative. I think she was hoping one day that I'd slip,
that I'd admit to breaking down in a sobbing jag, and that
she could use it as a lever to pry me away from the Union.
Never happened, of course, but she kept right on with it
every night.

And with every question she asked, the quieter I would
become, until she was raging against me with all of her
strength, and I was sitting back in my easy chair, eyes
closed, legs pulled against my chest in that familiar, comforting way. Anyone walked by, they would have thought
Mary-Ellen was screaming at a corpse.

Again, perhaps this was something of a sign.

———

The neighborhood children are playing in the street below
once again, jumping rope and singing songs. This time, the
tune and the words are different:

Tell it to the mama
Tell it to the son
They'll all be gone when the day is done
On come the wrinkles
On comes the sneeze
Old man dies on his old-man knees . . .

There are no old men anymore, I want to yell down to
them. Old men went out with cardiac disease and paper
straws. And even if there were an old man to be found, no
chance he'd have his original knees.

———

I don't know a single person who's died of old age, unless you count living long enough to be killed as dying of old age. My father had a fatal brain aneurysm the second year I was in the military, and Mom did her thing eight years later, still a young woman, only one too frightened to go on living all by herself. Wonder where I get it from.

Harold Hennenson sure wouldn't make it to his geriatric years; neither would that kid with the spitballs. Ejected himself right into the roof of the tank, the other soldiers in his machine said, just latched himself into the control chair, pulled one lever too many, and a second later wound up with ground beef from the neck up. The smoke I smelled came from the explosive charge that propelled the chair upward at over a hundred miles an hour. Of course, he didn't go anywhere close to a hundred miles; three feet did the trick.

After the military service, we were given four hours' mourning time, during which most of us sat in our control chairs and stared into space, trying to figure out which lever the idiot had pulled and promising ourselves that we would never, ever, do something as god-awfully stupid as that. Chaplain came down to see us, to console us in our time of grief, see if we wanted to ride with him back to the chapel for long-term counseling, but we all humored the guy and shooed him away. Nice enough fellow, but there's not a lot of use for consolation in the armed forces. When we joined up, each and every one of us knew that there was a chance we'd die during our service, and the loss of a private none of us knew all that well—and a moronic one at that—didn't have the platoon all choked up.

I like to think that if I were the one who'd ejected myself into the great beyond, the chaplain would have had his hands full with despondent friends who needed his company and guidance for weeks on end, but I know deep down that

Father McGuigan was taking that long trip back up the coast all alone one way or the other.

———

The whole incident is pretty similar to how Greg Kashekian, the Persian from across the street, met his own Muslim maker, or so the story goes. Great bit for the gossipmongers, but as I heard it from Sergeant Ignakowski, and I've never had any reason to doubt a single thing Tig ever told me, I feel I can repeat the tale here with confidence:

We were already out in Africa, and our first day—one of our only days, it turned out—of real combat had passed us by. On our side, we had six wounded and two dead, compared to a wholesale slaughter of the enemy, which sustained massive casualties the likes of which I'd previously seen only on television history specials.

Jake and I were personally responsibly for at least eighty-two casualties on the other side. I know this because Jake chose to let loose with a holler and a whoop with each kill, marking off a tick on the inside wall of the tank with a permanent marker he'd purchased in Italy for this very purpose. Our teamwork was impeccable; I drove, he shot, and in this way, we made our mark upon the desert.

By the next morning, the battle was over. We were elated. And, soon enough, drunk. Tig wasn't a fan of excessive inebriation, but he understood that his soldiers needed to work out their issues in different ways, and he was more than happy to let us get as boiled as cabbages while he sat back and sipped on a water bottle.

Harold, who was only forty-two days away from his own death but didn't know it, was more animated than I'd ever seen him before; he'd been tank commander that day, riding hard at the point of our vanguard, manning the scopes and leading us across the dunes. Harold was the first to notice the odd ticks on the horizon, and by the time the rest of the tanks had made their way to the top of the dune, the boy from the Bronx and his crew had taken out two enemy battalions with a pair of guided missiles and were well on their way to another hundred or so confirmed kills.

We cheered; we toasted; we sang songs about our virtues and virility. We were Vikings, and we'd pillaged and plundered with the best of them.

Tig left the tent to take a leak. I followed along.

"Pretty fucking sweet," I remember saying. The desert sands shifted beneath my feet as I urinated; it was either the wind or the whiskey.

"We had a good day," Tig said, slapping me on the back.

"Got a whole mess of 'em, didn't we? Two fifty-eight confirmed."

"Forget the numbers. You woke up this morning, and you're going to sleep tonight. In my book, that's a good day."

In recent months, I have adopted Tig's philosophy.

———

Somehow, the conversation got around to hometowns and the like, and when I told Tig where I was from, his eyes narrowed into little slits. Right away, I could tell he knew the place, which was odd, because even folks in the little cities three or four towns over hadn't heard of it.

"You know a Kashekian?" said Tig.

"Greg, Tilly, yeah, I know 'em."

And that's when he told me the story of how the dumb sod really died:

Greg Kashekian entered the military not much different than he left high school. He was still an arrogant bastard, but now he had a gun and a uniform and a new way in which to flaunt his size and strength. Like me, he joined the Marines, and like me, he was a whiz at that concussion test. Big skulls and small brains were common on our block; perhaps there was something in the water.

Tig said that from the first day, Greg had already charmed the rest of his platoon with his meager wit and bulging muscles. They were suddenly his best buddies, eager to listen to his stories of games he'd won and girls he'd bedded, and Tig had a rough time trying to get their minds off of football and women and back to the task at hand. Like me, Tig took an instant dislike to my neighbor, though he was still duty-bound to treat him just like the rest of the knobs.

The Persian also proved to be a whiz as a tank gunner, able to lock in and identify targets at incredible distances. By the time they'd finished training, Greg Kashekian had some of the highest marks ever given to a Marine private on that particular machine, and was recommended for a corporal position, to be awarded once he returned from his first stint in Africa.

If I remember correctly, his mother received the post-humous promotion certificate along with his ashes.

———

"Africa was quieter then," Tig told me that night. "They hadn't started in with the biologicals, and we hadn't yet firebombed the veldt. Nairobi was still stable. We hadn't seen any real combat yet, so most of it was maneuvers, some light recon missions. Tanks crawled over the desert, but weapons were kept locked down, and for two weeks, we didn't have a single casualty.

"Eighteenth day out there, we hadn't caught the slightest glimpse of the enemy, and everyone was getting restless. Some friend of a friend of one of the supply sergeants had snuck in a big load of nudie mags and Kashekian thought he was Santa Claus, buying up a whole stack and handing 'em out to his friends.

"Middle of the night, we called a readiness drill, and the platoon jumped outta their bunks and into the tanks, ready to crawl fast over the sand into a recon base we'd set up about twenty clicks south of camp. I hooked onto a halftrack and paced the group from the side, watching the drill and taking notes for the com officers who'd ordered the exercise.

"We're halfway there when I hear this charge go off and I look up to see a trail of ejection jets slicing into the air—a control chair flying up out of a nearby tank. I watched that thing leap up, hang in the air for a fraction of a second, and then start to plummet back to the hard sand below, dropping like a sparrow killed mid-flight. The goddamned parachute didn't open.

"I burned that halftrack fast as I could, racing over to the jumbled mess of metal on the ground, the whole way thinking about the tank and the ejection seats and the mechanical failures. It was gonna be weeks of inquisitions and testimony. Paperwork up my ass.

"But when I got there, I found that goddamned Kashekian, broken and bloody, still propped up in the mangled control chair, pants around his ankles, skivvies 'round his knees, one hand clutched around a copy of *Hootenanny Hooter Review* and the other 'round his johnson. He mighta been dead, but he sure looked happy."

———

Moral of the story: Growing hair on your palms could be the least of your worries.

———

The unofficial inquest determined that Greg Kashekian—homecoming king, illegitimate dad, patriotic American—had been using his hands when he should have been sitting on them, and that an errant tug had sent him hurtling skyward to his doom. The official inquest, on the other hand, labeled the death as accidental operator failure and informed all interested parties that the military would be looking into the problem. It would be bad press to let the folks at home know that their rock-hard fighting force was just that, so the matter was resolved and hushed up nice and quick.

I can't say I mourned for Greg Kashekian, but I did not rejoice in his death or manner of demise. To do so would have been to disrespect all members of the armed forces, and despite my feelings toward the individual, I won't knock all jarheads just to gloat at one Persian getting his comeuppance.

I will admit to visiting his grave upon returning from Africa and, upon finding that someone else had placed a jar of Vaseline and a copy of *Hootenanny Hooter Review* atop his headstone, wishing like hell that I'd been the one to do it.

———

Speaking of reading material, I was able to pinch a few books out of the library this morning which might help me on my quest to hunt down the hotel's other resident. *Trapping and Survival*, by James McQuarry, had a nice ring to it when I grabbed it off the stacks, particularly because the title combines the two concepts that currently comprise my entire lifestyle. Unfortunately, this early-twentieth-century tome has more to do with recipes for squirrel casserole than it does my current situation; at the very least, it might make for a nice starter in case I should ever choose to light a fire.

I've also got a copy of *The Adventures of Swiss Family Robinson*, this more for pleasure reading than any hints it might afford, though I seem to remember a part from my school days in which

———

Incredible. Amazing. And incredible again.

An hour ago, as I was typing that last section about Swiss

Family Robinson, the remote motion sensor in my back pocket began to vibrate. At first I spun around, thinking some critter had squirmed inside Tyler Street and was preparing to feast on my rump, but quickly I remembered what that buzzing meant. I leaped to my feet and into the hallway, grabbing my Mauser for long-range protection and the garrote for hand-to-hand combat.

Launching myself up the stairs as quickly as I could without making too much excess noise, I ran through the floors, devouring three, four steps at a time. By the time I reached the penthouse, I was panting hard—these last few months have taken their toll on what was once a Swiss watch of a cardiovascular system—but my precision heart was still functioning just as the brochures promised it would. I entered the top-floor hallway and grabbed the doorknob of the penthouse suite, aware that on the other side could be anything ranging from a dormouse to a rifle to a platoon of Credit Union Bio-Repo men waiting to tie me down, tear out my heart, and send me packing to a local pauper's grave. Suddenly, I wasn't sure anymore if I'd really felt the buzzing in my pocket or if it had been my imagination.

I held the Mauser out in front of my body, flicked off the safety, and kicked in the door.

———

Of my five wives, four of them were talkers. Gold-medal caliber, each and every one, tongues like whips when the mood struck right. The only quiet one among them was my third ex-wife, Melinda, and she stayed silent right up until the end.

Not that it kept any of the marriages from dissolving into crumbs, but I think the verbal sparring matches between myself and my former spouses added a bit of spice to what might otherwise have been boring domestic bliss. I do know that although each marriage ended with a ream of divorce papers delivered to my mailbox, every single one of my relationships began with a protracted conversation:

Beth: After one bout of paid sex and two freebies.

Mary-Ellen: After I stole her tuna sandwich and she slapped me.

Melinda: Before I broke into the nursing home where she worked and repossessed a Jarvik–11 from her favorite patient.

Carol: While trying to find our way out of a burning restaurant.

Wendy: In the cemetery, after her father's funeral.

And now, on the subject of the all-time great talking women in my life, it seems there's a new one to add to the list:

Bonnie: While we held each other lovingly at gunpoint.

CHAPTER 9

Down the barrel of my gun, caught in my sights: She stood in the middle of the suite, feet spread at hip distance, right arm outstretched, left arm supporting an old six-shooter clutched in her hand, the barrel not trembling an inch. A tight bun of shiny blonde hair curled at the back of her head, a single strand dangling down into her eyes, forcing her to blow up a column of air every so often to clear the view. Wrapped in a brown woolen jacket, collar brought up high around her long neck, caressing a strong jawbone. Long, angular face with soft features somewhat familiar, though unplaceable. Blue jeans tight at the hip, flared at the ankle.

"You're in my hotel," I said plainly, taking a step into the room.

She cocked the gun, making a big show of it. The hammer clicked back. "Four months," she said, and though the voice that came out of her mouth was sonorous and smooth, it sounded off. Edgy. "You?"

"Five months," I said. I'd been here no more than two.

"You're lying."

"So are you."

And still we held our guns aloft, aimed at each another. My arm, unaccustomed to holding anyone at gunpoint in quite some time, began to tire, the triceps trembling a bit; I couldn't understand how she was able to keep her pistol so rock steady.

The woman inspected me up and down—more than inspected me—devoured me—her gaze sucking in everything, lingering on my crotch, my chest, and suddenly, uncomfortably, I understood what the feminists had been on about all these years.

Eventually, her stare settled on my neck. On the tattoo. Impossible to miss, impossible to misidentify. But whereas most people's reactions would be shock, fear, anger, she simply said, "I'm guessing that's pretty old."

"You're guessing right."

"Still active?"

"Not as such, no."

She nodded. "That's what I thought." Again, there was something odd about her voice. Not the tone itself, but the way in which she formed her words. They were crisp, clear—perhaps too much so.

More time passed, and I paced my way about the room, keeping my Mauser aloft, my finger on the trigger. With every second, my arm grew wearier, and I had to bring all of my attention into focus to keep from dropping the pistol to my side. "Look," I said finally, "this is getting tiring—"

"For you, perhaps. You could always put your gun down."

"And then?"

"Then I'd probably shoot you," she said. "But I might not."

I held the gun higher. "I'm not here to hurt you," I promised.

"How reassuring."

Thirteen stories down, a jumble of cars had gathered on the street corner, honking and causing a terrible fuss, the cacophony floating up to the penthouse suite, forming a jangle of music for our little scene. An accident is what it looked like, three-car collision in the middle of the road. Ambulances were just making their way to the intersection.

"You steal a lot of artiforgs?" she asked me, taking her first steps in my direction. They were confident, but oddly stiff.

"I never stole a thing."

"I read some of that manuscript of yours," she said, and my Jarvik jumped at the violation. I'd assumed she'd just come in, scribbled that little note for me, and taken off; I had no idea she'd been through my things. "I know what you do. What you did. Make yourself out to be a real martyr."

"I'm just telling it like it was."

"There's no law you've gotta write your memoirs before you go," she told me, and as she walked I thought I heard a familiar knee joint popping and clicking.

"But there are a few about concealed weapons. What say we put these down?"

She pursed those pouty lips and took another look at my Mauser. "You first."

I nodded. "If you tell me your name."

"Bonnie," she said after a time. "I hope that suits you."

It suited me fine. I put down the gun, told her my name, and we got on with things.

———

Bonnie's actually been staying in the Tyler Street hotel for a little less than five weeks, and the penthouse has been only one of her domiciles during that time. Upon first arriving, she found a two-room suite on the ninth floor that hadn't been affected too badly by the fire, or so she thought until she came back from a trip to the bakery to find that half of her stuff had been buried by a crumbling pile of plaster in the master bedroom. From there she moved into a series of standard rooms on varying floors, none of which afforded her the privacy that she desired; either they were too close to the street below or the insulation had burned away, making them hot during the day, cold at night, and loud all the time.

"But I like it up here," she told me once we'd dispensed with the weapons and taken a seat across from each other on the penthouse floor. She sat down daintily, with a certain degree of care, as if she were made out of heavy porcelain and didn't want to chip her edges. "I can make a fair amount of noise without worrying whether street traffic is going to hear me, and as for the other hotel residents . . . Well, you're not exactly my worst nightmare on the subject."

As she spoke, talking mostly about herself while managing to reveal absolutely nothing personal, Bonnie displayed the same warm carelessness in conversation that had drawn me to the other women in my life. Once she got going, she didn't much care for pauses in speech, didn't wait to get my response, didn't ask if she was boring me or losing me or entertaining me. Still, it wasn't like she was talking just to talk; she was keenly interested in connecting, and though this was probably due to months of enforced isolation, it was flattering nevertheless.

We talked for two hours about the outside world, about the accident-prone intersection below the building, about the dilapidated condition of our current home, about film and music and art and friends—always about others, though, never about ourselves—before I excused myself to find a working restroom. When I returned to the penthouse, Bonnie was gone.

———————

I have a soft spot for women who take off on me. The more they're gone, the more I long for their return, and the more excited I become at the prospect of seeing them again. My ideal female is a gypsy circus performer with no roots in any town or country who enjoys making herself vanish inside the magician's velvet box, dabbles in faking her own death, and has been arrested at least three times for identity fraud, yet somehow repeatedly escapes from the maximum-security penitentiaries in which she's been imprisoned.

I suppose I could take out a personal ad, but my true ideal woman would never show up for the date.

———————

Beth had a habit of disappearing, as well, but back then, whatever dalliances she was off on were just starter recipes for my overactive imagination. Example: If she wrote me a letter telling me she'd gone down to Tijuana for the weekend, I'd instantly imagine her in the local donkey show, pulling ten guys up on stage at a hundred pesos a pop. If she said she'd gone to visit her mom, I suddenly decided that *mom* was a code word for "new boyfriend," and in my mind she wasn't shopping and girl-talking for those few days, but was facedown on some stranger's bed, getting it hard from behind.

I wrote postcard after postcard, simple little letters with a glaring subtext. I wanted more letters from her, more correspondence—anything, so long as it was in her handwriting and had her name scribbled at the bottom. I wanted it to come six, seven times a day. I wanted the military to hire an extra carrier just to be able to handle the volume of letters I would receive from my adoring wife. I wanted to cripple the U.S. postal service with the sheer bulk of twenty-pound paper stock. If she was writing letters all day, I figured, she couldn't be having sex.

And for every ten letters I wrote, one came back in response. So I'd up it to twenty, and to thirty, but the more often I sent one off, the less often Beth returned the gesture. I would venture to say that during the first six months I was in the desert, I wrote and sent approximately three hundred postcards and letters to my loving wife back home in San Diego.

I received eighteen.

One evening, in a sarcastic fit of rage, jealousy, and a fair amount of whiskey sours, I jotted off what was to be my final postcard sans attorney's fees. I wrote:

Dearest Beth,

If you would like your husband to rot in the desert while his wife fucks other men all over the Southern California area, please let him know at your earliest convenience, and he shall take great pains to help in this endeavor.

I set myself up, of course. The return letter came back quickly this time:

As you wish.

The divorce papers were stapled to the postcard.

––––––––

But while tank training continued, I was still laboring under the illusion that my notes home to Beth were doing the job of keeping her in line, and my spirits were high each day of practice. It didn't take long for Tig and the rest of the brass to figure out that I was crack at driving a tank and lousy at ammunition, so they gave me a permanent driving assignment and sent me out with a rotating series of gunners to see who I'd best be suited to work with.

One day, they put Harold in behind me, and though I was glad to have a mate on board, it was tough going from the start.

"Shove left," he'd call from the back. "I can't aim with you going right."

"Can't go left," I'd yell, trying to make myself audible over the noise of the six-ton machinery. We weren't fitted with talkie helmets yet, and even in the field they proved to be more prone to break than to work, so once inside the tanks, shouting was the best method of getting your point across. "There's a ditch left."

"Then rotate," he'd say. "Rotate!"

And more often than not, I'd rotate in the wrong direction, just to show him who was in command.

Sometimes I wonder if I'd been less of a stubborn bastard, Harold would be alive today. If I'd listened to him and actually worked *with* the guy, the brass might have assigned him to my tank rather than the one that got him dead.

Odds are Harold would have pissed me off enough to drive us all over the edge of the nearest sand dune, anyway.

They sent us back to base camp on weekends, probably because they didn't want to hear us bitch any more than they had to about sleeping in the control chairs. We'd hook up with our old platoon buddies, take off for twenty-four-hour trips into the Italian countryside, try to get some concept of what the outside world was all about. Of course, we all ended up at the same old places, doing the same old things.

To whatever degree the rest of us were taking to our assignments, Jake Freivald was positively flourishing. He'd gone from a thin, wisecracking NYC wannabe to a staid, filled-out soldier, just as likely to recite basic combat procedure as he would be to tell a dirty joke. Sometimes, he'd do it in the same sentence. The brass had taken notice of his ability and desire and given him extra duty in a recon squad.

"Recon is where it's at," he told me one night as we drank cheap red wine. "It's everything you saw in the movies as a kid, only more."

"More what?" I asked.

"More everything. More weapons. More tactics. More fun."

I asked him to give me details, to fill me in on the ins and outs of a job that sounded a hell of a lot more interesting than tank duty, but he was reticent on all matters recon. "Top secret, pal," he told me, then offered another suck off the wine jug to soothe my spirits.

"Tell ya what," he said, "if we both get outta here alive, and we're still talking to each other ten years from now, I'll tell you anything you want to know about patrols and recon, okay?"

We shook on it.

———

That was on October 14. Exactly ten years later to the day, I pulled a few strings at the Union to get Jake and myself assigned to run out an entire gastrointestinal system from an ex-football player out in Milwaukee. Workload was heavy that month, and it had been two weeks since we'd seen each other, so we spent the beginning of the job catching up, letting each other in on recent scores and jobs. I was married to Melinda at the time, and Jake liked to get in his jabs about my love life, chastising me for hitching my horse to yet another faltering wagon.

I waited until we'd stabilized the client—six-six, two-eighty, and thank the Lord we brought more than two Tasers with us, because that beast sucked up enough electricity to power the White House Christmas tree—and had already begun the messy extraction process before I let Jake know the importance of this day.

"Been ten years, huh? And you've been waiting . . ." He shook his head, seemingly more amazed that I remembered the date than at the swift passage of time.

"Ten years on the nose," I said, meanwhile trying my hardest to isolate the football player's aluminum esophagus catheter; I didn't want to scuff up the 'forg or bring anything back to the Union that wasn't their legal property to begin with. "And I've been waiting all this time, dreaming up the things you did or didn't do out in the field. So now you've got to tell me—what was recon like?"

Jake put down his scalpel, resting it on the smooth, blank forehead of the prone client. It balanced there like a seesaw, slowly rocking back and forth. "Back then, I thought it was fun. I thought it was dangerous, exciting. Sneaking in and out of locations, isolating targets, identifying enemies. The kind of thing every boy dreams about but never actually gets to do.

"But compared to Union work," he said flatly, "recon is accountancy."

———

So much for illusions. I've got a strong history of crumbling expectations, which is why this time around, I'm not counting on anything going down with Bonnie. For one thing, she keeps flaking off on me, and despite my predilection for such things, a woman this chronically invisible can't be good for any relationship. For another, we're wholly unsuited to each other. I've been wearing the same clothes for the last four weeks; she changes outfits whenever she bathes, which is, naturally, at least ten times as often as I manage to do. She's got a collection of dresses to match her six different pairs of pantyhose, which she dons at least every other night, despite the fact that, if she's lucky and does her job right, no one will ever see her. Furthermore, I'm fifteen years her senior, easy, and a man on the run from the Credit Union doesn't exactly make good husband material. Wendy, my fifth ex, found that out, and quick.

But I wasn't at all disappointed when Bonnie poked her head into my apartment two hours ago and asked if I'd like to grab some dinner up at her place. "Can you bring a tablecloth?" she asked. "My dining-room set is a little rusty."

By the time I put on my formal wear—consisting of the one remaining cotton shirt and chinos that had no discernible odor and few bloodstains—and tromped my way up the stairs, tarpaulin under my arm, Bonnie had already lit some well-placed candles, each illuminating a small corner of the room, keeping the rest in enforced twilight. The shadows played across her bright yellow-and-orange sundress, as if daring her to light up the room.

I brought up the tarp, whipping it up and out to spread across the metal table in the center of the room, and a small object flashed through the air, forcing Bonnie to duck as it flew by her head and *thunked* into the far wall.

"Forgive me," I said, plucking the scalpel out of the drywall and tucking it into my waistband. "I thought I cleaned this thing out."

While Bonnie used a small Sterno can to heat a pot of noodles she put me on chopping duty. Somehow, somewhere, she'd scored a grocer's dream—tomatoes, onions, cilantro—and was eager to teach me to make the perfect marinara sauce. For a while, I used a plastic butter knife, the only cutting tool she had, but soon whipped out the scalpel and went to town. Bonnie didn't say a thing when I resumed chopping away with a furor, but I did catch a few sidelong glances.

When the palate has come to accept Dumpster leftovers

stolen from alley cats as an average night's meal, fresh pasta and marinara sauce becomes nothing less than a gourmet orgasm. I barely spoke as we ate, slurping up noodles without benefit of chewing, sucking down as much nutrition as was possible within the shortest amount of time.

"Where did you get this?" I asked between gulps.

Bonnie said, "There's a market about six blocks down."

"And they threw this stuff away? Incredible."

She fixed me with an odd stare. "Threw it away?"

"Oh," I said, catching her game. "So you stole the food. Kudos."

Again, I wasn't getting through. "No, no," she insisted. "I went down to the market this afternoon and bought it."

How could I ever consider a relationship with this woman? We don't even speak the same language.

———

It wasn't until we were finishing up the sponge cake she'd purchased—not stolen but actually *purchased*, I understood now, from a real store with cash and a checkout line and everything—that I noticed that strange lilt to her voice once again, and couldn't help but ask her about it.

"It's a Vocom," she said.

"What is?"

"My larynx. Vocom Expressor, actually, one of the newer models."

Now that it had been isolated for me, I could hear the mechanical tone to her words, the way that everything was pronounced perfectly, artificially, with no slurs or tics. Smooth. Vocom's a grade-A company with an excellent customer-service staff.

And then, as if to prove it to me, Bonnie reached into her pocket and pulled out a small remote control, no bigger than the one for my Jarvik unit, though outfitted with many more buttons and dials. A push here, a spin there, and when she opened her mouth to speak, Bonnie was no longer Bonnie.

"It has a four-scale frequency modulation," she said in a smooth, meaty bass that thundered from her throat.

"Do you do that often?" I asked.

"Recently," she squeaked, adjusting the device to a chipmunk trill. "Sounding like someone else comes in handy when you don't want to be found."

———————

I'd run out some Vocom systems before, though these jobs were usually given over to the Ghosts, mainly because of the artiforg's ability to record the last forty-eight hours' worth of the clients' speech. Sort of like the black box they put in planes, but the Vocom Expressor only retained the words coming from the client, not from whoever they were conversing with. As a result, transcripts from Vocom boxes tend to be stilted, one-sided affairs, with so-called conversation experts left to decide what the other party had been going on about.

Once, toward the end of my career, I'd been sent in to repo a bladder from a Kenton client who'd overstayed the grace period by a good four months. Now, I'd been told that this guy had maxed out his credit all over town with a host of other manufacturers, but my job was with Kenton, and Kenton only. Even if I cut the guy open and came across an artiforg stomach or lung that I knew to be overdue, it wasn't my job to take 'em out. There are guys who work like that, freelancers who'll rip out any old thing and drop it off at the supply house in hopes of getting a cut of the commission, but I worked straight, and if my papers ordered me to lift a Kenton bladder, then a Kenton bladder I would lift.

Some folks don't move when you open them up; some

jerk all over the place. "Dead herring," "live tuna"—those are the repo terms. This guy was somewhere along the lines of a weakening trout, movement-wise, but he babbled through the whole thing, even though I'd gassed him down proper. Shot him up with an extra hit of Thorazine, then applied the Tasers, and even though his senses were shot, the fool didn't stop gabbing about how sorry he was, how he'd make everything right again, even as I dug the scalpel deep into his midsection. I didn't know what he was talking about, and I didn't care. I preferred to work in silence, and he was mucking up my day.

The bladder was there, in perfect condition, and as I reached for my tissue clippers, I suddenly heard a woman's voice echo through the room; as a reflex, my bloody hand dug into my jacket, flipping the Colt I used to carry into firing position even as I spun in a circle, ready to take aim and defend myself however necessary.

The room was empty.

Another cut, back to business, but a second later, a deep, throaty shout blasted into my ears, an anguished cry sped up to quadruple speed while still retaining its low tones. Another spin, another probe with the pistol, and nothing.

Then I isolated. Concentrated. Looked down at the client, locked in on his voice. It was coming from him, all of it, and just to make sure, I flipped the scalpel at his neck, drawing a new river of blood but locating a glint of silver and the Vocom beneath. It wasn't the Expressor model— those are relatively new on the market—but one of the old Communicator types, non-upgradeable. Just then, I felt something crack beneath my foot, and I looked down to find that I'd been stepping on the Vocom remote operating device all along; I'd been changing the voice as I worked, spooking myself in the process.

And somehow, I'd activated the recall procedure, which

explained why the sap never stopped talking—the Vocom was in playback mode, the larynx still reciting its own transcript of some prior conversation. Unable to figure out how to make it stop, I resumed work with this new soundtrack playing at full volume.

By the time I had the bladder tucked away in its protective Styrofoam container and ready for shipment back to the Kenton supply house, the client was certainly dead; all breathing patterns had ceased, his limbs were finally still, and I was unable to detect a pulse. But the Vocom, hardy artiforg that it was, continued its chant.

"Baby, you know I love you," the dead man yelled as I made my way out the front door. "Come on back, I swear I'll never hurt you again."

———

That's one of the things I had sworn to Melinda when she left me, that I would never hurt her again, that I would guard her against pain and suffering and the ravages of dealing with a chronically absent and absentminded husband, even though I knew that it was a promise I could never live up to. I've always done that with promises: One side of my brain does the swearing, the other secretly crosses its frontal lobes.

Of course, I didn't know until that night twenty years later how badly I would break my oath to Melinda. Even then, there was no way for me to know.

———

Bonnie had mentioned that the Vocom wasn't her only artiforg, and in my desire to learn what I could about my fellow tenant, I couldn't help but wonder if she was a fellow Jarvik host, too. But before I could convince her to let loose about the rest of her implantations, Bonnie's brow furrowed, and I noticed her neck arc slightly to one side, like a dog keying in on a far-off howl. She hushed me up quick with a delicate finger to my lips and tiptoed over to the penthouse window.

Keeping my eyes locked on the street beneath, I followed right behind. Didn't notice anything out of the ordinary, but stood still out of deference to her intuition. All but one streetlight had been busted long ago, darkness brought to the city streets courtesy of your friendly local hoodlums, and shadows crawled the pavement, obscuring anything I was meant to see.

Don't look, Bonnie mouthed to me, stepping back from the window. *Listen.*

And listen I did. Straining myself into silence, trying to project myself to the street below. In the distance, a mutt barking. A husband, yelling at his wife that if she screwed half as good as she cooked he'd sleep at home more often. A car, screeching as it sped through the intersection, cornering on the sides of its tires.

Nothing, I mouthed back.

Reaching out, Bonnie grabbed hold of my ear—her fingers were cold, long frozen sticks grabbing my flesh—and twisted the lobe back and forth. "Are these natural?" she whispered, and I nodded emphatically.

"Oh," she said, her voice low and compassionate, as if she was pitying me my unenhanced state. Digging into her jacket pocket, Bonnie fumbled around, metal clanging against metal, and soon came up with a compact pair of headphones: one wire, two pads.

Forcibly turning my head toward hers, she pulled me close and placed the instrument across my scalp and over my ears, fitting the speakers into my ear canals. Now all external noises were cut off, only my breathing amplified, and I nodded back at Bonnie as she nodded at me. The headset wire dangled impotently to the floor, electric lead scraping against the ground.

I took a glance back down toward the street—was there movement? Was it human?—and moments later, my hearing returned. Only this time there was depth to it. Range. Sounds I hadn't heard before, heard ever, made their way into my mind, filling my ears with noise. In that house with the yelling parents was a young child begging for them to stop fighting, for Daddy to quit yelling at Mommy already; the dog in the distance was barking at a softly mewling kitten.

I turned to find the wire from the headset around my ears leading up and into Bonnie's ear canal, dug in tight like a snake wiggling into its hole. As I stepped closer, I noticed that her lobe had cracked open a notch, the metallic edges glinting in the moonlight, and a panel near the eardrum had slid aside to allow for the wire's insertion. A Vocom corporate logo beamed out in a brilliant gold leaf just inside the socket.

"Artiforg ear?" I guessed, my voice doubling back to me through what was now Bonnie's hearing—my hearing—our shared hearing.

"Both of them," she said, and the words had a peculiar echo tone, sounding to me like *I* was the one doing the talking. "Now shush up and listen."

As I concentrated on the street below, Bonnie fiddled with the control panel inside her lobe, amplifying the ambient sounds by meager increments, filtering out the chaff. These speakers packed a wallop for their size; one slip of her fingers and she could blow my natural hearing out of commission, but the lady was careful, and soon we were past the dogs and the families and the cars below and focusing in on roach burps and mice titters.

And as we amplified and screened, amplified and screened, the workaday noises of the city were filtered out, until only one sound rode high above the rest: a high-pitched hum, warbling, shaky, underscored by a rhythmic, persistent *ping*. The music of electronics, and I recognized that sound from years of utilizing the only machine capable of making that noise, the tool that all Bio-Repo men cherished and all deadbeat clients feared:

We were being scanned.

CHAPTER 10

I whipped off the headphones and fell to the floor, cupping my gun, checking the ammo and restocking the clip even before my knees hit wood. Glancing up at Bonnie standing there in front of the window, such an easy target, such an easy shot, I motioned her down, grabbing for her arm in an attempt to drag her to safety. But she pulled away, laughing and shaking her head.

"It's too far away," she said to me. "They were scanning someone else, not us."

"I heard it—it was downstairs—"

"It was downstairs and two miles away. I keep this ear set to local standards," she said, pointing to her left, "and the other on long-range; I picked up the hum on the right ear. They're way too far away to pick us up."

I needed to check my weapons, prepare for the battle ahead. She still wasn't getting it. "There's no such thing as too far," I told her.

"Scanning range is one eighth of a mile—"

"Standard, yeah. But no one works off stock equipment."

That, at least, got her attention; she moved a few feet back from the window. "How far?" she asked.

"Far enough."

———

A scanner's legal range is one eighth of a mile in a single linear direction. The Supreme Court has repeatedly handcuffed the Bio-Repo industry, knocking down scanners with wider circles of influence, claiming that they represent an excessive infringement upon the right to privacy. They cite some constitutional amendment—I'm not sure which—that the Union has been trying to get repealed for years now.

But few Bio-Repo men actually use regulation scanners. We've got our own black market, a thriving industry that realigns the specifications of the devices so that they can be used up to a distance of two miles, as well as examine multiple directions at the same time. The scanner I used while on the job—Beth, I called it, for the manner in which it could do all number of people at once—was set to a mile and a half, and could give me facts and figures on the artiforgs of five different clients within seconds of each other. Jake was the one who had it recalibrated for me, and at a fraction of the price it usually cost.

Jake's scanner had a range of three miles, if I remember correctly. He paid more than fifty grand for the upgrade, and said it was worth every dime. Said it could sniff out an expired artiforg in every cardinal direction at once. Said he'd never lost a client once his scanner locked on. Not once. Good a reason as any to stay indoors.

———

As I went through my mental calculations, trying to figure out how long it would take me to run downstairs, grab my weapons, and either make a stand or run for it, Bonnie took the initiative. She scooped up a blue tarp lying on the floor and headed for the door to the hallway.

"You're running?" I asked her.

"Not exactly," she said.

"If it's a fight you want, it's a fight you'll get. These guys—the Union—they don't back down. You'll need more than a tarp."

"I know," said Bonnie, "but I also know my hotel. Come on downstairs, and I'll let you in on a little secret."

———

Tony Park's scanner, it turns out, has a radius of 2.6 miles, more than enough to do the job on that particular day. I heard him before I saw him, stomping up the stairs, making no effort to conceal his approach. The repeated *ping* of his scanner became louder and more frequent as he stepped off the landing on the sixth floor and made his way down the hall, huffing and puffing with the exertion.

"Making too much noise," I called out. "I'm in 604. In case you want to hurry this up."

His florid, ruddy face appeared before the rest of him, peeking into the room from the hallway, as if expecting some sort of trap. Like I'd be the kind of guy to spring that on him.

I sat at the far end of the room, cross-legged, casual as could be. To my right was the Taser, resting simply on the bare wooden floor. The blue tarp Bonnie had taken from the other room covered the middle of the floor, plates and makeshift silverware scattered as if in the aftermath of a grand picnic.

"Good way to get yourself killed," I said to Tony, "making all that racket. You could do with a little cardio work now and then, too. Bio-Repo lesson one: Never be too hasty."

Tony took a step into Room 604 and cracked his neck. "You got some property that ain't yours. And I'm gonna have the time of my life taking it back."

The tattoo on his forehead, I noticed, sported an extra

thunderbolt. "You get a little promotion there, Tony?" I
asked, still cool as November.

"Bet your ass I did. Since some punk-ass couldn't handle
his shit, there's been some extra work around lately."

"Glad to be of service," I said, uncrossing my legs and
making a show of stretching my hamstrings as I stood. "So.
Should we get on with this?"

"Gladly," Tony growled, and went for his Taser.

"Typical," I sighed, and made a show of leaning back
against the hotel window.

True to form, Tony stopped mid-draw. He was always
under the assumption that I was looking down on him; of
course, he was always right. "The hell's that supposed to
mean?"

"Nothing. I'm just saying you've got me here, in a room,
just us, no protocol necessary, no forms to fill out, the
chance to do what you've always wanted to do, and still you
go for the easy way out. It's a bit . . . typical, that's all."

He must have known I was goading him, but didn't
care. Tony outweighed me by at least thirty pounds of
pure muscle; I didn't have much of a chance in a fair fight.
Fortunately, this wouldn't be fair.

Tony didn't bother with words; he grunted like a hippo,
lowered his head, and charged, headlong, meaning to take
me down and rip my heart out with his bare hands. I stood
my ground, flexing my knees as if to welcome the oncoming
blow, Tony rushing across the wooden floor of Room 604,
straight at me, right across that blue tarp—

Which is when he plummeted through the rotted-out
floorboards beneath. The tarp went with him, sending the
plates and silverware flying, shattering against the nearest
wall as Tony fell through the next three stories, his massive
bulk smashing through the rotted wood on each successive
floor. By the time he landed in Room 204 with an audible

thunk, I was relatively sure he wouldn't be bothering us—or anyone else—any longer. We'd go down, make sure he was finished off, and, if not, do the job manually.

At least, that's how it was supposed to happen.

Bonnie, who'd been standing in the shadows in the far corner, shotgun in hand just in case Tony'd chosen to run around the tarp instead of straight over it, stepped to the edge of the hole and peered down. "He's not moving," she said, and looked up at me with a smile sweet enough to send me running for a new pancreas. "That was entertaining."

Before I could answer in kind, though, I heard the sharp crack of wood, saw the splinters pop up from the floor. Bonnie spun just in time to see the ground beneath her give way, the rotted floorboards unable to cope with the trauma of Tony's fall. I didn't even have time to scream, "Look out!" before she'd vanished through the hole.

———

Like I said, I've got a soft spot for women who run out on me. They just don't usually do it so vertically.

———

She landed on top of Tony, which was something of a double blessing. In addition to cushioning her fall, she must have contributed to Tony's already massive internal bleeding. By the time I ran down the stairs and found my way to 204, a steady stream of blood was pouring out of Tony's nose, and his chest was making thick gurgling sounds. I'd heard it many times before—he was minutes away from choking on his own blood. Now, I've got no love for the guy, but I'm not a monster, and even though I'm pretty sure he was unconscious, that's no way to go out. I quickly ended it with a well-placed scalpel, and within moments, he was done.

Bonnie was another matter entirely. Blood and 'forg fluid leaked out of a wound on her right leg; she'd taken the brunt of the fall upright, messing up her artificial knee something fierce. The light was too dim for me to see much, but it wasn't like I was going to try and fix it here. If there was one thing I knew, it was this: If Tony Park had found us—if that dumb galoob with the forehead tattoo had enough wherewithal to track me down—then the rest of the Union cadre couldn't be far behind.

It's time to leave home.

CHAPTER 11

I'm pretty sure this place used to be a Laundromat; though there are no longer washers or dryers here, I've noticed some heavily spray-painted vending machines that still smell more of detergent than they do of urine, and in this part of town, that's a blessing.

I half-carried/half-walked Beth through the city streets, resorting to occasional slaps to keep her as awake as possible. The longer we were on the streets, the more likely we'd be tagged by some happy-dappy Bio-Repo guy out scanning for his jollies. I'd packed all my weapons—and, of course, my trusty Underwood typewriter here—into a duffel, and between the weight of the metal and Bonnie's slumped form, it was slow going.

This joint seems safe enough, though—a small, protected room in the back of the main space, easy access to the alley behind for a quick getaway. Only one main entrance through smoked plate-glass doors out front, easy to see out but not so much in.

Bonnie's still asleep. When she wakes, we'll go to work on that knee. Until then, I'll type. I can feel the noose getting a little tighter with every passing day. Eventually, some-one's going to kick the chair out from under me, but until then, I'll keep putting it all down on paper. It's outdated, I know, but it's all I've got. At this point, I'd rather be obsolete than forgotten.

———

After Beth's divorce papers showed up in mail call, I applied for a forty-eight-hour leave and threw myself into the deepest, blackest bender I could work up. Most of my time was spent badgering the proprietor of the local liquor mart near base to sell me more alcohol, and after a protracted series of arguments, he could tell I wasn't going to leave him alone, so he up and gave me two pints of tequila, a fifth of scotch, and a case of this odd African beer, just to get me away from the store. Sometime during my stupor I must have run into Antonio, the old Italian who liked my clothes, because when I returned to base, ranting and raving about the whore bitch who'd left me, I wasn't wearing a stitch. It was nighttime, and the African desert was two degrees Celsius.

Lucky for me, Tig caught me before the higher brass did and sent me into barracks to sleep it off inside a control chair. When I was finally sober enough to manipulate my limbs, Tig placed me on bathroom detail as punishment, which was actually the ideal place for a hangover of Roman proportions, mainly due to the proximity of magical porcelain receptacles. As soon as I'd vomit and clean out one of the toilets, I'd stand and be ready to desecrate the next one over.

All this blubbering over a girl—a prostitute, no less, a whore if we're calling a spade a spade—may seem like petty nonsense from a man who would, ten years later, feel no remorse at taking a child's lung implant because his father frittered away the monthly artiforg payment at the dog track, but at the time I was still not much more than a boy who had lost the only woman he thought he could love forever.

It got much worse before it got much better.

———————

The day Harold Hennenson died was a warm one. Most days in the desert were warm, of course, but I remember it as being particularly hot that afternoon, sweat dripping down my cheeks even before I climbed into the stifling atmosphere of the tank. We'd eaten a hearty breakfast of MREs in foil, made our guesses as to the actual content of the meal, and been given stock orders from the commanding officers to resume the maneuvers we'd been at all week.

The enemy, we were told, was retreating faster than we could advance, and it was up to our division to claim as much territory as possible in the most rapid fashion we could muster. The military didn't want any dead space; they looked upon a neutral zone as nothing but a vacuum for other foreign interests to fill, and the last thing America needed, we were told, was to engage yet another enemy out here on the sand.

We were running after them, more or less, charging with our guns held high, sighting only their rumps as they ran away wholesale, only a few lone snipers and gung-ho religious nuts staying behind to fight us off. I remember one fellow who came charging out from behind what must have been the only palm tree—the only tree—the only living thing—for miles, finger hard on the trigger of his Uzi, spraying the advancing line of American tanks with rapid-fire ammunition, screaming something in his own language that could have been anything from a religious battle cry to a nursery rhyme; I've never understood what the hell those people were saying.

Don't know who targeted him first, but three of our tanks released million-dollar heat-guided rockets at the exact same time, each one exploding in a bright wash of fire that hardened the desert into a thick, twisted mass of burnt glass and obliterated any mortal sign of the lone gunman.

Three missiles, one man: The modern Marines in action.

But the day Harold died, there were no fireworks or heroics; just a row of tanks rolling through the desert, side by side, a giant kick-line of metal strutting its stuff across the dark continent. There were eight of us per rank, stretched out across a three-mile-wide expanse of land, gunners in back manning the turrets, keeping the watch out for an enemy we knew would never show.

My concentration was focused on the terrain ahead and the topographical map laid out before me, the three-dimensional image floating in front of my control chair ray-traced in bright green lines. Each of our machines was represented by a dot—blue for mine, red for Harold's, and so on—and the hills and valleys of the desert peaked before my eyes long before the tank ever made the climb or descent, enabling me and the other drivers to chart our course in advance.

The talkies were on the fritz again, static hissing through any communication we attempted with each other, our frequencies limited to local range. This was a common occurrence out in Africa; some thought it was the sand, the dust storms. I had a hunch it was crap engineering due to a little bit of nepotism in the military bid process, but kept my feelings on the matter to myself. As a result of the headset malfunctions, I could converse with Jake holed up at the gun in the back, but was unable to relay information to any of the tanks around me.

I could hear some of the other tank conversation, though, in the odd moments when the crackling died down, and was relieved to hear that while imagining themselves safe in their confines, the other soldiers talked about the same stupid stuff we did in ours: money, girls, and the things we'd done to get them.

"How's the back?" I radioed to Jake, who'd been passing the time by sighting and summarily destroying any insects unfortunate enough to pass by his scope.

"Clear. Like always. Second line of tanks are in some goddamn awful shape, lookin' like a buncha runners at the end of a race. Tig would kick their asses good and proper, he saw that."

"Not our problem," I said. "Long as our line's in order, we're doing our jobs."

I remember pulling up a second view of the topographical map, a small display winking into existence next to the first; as the original map scrolled forward, this one scrolled backward, marking the progress we'd made. A second line of colored blips steadily made its way across the desert, only this one was as convoluted as Jake had said, the tanks all out of alignment.

Static on the talkies, and I heard a nearby missile gunner, a kid from Omaha named Percy who would wind up spending the bulk of his post-military life in a military jail, saying, "I'm getting feedback from the second row. They're slowing down on the right side."

"Why?"

"Can't make it out. Something about . . . there's a . . . a drop . . . ?"

A third map popped into place, hovering above the first two—more desert, the altitude graph climbing sharply, oddly, and I turned my legs in such a way as to pan the entire map to the right. The soothing blue digits

on the map's altimeter quickly darkened into a flashing
red, and as I swung the map around a full 90 degrees, I
saw in bright green lines, boldly drawn through the air
in the small tank compartment, the rise and fall of what
we would later find out was the largest sand dune ever
seen in Africa. Harold's tank was heading directly up its
sloping face.

"They're not turning," said Percy. "They don't see it."

"They can't see it, they're *on* it," another gunner piped
up, and now it was getting hard to hear, the static was so
strong. "Its huge . . . can't see the . . . but it. . . ."

But Harold's tank kept on rolling, climbing up the
dune, unaware that they were 300 meters from the edge—
unaware that there even *was* an edge. Our topographical
information came from a network of all the tanks' radar
put together, which allowed the drivers a full 360-degree
view of the terrain. If that network was out—which is
what the Marines later surmised happened to Harold's
tank—then the immediate area in front of the machine,
especially if it was on an incline, was off-limits to the
driver. Radar doesn't turn corners, and it doesn't bounce
off clouds.

The talkies cleared up for a moment, and I used the time
to frantically dial into Harold's frequency, hoping to get a
message across to his tank's driver. But the crackles started
up as soon as I locked in, and though I could hear their
words, I know now they could never have heard mine.

" . . . sweet babies falling for these muscles . . ." I heard
Harold saying, bragging to the other kid in his tank, the
static cutting into his words. "Gonna get me a . . . when I
get on back . . . gal for me. Hey, you think . . . with the same
. . . am I right? And you know . . . he's the driver three tanks
over? He's a buddy of mine, got a great gal down . . . maybe
she's got a friend . . ."

I punched buttons. I spun dials. I screamed and I yelled and I shouted into that talkie headset, and I know neither Harold nor his driver ever heard a word of it. In a last desperation attempt, I violated Marine policy in every possible way by unbuckling myself, squirming out of the control chair—Jake yelling at me, screaming at me to sit and drive, for chrissakes, drive—and blowing the top of our tank, climbing out and up, imagining that somehow I could leap onto the sand and outrace Harold's machine, banging on the side, scrambling up top, pulling open the hatch, and applying the brakes myself just inches before the tank made its fateful dive.

As it was, I opened our hatch and reached air just in time to watch Harold, his mates, and 54 million dollars' worth of Marine equipment plummet over the edge of the sand dune and fall 200 feet before exploding on the sand.

The sandstorm was what did it, they said. Mucked up the talkies, mucked up the topographical displays. Billions of particles no bigger than flea snot, bringing down the mighty force of the marching military. Maybe the enemy should have tried to harness the power of the desert rather than resort to modern-grade weapons in order to fight us off. It doesn't come much lower-tech than sand. Perhaps next time they'll wise up and try stoning us to death.

Nostalgia, of the good kind:

Peter, my son, did a report for his third-grade class on the disciplinary procedures of cultures before the common age. I wasn't usually around to help out with homework, especially during that part of Peter's life, but he was in my custody that weekend, as determined by the courts, and I was obligated to take care of the little pisser for at least those two days every other week. He hadn't learned to hate me yet, and I like to think it was for a good reason: At that point in his life, I hadn't yet done anything to incur his wrath.

I was sitting in my workroom, going over a few last bits of paperwork from the last artiforg I'd brought in, and Peter ambled over. It was late, and he was already dressed in his pajamas, feet and all.

"My teeth are brushed," he announced, "and I washed my face."

These were bedtime procedures Melinda insisted upon; I always forgot about them, but Peter was a good-enough kid to remember on his own.

"Great, champ," I told him. "Run off and I'll see you in the morning."

But he stood there, a sheet of paper in his right hand, and waddled to where I was sitting. "Dad," he said, "why did the Romans stone people to death?"

"Because they didn't have any guns," I answered.

I think he got a B.

When Peter was younger, just a tyke who didn't want to go to sleep, who wanted to stay up with Mommy and Daddy and dance and play, Melinda and I used to sing nonsense songs to him in place of lullabies. He was never interested in the conventional "Rock-a-Bye Baby," but he did close his eyes and drift off to our own improvised tunes.

Melinda was much better at it than I was; her songs, at least, made sense. But Peter's favorite, the song he'd ask for over and over again once he got old enough to put in requests, was a silly little number I'd constructed one restless evening when he had a cough and a fever and nothing else was working.

It was like a Dixieland riff on a Hawaiian melody, jangly and fun and soft, and I still remember the words today:

I want to swim in the sea with the bears and
     the hummingbirds
Swim with the goats and the lions who know all
     the words
Swimmin' 'round like a busy bee . . .
I want to swim with the dogs and the monkeys and
     the kangaroos
Swim with the peacocks and the badgers
     and the lions, too
And I want them to a-swim with me . . .

Melinda and I sang it to each other well after the first movement of our marriage had come to a close, the love of our son the only thing that still bound us as a couple. I wonder if Peter still remembers it. I wonder if it still helps him go to sleep. I wonder if he remembers that his pop made it up.

————

Tig asked if I could write a little something to be sent back to Harold's parents along with his ashes. There wasn't much to say, I told him. At least, not much I could say to his parents. We'd hung out together, sure, gone to bars and clubs and whorehouses. Fought side by side, talked about what we wanted out of life and how we thought we'd get it. Where we thought the world was going to and whether or not it was going to leave us behind. But that wasn't anything to write home to parents, was it?

I eventually wrote:

Dear Mr. and Mrs. Hennenson,

Your son Harold was the finest man I ever knew. He was brave, he was strong, he was courageous, and if it weren't for him, I wouldn't be here writing this letter

*to you now. Me and the boys owe our lives to Harold,
and you should always know that he was, in so many
ways, a hero.*

And then, just so there could be some element of truth in
this little elegy, I scribbled:

P.S. He also had an incredible set of abs.

Noise outside. Screaming?

Bonnie and I are leaving the Laundromat. We just got here,
but we have no choice. Our first night will be our last.

She was awake and waiting for me in the darkened alley,
tourniquet around her knee. I burst through, scalpel in one
hand, Mauser in the other.

"Did you hear it?" she asked. I noticed that she, too, was
armed, her .38 clutched in that delicate hand, nail wrapped
around the trigger guard.

"Yeah. You're walking?"

"Well enough."

Another wail shot out from nearby, clearly female,
clearly in distress, clearly none of my business. "We
should stay put," I tell Bonnie. "We should hole up and
stay put."

"And if she needs our help?"

"No one needs *our* help in particular," I pointed out.
"If she needs help, someone else who's not on the run can
do it."

Bonnie wasn't having any of it. She fixed me with a
look intended to make me feel like pigeon droppings, and
it more or less worked. "It's not a Bio-Repo man," she said,
"or she wouldn't be screaming. She'd be passed out—you
know the drill."

On that, she was right. But I didn't cotton running into any officers of the state, either. They might like to know what we'd been up to cruising the streets of skid row at night, a couple of nice folks like us, and then questioning would lead to detainment, which would lead to a ride downtown, which would lead to my credit file, which would lead to . . .

"And the cops won't be coming by to check it out," promised Bonnie, following my thoughts. "They gave up on this area a long time ago."

Another scream jumped through the night to punctuate Bonnie's sentence, and within moments we were headed across the street, against my better judgment.

———

Altruism, to whatever extent it actually exists in modern society, is not a required trait for the Bio-Repo man. The personality tests they make you take when you apply for a Union job are designed to detect a certain degree of deviant pathologies, a smidgen of mania, and a healthy dose of clinical apathy, which is the scientific way of saying you just don't give a shit. The petitioner who passes all these ink blots and name games will be allowed into the training program, but will be watched to make sure his levels don't get wildly out of control, spewing brain chemistry this way and that; the Union has no urge to license sociopaths with scalpels.

But altruism can't be found in any of the Union training manuals, and for good reason. There's no time to be nice when your ass is on the line; more often than not, it will get you killed. Gas, grab, go—the Bio-Repo man's mantra.

I have violated this rule in the past. Without fail, it has been because of a woman. There is a trend here.

———

The building across the road from the Laundromat used to be an office plaza, and the very same series of city fires that ravaged Tyler Street must have wreaked havoc with the office plaza as well. Wide, open courtyards with canopies of trees and natural vines, sparkling fountains—it must have been a lovely place for the suits to come and relax during their fifteen minutes of lunch break every day.

But now the courtyard is blackened and dirty, weeds poking up through the cracks, prickly things that stabbed at my legs as I rushed by them. Bonnie and I moved through the main enclosure—Bonnie limping, grimacing with every pained step—toward the back of the plaza, toward the screaming, picking up the pace with every new howl. But the faster we went, the faster the shrieks came, and the faster the shrieks came, the more I wanted to turn around and hole up in the Laundromat. This was not cowardice; this was intuition.

Three floors to the plaza, though half of the building had crumbled to a single story, rubble filling the rooms beneath. We stood by the entrance, waiting for another burst of noise to indicate our next direction. I was double-fisting it: Taser in my right, Mauser in my left. I'd moved the scalpel into my waistband for easy access, the tip of the blade digging lightly into my groin. Bonnie was still holding her .38, but loosely, as if she didn't expect that she'd have to use it. Dumb move. Always expect to use your weapon. When you don't, that's when you'll need to.

A scream, directly in front of us.

"In there," Bonnie said, and moved confidently into the building, ducking her head beneath the partially collapsed door frame and disappearing into the darkness. I flicked off the safety, held the Mauser down by my knee, and followed.

————

His neck was mostly missing, which explained why the girl was screaming so much.

"Calm down," I said to her, trying to pull her away from the blood and the gore and the messiness. "Calm down, stop yelling. Get a hold of yourself."

But my bear hug only intensified the fit, her head slamming up and down, chin pounding her own chest, long blonde hair flapping through the air, making me sputter as it flew into my mouth. "Can you do something?" I asked Bonnie, but she just stood there, stroking the girl's hand, whispering into her ear.

The guy on the floor was dead, no doubt about it, and from what I could tell, his thyroid was gone, too. It's not a big organ, the thyroid, but when you've got as good a knowledge of anatomy as I do—and in specific, a knowledge of where organs should be when organs are not—a heap of blood and tissue doesn't matter. There's a hole where there shouldn't be, and in that hole went a thyroid gland. More likely, in that hole went an artiforg.

"Tell me what happened," said Bonnie.

The gal had calmed down considerably since we first arrived, but she still took great gasps of air as she spoke, trying to get it all out. "He—he—I was bringing him—bringing him lunch—and I came in and—and I found him—I found him like—like this . . ." The crying began again, and Bonnie hugged her close.

I was superfluous. Stood there watching these two women hugging each other, not in the least aroused. In one corner of the room, next to an overturned wooden box with food stains on it, I spied a familiar yellow sheet of paper, bloody fingerprints marring the corners. Using the blade of my knife, I drew the paper up from the floor, running it along the wall to eye level so I could get a good look at it.

Official Credit Union Repossession, it read, and then, below it: *One thyroid gland. Payment 120 days overdue.* The details came next: client name, age, last known address, the works.

Before I could absorb the rest of the sheet, the girl snatched the paper off the wall and knocked away the knife, nicking her thumb in the process; the blood dripped off her hand and joined the pool on the floor. "This is what they gave me," she sobbed, waving the paper through the air. Bonnie came up behind her, eyes moist.

"It's a receipt," I explained. "You get to keep that. For your records."

Still, she kept sobbing. "They gave me this and they took my boyfriend . . ."

"They took your boyfriend's *thyroid*," I said, the sentences flowing from my mouth in a rapid patter, a torrent of words I had repeated hundreds and hundreds of times over during my career. "They didn't take your boyfriend. They took their merchandise, and the Credit Union has a right to their merchandise, just like you have a right to yours. If they didn't reclaim their unpaid belongings, they'd never be able to continue as a corporation, and then all the people who need medical help would be unable to get it. Furthermore, under the Federal Artiforg Code, section twelve, number eighteen, they and/or their agents are under no legal right to resuscitate the bearer of said merchandise if payment had not been met by the—"

That's when she started crying again. I have this way with women.

———

The Federal Artiforg Code was the Holy Book to those of us who lived under its protective umbrella. Some six hundred pages long, it detailed every possible scenario between manufacturer, supply house, direct marketer, client, and organ, and served as the ultimate tome in all cases arising from error or miscommunication. Many was the time that I'd had to sit in a stranger's living room and recite article after article to some widow or soon-to-be widow, only to be hit or kicked or shot at even after all the trouble I went through memorizing the damned thing. They didn't appreciate the hard work, not a one of them.

Granted, some had legitimate grievances, and I can only hope that those who took these matters up through the proper channels were properly remunerated. A telephone number was listed on the bottom of every repossession receipt—a toll-free number, mind you—and business hours were every Monday through Saturday from nine until six; if there was a problem, these people would listen, get to the bottom of the situation, and sort it all out within a few weeks' time.

Ran out a small intestine once, back when Kenton was still making the IS–9, and due to a clerical oversight, I was out of ether. So I tagged the guy with a Taser, shot him up with a few hits of Thorazine, and he was out for the duration of the extraction. Problem was, his wife came home midway, and she didn't stop screaming at me how they'd made the monthly payments on the intestine, how the paperwork had gotten all screwed up, how it was all a mistake. I was sympathetic, but she wasn't letting me do my job, so I had to Taser her as well. It was legal—section 10, article three of the F.A.C., interference with a licensed repossessor—but I didn't enjoy it.

So I repo'd the IS–9, brought it back to Kenton, got my commission. Two months later, I'm called in, and they tell me there really was a mistake, that the guy had not only paid up on the device, he'd actually been paying a little extra off in advance. Real swell customer, great credit history, just a screwup down in records. The wife had called the toll-free number after I left and the customer-service folks, ever vigilant, didn't give up until they found the problem. Kenton sent me back.

I returned to the house bearing baskets of fruit, gifts for the client's kids, free artiforg certificates for the widow. Refunded the full amount they'd already paid for the organ, plus a few extra thousand bucks on top to ease the pain of loss. Federal guidelines require only a refund in case of a foul-up; the additional money just goes to show what great management they've got at Kenton.

I felt like Santa Claus, handing out toys to the children, money to the widow.

And I still got to keep my commission.

————

But this girl wasn't having any of it; her screams fell into sobs, which fell into weeps. I tried suggesting that she stand up, jog in place, try to walk it off, but she was inconsolable. Bonnie, who had been with her on the ground, lying next to the girl in an attempt to get her to talk out the pain, stood and brushed herself off. She had the yellow receipt in her hands.

"It looks in order," she said. "Jessica told me they've been hiding out here for a few weeks. Her boyfriend is— was—an electrician, but with the recent layoffs, he lost his job, and after food and house payments, the thyroid . . . well . . ."

"I know the story," I said. I'd heard it all before. Food, water, and shelter is what they teach kids in school. The three necessities; take care of those, and you're good to go. Liars.

"So they were found out."

Bonnie nodded. "This morning, when she went out to look for something to eat. She said they'd been hearing noises but thought the building was safe. She left, grabbed some bread and cheese down the street, and came back to . . . this. It was the first time she'd left his side in ten days."

"Only takes ten minutes," I explained. "Five for a gland."

This set the girl off on a new sobbing jag. While Bonnie attended to her, I took back the yellow receipt and soaked in another good look. Never understood why people forked over money for artiforg thyroids; pills work just fine as a replacement. There's no need to go to all the pain and trouble of an artificial organ when you can just suck down 30 mg of levothyroxine twice a day and be done with it.

At the bottom of the repo receipt is where they keep the official stuff, coded in such a way that only Credit Union employees can read and understand it. From the string of digits typed neatly along the edge, I learned that the client had a credit rating of 84.4 when he applied for the thyroid—respectable in today's financial climate—and had been awarded the artiforg at an interest rate of 32.4 percent over a period of 120 months. Again, quite fair, all things considered. My Jarvik unit was offered at 26.3 percent, but that was a special rate afforded me by my former employers. I still won't be sending them a card at Christmas.

But here's the reason why we're moving, the excuse for packing up our goodies and hoofing it out of the Laundromat and away from this part of the city as soon as dawn breaks and the sentinels go back home to sleep off the sunshine:

In the bottom right corner of that yellow receipt was a signature, right where a signature should have been. This is where the Bio-Repo man in charge of the case signs off that the artiforg is back in Union possession, that the client has paid his debt in full, and that the account is now considered closed.

I recognized that signature right away; I'd scrawled my own name next to it many a time.

It was the signature of the repo man I least want to run into. The one who has the best chance of locating me and successfully finishing off the job.

It was the signature of Jake Freivald.

CHAPTER 12

Jake came over to dinner one night when I was still married to Mary-Ellen; we'd gotten off a messy job, full respiratory system, both lungs included, and I'd invited him home without first asking the wife. But we were still in our honeymoon phase, so she was reluctant to cause a scene when I walked in the house with a friend at my arm.

"You remember Jake," I said, ushering him through the door, suddenly not sure if the two had ever met. "From the Union . . ." I wanted to point out that I'd also known him nearly my entire life, that we'd spent an entire tour together in Africa, but I'd already gotten the signals from Mary-Ellen that the military lifestyle was an off-limits conversation. So I settled for, " . . . and earlier."

"Of course," she nodded. She may have been covering up. She was good at covering up. "Come in, I'll set another plate."

Dinner was a civil affair, I remember, full of bland talk about movies and politics and religion and all the casually safe topics, but it was afterward, during dessert and coffee, that someone threw a match into the fireworks factory. Jake started talking about work, about some client he'd recently deprived of a bladder or something, and Mary-Ellen started in with her questions, peppering him with jabs, swinging the occasional roundhouse:

"You don't mind killing these people?"

"How can you go home at night and sleep?"

"Do you take a lot of showers to wash off the filth?"

"Where is your sense of decency?"

"Are you even human anymore?"

I didn't bring home any houseguests after that.

————

But Jake took it all in stride, answered every question Mary-Ellen threw at him, and the quieter I got, the more the two of them sunk into the fight, sparring back and forth. Jake would get backed into a corner, and then rise up and battle his way back to victory before tackling the next niggling point. It was exhausting, watching these two go at it, and by the time three hours had passed, I'd passed out in the easy chair, a beer on my lap and a pillow over my head.

Later that night, after Jake had gone back to his flat and we were all alone, I apologized to Mary-Ellen for letting things get out of hand. "I'm so sorry," I said, figuring I'd never be allowed to bring another buddy back to the house. "You must have hated him."

She was getting ready to go to bed, I remember, pulling back the sheets, and she stopped for a moment, comforter held in one hand, turned to me, and said, "No. No, I didn't hate him at all."

I was surprised. "Even though everything he said about the Union, and —"

"He had passion," she explained, tucking herself into bed, pulling the sheets up under her chin. "It was poorly guided passion, but it was burning in him, and I can respect that."

"So he didn't disgust you." I wanted this firm, on tape if possible.

"Passion never disgusts me. Apathy disgusts me."

Wow, I thought. *She's coming around. This marriage might work.*

It wasn't until the lights were out and we were already on the verge of sleep that I thought to ask, "What about me? How do you like my passion?"

No answer came. She must have been asleep.

———

He was also there for the birth of my son. I'd been working twenty-hour shifts, trying to work in a sweep of the Big Hundred, cracking down on the worst of the deadbeats. Dragged myself into the hospital when I got the call, groggily watched Melinda push Peter out into the real world. As I mopped down her forehead with damp towels, three jobs came up on my pager, informant tips on client sightings.

It's a good thing Jake was there, too. We asked if he wanted to be the godfather to Peter, and as soon as he accepted, I charged him with the duties of taking care of my wife and newborn son until I could get back from the office. It was a busy, busy week.

———

When Harold passed away, Jake was the one to speak at the small military funeral. I've never been too good in front of an audience, and Jake was the only other guy I could think of who'd known Harold for longer than four or five months. The new recon unit had flown him down from Northern Africa—he still couldn't tell us what he was doing up there, but we imagined all manner of intrigue and suspense—and into Namibia for the day, just so he could see his friend's ashes off properly. The military had stuffed them into a small ceramic jar, though Tig admitted that they were not entirely sure that it was solely Harold's mortal remains inside there.

"There were three men in that tank," he told Jake and me as we walked to the makeshift tent-cum-chapel. "And it was all one ugly mess. We had to take a guess, consolidate, and divide."

Jake's speech at the service was quite moving. He talked about love and honor and the brotherhood of men, about discipline and training and the knowledge that Harold had done his duty to self and to country.

"And I only wish," he concluded, shooting me a sly wink, "that when it is my time to leave this green Earth, that I, like Harold, will be surrounded by my friends in death as I was in life."

We all said *amen*.

————

Melinda was cremated, I believe. Peter never told me where the funeral was. He didn't even try to call—I know, because I picked up the phone on the first ring during those lean days, just in case a sweepstakes manager or lottery announcement was on the other line. The last words I ever heard him say to me were *and that's always been the problem*, just moments before he stormed out of the local Snack Shack. After that, nothing. I wonder if he'll attend my funeral. I wonder if he'll take the call.

But I remember a conversation I had with Melinda during the good years. Peter wasn't even born yet, wasn't even conceived. It was after a particularly furious bout of lovemaking, and we were having a little pillow talk, the nightly gab shows not having started up yet.

"Do you think there's sex in heaven?" she asked.

I grunted affirmatively.

"And do you think you need your body for it?"

I shrugged and fiddled with the remote control. "Always need your body."

"But in heaven you don't," said my wife. "It's just souls, no bodies."

"If there's no body," I said, "there's no sex. Sex organs are on the body. Mouths are on the body. No body, then no sex organs, then no point to sex, no point to anything."

But Melinda disagreed. Propping herself up against a pillow, naked breasts firm against the sheet below, she leaned over and conked me on the head. She always did this lovingly—at least during the happy times. It was her sign to me that I was being a numbskull, that I hadn't thought things through. "You don't get it, knucklehead. The body's just there to support the rest of us. What you do for a living—dealing with those artiforgs—it's all just a support system. A cottage industry for what really makes us tick."

I like to think that she was right. And I would have responded, but soon our talk show came on, and we stopped worrying about ourselves and each other and started worrying about celebrities.

My artiforg, in a nutshell:

> One (1) Jarvik Unit, Model 13.
> Standard features: Replaces all of client's heart
>   functions, including pumping, sucking, and
>   distributing blood supply. All major vein and
>   artery connections are standard in titanium
>   silicone. Four color choices: Cardinal, Key Lime,
>   Pinewood, Bluebird. Automatic rate monitor to
>   determine degree of bodily function/action and
>   blood regulation. Realistic heart sounds. Realistic

pumping motion. Conditionally guaranteed for
5 years/150 million beats.

Optional features, specific to the Jarvik–13: hip-
welded control to raise or lower heart rate, if
desired, with built-in high and low limits.
100-year battery, rechargeable. 6 TB music player,
prerecorded with eight thousand of the client's
favorite songs, the music relayed via sonic bone
conduction into the jaw.

Cost: $152,000, dealer's invoice. Options bring it to
$183,000.

Financing direct through the Credit Union, annual
percentage rate (APR): 26.3 percent, or 25.8
percent if automated payments are chosen.
Approximately $36,000 down payment (20
percent), with outstanding balance of $147,000.
Artiforg insurance: $4,800/year.

Monthly payment, Principal & Interest: $3,815.62.

Payments to date, total: $39,413.

Amount paid to interest: $36,103.

Amount paid to principal: $3,310.

Outstanding balance: Infinity.

————

Oh, yeah—I forgot the most important statistic.

Months delinquent: Enough.

————

They tell you all about the late payment penalties and the
pressure and the possibility of eventual repossession up
front—that's the law, after all—but most clients are so
elated once they find out they've got the loan that they're
ready to sign most anything put before them. Still, it's
better than the old days, when poor slobs with liver damage
had to put themselves on a list and wait for some other

poor slob without liver damage to die in some horrible yet liver-preserving way, so that they might be matched up for a human-human organ transplant that eight times out of ten was rejected by the host body anyway.

During the repo training seminars, they threw a basketful of statistics our way; out of the thousands that fell out of my brain as soon as they entered, one managed to stick in there: At any given time during the days before the Credit Union made widespread artiforg implantation possible, there were 120,000 people in the United States alone waiting for someone or another to die off and give up the goods. And despite the impressive methods with which many folks knocked themselves off during those years, there were never enough donors to meet the requirements, so a staggering number of citizens—some good, some bad, all dying—got sent on their way for want of a few organized cells.

But my point is that this is an anachronism; today, only the very poor or those who have abused their credit to the point of criminal activity are unable to secure loans for their artiforgs. Some cut-rate houses even cater to those with less-than-stellar credit histories, attaching their material goods as collateral. Heard about one place overseas which lends out Jarviks by the boatload, and all you have to do to get one is sign a note of indentured servitude of ten years. Decade of work for a new lease on life—that's not a bad trade.

So when the Credit Union people approach with a ream of paper and a pen, the instinct is to clam up and sign, sign away. That's what I did.

———

Two caveats:

A) I had no illusions. I knew the penalties for not paying. I knew them when I signed the forms, I

knew them when I stopped sending my checks,
I know them now that I sit in this abandoned
Laundromat.
B) I didn't have a choice.

Propped up in a hospital bed, on a steady, lovely mor-
phine drip, my new Jarvik–13 implanted by a team of doctors who made the decision for me, without me, as I lay
dying on a gurney. Jake and Frank standing there, smiling,
bearing flowers, glad to have me alive, glad to have me back
on the team again. The artiforg was in me, full implantation,
and what was I to do? Rip it from my chest? I was out of
practice.

———

Bonnie just came into the back room to tell me she's heading off to bed for the night. I told her, "Okay." She said that
she was feeling tired, and that she'd be better after a night's
sleep. I said, "Good idea." She stood around for another
second, and then said that the floor was cold, but she'd find
some way to stay warm. I offered her the use of the tarp.
Bonnie sighed and left.

Five minutes later, I figured it out. I hit myself in the
head, but it just wasn't the same.

———

After Harold's death, the war was a long string of non-
events, one after the other. We never got to storm a city, to
lay waste to a village, never committed any of the terrible
war atrocities that show up in the news magazines or heroic
war efforts for which they throw city-wide ticker-tape parades. The tanks rumbled across the desert, gobbling up
space, advancing the American line by sheer force of inertia,
and day by day, the enemy was kind enough to retreat without putting up too much of a fuss.

One night in April, I drove the tank over two snakes and

an unidentified furry creature. Those were my confirmed kills for the week. My tankmates threw me a party.

Meanwhile, that same night, 8,000 miles away, Father was putting his feet up on the green corduroy ottoman in his paneled den, a brandy and milk in his fist, settling in to watch a flick on the late show and fall asleep before the second round of commercials even started when a large blood vessel in his brain chose to burst and send him packing on a one-way trip out of our dimension. Mother was in the kitchen, fixing up some decaf. She didn't hear when he dropped the remote control on the hardwood floor. When she found him two minutes later, he was brain dead. By the time the ambulances arrived, so was the rest of him.

They shipped me back overseas for the funeral, though I would have preferred to stay in the desert. It's not that I didn't want to see my pop off—we loved each other, in our own modernly dysfunctional manner—but I felt out of place back in the old hometown. Where was the sand? Where were the frightened locals? Where was my control chair? This bed was too flat, too simple—where were the buckles to hold me in place?

Sam Jenkins worked with Father down at the office; he was a middle-aged guy who would hold donuts with one hand and diet sodas with the other and always had some story to tell me about his twin daughters that wasn't in the least amusing yet had to be repeated at least three times. Before the funeral service, he came up behind me, slapping a meaty hand down on my shoulder. His breath reeked of carbonated saccharin.

"How you holdin' up?" he asked, squeezing as he spoke.

I said, "I'm fine, sir."

"Good lad. What've they got you doing out there in the desert? Killing some baddies for us?"

"Some," I said.

"Good lad."

Held it together through the next few hours, sitting patiently as they said nice things about Father, making a show of fighting back tears when they lowered him into the ground, holding onto Mother when she needed holding. But after the funeral, when the line of well-wishers grew so long I couldn't see the end of it, something in me snapped at all the measured words and polite phrasing.

"Honey," drawled my great-aunt Louise, who, eight years later, would come into a fair bit of money in the stock market and have every plastic surgery operation ever devised, "it's sooo good to see you." At this point in time, pre-surgery, she was fast approaching disintegration, her skin sagging beneath too many years of sun worship and questionable skin cleansers. "Honey, I want to know what they're doing to you out there."

"They're not doing anything," I swore. "It's just a job."

"Ach," she spat. "Such a job, hurting others. You're not hurting others, are you, honey?"

And there it was, out of my mouth before I could stop it. Then again, even if I'd given it six days, thought, I probably would have said it anyway. "With my bare hands, Auntie. Every chance I get."

————

I was able to convince the military to send me down to San Diego before they shipped me back overseas; I told them there were funeral services going on down there for a cousin who had coincidentally died on the exact same day, and that I had been conscripted into pallbearer duties. Even went so far as to scour the obituaries and find a dead guy who matched up with my story.

Soon as I stepped off the plane, I corralled a taxicab and had them take me into the Red Light District. I was dismayed to find that my palms remained dry, my heart-beat steady. All the allure I'd always felt on the trips to the Red Light, the ticklish knots in my bowels—they were gone. During the day, I could see all the chipped paint and cracked skin. The neon was just a series of tubes, empty, meaningless. For all of my so-called marriage to Beth, I'd never really been to her place of employment during the day before; the few times I'd gone to see Beth when the sun was up, I wasn't quite *there* there. I was *Beth* there, which meant most of me was off in some other world that smelled like lilacs and kissed up a storm.

Though I'd had them in my possession for months, I had yet to sign the divorce papers; something in me rankled every time I put pen to the red line, and even after a hundred tries, I wasn't able to get the job done. My hand shook, trembled, and refused to make a mark.

But I had a plan. I brought the papers with me on my trip back to the States, and as I stepped out of the taxicab and into the heart of San Diego, I reviewed it all in my head like a general going over battle strategy: I would storm into Beth's "office"—this is the term I preferred back then, her office—throw out whoever she was "meeting with" at the time, scoop her into my arms, kiss her with all the strength my lips could muster, and we'd laugh and rip up the papers together, her and me, my hand on one side, her hand on the other. Sunset, children, happy ending.

As the military would say, my mission was accomplished with a 5 percent success ratio. I definitely stormed into her office, no doubt about it.

And that's where I found Debbie, a sweet eighteen-year-old from Texas who'd just started in the business. And that's where I found the two beefy guys Debbie was servicing at three hundred bucks a pop. And that takes care of the second time I was ever knocked unconscious.

Never saw her again. Beth, I mean. Never saw Debbie
again, either, though I hope the ugliness that went down
in that room scared her off of the whoring for good.
Beth's apartment, I soon found out, had already been
rented out to another tenant, and her usual hangouts were
devoid of her presence. No one wanted to help me find
her; obviously, they'd heard stories. Obviously, she'd
made things up.

I trolled the city for two days and nights, casting out my
net, showing pictures to everyone I came across. Most of the
photos I had of Beth were of the boudoir variety, but I figured if anyone was going to recognize her, she would have
to be *au naturel*. The tales they tell, if they tell them at all,
of a deranged lunatic walking the streets of downtown San
Diego flashing obscene photos at passersby were inspired
by yours truly. I thought I caught a glimpse of her hair once,
turning a corner and bobbing down a side street, but by
the time I caught up, the road was empty, save for a small,
withered bag lady who offered to jerk me off for an order of
mozzarella sticks.

I signed the divorce papers on the plane back to Africa.

All these years later, I've forgotten what she looked like.
I've got the basics, but it's nothing more than a stereotype.
Blonde, leggy, stacked. Hooker 1A, sans the fishnets. Beth
hated fishnets.

I remember Mary-Ellen; at least, I remember Mary-
Ellen's long legs and Mary-Ellen's arms and the way Mary-
Ellen's stomach dipped down after her ribs but then rose a
little bit by her hips, a delightful pouch of flesh that I must
have kissed a thousand times in the six months we were
together, and I remember Mary-Ellen's crooked chin and

her pert nose and her blue, blue eyes, and even if I can't put it all together, isn't that just as good as remembering Mary-Ellen?

I remember Melinda, of course. I did, after all, see her somewhat recently.

I remember Carol, and the way she made me feel like I was the one who needed all the remembering. I remember how she'd pull me close in the middle of the night, then shove me away just as I was finally getting comfortable with the proximity. I remember Carol because she wouldn't have it any other way.

And Wendy, who should have been the most memorable of them all, who took me half a lifetime to find and a few short years to lose, is rarely on my mind these days. I can call her up, examine her as I wish, but only one section at a time. If I try to take Wendy as a whole, I lose it and have to start all over again. I can pan up from her feet to her hair like she's the ingénue in an old-time movie, or leer up and down from breasts to face and back again, but there's nothing full-on, and it's all fleeting.

And now there's Bonnie, and that's a mystery to itself. Bonnie's just out in the other room, but even though she's only 60 feet away, I'm having problems isolating her, separating her image from those of my ex-wives. It's all a great process shot, a nose from this one, lips from that one, a merger woman gone awry.

There's something about her that keeps drawing me back to my prior life, something that wants to help me connect her to the things I used to know and the things I used to do. It's not there yet; I can feel it creeping up on me, but every time I chase after it, the memory runs away, like a child playing tag. I'll get there eventually.

I could, of course, walk out to the other room and find

out what Bonnie looks like in the flesh. Ask her why the hell she seems so damned familiar. I doubt she'd mind. I know *I* wouldn't.

But it's late. And I'm tired. And tomorrow is moving day.

CHAPTER 13

A nature special on the modern Bio-Repo man would go something like this:

He is omnivorous by nature, almost definitely male, likely to be without a mate. He feeds on processed foods and beverages, or on the leftover comestibles of his clients when his time is scarce. Always looking over his shoulder for some unseen adversary, he is cautious, wise, cunning. He wears a watch, sometimes two, always synchronized with local time. The Bio-Repo man, with his array of tools and weapons, is able to see in the dark, scan foreign objects at great distances, and outpace his clients in nearly any foot-race. He tends to drink too much, smoke too much, mistreat his body in every way he can imagine, and when his creativity has run dry, he will solicit advice from others on how to continue the abuse.

When the Bio-Repo man follows his clients, he blends into the shadows, working with the night in a friendly partnership. Few can see him. Fewer can escape him. The only sound he makes is that of ether hissing from one of his portable canisters, and by the time the client has recognized this noise, it is usually too late. The calling card of the Bio-Repo man is a yellow receipt laid across the fallen body, signed in triplicate.

The Bio-Repo man is nocturnal.

———————

All of that, by the way, would be underscored by music, preferably in a minor key. It's crucial for a Bio-Repo man to maintain a proper air of mystery.

———————

Having lived that exact nature special for the better part of my life, we knew enough to leave the Laundromat during the day, when all good Bio-Repo men would be home sleeping off their lives. When the sun popped up sometime around six, Bonnie and I crept out of the crumbled building and tried to blend in with the rest of the skid-row bums who were just getting ready to begin their long day of begging. Bonnie, whose face had grown more and more maddeningly familiar with every hour we spent together, had loaned me a long duffel bag in which I transported many of my weapons, though I kept my scalpels and the Mauser tucked away in various pockets. Bonnie was packing heat, too, though it was impossible to tell exactly what she had on her and where; the weapons disappeared perfectly into her form-fitting overcoat.

Twenty minutes down the road, we found a dingy, poorly lit diner, grabbed a booth in the back, ordered eggs and toast—Bonnie was treating—and tried to figure out where the hell we were going.

"A safe house," I suggested. "A buddy we can hole up with."

Bonnie shrugged. "I've lost most of my friends."

"I never had many to begin with. Not outside the Union. And we're not going down that road."

She nodded, pursed her lips. "How late are you?"

"Late enough," I said. "After three months, what's it matter anymore?"

She took a sip of the warm tap water they'd offered us. "You ever talk to a credit manager?"

My laugh was unintentional; it just slipped out. "My credit manager is my old boss. Once I skipped out on the job, he wasn't about to start cutting me deals. You?"

"Sure," she said. "I had three different managers—"

"I've never even heard of that."

Bonnie smiled, and the rest of the diner dropped away. Nothing else mattered. "I'm full of surprises. So how bad do they want you?"

"I'm on the Hundred Most Wanted List," I said, feeling in a perverse way as if I were actually bragging about it.

"Oooh, a bad boy."

"And then some. I'm number twelve."

If Bonnie was impressed, she didn't show it. Just went on sipping her water and taking in the diner. Staying safe.

"So what's new in you?" I asked. "You've got the Vocom, some ears—anything else?"

"A few," she said. Was she deliberately being evasive?

"Such as?"

Narrowing her eyes into tight little slits, I got the feeling that she was inspecting me again, trying to get ahold of me. For a moment, I was pretty sure I could hear mechanical lenses focusing, spiraling in and out. "You get to choose three body parts to ask me about today," she said.

"You've got three more artiforgs in there?"

"Choose."

So many organs, so little time. I already knew about her ears and her larynx, both top-of-the-line Vocom models, so I decided to make my way across the face. "Eyes, nose, mouth."

And this is what she said:

————————

"Both of my eyes are Marshodyne Dynamics, each with standard 100× zoom capability and full-spectrum color enhancement. The left one has an additional lens that slips into place when I blink three times in succession, and can increase the long-distance zoom capacity to 300×, but that's when I tend to get headaches. The right eye has a macro feature that allows me to go microscopic, up to 200×, but that one makes me nauseous. If I use them both at the same time, I mostly end up walking in circles, slamming back aspirin, and puking. I got the financing from Marshodyne through the Credit Union at a rate of twenty-nine point eight percent.

"The cartilage of my nose is a silicone variant made by the Boone Corporation out of Virginia, but the actual sensors and nerve pathways are Credit Union generic. The sensory modification on those is slight, but I'm able to block certain foul odors and enhance certain sweet ones. Recently, it's been pretty useful. The financing came straight from the Union, and this was at a special rate of twenty-seven point four percent.

"And my mouth is basically a department store of brand-name artiforgs, but since you seem interested, I'll give you the whole tour as a freebie. Lips are my own, but the sensors are Kentons at thirty-two percent, the tongue is a variable polymer of some sort with fourteen times the number of taste buds and shutoff features a lot like those nasal ones—that's also Credit Union generic at twenty-eight point four percent—and the teeth are a plain set of dentures my ortho-dontist ordered up for me. No finance charge on those.

"Does that answer your question?"

————————

That's when I figured it out: As Bonnie spoke at length, giving me a litany of artiforg details, she leaned forward to replace her juice glass, and the motion of her arm brushed away that frustrating strand of hair that always fell into her eyes. As it dropped to one side, I finally got a good shot of her face for the first time since we'd met, and suddenly, instantly, I realized why she looked so damned familiar.

"You're number one," I gasped, lowering my voice as some other patrons turned and looked our way. "You're right up at the top —"

"And you might wanna keep it down."

"I saw the list," I continued, dropping to a whisper. "In the Mall lobby, I was looking for my name—"

"I know, I'm number one on the Big Hundred. You think I'd be alive this long and not know a thing like that?"

Before I could say another word, the waitress arrived with our breakfast. The heavy plates hit the table with a *clunk*, and I took a stab at the bacon strips before continuing on.

"How long have you been running?" I asked, keeping volume in check. "Must have been awhile, to get listed that high."

"It's not the time," Bonnie corrected me. "It's the quantity. Later, you can ask me about my torso."

———

My favorite Credit Union commercials, in no particular order:

1) "What's New In You?" Even though the phrase is practically a mantra these days, I'd be surprised if anyone remembers the ad itself. It was one of the earliest Credit Union spots, the one with the three little multiethnic kids singing about their newly implanted artiforgs. They tap-danced all over the great structures of the world, bringing life and love to the

people of Earth. A new pancreas at the Taj Mahal, a shiny new bladder at Big Ben, everyone showcasing their excellent health after a speedy operation and recovery. More than the commercial itself, I've always been impressed at how easily the phrase slipped into the popular culture. Now, it's almost more proper to say, "What's new in you?" than it is to greet someone hello. The marketing folks got a big holiday bonus for this one.

2) The introduction of Harry Heart and Larry Liver. I know it's outdated, I know they've been marketed through the roof, that everyone's sick to death of the cartoon and the plush toys and the theme park and the fast-food tie-ins, but I can't help but love this rascally duo's animated adventures. *Harry and Larry's Magical Journey* was the first six-minute infocast to hit the marketplace, and it did wonders for the Union's image. The best part was when Harry and Larry squared off in the boxing ring made out of ligaments before realizing that they worked better together than they did apart. Moral lesson for kids, right there.

3) "Ask me about my brain." Probably the funniest commercial to come out of the Union marketing department, though it was actually a supply-house ad for Kenton's first Ghost system. It's the one with the guy who has that incredible memory and runs around town with the film undercranked, moving ten times normal speed, and when he gets back to the office and they ask him what he did, he blurts out this laundry list of his adventures without missing a beat. And like, "What's New In You?" it created a new phrase for every artiforg patient, a way in which they could introduce their new organ into conversation. Finally, there was no shame in having an implantation.

I'm sure there are more, but these three stick out. Maybe it's because I've forgotten all the others. My memory, in general, isn't what it used to be; perhaps I should have gotten that Ghost system implanted when I had the chance. Nowadays, all I can say is *Ask me about my heart*, but after more than a year of that, the glamour has sort of worn thin.

———

Funnily enough, the first Credit Union commercial I ever saw was during a rerun of *The Six Million Dollar Man*. Not the original, or the remake, but the second remake that ran for three seasons, back when they'd first given up on original programming. The commercial was for a heart, I think, the Jarviks being ahead of the game when it came to safe implantation, and I remember being not so much surprised at the irony as I was saddened by it. The truth is, even with the excellent credit history that Steve Austin no doubt sported, there's no way he'd get out of that hospital these days for a penny less than 12 million.

———

None of my wives had any artiforgs, with the exception of Melinda, though she did not have the implantation while we were married. Back then, she was all natural and proud of it, scoffing at the clients whose houses I visited nightly.

But when Peter was around twelve and over at my apartment during a court-ordered weekend, he let it slip that his mother had been into the hospital for some surgery.

"What sort?" I asked him.

"Kidneys," he said innocently, with a hint of wide-eyed excitement. "She got some new ones!"

"What kind?" I asked, trying to make the question seem nonchalant. I didn't know back then that nothing is nonchalant to a twelve-year-old.

"Gabelmans," he replied. "My friends are *so* jealous."

And that was how I found out that Melinda was packing metal. I suppose it was better for me to know then as opposed to finding out later on, but I wonder if things would have changed had Peter kept his big mouth shut.

Probably not. I would have killed her either way.

———

Bonnie had a place we could go. Rather, she had a friend who might know of a place we could go, which was good enough for me, as I was fresh out of ideas.

"So you'll call him?" I asked her as soon as we were a few blocks away from the café. Most of my attention was taken up by the throngs of people that passed by; I inspected every one of them for the hardened grin of a Union stooge, waiting for the hum and beep of a scanner to give us away.

"No phone," she told me. "But we can go to his place. He can probably help with my knee, too."

"No," I said emphatically, "we can't trust anyone else—"

"He's clean," she promised. "He's outside the Union."

Outside the Union. This was the preferred term for a black-market artiforg dealer, and though I'd done some repo work for them, I didn't like the type. Usually they're ex-loan officers who score a deal with a shady buddy back at a supply house; they steal the artiforgs off the manufacturer's shelf, then sell 'em at discount prices with cut-rate financing. The more ambitious and sleazy "Outsiders" follow licensed Bio-Repo men to their assigned jobs, then wait until they've done the dirty work and scurry inside to pick at the bodies for remaining parts. A Union man only takes what he's assigned to; the Outsiders scavenge the rest.

But in terms of our personal safety, we were clean. This guy was bound to be as much on the lam as we were, and would have no interest in calling the Union down on our asses, no matter the reward money.

And what other choice did we have? We went to see the Outsider.

————————

For most of my professional life, I spoke every foul word against the Outsiders that I could; they were the competition, and their tricks stole food off of our tables. Special task forces were formed every so often to search out their nests and hunt them down, but most of the time we came up empty-handed. We were the lions, and they were the vultures. But if it hadn't been for their meddling, I never would have met Melinda.

Sixth year on the job, and Mary-Ellen was all but a memory to me, a slight twist in my stomach that could easily be put off to indigestion. Work was going well, and I'd recently been promoted to clearance level three, which meant that I would be allowed to undertake certain repossessions that previously would have been off-limits to me. This included high-level professionals and celebrity clientele, as well as repossessions under difficult extraction conditions.

To that end, my supervisor called me into his office and handed over a case file that had all the trappings of an easy night. An elderly woman, her time all but expired, had stopped payments on her Jarvik unit a few months back; the Union wanted it out before she died and ended up buried with the device. There had been situations like that before, ugly little scenarios necessitating messy exhumations that wreaked havoc in the PR department, so it was up to me to recover the unit before anything untoward occurred.

The nursing home was on the edge of town, next to some low-rent apartment buildings, a gas station catty-corner. Litter on the sidewalks, the hedges untended, cars zooming by on the busy street below. Three meals a day, all gruel, recreation room stocked with two board games missing a third of their pieces. This was where loving children sent their parents and grandparents in order to exact revenge for not getting the Auto-Go toy car they wanted for Christmas lo those many years ago.

————

Note to Peter:

Kill me if you want. That's fine.

Hunt me down and exact revenge. Torture me. Make me scream. I'll understand.

But if you put me in one of those places, if you hole me up in some home and keep me rocking with sixteen pills an hour, then you're outta the will, sonny boy.

————

Mrs. Nelson's Jarvik unit was a Model 11, one of the mid-range prototypes without all the whistles and bells. Her precise artiforg information had been loaded into my scanner in order to make it easier for me to locate her among what were sure to be countless numbers of artificial organs inside the nursing home. It was futile for me to try and gas down the place; I didn't have the ether, and the old folks weren't about to try and fight me off. I didn't enjoy repossessing from the elderly. Their time was short, they knew it was coming, and here I waltzed in to rob them of whatever moments they had remaining. Still, they should have paid the bills.

I took a front-door approach, walking into the lobby, shushing the front-desk girl with a simple touch of the lips. She was new. Sat straight up as I approached, fear ratcheting her to the chair. Just for fun, I flicked on the scanner. It beeped. She jumped. I blew her a kiss and moved on.

Jake had already gotten my scanner modified a few years prior, so I was able to soak in great circles of information as I walked through the hallways. It was hot, so I'd worn my black tank top that day, the Credit Union tattoo blasting out from my bare neck. Residents shuffled down the hall, some with walkers, some on their own, each looking at me and muttering, some turning away in a futile attempt to cover up their own unpaid artiforgs. "I'm not here for you," I told those who looked the most frightened. "Go about your business." It eased their worry. They might end up as my clients next week or next month, but there was no need to let them know that.

The pings came at me from every side, and I read off the specs as fast as I could, looking for Mrs. Nelson's Jarvik–11. There were too many artiforgs to take in at once. Decreasing the range of the scanner, I stopped in the middle of one hall, turning in slow circles, trying to isolate. When the number 11 flashed past, I did a quick rewind and locked on. By the time the specs had flitted across my screen in full detail, I was at the room.

Two women. One old, one young. One with an artiforg, one without. One in bed, one in a chair. One sleeping, one wide awake. This wouldn't be too hard to figure out.

The younger one, a nurse, I guessed, started in with me. "You're in the wrong room," she said. "Please leave."

"I'm sorry, ma'am," I said, "but I have a job to do for the Union. You might want to leave, yourself. It can get messy."

She stood up to me then, came right for me, but I held my ground. We ended up nose to nose. She was tall, nearly my height, with a thin, pointed face and a head full of auburn hair. Her posture was incredible. "I know who you are and I know what you do, and I'm telling you, you've got the wrong room. This is Selma Johnson, and she doesn't have what you want."

Checked the scanner, and the old lady's Jarvik–11 pinged back at me. Early model, no options, four chambers pumping away to eternity. Couldn't draw a serial number or name, for some reason, but recalibrated scanners were known to malfunction in certain areas. Give and take of technology.

"She's got the Jarvik–11 I've come for," I said, trying to circle around the nurse and make my way to the woman on the bed, "and I need to get it back before nightfall. It's a job, lady."

"I know it's a job, but you're still wrong, you knuck-lehead." This was the first time Melinda ever used her pet name for me, and even then, long before we would marry, it sent chills of pleasure down my spine.

This was also when I learned how stubborn my third ex-wife could be. I could have just Tasered her into uncon-sciousness, I know, but something in me let the conversation go on without electrical stimuli. It was as if I wanted to fight with this woman. It set off the pleasure centers in my brain, like arguing with her was something I'd been missing all my life.

Carol's therapist had a field day with that one.

————

"It's an Outsider implant," Melinda said finally. "All right? You can't take it back for the Union because it's not theirs."

"It scans the same—"

"Oh, and no one has the same artiforg," she said sarcasti-cally. "Can you pull a serial number off of it?"

"Well," I began, "no, but—"

"Because it's black market. I know—I helped her find the Outsider to do it." I was stunned—most people are too frightened to talk to Bio-Repo men in the first place, let alone admit to steering others toward Outside help. But this girl—this *woman*—was a cyclone of righteousness. Suddenly, the room was hot.

"Do you want to go grab some lunch?" I asked her.

"Will it get you to leave the room?"

"Yes."

"Then yes, I would," said Melinda.

And, after she led me up three flights of stairs to Mrs. Nelson's semiprivate suite and stood by with her arms folded as I repossessed the Jarvik–11 that did, indeed, belong to the Credit Union, my third ex-wife and I went on our first official date. We sat in a booth and ate sandwiches and talked about the day. I left the heart in the glove compartment.

———

Speaking of life-changing meals:

Three days after the war ended was the first time I ate any African food. We'd been stationed there for nigh on two years, and not counting the meals in the field, that would have given us approximately 212 chances to sample the native cuisine. Not once did we try it, though, until those days just after the war.

We reached Windhoek, Namibia's capital city, well after nightfall, rolling our tanks down the narrow, rocky streets, waving to the surprised townies as our heavy metal crushed their roads into rubble. Me and a few of the other guys who'd driven the last few clicks into town were given forty-eight hours to party it up in a city that hadn't seen a disco ball during its thousands of years of existence, but we made it our mission to find some exhilarating way in which to celebrate the end of the African conflict.

They did not have a red light district. That was fine by me. I didn't need another wife.

But we did find an all-night eatery, a tight, curtain-lined restaurant that served great, heaping bowls of steaming meat covered in a succulent sauce. Potato-like vegetables swam in the mixture, their unpeeled knobby brown roots scratching at my throat as they went down. The meat was tough, gamey, but satisfying, and even when one of the gunners who spoke a little Afrikaans figured out it was goat, I kept on chewing and swallowing, chewing and swallowing. *This is what I should have been doing all those nights in those little desert townships*, I thought as the stew filled me up, warming me from the inside. The waiters kept coming, bringing plate after plate after plate—even as I was suddenly shamed because I'd been eating so ethnophobically all the way through the war—and I sucked it all down like a crash dieter given one last reprieve.

Twelve hours later, I was doubled over a good old U.S. toilet, revisiting my repast, as was every other man who ate in that god-awful establishment. We may have ruined their homeland, but they took out our digestive tracts.

———

Something took out Bonnie's, as well. On the way out of the café, I badgered her into letting me guess at three more organs, and this time, I went internal. Stomach, liver, kidneys.

"My stomach" —Bonnie sighed as if it bored her— "is a Kenton ES/18, Lady Mystique model, with a three-point-two-cup capacity. The model I purchased was the best at the time, but it doesn't have an expansion/contraction regulator like the new ones. Still, after I eat enough food to fill the artiforg, it sends a message up to the esophagus—which, since it's part of the whole system, I might as well let you know is also from Kenton—and effectively shuts down the swallowing muscles of my throat. It also happens to be robin's-egg blue, my favorite color. The unit was on sale the day I went in for the surgery, and we secured a loan directly from Kenton at twenty-two point six percent.

"My liver is a Hexa-Tan, which is a specialized supply house out of Denmark. It doesn't do anything other than clean the toxins out of my system, and the loan came through a number of international intermediaries working with the Credit Union, financed at thirty-four point two percent, with a point-one-percent drop every year due to excellent payment history.

"And my kidneys . . . my kidneys are two different models. The left one is a Credit Union generic, twenty-four percent flat, and it's been starting to run down a bit recently, but my insurance has lapsed and I can't get into the hospital to have them take a look at it. The right one, which was implanted six months later, is top-of-the-line Taihitsu, with every option included, from a built-in ketone monitor for diabetics to this little device that adds a nontoxic dye to the urine so I can fool my friends into thinking I'm pissing out blood or blueberry juice or whatever. I haven't used that option yet. Either way, the loan was eighteen point two percent, the lowest on my body."

I had a feeling she could go on forever.

———

Taxi drivers are notorious for snitching to the Union; some make more than 90 percent of their take-home pay from reward fees. I had a network of cabbies on my personal payroll, fellows who didn't mind hauling in a couple of extra bucks by getting on the horn and alerting me to where they'd dropped off a wanted client. Now, if they recognized a face and *really* wanted to pull in the dough, the smart ones took a "shortcut" to wherever the client asked to go, and a few minutes later pulled up at the Union back door instead. I'd be at the curb with a short-range Taser long before the deadbeat figured out that this was his time to make like a gazelle.

One time, just a couple of days before the end, when Wendy was leaning on me hard to transfer over to sales, we had a barbeque over at the house. Just me, Jake, Frank, a couple of the other repo guys from down at the shop, throwing a football and shooting the shit. There was beer, hot dogs, steaks, a fun afternoon to be had by all. Peter had even shown up; by that point, he was already in school, and Melinda had gone off on some trip or another and hadn't come back yet. We were starting to get concerned, me and

Peter, but Melinda had a habit of doing that sort of thing; she'd show up in a few weeks, no doubt, talking about her latest jaunt to Peru or how she helped out an indigenous family in Louisiana.

So there we were, kicking back and relaxing, when a call came in. I answered it to find a cab driver I used as a frequent snitch on the line; he said that his engine was running a little hot, which was his code that he wanted to make a delivery to the Union.

"I'm not at work," I explained, waving to Wendy, who stood nearby talking to Peter. "It's not a good time."

"I think it's running at least a six or seven," said the taxi driver. Six or seven months overdue, according to the un-licensed scanner I'd given him a few years back. That was bound to be worth some serious money to the Union, even if it wasn't one of my official assignments. I didn't need the cash, but it's hard to turn down bills when they come straight at you like that.

"Outside in five minutes," I said, and gave him my home address.

I hung up and returned to Wendy and Peter, giving my wife a peck on the cheek. "I've got to run out for a few min-utes, pick up some more beer. Be back in a flash."

I nodded over to Jake, across the backyard, who instantly picked up on the situation and followed me through the house and out the front door. He'd grabbed the filet knife from the grill, the blade dripping with beefy juices.

"Isn't that a little unsanitary?" I pointed out.

"So we'll shoot him up with antibiotics." Jake always had an answer. "Heads up, here they come."

The cab roared into the driveway and screeched to a halt, and the fare was already freaking out. He barely had time to bark out a "no" before we had the door open and hit him with a Taser. As Jake and I worked, locating and reclaiming a half-year-overdue kidney, I could see the cabbie peering at us in the rearview mirror, watching us do our thing.

I tossed him two hundred bucks for the delivery, and an extra fifty to get rid of the body. But as I pulled myself out of the cab, BBQ apron bloody and stained, I saw Wendy standing at the front door, watching the entire scene with a look of disappointment on her face. She turned on her heel and headed back inside.

"Come on, baby," I called out, "don't be like that. It's only a kidney."

"Yeah," Jake added. "He's got another one."

————

So Bonnie and I were loath to risk our lives by hopping a taxi to her friend's place. And since it was clear across town, and walking a hundred blocks with a duffel bag full of artillery was out of the question, public transportation became the only option. One of the first things they taught us in repo training is that subways make a great place for deadbeats to hide, because the crush of people makes it difficult for a scanner to isolate one artiforg from the rest. Density was what we needed; we headed underground.

I suggested hopping the entrance carousel; instead, Bonnie once again paid for us both, and we walked onto the platform like genteel citizens. I didn't know how much loose change she had on her, but I imagined that it all must have been of the nickel-and-dime variety; otherwise, she'd have bagged 'em, tagged 'em, and paid off those organs long ago.

————

Sixth year on the job, and I was sent by the BreatheIt Corporation into a housing project in order to repo a pair of lungs. BreatheIt was a new supply house at the time, and rumor was that a majority of their capital had come from certain extra-legal sources who were interested in laundering their money to a golden shine. I didn't care; they were paying me a commission 6 percent higher than standard Union rates, so I was happy to shut up and do the job with a smile.

I'd been to housing projects all around the country, of course; as a Bio-Repo man, you live practically every working day in some diseased pit or another. But Reagan Heights was one of the worst, vermin-speaking, that I'd seen in a long time. It was like the rats rented the place, only they had a bad human infestation. I double-parked my car in what was essentially an automobile graveyard, ancient rusted domestics from forty years ago left to rot away into three-wheeled heaven.

The Federal HUD had long since been disbanded, of course, and the state-funded departments that sprang up in its place never quite got on the ball in terms of bringing functional aesthetics to the ghetto. I walked past towering high-rises competing for space with small, low-slung duplexes and blocking out their light, depriving the whole ugly mess of any sense of coherency. Pinks and greens and yellows, all faded, all chipping, fought with the browns of the untended, out-of-control lawns, and the building names and street numbers had all but fallen off of the stucco, making identification difficult, if not impossible.

But I knew where I was going. I'd followed the guy home from the porn shop.

Couldn't gas down the place, because his duplex was connected to others via a common air shaft, and I'd heard the high-pitched clatter of children nearby. The last thing a new company like BreatheIt needed was to gas a couple of kids onto the evening news. I picked the lock, slipped in the front door, and found the deadbeat in an easy chair, preparing to pleasure himself.

I waited in the shadows, watching as he placed the nudie

mag on the rickety end table, unbuttoned his filthy jeans, and pulled them down to his ankles. Immobility.

"Breathing okay?" I asked as I stepped into the light. The client fell hard into the chair, shoulders shaking. I lunged out with a flashlight, shining it into his eyes, forcing him to scrunch up his face. Pantsless, shaking, squinting—this could not have been his finest moment.

"I—I'll call the cops—" he stuttered, making feeble attempts to reach a phone halfway across the room. I pulled out a Luger I was fond of at the time, complete with a long-barreled silencer, and shot the phone three times before it fell to the floor, smoking.

"You've got some property that doesn't belong to you anymore," I explained, calmly removing the paperwork from the inside pocket of my leather jacket, "and I'm here to take it back." As long as there was no ether involved, it was always easier if you could get the clients to sign off on their own repossessions—less red tape back at the office—but it was a rare occurrence.

Now, either this guy was on narcotics or I wasn't looking as fierce as usual that night, because the son of a bitch actually tried to fight me off. As I approached the trembling man, yellow receipt and pen in one hand, Luger in the other, he leaned back in the chair and kicked out with his naked legs, landing a solid shot to my midsection. I doubled over.

It only took a second to recover, but by then he'd managed to waddle out of the easy chair and hop for the far bedroom. Reaching down to my boot, I lashed out with the Taser, the darts soaring across the room and slamming into the door frame just as he leaped through. Sighing, I calmly strolled to the door, reloaded the Taser gun with two fresh darts, and entered the bedroom.

And there he was, sitting on the floor, still in his skivvies, cracking open jar after jar of loose change. It was a swimming pool of nickels and dimes, cascading around his legs in tinkling waterfalls. "I got—I got the money," he stammered. "It's all here, right here."

"I'm not counting that."

"I'll count it," he whined.

"And I'm not trusting you." My first move was for the Taser, but a niggling thought soon stopped me. I didn't quite remember BreatheIt's policy on late payments. Kenton, for example, would rather the Bio-Repo man take the money, if in full, than repo the organ. I didn't want to botch my first job for this new supply house, and I didn't want to call the office and profess my ignorance on the matter. So I played it safe.

An hour later, and we were at a local bank. I'd stolen some pillowcases from some of Reagan Heights' more absent tenants and made the guy fill them with his change. Sixteen pillowcases, all told, and I held him at gunpoint while he dragged the change up to the bank's bulletproof window. The teller wasn't too keen on counting change that hadn't already been rolled, but I had a nice discussion with the bank manager, and after dispensing a few free artiforg credits, all was settled. We were given a helpful V.P. to assist us in a back room.

According to the receipt, the deadbeat's bill, with late payment penalties and all, came to just over sixteen thousand dollars. The kicker is, he almost made it.

"Fifteen thousand, eight hundred and twelve," said the kind woman with the bouffant hairdo. "And forty-five cents."

The client was thrilled. His face, previously blanched of color, returned to a normal hue, and I thought for a moment he was going to hug me. "Take it," he said, pushing the mounds of change toward me. "Take it all, and I promise to pay every month."

"You're two hundred short," I pointed out. "That's not payment in full."

He started screaming then, shrieking like an alarm siren, begging the bank teller to help him, but she wisely scooted out of the room as I brought the Taser to full power. The bank employees were good enough to stay out of my way during the fifteen-minute extraction, and as I shuffled out of the bank with both BreatheIt lungs still pumping away beneath my arms, they told me not to worry about the mess, that they'd clean up.

I could have loaned him the two hundred bucks, I guess, but I had a feeling that the guy wouldn't be good for it.

———

Sometimes, despite my best efforts, I allow trust to jump the fence and play for my team. Trusted my wives; that worked out swell. Trusted my staff sergeant; good sense there. Trusted my boss and my friends at the Union; jury's still out on that one.

———

"You want to know how I got here," Bonnie said to me once we were on the subway. It wasn't a question, and she was correct.

"Tell you mine if you tell me yours."

We kissed on it. Our first. A light peck, lip to lip, the electric hum of her tongue stopping just short of mine. We were the only folks on this side of the train—number one and number twelve on the Union's Hundred Most Wanted List, a fortune in flesh and metal waiting for any smart snitch to get a glimpse—yet we were somehow able to relax enough to stretch out across the seats, lean back, and tell our tales.

Bonnie went first:

———

She had been a housewife, plain and simple, the loving spouse of a Union-registered surgeon, an internist who specialized in quick, nearly painless pancreas and kidney implantations. They had a lovely home in the hills and a winter cabin in Park City that wasn't too big, wasn't too small, but was perfect for short ski trips with friends. She and her husband owned three imported automobiles, one domestic convertible muscle car to tool around in on the weekends, and a small sailboat they kept in a rented slip up in Vero Beach. They had no children of their own, but showered their love and affection on their nieces and nephews, planning elaborate birthday parties and holiday trips, purchasing toys and clothes and games for them, waiting for the day when the little red line on the early-pregnancy detector would finally turn into a plus sign, and Bonnie could give birth to the child of their dreams. The obstetrician said it would come any day now, as long as they held a positive attitude and kept trying. "Have a lot of sex," he told them. And they followed doctor's orders.

Two years passed, then three, and though they'd had enough sex to make it a chore, there was nothing. That's when the tests began, long complicated procedures involving tubes and blood and needles. "I was a baked potato," Bonnie said to me on that subway train. "They kept poking me to see if I was done."

One afternoon during the third year, as Bonnie was doing her weekly shopping in the local grocery store, she felt something warm and wet running down her leg. Her first thoughts went to blood, mucus, any of the signs of miscarriage she'd come across so many times these last few years. But as she looked down at her pants, she realized in horror that it was urine, and that she had no way of stopping the flow.

That's when the tests really intensified, and that's when they found the growth. The cancer had begun not in Bonnie's bladder, but in her uterus, and the only way to stop the spread, they told her, was to remove the uterus and bladder at once, replacing them with top-of-the-line artiforgs from Kenton. Her husband, a wealthy man with an excellent credit history who loved his wife very much, quickly convinced her that this could be the only sane, rational course of action.

"They opened me up," Bonnie said. "And they put 'em in. They said the artificial uterus was better than the real thing, that it had special womb-forming gen-assists built into the lining, that I'd be pregnant before I turned around, but I knew that wouldn't be the end of it."

And it wasn't. The cancer spread.

By the time she went back for a checkup, malignant cells had taken over her ovaries, destroying the eggs along with their nest. Emergency oophorectomy. *Now* they had that cancer beat, they told her, and even though Bonnie's eggs were gone, the scientists assured her that they could find a way to combine some of her DNA with her husband's sperm, and as long as they found a suitable egg donor, the two of them could still be natural parents.

Until her stomach went, too. And her liver, and her pancreas. And her spleen and her kidneys and . . .

They'd never seen anything like it, they said; the cancer moved in a blitzkrieg, storming each part of her body, seemingly taking it without a fight. Her organs were France, and the cancer ravaged the countryside of her body.

But the faster the disease spread, the faster her husband ordered new artiforgs, securing loan after loan after loan for his dear, dying wife. Two more years passed in this way, her days filled with trips to the hospital and supply houses, her natural organs replaced one by one with perfectly designed replicas, as good as or better than the originals.

By the time they were all done, by the time the cancer truly had been excised from her body, Bonnie was 74-percent artificial.

"My skin is my own," she told me, "and a lot of the fatty tissues, lucky me. I got to keep one breast, and for the other they implanted a Quattrofil, inflated to look exactly like the real one, only it's got a refillable milk pouch to help me breast-feed more naturally. Ha. A lot of my bones are natural, but they said that as I got older and osteoporosis took over, I'd need to have those replaced, too, or the titanium support beams that make up the rest of my body might overwhelm my whole frame. The skull is mine, though most of the sensory sections of my brain are shot through with Ghost wires, and around half of my tactile experiences are stored in a suspension gel accessed by a solid-state processor. Sometimes, when I'm thinking really hard, I can hear my memories squishing around for space. The infrastructure is all there, but it needed a lot of reinforcement.

"Basically," she said, "I was retrofitted back to life."

But here's the best part:

"And your organs . . ." I asked, "the big ones . . . ?"

"All artiforgs—with one exception. The cancer raced through my body, hitting everything it could, but for some reason it left my heart alone. Every time they opened me up, they expected to have to fit me with a Jarvik, but the cells in there stayed pure. Still, the doctors wanted to set me up with one, figuring if the rest of my body could live to a hundred and fifty, why not my heart, but I refused. If it hadn't been touched by the cancer, then I didn't want it out. The doctors were reluctant, but they couldn't go against my wishes. My husband tried to talk me into it—what's another artiforg in a body filled with them, right? But I can be bull-moose stubborn when I want, and the discussion was over before it started. So that's where I am today—real heart, fake container."

I laughed then, loud and clear, my first good laugh in months. It started low, in my belly, and exploded up through my mouth, startling Bonnie and drawing the attention of the few other passengers who'd boarded the train. But I didn't care—I laughed and laughed until my sides ached, unable to explain to Bonnie why it was all so damned funny.

I had an artificial heart. She had an artificial everything else. No wonder we connected from the start. Me and her, we were the perfect jigsaw puzzle.

CHAPTER 14

For the first two months after I returned from Africa, I sat around the house a lot. Stayed in bed for hours, curled up in a control-chair crouch, fiddling with crossword puzzles, reading the funny papers, worrying Mother to no end. She'd come down and try to get me to dress, shower, look for a job, but I wasn't interested. I told her it was because I was trying to sort the war out in my head, trying to figure out how the experience had affected me. This, naturally, was a lie. I was a lazy bum.

Checked out some mech jobs over at the local chop-shop, but the work was too upfront, too humdrum. They wanted me to work with engines, recalibrating parts no bigger than my fingernail; my only experience with machines was on a macroscopic scale. Treads, gun turrets, ten tons of metal streaming down the desert sand. Mech jobs were literally too small for me.

The higher-tech firms weren't interested in my services, either, and I couldn't blame them. With the exception of some warehouse duties in high school, tank driving was the only real job on my stunted resume, and it didn't get me very far with the business set. Not that I wanted in on that life. Or on any life. Hell, I didn't know what I wanted.

Until the day I caught up with Jake Freivald. He'd served a few extra moths, finishing up his recon assignments, clearing out whatever messes they'd begun now that the war was over, and I hadn't spoken to him in all that time. It wasn't until I hit a local bar—alone, depressed, and looking for companionship of nearly any sort—that I had any idea he was even back in town.

I walked into the tavern, sat at the bar, and the first thing I heard apart from the jukebox was, "You little sack of shit." Behind my back, aimed at me. I prepared for a fight. Wasn't particularly in the mood to throw down, but was grateful that at least I'd be doing something productive with my time. "You goddamned ugly piss-poor moth-eaten mother-crappin' sonofoabitch."

I turned, hands already balled into loose fists, but it was Jake, just Jake, laughing it up with some cute redhead on his arm, but soon enough he'd lost the girl and sat down next to his oldest friend. We drank, and then we drank some more, and we caught each other up on what we'd been doing for the past few months. My story was bland as toast, the days of boredom blending into one another. Jake had gotten in some action during the final cleanup phase of the operation, but since he'd rotated back to the States, it had all become something of a drag.

"I mean, don't get me wrong," he said after the fourth or fifth beer, "I can get down with the military pension and all that. A grand a month for sitting on my ass won't get a complaint outta me."

"Hell, no."

"Hell, no, indeed." Jake finished off his beer and ordered another. "But it's not like I've got any hobbies."

"Any legal ones," I offered.

"And you're bored fucking stiff, I can tell that just from looking at you. Probably shit your pants with glee if someone burst in here right now with a machine gun."

I couldn't argue with him there. "So?"

"So . . . nothing. You sit, I sit, we find some goddamned desk job and go about living the lives we're supposed to live, I guess." He couldn't have sounded more depressed about the concept.

"I can't see you running with the shirt-and-tie crowd," I said.

"Over them, maybe." Jake smirked. "In a tank."

He held out his thumb, and I pressed mine against it. At that moment, it was us against the world, two lost soldiers in search of a war they'd never find again.

"I miss the rush," Jake softly admitted.

"I miss the structure," I said.

Jake finished off the last of his beer and, for good measure, took a swig off mine, as well. "I miss the kill."

———

They always put the come-on ads in bathrooms; I imagine it's because they're trying to take advantage of the inebriated or the incontinent or both, but the Union marketing people have their shit together and I can't argue with it.

Even back then, when the ads were just ink on paper tacked to a wall, they knew how to tweak the right people at the right time. Jake and I had no idea when we walked into that crapper that the next phase of our lives had already begun.

There we were, six or seven sheets to the wind, barely standing up as we pissed into adjacent urinals, trying our damnedest to coax our bladders into action, when our eyes fell on the poster on the wall in front of us:

LEARN A TRADE. JOIN THE UNION. FULFILL YOUR DESTINY.

It was destiny. Said so right on the poster. Who were we to argue with Fate?

———————

There was no Mall back then; the Union and the supply houses were individual operations, each content to scratch out their own little corner of the slowly burgeoning artiforg market. Arnold Kurtzman had yet to open up his storefront, and the business, while quite legal, was still looked upon as shady by doctors who had been raised in a world where medical ethics hadn't yet caught up with technology. That which seemed morally questionable became, by default, morally reprehensible, no trial, no jury.

The Credit Union headquarters was located in what would have then been considered a bad part of town, but has today been re-gentrified into a sparkling example of urban "recommitment." In other words, it's stocked with big box stores, chain restaurants, and the families with babies who cry in them.

Back then, it was all auto mechanics, liquor stores, and pawn shops, but no one really bothered anyone else, and if you didn't mind a little dog shit on the streets, it was fine for walking at all but the darkest hours.

Jake and I headed up to the Union building, a large warehouse abutted by two empty lots. A bunch of guys stood on the stoop, smoking cigarettes; some I recognized as guys from the neighborhood, some I didn't, but all had the same air of practiced boredom that I had been cultivating since I got back from Africa. Finally, I felt at home.

Jake recognized a guy who'd lived down the block from him a few years back, and he introduced the guy as Big Dan. He was at least half a head and sixty pounds bigger than me, so it's not like the name was particularly ironic. On the side of his neck was a jumble of scar tissue with a colorful play of shimmering lights washing over it. It was the first time I'd seen a Union tattoo up close, and I was transfixed.

"The rest of these knobs are waiting for their number," Big Dan explained as he led us past the line of young men. "I'm gonna take you in personally."

Turns out Big Dan had stumbled onto the Credit Union three weeks before we did, and was already a member of their training program; as such, he was able to wheel us in past the security guards and straight up to his boss's office, where he demanded that we be given jobs.

"Do they have any special skills?" asked the supervisor, a man who would die four years later in an airplane crash when the pilot's Ghost system malfunctioned during landing.

"We drove tanks in the war," Jake explained, not letting me get a word in. "And I did some recon work . . . which I can't tell you about, but let's just say we're qualified. So shut up with the questions and give us a job, okay?"

So they gave us jobs. I was elated, even more so when I was issued my first Taser, scalpel, and empty ether canister. I was amazed that Jake's brash ploy had such an effect on the bosses that we were given employment over all those other potentially qualified candidates.

Turns out everyone got a job that day; they were hard up for men. The organs had been selling like organs.

———

The Credit Union has always done a good business. From the first year of their inception, even with all the built-in liquidity drops, they have never once taken a loss on quarterly earnings. People buy artiforgs, plain and simple, and with today's generous interest rates, there's no end in sight. There was one point about eight years back when the average loans were coming in at 40, almost 50 percent, at which point a lot of people chose to take their chances with modern medicine rather than the repo corps. End up with more than one artiforg, and the payments can stack up quick. So the Union scaled back the percentages until the applicants started flooding back in. It's a delicate balancing act, but they've got it down to a science by now.

"I've got a few million dollars of machinery in me," Bonnie said as our subway ride came to an end. We hopped off the train and onto the platform, heading out of the station. Outside, a light rain had begun; we saw people entering the underground tunnels, shaking off their umbrellas, muttering about the weather.

"But you paid the loans off?"

"For a while. My husband was very wealthy—*we* were very wealthy—and we'd invested well." She paused, shook her head. "Actually, *I'd* invested well, with his money. He didn't know a thing about the market, but I put us in the right places at the right times. Had a lot of money in Union and supply-house stock, actually. We got lucky. Lucky enough, I guess, because interest alone was enough to keep us in the clear with the supply houses."

"So far, so good," I said as we made our way onto the street. The rain was coming down harder, pelting the ground in big, heavy drops. I lifted the duffel over Bonnie's head, weapons and all, protecting her as we walked.

"So far, so good," she agreed. "But it wasn't enough. By the time I had recovered from all of the implantations, I was too far gone to have a baby. We tried IVF, we tried full fetal, everything short of growing the kid in a petri dish. Sure, they could implant a seed in that artiforg womb, but what kind of child could come out of a metal mom? It never took, and I was never surprised.

"I think that's when Ken started to die a little. He still loved me, I know that, but there was a part of him that could never be fulfilled. He wanted a baby, and I was keeping him from it. We talked about adoption, but he wasn't really into it; I could see that far-off look in his eyes; he was dreaming of dresses and football and chats about the prom. I wanted to make it right for him, to give him whatever he wanted, but it wasn't in the cards for us anymore. And somehow, it was my fault.

"Two months later, he left me."

————

I was thinking we should find a way to hook up Bonnie's ex-husband with Beth, Mary-Ellen, and Carol. They'd get along like gangbusters.

————

We were nearing her friend's apartment, but Bonnie continued with the story.

"He disappeared one night when I went to sleep. Left me a note, twenty typed pages, and yeah, clearly he'd been putting some thought into it for a while, but that's all there was. Fifty grand in cash, but I didn't want his money. That's not what I was looking for.

"I guess it would have been pretty damned easy to just give up, but I'd already beaten up this cancer that no one beats up. Let them put all this metal in me. For Ken. For the baby we were supposed to have. So maybe it was better. I knew that Ken would try to cover, that he'd keep paying off the loans, but once we were separated, I wanted it to be a clean break. I didn't want him to have to tell his new wife that they were in the hole for eighty-nine thousand dollars a month due to a missing ex. I got cancer on my own, so I'd deal with it on my own, repercussions and all. So I had the automatic payments switched to a personal account. Once the money in there ran out, the delinquent bills would start piling up, and then they'd be after me."

"How long ago was that?" I asked her, amazed that there could be a woman this generous and kind and wonderful and screwed up all at the same time.

"Three years," she said, staring up at the high-rise across the street. "Give or take. Come on, let's go inside."

———————

Mary-Ellen left me, after a fashion, but not with such benevolent intentions. Our marriage lasted for eight months and three days, counting the period when I was still sleeping in our home—on the floor, by myself—yet not quite legally divorced. Housing crunch.

I came home at four in the morning after having worked a double shift, covering for Jake, who was off on some fox hunt of one of the Big Ten. Every once in a while, the Credit Union gets on a completist streak and sends out teams of Bio-Repo men to corral the most wanted; that year, we managed to round up 95 percent of the Big Hundred before finding new deadbeats to take their places. Commissions were good, but time was scarce.

I'd done five full repos in twenty-four hours' time, with additional trips back to the Union for more ether and supplies. So I was beat when I got home, too tired to notice that most of the furniture in the living room was gone. Didn't care about the missing television, either. My feet took me right into bed. Rather, they took me right to where the bed should have been. It wasn't until I lay down on the cold, hard floor that I realized something was amiss.

Crashed around the house for a while, looking for an answer to this little puzzle, unable to find an explanation. I was already starting to accept the fact that my second marriage had come to a close, but I couldn't believe that Mary-Ellen would be so coldhearted as to vanish without leaving a note.

When I finally gave up and stumbled into the bathroom to splash some water on my face, I saw the blood on the mirror. My first thoughts went to suicide, to a dead wife in the bathtub, wrists slit, a heady mixture of blame and guilt making me dizzy. But it was red lipstick and nothing more, scrawled across the bathroom walls in pure horror-movie fashion.

Good-bye, you bastard, it read, stretching from the shower to the sink and back again. *There's a meat loaf in the freezer.*

———————

Concomitant with my five divorces were, of course, five teams of lawyers. Some, like those who represented Wendy, were kind enough in their own way, allowing me time and space to work things out on my own. Others, like those who represented Mary-Ellen, deserve to be ripped apart by ravenous hyenas. And if hyenas are out of season, tigers will do nicely.

But they were just the soldiers and Mary-Ellen was the field general, using her team of attorneys to rip into my bank accounts, my Union stock portfolio, my future earnings. For a woman who claimed to want nothing to do with the repossession lifestyle, she was more than happy to take her share of profits.

I didn't fight it. After Beth, I never fought any of it. If these women didn't want to be with me anymore, then who was I to argue? Someday, I knew, I would find a woman who would fit me perfectly. Who cares if it hadn't happened yet? I was a young man.

———————

The Outsider lived in a four-room flat on the third floor of what seemed to be a structurally sound building. It was good to see running water again. The apartment, though sizable, was separated by a gaggle of Chinese paper screens, set up so as to create a huge maze out of the living and dining areas. As I worked my way in through the front door, I managed to squeeze myself around the barriers, my chest brushing up against them as I slinked past.

He was broad of shoulder yet wiry and slim, the muscular definition above his chest a stark contrast to the rest of his body. Like he'd spent a lot of time shoveling coal or plucking chicken feathers but not much else. A red bandana wrapped around his forehead to keep the sweat out of his eyes, tied back against a thick mop of braided hair.

Bonnie introduced us. "This is Asbury," she said, and I shook the man's hand. It was wet, slimy.

"Sorry," he said, wiping his palm off on a filthy apron before going back for another shake. "Working on an op, and the juice done leaked a pop."

In the distance, I caught a glimpse of an artificial backbone lying limp on a card table; cerebrospinal fluid dripped to the floor below. "In and gone," I said, switching into the once-fashionable repo-slang this guy was so fond of using. It was ten years old, this stuff, but it floated naturally off my tongue.

He shot a smile up at Bonnie, clapping her on the back. "You brought me down a wood nymph, I like that."

"No," she replied, "he's not an Outsider." She pulled down the high collar that hid my tattoo, exposing it to Asbury's gaze. "He was with the Union."

Asbury was instantly on the defensive, backing up a step as he eyed me warily. "Why'd you drag me a U-man, baby?"

Palms up, I clarified. "I'm not with them anymore. I quit the rap."

"You quit," he asked, "or you were quitted?"

"I was quitted," I said. "About six months on the back end."

He nodded, getting a good look at my eyes. Probably trying to see if I was lying or not, but there was the distinct possibility he was sizing me up for artiforgs, wondering if I could be of any financial value to him down the line.

Eventually, he dropped his guard and allowed me farther into the flat.

"*Mi casa, cabron.*"

We had lunch inside his small kitchen, standing up at the counter, our shoulders rubbing up against one another as we talked about the outside world, about the Credit Union, about Bio-Repo men and about the black-market artiforg business. Freshly sliced luncheon meats rolled into cylinders, shoved down with our fingers, washed back with seltzer and lemons. It was the best meal I'd had in weeks.

"I can snatch a pumper from a shelf and spin it to quarter value," Asbury boasted, trying to convince me that he was doing the world a favor, "fly it into the op for half, and still make a credit on the upside."

"Or the client can do it legally," I said, my mouth going through the words I'd said a thousand times. "Get full benefit of warranty and customer service."

"How's a *vato* in the ghetto gonna up-front the Union?" he asked. "Downtown, all they care about is the equity. Me, the only equity I care about is hanging in your skin."

"Asbury's right," Bonnie chimed in. "He's recycling. Plus the client gets a cheaper artiforg, so everyone comes out a winner."

"Except for the supply houses," I pointed out. "It's their merchandise, after all."

I expected an argument, but the Outsider just laughed and turned to Bonnie. "They quitted him, all right, but they shoulda quitted him harder."

————

He had nodes in his head, implanted sockets, which meant Asbury did some serious Ghost work in his spare time. Most spooks are satisfied to use headsets and earplugs; only the diehard riders got their own artiforgs and connected directly.

As we finished up with the meal, I couldn't help but ask him about it.

"You licensed to pimp for the Ghost?" I asked.

"Licensed?" He laughed. "No, U-man, I'm not 'licensed.' But I'm down with the Ghost. Full sense implants, get a ride every one or two, pick up a system and curl it out. You?"

"No," I admitted. "Pulled 'em out, but never taken the ride."

Excited now, Asbury pulled me across the kitchen and over to where a dining room should have been. On another rickety card table was a thin, rectangular box with flat wires like bunched linguini leading out from the center. Ghost processor. Asbury hovered over it like a kid waiting for a plate of cookies to cool, his fingers barely caressing the metal. "Witness."

I backed away as he held the wires out to me. "I'm no spook," I insisted. "Node free."

Asbury had it covered. He reached under the table and rummaged around in a large cardboard box filled with plugs and cords, eventually coming up with the smallest pair of goggles I'd ever seen. I'd heard of sets like this during some of my repo training, but I'd never had to pimp out a visual system before. Furthermore, I had no interest.

But we were here looking for help, and the last thing I wanted to do was offend the guy. I figured there couldn't be any harm in seeing what all the fuss was about. Some of my pals back on the repo force went full-time spook after riding their first Ghost systems; there must have been something entertaining about the experience.

"You put them in like contact lenses," Bonnie explained, helping me to keep my eyelids open as I popped the sensors onto my eyeballs. Thin metallic leads ran from the bottom of each lens across my cheeks down to a frayed, open end, and Asbury twisted these onto the wires stretching from the Ghost system. From my perspective, nothing much had changed.

"This guy was a racer," Asbury explained to me, his hand firm on the controls. "Fritzed on the Q. Got sixteen hours visual Ghost time in here, forty-two audio. You get the vids 'cause the 'verb's too intense."

I was going to ask a question, but he turned on the box. Suddenly, I found myself pimping for the Ghost.

———

Woman on the floor, falling away from me. She tried to stand up but fell back down hard, hitting her head on a chair. Her belly was thick, full. Pregnant. Puddles of mystery moisture obscured the crumbling wood floorboards, and a cat zipped across the room, hair on end. All of this was mute, completely silent. No thunk, no ouch, no meow, just the hum of the Ghost system and the taut breath of Bonnie and Asbury behind me.

"Are you okay?" Bonnie's voice, but she wasn't in the room. She was in the Outsider's apartment, I knew, but in here it was just me and this half-naked woman and a cat that kept jumping on the counter and off again and on again and off again.

"Doing fine," I replied.

The room shifted, came closer into focus. I saw an arm rise up—from the vantage point, it should have been my own, but it clearly was not. On the filthy fingertip, nails long and unfiled, was a sparkling red powder, glittering in the glare from the exposed overhead bulb. It came toward my mouth and disappeared beneath my field of vision.

"This here's when he drops the Q hard," said Asbury. I could feel his hand on my back—*my* back—and he said, "Keep it tight."

The floor suddenly burst open in a flash of light, exploding out, molten lava streaming from the gaping wound and flowing across the ground. The pregnant girl was caught up in the flow, the liquid heat racing past her knees, but she didn't notice. Bent over double, she vomited once, twice. The cat sprouted four extra legs and hopped back off the counter, climbing the walls and ceiling before dropping down next to me. Its mouth opened in a hiss, fangs dripping with green saliva, but all was still mute.

Everything pushed away; the body I was looking through must have leaped backward, and suddenly I was staring at the sky through a hole in the ceiling, at a pure, white light streaming down from above. A phalanx of angels with automatic weaponry descended from on high, their guns aimed at me, at the pregnant girl, her belly now distended to encompass half the room, growing with every second, at the cat/spider, caught up in the lava flow, burning as it danced from her to me, all of it rising up, into the air, coalescing into a giant fiery pillar, towering hundreds of feet above my head, ready to crash down and crush me, finish me off—

And I was back in the Outsider's apartment.

"We broke your cherry, repo man," said Asbury, gingerly plucking the contacts from my eyes. "I'm gonna tell all my friends at school."

———

I've had spooks push their machines on me before; like Q users, they're always trying to sucker squares in on their act. The only good thing about a Ghost machine is that you can only ride one sense at a time. Eyes, ears, the rest—you choose, and you plug in. One customer, one sense—it's a safety valve. I got the visuals on my ride in Asbury's flat, but I'm sure if I had the whole experience assaulting me at once, I would have gone just as mad off the drug as any normal Q user.

But now I can say, as my life approaches its potential end, that I have pimped for the Ghost, and that it hit back

hard. Doesn't sound all that impressive, but in the right
circles, it'll get me a free round of drinks.

———————

Asbury ran us past his workstations—tables filled with artiforgs in various states of disrepair, tools I'd never before
seen outside the Union compound—eventually leading us
over to a comfortable couch. It was good to sit on fabric
again. Meanwhile, Bonnie let him have the entire story—
we'd been holed up in good digs but the Union was closing
in, and we needed a new place to crash.

Asbury listened, nodding and shrugging in the appropriate places. He sympathized, he told us, but didn't know what
he could do, short of offering up his own apartment for a
hideout. "There's cavities up in this hole can't no scanner
ping you," he promised. "And I got open time to boot."

But Bonnie wasn't interested. "That's not fair to you," she
said. "You're in enough danger with us coming here as it is."

The Outsider thought for a moment, snapping his fingers
as he stared off into space. I wondered how he and Bonnie
knew each other. Was it a friendship from her marriage? I
doubted it. Afterward, then? Had they slept together? Were
they lovers? Suddenly, jealousy had taken over, and I was
ready to interrogate them, then and there.

But Asbury spoke first. "I'm thinking on this one hole,
but I gotta crunch down on this man's data before I let it go.
It's high on the top."

Bonnie turned to me to translate, but I understood the guy
fine. He wanted to know who I was before he let me in on
his secret hiding place. He wanted to know how I'd come
to the situation I was in. He wanted proof that I wouldn't
snitch him out.

He wanted to know why I was a Bio-Repo man on the run.

Fair enough. It was my turn to talk, anyway.

And this is what I said:

CHAPTER 15

About a year ago, I ran out a set of glands from a pair of circus twins who'd contracted the same genetic malady on their thirty-fourth birthday. Their hypothalamuses had begun to shrink, and it was all doctors could do to get double artiforgs implanted on the same day. They were trapeze artists, good ones, too, who regularly defied death by flying 50 feet above the midway floor, letting go of each other's hands, and landing in a two-foot pool of water surrounded by glistening iron spikes coated with *curare*. The circus had been upgraded since I was a kid.

But it wasn't as profitable. Folks preferred to shop or stay at home watching the tube than witness risky, live-action spectacles. For those who were interested in such things, there were always demolition derbies and rodeos. Ticket sales were down; insurance premiums were up.

Which might explain why Hans and Edwin, the Flying Moellering Brothers, were unable to keep up the payments on their new hypothalamuses, and why I had to track them down in a small Midwestern pay-by-the-hour motel. For a fiver, the clerk told me what room they'd checked into. I didn't think they'd pose a problem, so I didn't bother gassing the place down. We all make mistakes.

Hans hit me over the head with a trapeze bar as I entered the room, a glancing blow that momentarily stunned me, but I caught the stick as he tried to bring it back up and whipped it out of his grasp. Swung it around in the other direction, caught him halfway down the face. Hans stumbled across the room, clutching his head, moaning in pain.

Edwin, meanwhile, was crouched down behind the far twin bed. I could see his shoulders working at something, twitching like he'd just been shocked. I heard the clicks and the sound of a clip popping into place, and ducked just in time to feel the bullets whiz through my hair. Six shots, each one with my name inscribed on it, and yet each one passed me by. I let Edwin empty the gun into the door behind me.

"You're a lousy shot," I said, and stood back up again. Hans was still trying to regain control of his limbs, and Edwin was furiously attempting to eject the clip from his automatic. He never got the chance. I leaped over the bed, bouncing once on the mattress, and sunk a knee into Edwin's back, pinning him to the floor. I snatched the gun by its barrel and pocketed the weapon.

"We can pay you," Edwin grunted, his face pressed into the thin, stained carpet. His accent was weak, but still there; he hadn't yet excised his Teutonic roots. "We pay you, and you say you couldn't find us."

I could feel Hans moving in behind me; I spun, kicking out with my legs, my foot cracking into his knee, buckling it, snapping it. The wiry German fell to the floor, screaming in pain. In his hand was not a weapon, but a small wad of cash he'd been trying to push on me.

"I don't work that way," I explained to the writhing man. Then, grasping the bills in my hand, I shook them in front of his face. "Is there anyone you'd like me to give this money to?"

Edwin shook his head, tried again. "You keep it—you keep it, and go away."

"I said I don't work that way." Then, emphasizing every word: "Do you have a next of kin?"

Clients hated the next-of-kin question. It always sent them blubbering. I cut off Edwin and Hans' sobbing with a quick double-shot from the Taser, grounding the Flying Moellering Brothers once and for all. I started in on my work.

———

Wendy was a wreck by the time I got home. She'd heard about the job from a friend of ours, who'd heard about it from a guy named Chip, who'd heard about it from Frank. All of this in under four hours, but when you nearly get whacked on a gig, it makes the rounds pretty quickly. Everyone's got their stories, and the bad ones travel faster than the good.

We'd already been discussing a potential transfer for a while, Wendy suggesting I move over to sales, me resisting, her suggesting again in a slightly stronger tone, and then we'd let it drop for a week or two before starting the cycle back up again. I couldn't argue much with her points: It was safer, it was more befitting of a man of my advancing age, and it would afford me the chance to do the things I really enjoyed doing, such as breathing.

But the Moellering Brothers incident threw her over the edge, especially because by the time the information had come her way, I'd been shot/smothered/decapitated, which is understandably upsetting to a spouse. She grabbed me tight as soon as I walked in the door and only let go to punch me, hard, in the chest, for putting myself in such a dangerous situation. Wendy was no innocent when it came

to the repo game; she knew full well that there were ways
to anticipate and ways to prep, and that I'd probably gotten
sloppy somewhere in the planning stages.

"Tell me you'll transfer," she pleaded that night. "Take a
job with sales. Frank'll let you, I know it."

"It's not what I do," I explained.

"It's not what you do right now. But you *could*."

I was prepared to fight. Hell, I'd done it with every other
wife, every other time. No reason I couldn't continue the
pattern.

But I was tired. It was probably the worn-off adrenaline
from the Moellering Brothers that had me in such a recep-
tive state, but I couldn't work up the energy for a proper
argument. Rather than go through the trouble of getting
myself all riled up, I suddenly heard myself saying, "Okay.
Okay." And once more, as if I couldn't even believe it
myself: "Okay."

———

Jake and Frank did their best to change my mind. Presented
rational, cogent arguments as to why I'd wither and die in
sales. Why repo was the only place I belonged. But they
knew it was a foregone conclusion. Jake, in particular,
seemed resigned to it.

"The money's not as good," he pointed out. "Nowhere
near as good."

"I know," I said. "But I've got enough money as it is."

"Even with the five divorces?"

"Four," I said.

"Four *now*."

Sure, I'd be losing about a third of my salary by switching over to sales; the commissions were nowhere as high as
they were in Repo, but neither were the dangers. My mind
was set, and Frank put in the paperwork.

"You've got about two weeks before this goes through,"

he told me. "You want to take vacation time before you start, or you want a few last pink sheets for the road?"

"Screw vacation," I said. "Give me some pink sheets."

See? It's true what they say—too much work *can* kill you.

———

The next couple of weeks were a blur of ether and blood, as I tore into the city with a vengeance. I must have logged two months' work of repo jobs in twelve days. Most nights, I didn't bother coming home; I'd do a gig and sleep in the car for a couple hours before heading off to the next. Wendy didn't bug me about it; I think she knew I was just getting the final vestiges of the job out of my system.

Jake and I even had some fun running out a couple nests we'd located down by the old high school. Twenty or thirty debtors hiding together, hoping to find a way out of the system, out of the country, maybe make it to one of those islands where everyone still roams free and clear and fleshy. But the very nature of their operation, huddling so many people with so many past-due artiforgs in one place, made it easy for us to locate and track. We took fifty-seven artiforgs out of twenty-one hosts in just under four hours. I'm pretty sure Jake put a down payment on a powerboat.

I was finally coming to the end of my rush, the endorphins of nearly two weeks of fight-or-flight wearing off, when Frank gave us two more pink sheets. I scored a guy who was five months over on a knee replacement—with that kind of extraction, he had a pretty good chance of limping down to the local hospital for a patch-up job—but Jake grabbed a winner.

"Captain Krunkybean?" Jake scoffed. "That's the guy's name?"

"You're shitting me," I said, snatching at the sheet, checking the stats. "You got Captain K?"

"You know him?"

"Know him?" I said. "I used to watch him every Saturday morning. You're telling me you don't know who Captain Krunkybean is?"

Jake shook his head. "This is a guy from the war?"

"It's not that kind of captain," I said. "It was a kids' show. You never saw it? Shit, man, he was a legend around here. He'd show cartoons and had that puppet zebra, and they'd get kids to come in and tell jokes. I always wanted to do a knock-knock joke, but my parents were too busy to take me down to the studio."

Jake just shrugged; it didn't ring any bells. "So, you want him? I'll trade for the knee."

"Hell yeah, I want him." I swapped out pinks with Jake, and took a good look at the sheet. Jarvik unit. Considering the good captain's age, it wasn't all that surprising. "He deserves to get his heart ripped out by someone who appreciates his work."

————

The captain was holed up in a grocery warehouse district, according to the pink sheet. A snitch had placed him in the general location before losing the scent. Easy enough. I rolled into the area, cut a hole in the chain-link fence to allow myself access, and got situated. Few lights, no dogs, lax security. Large buildings on the perimeter surrounding smaller, one-story warehouses and office buildings on the inside. A fortress of produce.

I flipped on my scanner and started walking. You work the job long enough, you tend to get a feel for hideouts. Knowing where bodies fit, where humans naturally choose to make their caves. I knew, for example, that the most interior of the buildings would be empty; deadbeats always think they'll get one ahead of the Union by not choosing the most obvious location. So I settled the start of my search somewhere in the middle, concentrating on the medium-size office buildings.

My scanner, thanks to Jake, could not only ping multiple artiforgs at once; its search beam could penetrate almost any substance with the exception of lead. Superman had his weaknesses; so did I. But there wasn't a lot of solid lead construction around anymore; if folks needed to build something strong, they used titanium, which weighed less, worked better, and, fortunately for me, was not impervious to a scanner's rays.

I found the captain quickly enough. As I approached the fourth building along the left side, waving the scanner's beam left and right, a ping came back to me, filling the screen with a flurry of facts and figures. Jarvik–11 unit, model 2a, datebook and calendar option enabled. Manufacture date of four years prior, which was surprising to me; most folks who go welsh do so after a year, tops. Anyone who can pay for four years of artiforg service can usually eke out the rest of the cost, too. Then again, folks can be riding full speed on top of the world, hit one short bump, and fall headfirst onto hard times.

I would find that out soon enough.

————

Chose not to get a visual. The pink sheet said he'd been holed up by himself, and I had no doubt that the captain's lonely status hadn't changed. Maybe he still had Mr. Zebra in his front pocket; if so, the striped fella was about to get a visit from the sandman. From outside calculations, I estimated the size of the office to come in at 900 square meters, but played it on the safe side. I plucked three ether canisters from the pack, each with a 400-square-meter fill. Gas was cheap.

No window on the outside, so I took my time carving out a hole for the tube in the wooden door, slicing away bit by bit with the pencil laser, trying to keep the smell of burning wood to a minimum. Even though Captain K was of advancing age, he probably still retained enough of a sense of smell to be on the lookout for an odd whiff. One wrong move, and he'd be out the back door and running before I even noticed. I had too much respect for the guy to have to chase him down; he deserved some dignity.

After twenty-five minutes of this—my scanner keeping a silent watch on the artiforg inside all that time—I'd scraped out a large enough knot in the wood through which to insert the plastic tubing. Then it was the simple act of attaching the ether canisters one by one, twisting the release knob, and letting the odorless gas do its work. I waited fifteen minutes, slipped on my respirator, and went inside to finish the job.

It seemed so easy.

————

His body was prone on the floor, chest up, arms splayed to each side, just the way I liked 'em—unless I was doing kidneys. He wore a rumpled blue tuxedo shirt and pants, no jacket, as if he'd just come home from playing a wedding gig at the American Legion dance hall. His features, though wrinkled and worn by time, were still the same round, friendly ones I'd come to love as a child, and part of me wanted to revive him and ask all the questions I always wanted to but never had the chance: How do you make Mr. Zebra talk? Does Polly Persuasion really believe all those things she says? Why don't you ever wish me happy birthday on the air like you do for the rest of those kids?

But I had a job to do, so I sliced through his clothes, exposing a body covered in thick, graying hair. Next came scalpel, scissors, suction to clear away the blood and let me see what I was doing. Expandable lamp, set up next to the body, throwing a pool of light on the chest. Hammer to crack the ribs, a manual bone saw to finish the job in case I had problems getting through the sternum. The captain remained still, not a movement or peep, and I wondered for a second if he was already dead, the Jarvik continuing to pump blood through a corpse. It didn't matter, though; the heart was still beating, and that was what I had come for.

The early Jarvik models were notorious for continuing to run long after they were taken from the host bodies, and I knew a number of Bio-Repo men who lost fingers when the titanium valves bit down on flesh and bone. So a few iterations back, they installed electro-pulse monitors that, aside from properly mimicking the heart's electric beat, enabled a Bio-Repo man to shut down operation when the correct voltage was applied. Like all good Bio-Repo men, I kept my defib unit in the trunk of my car, and brought it along on every potential Jarvik job. Today's was no exception.

But here's where it gets a little fuzzy. I remember pulling the defibrillator out of my pack and setting it on the ground. I recall flipping the unit on and hearing the familiar hum of the electric charge. I grabbed the shock pads by their handles and rubbed them together, partially to build up friction, mostly because this was how I'd always seen it done on television. Set the dial to 300, enough to jolt anyone out of this world, and sat back for but a moment, contemplating how easy this job had become, how perfect it was to be so good at a profession that helped so many and paid so well, and how I'd miss it, every day, and in every way.

My hands firmly clenched around the handles of the shock pads, I pressed the unit into Captain K's hairy chest, and, with a flourish, depressed the thumb buttons that would send the beautiful streams of electricity racing through his body.

And that's when my heart stopped.

Oh, I thought indifferently. *So this is what it feels like.* And that takes care of the fourth time I was ever knocked unconscious.

I was legally dead for an hour.

"Last job took you down," Asbury said in a low whisper as I neared the end of my story.

"Third to last," I replied. "I still had a few more on the docket. If I would have ever made the transfer at all, I don't know. But, yeah, that's how it happened. Somehow the defib unit got reversed, the wires got crossed. A glitch in the system. The shock hit me instead of the client."

Bonnie ran her hand along my back, edging herself closer. "But you lived," she said.

"More or less," I said. "The warehouse manager for the building had forgotten a file back at his desk, so he drove in to pick it up. Saw my car, saw the light on inside, called security, and soon enough they were carting me off to the hospital."

"Which is where," Asbury concluded, "they dropped your 'forg."

I nodded. "They brought me in dead, they shipped me out alive. Came in on a gurney, full cardiac arrest, and they knew there was too much dead tissue on my own ticker to get it running again. Hospital policy called for an artiforg implantation, and so they went at it, picking out the newest Jarvik model for me. By that point, someone had seen my tattoo and figured out I was a Union stooge, so they were sure to give me extra-special care.

"I woke up in the intensive care wing to find my Union supervisor and my buddy Jake standing over me, bearing gifts and flowers and swearing like hell that they'd treat me just like they always did, that they wouldn't let my new situation get in the way of our working relationship."

"And did they?" asked Bonnie.

"More or less. These days, mostly less."

It was only a day later that they came to me with the papers to sign, the fabled yellow sheet documentation. I scribbled where I was supposed to and the assigned Union salesman pulled off the yellow copy to reveal the pink sheet below, which he quickly folded into a compartment in his briefcase. That pink sheet would be ferried back to the shop and kept on file until the Jarvik had been paid off, or until it got assigned to a Bio-Repo man for collection.

Naturally, I tried to put it out of my mind. Unfortunately, not trying to think about a pink sheet is like not trying to think about a pink elephant. Go ahead, try either one.

Wendy had to take out a second mortgage on a lake home that had been in her family for generations. But the down payment was taken care of, so all I had to worry about was the thousands of dollars a month it would take to keep my heart ticking and my credit in the clear. There was no possible way that a sales gig was going to allow me to pay off all my alimony, keep Wendy and me in the house we'd just managed to afford in the first place, and continue payments on my brand-new heart. A desk job was out of the question.

I'd have to go back to repo.

My hospital stay was short; the day after I signed the Union loan papers, they shipped me back home to work on the rest of my recuperation. They said I'd be allowed to move around in a week, be back on the job in a month. After fourteen days of staring at the television screen, I made the decision to ignore my physicians. I went back to work.

Everyone at the Union was glad to see me; I got back slaps all around. But as I walked through the corridors of the main offices, I could sense a shift in tone, as my co-workers would look at me and wonder if I'd be the next poor sap on their pink sheets. Like I'd finally given up and had a sip of the Kool-Aid.

Frank was surprised to see me back so soon. He hadn't expected me for at least another week. "I don't know what I've got for you," he told me. "All the Level Five jobs are assigned already."

"Then give me a Level Four," I said. "I got Union merchandise in me now; I need the cash."

After an hour of badgering, I got him to assign me to a chain job, taking off limb prosthetics. I was sent into the field with two Level Ones, nineteen-year-old recent trainees working the early, easy jobs. The kind of thing that any street thug could do, only with the benefit of a neck brand and legal protection.

One of the kids, a six-footer named Ian, was properly scared of me. He'd just been promoted from a gig working the Harry the Heart costume out front, and had watched me come back to the shop multiple times with blood on my hands and scars on my skin. He had a romantic and inflated notion of what the job was about, and deep in his heart of hearts, believed that it would make him a better man.

The other was a ruffian called Garrett, who didn't so much speak as he did grunt or laugh, as he did bray. His main goal in getting his hands dirty seemed to be getting his hands dirty. To be fair, a lot of Bio-Repo guys liked the bloody aspects of the job; it was never something that particularly appealed to me, but I recognize that the career draws applicants from a certain psychological pool. Garrett came from somewhere near the shallow end.

The job was an arm and leg prosthetic, both left side of the body, off a guy who'd lost a fight with a freight train. Something about a crossing, a malfunctioning guard gate, and a settlement with the county, which paid off the

20 percent down and five years of payments, but after that, it all went to hell.

I showed Ian and Garrett how to gas down the house—Ian watching every move of mine with almost fanatical interest, Garrett clearly wishing he could just bash down the door and take the guy head-to-head—and we moved in.

Once inside, we found Mr. Ewen, our client, facedown in a bowl of tofu, and his pretty wife faceup on her back. While Ian and I prepped the client, Garrett took his time examining the missus, and I grabbed him just before he started getting handsy. "Molest the innocent on your own time," I told him, grabbing him by the collar and forcing him back onto the job. "The Union ain't paying you to grope."

Teaching's never been a specialty of mine, but I took the time to impart my years of knowledge to the kids, showing the best places to cut and remove the implants in the least amount of time, shedding the fewest pints of blood.

But when it came time to make the first incision, my hand shook. Just a bit, but it was there, a distinct tremble where before there was only solid, swift motion. I ignored it and pressed on, and soon enough we were in deep and doing our job. But as I cut and grabbed, working alongside these teenagers, these people who would one day replace me, I couldn't shake it from my mind. My hand had trembled. There it was. The beginning of the end.

————

"And then . . . ?" asked the Outsider. "They rip your cord, or what?"

I shook my head. Too much information divulged already. "No, I got jobs, all right."

"So what's the problem? Scoring gigs, pulling cash . . . ?"

"Got one job too many," I said, and left it at that.

Asbury was about to ask a follow-up, but Bonnie—dear Bonnie, who is sitting beside me as I write this, reading some arcane artiforg instruction manual—shot him a no-no glance, and he backed off. Instead, he wandered back into his kitchen and rummaged through a drawer, papers flying through the air. Eventually, the Outsider came up with a pencil and scribbled something down on a blank notepad.

It was an address; he gave it to Bonnie. "You flip over here, find a gal named Rhodesia, and they'll hole you up right."

I caught a glimpse of the paper—it was an address on Greendale Street, one that I recognized from my past. "That's the Gabelman supply house," I said. "Are you insane?"

Asbury laughed and tossed me a liver. It was a Taihitsu, top of the line. "The Outsider's got insiders, repo man. Supplies is top of the pops for holing—'forgs all got serials on 'em, so you can't get scanned."

He was right. Like the liver I held in my hand, every artiforg sitting on a supply house shelf was already outfitted with a ping chip; any scanner trying to pick up my heart would also register the thousands of other organs surrounding me. Even Jake, with his scanner tricked to the moon, would have difficulty locating us inside the Gabelman compound. It would be like trying to find a haystack in a pile of haystacks.

But a Union-affiliated supply house wouldn't do as a permanent place of residence, and Asbury knew it. He turned to Bonnie and said, "You keep tight for a few spins, then flip over and find me. I'll crunch up some new digs."

She gave him a hug—chaste, not lingering—and passed him down the line. I went to shake the man's hand, but he pulled me tight and wrapped his arms around my shoulders. "Take care of her," he said, falling out of dialect for the first time. "You do that good, and you and me will be all right."

Will do, Asbury.

Wendy knew I was leaving. I didn't want to crush her like my four ex-wives had crushed me, so I told her up front, leveled with her. The bills had gotten out of hand, my career as a Bio-Repo man was all but officially over, and they'd be coming for my Jarvik as soon as the last issuance of Final Notice went past the thirty-day grace period.

"You can find another job," she protested. "In another field."

"No training," I said. "I'm too old to start up again."

"And you can't . . . you can't go back to the Union? They want you, I know that. You could do a few more jobs, we could eat light, pay off the heart sooner . . ."

She was right; the Union did want me back. After I healed up, my supervisor was true to his word and started assigning me Level Five jobs once again. They would have loved to see me continue doing what I did best, and they would have paid me terribly well for it, just as they had been doing all those years. Probably would have made me a Level Six, too. But I couldn't do it anymore.

Lucky me. I lost a heart and found a soul.

CHAPTER 16

It's late.

The Gabelman supply house is a sprawling industrial complex, a conglomeration of different manufacturers under one common roof, sharing utilities and factory space, often pitching in to offset the combined overhead. Most of the American boutique artiforg manufacturers fall under the Gabelman umbrella, including Struthers, Thompson, and Vocom. Struthers, for example, has resisted expansion for years, despite their award-winning line of epiglottises. Every time they win a Rachman design award, the offers come pouring in, and eager investors clamor for the company to go public. But the Struthers family, which in previous generations had been manufacturers of fine wooden baby furniture, has been putting out some of the best handmade organs for twenty years now, and a large market sale could only hurt the corporation. Same with Thompson, Vocom and the rest; they want to stay small enough to keep the company, yet be able to have a large-enough distribution system to go up against full-scale competitors like Taihitsu and Marshodyne.

That's where Gabelman comes in. They act as a middle-
man, of sorts, making the boutique organs available to the
general public, as well as to lending houses like Kenton and
the Credit Union. Of course, both of these organizations
have their own artiforg manufacturing plants as well, but
they're happy to lend out anyone's organs if the client's got
a down payment and credit to match.

Confusing, and that's how they like it. An enterprise
schematic of the modern artiforg industry would splinter
all over the chart like a drunken spider's web. It's nothing
more than corporate incest, and these houses are the kissin'
cousins of the business world.

But it all makes for a hell of a place to hide. The warehouse
aisles are 20 feet high, stretching for 30 yards in each direction before doubling back and doing it all again on the
next row over. Three shelves per aisle, each one 6 feet deep,
perfect for full-body rest, a king-size bed stretching as far
as the natural eye can see. These warehouses are nothing
but overgrown hangars with a wholesaler's flair for design,
and if the stories around the Union are true, the buildings
that now house the Gabelman artiforgs were once used
by the U.S. military to engineer stealth devices during the
twentieth century.

I don't know about that. I do know that the fourth shelf
on the left, three tiers up, is an excellent place to get some
typing done. The echo is muffled by a fortress of surrounding artiforgs, a wall of livers and hearts and eyeballs and
spleens that took me an hour to construct, and would take
only an errant tug on the wrong pancreas to undo. It is not a
toy. Bonnie has already been reprimanded more than once.

We'd arrived at the back entrance of the Gabelman
complex an hour after leaving Asbury's; his friend was
waiting there for us, red carpet and all. A security guard,

nothing fancy, running her part of the operation from inside the three-foot-by-three-foot guardhouse. "Come inside," Rhodesia hissed as we approached. "Don't run."

"We're not," said Bonnie.

"Just don't."

She hustled us inside and down a long corridor, leading us past shelves filled with the best of what the modern artiforg corporations had to offer.

"This is a backup facility," Rhodesia explained. "They don't come in here 'less there's a big crunch on merchandise, and then they call me ahead of time."

"Doesn't anybody check it?" I asked.

"They is me, and no, I do not. You'll be safe for a couple of days."

So we're huddled up here, waiting out our time. Bonnie is busy leafing through instruction manuals as I type, looking over my shoulder every now and then to get in a quick peek. I don't mind. After every glance, we kiss. Tonight, I hope, more will follow.

Bonnie just saw me type that last bit. Her face registered surprise at first, that delicate mouth falling into an open *O*, but it was all for show. Bonnie nodded slowly, leaned in close, and now I know what an artificial tongue tastes like: honey.

Silicone, too, but mainly honey.

———

Out of all my ex-wives, Melinda and I had the most adventurous sex life. She was insatiable at times, in heat more often than I could cool her down, and even those days when I came home from work with knuckles dragging along the ground became wild nights in bed. Or in the car. Or in the park. Or the grocery store.

It all slowed down after Peter was born, but I attribute it more to our dissolving understanding of each other than to the birth of our son. We could have bought a puppy instead and still been divorced two years later. Melinda was increasingly under the impression that I was selfish, that I didn't listen to her needs. I was increasingly under the impression that she whined an awful lot.

But some things she said stuck with me. Some time after Peter's first birthday, when things around the house first fell into entropy, Melinda suggested we take dance lessons to help our relationship. I didn't see the logic, but was too tired to argue. So twice a week before work, we'd drag ourselves down to the local studio and get instruction from a woman who was elated that she could educate a real-life Bio-Repo man in the art of graceful movement.

Melinda, for all her fine qualities, did not take well to dance. She was like a kid at a wedding, excited and gung-ho, but entertaining mostly on an *isn't that adorable* level. She felt the music, certainly, and had an innate sense of rhythm and beat, but she was unable to master the footwork beyond a basic box step.

I, on the other hand, picked up on the moves like I'd been waiting to learn them all my life, as if there were an open box inside me and dancing was a gift that fit perfectly. The tango, the waltz, the mambo, it was all natural as breathing. If there was a one-two-shuffle-kick step, then I hit it with surgical precision. Spins, twists, turns, I nailed it all. Barely broke a sweat.

But when it came time to put the moves together, I was as useless as my wife. My individual motions were perfect, but the true concept of dance remained elusive.

"There is no sense of unity," our instructor told me the last time I attended class, isolating my problem. "I see in you only the fragments. You can take the finest movements, the most beautiful snippets of motion, and perform them beautifully, but if there is no cohesion, then there is no dance."

I never went back to class. Melinda told the instructor I'd come down with the flu, but I know she knew the truth. What was the point of practicing something that went against everything I understood?

———————

Melinda blamed me for the failure of our marriage, and used the dance situation as an example of what had gone wrong. "You can't put things together," she yelled at me one autumn evening during dinner. Peter was playing in the living room. "Everything is pieces to you."

I had twelve different arguments to refute her allegation, but in the heat of the moment, I was unable to form them into a single, logical defense. Rather than make her point for her, I stayed silent and ate my potatoes.

———————

Carol's therapist said it, too. "Our tests show you have a knack for deconstruction."

I didn't understand what he meant, so I nodded.

"Do you find this to be a problem?" he asked.

"Not if Carol doesn't," I said, deferring to my wife.

"Carol," asked the shrink, "do *you* find it to be a problem?"

"Not really," she sighed. "I just wish he wouldn't be such a bastard."

———————

That's four out of five wives who've used that term to refer to me, in case anyone's counting. I wear it like a badge of honor.

———————

Carol and I met when her brother-in-law's restaurant burned to the ground. I'd stopped in for a quick bite between jobs, a liver extraction I'd just finished and another, very similar job, uptown. The joint was a new one on me, but I had no allegiance to one restaurant over another; as long as it stayed down, food was food.

Still, cleanliness is a matter of course with me, and I

can't abide poor health practices. I was halfway through my ravioli entree when I crunched down hard on some foreign object. Near to gagging, I plucked it from my mouth and discovered the jagged remnants of a woman's fingernail. I threw down my napkin and pulled back from the table.

"Is there a problem, sir?" asked the waiter, scurrying to my side.

"The kitchen," I said through clenched teeth. "Where is it?"

"If there's a problem —"

I grabbed the young man's thumb with my right hand, his wrist with my left, and made like I was playing jack-in-the-box. His face soured into a grimace as I twisted, his knees buckling. "The kitchen," I repeated.

The chef was outraged at my presence in his workroom, but soon saw a light very similar to the waiter's. He summoned the owner.

Chet was as apologetic as could be, and together we went on a search of the kitchen staff, inspecting the ladies' hands for missing accessories. We worked our way through waitresses and bus girls and sous chefs before I saw the light go on behind Chet's eyes—he had an idea. He led me into the back room of the restaurant, toward an office, where his sister-in-law was working on the books.

He said, "Lemme see your hands, Carol."

She didn't even ask who I was; didn't seem to care. She sighed and held out her perfectly manicured hands, sans one index fingernail. I was relieved to see the entire set was acrylic; all I'd munched on was some hardened plastic.

It is no coincidence that I did the cooking around the house.

———

Years later, long after Carol had left me, Chet and I would remain pals, drinking ourselves into tales of nostalgia. He never liked Carol, he said. Just put up with her because his wife was her sister. Didn't understand how I could screw someone that cold.

"She warms up," I said.

"So does a block of ice," said Chet. "And then whaddaya got?"

————

Carol had been sampling the ravioli in the kitchen when the nail fell off, and we were in the middle of extracting an apology from her when the screams started. It was commonplace clamor, at first, the chaos of a popular restaurant kitchen, which quickly turned into shouts of urgency. Chet, Carol, and I glanced at one another and ran for the door. I imagine they wanted to investigate the problem; I just wanted out.

But none of us was going anywhere. By the time we got to the kitchen, the grease fire that had started on the range had spread throughout the room, flames licking at the ceiling. I was barely able to shout out a "No!" before a busboy ran up with a tray full of water and launched it at the blaze. The flames spread and instantly flared up into a new conflagration, and through the building smoke, I could see the head chef knocking the bus boy around for his foolishness. Chet entered the fray, yelling orders this way and that, screaming for a fire hydrant, salt, anything.

My pack was still slung around my shoulder, and inside it, three canisters of heavily pressurized ether. These were not items I would wish to introduce to heat anytime soon. Grabbing Carol's hand in mine, I dragged her backward, away from the kitchen, into the back office of the restaurant.

"What the hell are you doing?" she snapped, yanking her arm away.

I wanted to reply with something witty, or at least a movie-star grunt, *Saving your life, lady*. But all that came out was, "Shut up." It didn't work, but she followed me.

"You think you're a hero?" she asked me as I led her through the corridors.

"Hell no," I responded. I just wanted out.

"I've got books back there."

"And they can burn. Is there a back door in this place?"

Carol shook her head. "It's boarded up. Street bums kept sneaking in and stealing food from the kitchen."

"Boarded I can deal with," I said, and told her to lead me to it. On the way, she asked me what I did—"You a cop or something?"—and I flashed my neck tat in response. Rather than shy away like most folks, she came at me harder. Carol was the only one of my wives who didn't have a problem with my career. She loved my job; she just didn't love me.

We got out of the restaurant by using my pencil laser to bore away at the hinges of the emergency exit door; a well-placed kick sent the whole thing flying, and we were safe in the back alley. Rather than head our separate ways, we hung out by the trash cans until the fire trucks arrived, coughing out the smoke that had made its way into our lungs, Carol eager to hear about my life with the Union, me eager to impress the beautiful woman in the soot-stained sundress.

I took it slow with Carol. We didn't marry for nine whole months.

Jake was the best man at each of my wedding ceremonies. He had one tuxedo that managed to fit him throughout all those years, his muscular body not changing a bit when everyone else's metabolisms slowed like snails.

He was also a witness to each of my divorces, except for the last. The Union paid for him to get a notary certificate a few years back, and though he didn't do much in the way of stamping and embossing, it did come in useful for certain Union loan claims. He was able to process three or four fewer documents per artiforg than the rest of us, a good hour's worth of work, which gave him an advantage in securing new jobs. But he didn't charge me a cent when it came to notarizing my divorce papers. That's what good buddies do for each other. He'd even offered to be the official on record when Wendy and I got hitched, but she was intent on having a man of the cloth perform the ceremony. I told her that Jake had spent a few years in Catholic school, but she wouldn't budge.

I wonder, if Jake finds us here—if he's got us trapped and there's nowhere to run—if that offer of officiating still stands. If he somehow tracks us down amid this garden of organs, I wonder if he will consent to marry Bonnie and me. It won't be much I'll ask for, just a simple ceremony, five minutes at the most, and then he can knock us out and repossess as much as he wants.

I should probably discuss the matter with Bonnie beforehand.

———

Carol had her own house, a beautiful Victorian down in Alabama, and for a while, I transferred to the Union offices down there, just to get a feel for the place. Union transportation was such that I could live practically anywhere and still make it back to the main offices every now and again in order to drop off artiforgs and pick up assignments, but I thought it would be best to get to know my fellow workers in the 'Bama office.

I don't know if I was expecting a different kind of Bio-Repo man, or if I thought that the genteel ways of the South would have somehow affected the average working day. But it was gas, grab, and go, like anywhere else. Sure, there were more company barbecues, and the accents tickled my ears for a few months, but the Bio-Repo men down there didn't strike me as any different from those back home. I didn't make friends. A few of them had heard of me before; they stayed out of my way. The others weren't interested in the newcomer.

That's one thing I tried to tell Carol's shrink, right off. "We don't change," I said to him on that first visit.

"Those of your profession?" he asked.

"Those of my gender," I replied. "Hell, those of my *species*."

———

She was a businesswoman, Carol was, and she bought and sold small companies more often than I changed my underwear. I would come back from a three-day repo stint out West to find, say, her gourmet foods storefront empty, the cheeses and patés all sold off, and Carol in the back room of another shop a hundred yards down the street, doing a thriving business in yarn manufacturing. I couldn't keep up with the financial transactions, and one day, I asked her how she managed to flit from one career to the next.

"It's all the same career," she said to me, surprised that I'd asked the question. "I sell."

"But you sell so many different things. Doesn't that make it difficult to know the market?"

"Do you find it difficult to repossess a kidney and a spleen and a liver in the same night?" she asked, turning my question back at me.

"No, but that's not the same. I'm taking things out."

"So am I," said Carol. "But in my case, it's cash from their wallets. And I don't need a scalpel for it; that's why God gave me a tongue."

———

I am 95 percent sure she meant that she talked customers out of their money. Ninety-nine on the good days.

————

Bonnie just finished up reading the manual for a Yoshimoto Pulmonary System. "Fascinating," she said, laughing as she read the poorly translated directions to me in a poor Japanese accent. "In happy operating procedure, the breathing is like fresh air through the body. In unkind operating procedure, the fresh air is gone sad."

Fresh air gone sad is a beautiful way to describe the death process. Leave it up to the Japanese to make a poem out of everything.

————

Bonnie has just told me to put away the typewriter and go to bed, but I think she actually used the words "*come* to bed." This time, I will not be quite so dumb. I will listen to the scream of instinct inside my head. I will go to Bonnie now, lay her down on a mattress of livers, and allow nature—at least, whatever remains of it—to take its course.

CHAPTER 17

Two days have passed. Yesterday, there was no typing. Yesterday was a day for me and Bonnie, no tools allowed. We sat on our shelf and talked about ourselves, each other, the past. I can now say that I have only loved seven women in my life, including my mother, and I married each one of them, excluding my mother and Bonnie. It's a good thing the list is modular.

As soon as we woke up in the morning after a night filled with carnal delights, we went at it again, two hungry kids just starting to figure out what it was all about. She told me a little more about her ex-husband, stories of how she'd made it on the streets all these years, undetected, tales of a life hunted by the Union.

And I told her about my own run from the cadre, about the way I'd managed to escape their nets, about my trip to the Mall, about my life since the day I gave up my job and went on the lam.

And, because to do otherwise wouldn't be fair, I told her about Melinda. It was the only thing I'd kept to myself since going on the run, and it felt good to finally get it out, like releasing a breath I'd held in my chest for months.

It started with a discussion of my last days with the Union. She couldn't understand why I'd been fired.

"Because I wouldn't take the jobs anymore," I explained.

"You wouldn't, or you couldn't?"

"Either. Both."

"Why?" she asked, and that's when I told her about the very last time I saw my third ex-wife.

――――――

My chest had all but healed from the implantation, and according to the digital readout welded onto my hip, the Jarvik–13 unit pumping away in my chest had two hundred more years of good, steady work in store for me. Frank had been pleased with my recovery, and after I worked my way back into full health, we returned to the easy give and take that we'd had before the accident. He cast jovial aspersions about my character; I made jokes about his mother. We got along fine, me and Frank.

The Jarvik payments were steep, a couple of thousand bucks a month, and with the mortgage on the house and rising fuel costs and food . . . Hell, I knew I sounded like the deadbeat clients I dealt with every day, but finally I was getting some idea of what they went through. Still, I managed to pay my bills, on time and in full, and kept my credit rating in the clear. That's what you do, because, well, it's what you do.

But I knew that I was only one or two jobs away from serious default, and should anything go wrong or take longer than expected, that I could be in serious trouble. Even a holdup of my commission at the Union paycheck offices could land my payment past the grace period, and the penalty charges could send me over the edge. I kept my wits about me, though, and the jobs went down like they should have. Quick, easy, painless.

Except for the tremble. On every job, to varying degrees, it would be there, hovering over me like a spirit, waiting to strike at any weak moment. I'd be sliding a scalpel through tissue or twisting a stubborn nut, and I'd feel it roll down my arm, a miniature quake whipping through my forearm, down my wrist, and into my hand. Even when it passed, it would still be present in my mind—when will it come again? Will it be worse the next time out?

One day, after I'd successfully brought down a ring of Outsiders who'd been scavenging Kenton accessories off our clients, Frank called me into his office.

"New job," he said, "fresh off the line."

The dossier cover was familiar to me. Purple with white stripes, a Gabelman job. I opened the folder, scanning the important stats on the pink sheet inside: Double kidney job, a full year delinquent, last seen downtown. Commission was three thousand on top of standard, which would keep me out of the hole for a few more months. I took it on the spot. The photo of the client was of a security-camera candid shot; they must have grabbed it from an ATM or stoplight video. It didn't really matter one way or the other; once I got close enough, the scanner would give me all the information I'd need.

In the litany of almost-beens that make up my regrets in life, not taking a closer look at that pink sheet has got to rank in the top three. The other two deal with a forged lottery ticket and a girl from Bethesda, but that one little oversight will haunt me forever.

Jake saw me off. I was in the Union locker room, assembling my gear. Back then I had a leather carrying case that Carol had given to me; it had pouches made specifically for ether canisters, straps that held down scalpels. Custom-made by some fellow in Turkey. It smelled like cow urine, but it was the best bag I ever had.

"How's the ticker?" he asked. "Keepin' up to Greenwich time?"

Jake had personally recalibrated my Jarvik to good old U.S. measurements, but he liked to tease me about the original settings. "Workin' great," I told him. "Heading out for some kidneys. Any buzz your way?"

"Nah," he said. "I've got a few local jobs, nothing big."

Slinging the pack up and around, I prepared to hit the road. "Till tomorrow." I held my thumb out, and Jake pressed it with his.

"Till tomorrow," answered Jake.

———

The beauty of working downtown, at least for a Bio-Repo man, is that the straight, simple layout of the city allows for an easy taxi ride up and down the streets, scanner set on a relatively tight range in order to weed out the fool's gold. I hit a few bum organs on Fillmore, scared a couple of old men to death when I pinged one kidney on each of them, but for the most part, it was smooth all the way, and I tipped the cabbie an extra fifty just for letting me sit and ride.

It was down near the south side of the city where I got the double set of pings. Two kidneys, Gabelman licensed, same manufacture date, within a foot of each other. This was the deadbeat I was looking for.

There wasn't much in the way of modern business accommodations down here; the last fire had pretty much taken care of all re-gentrification efforts. But some of the local merchants had managed to scrabble together a few makeshift stores, fruit carts, junk stands. Languages with which I was unfamiliar flew at me from all directions, come-ons to buy their crap, harangues when I wouldn't. All I had to do was flash the neck brand, and they shut up. Most of the time, I simply walked on by.

As I approached the general area where I'd first pinged the artiforgs, I steadily decreased the range of my scanner, localizing with every step. I carefully picked my way through downed rubble, hunks of concrete nobody'd yet bothered to haul off the streets. Ash and charred bricks surrounded me on all sides, a decrepit building abandoned and forgotten, trash to the careless, spooky to the ignorant, off-limits to all. *This is perfect*, I thought. *The kind of place I'd choose to hide out.*

Call me a prophet.

———————

The Oceanic Plaza had fallen prey to two different fires, separated by five months of lag time. The first was electrical, a power-substation gaffe that got out of control and took out an entire wing of the six-building complex. The second was probably arson, an explosion that rocked the rest of the plaza into rubble. By that point, the corporation had cut its losses and vacated the area, and no one was left who cared to investigate. The Oceanic folks had a twenty-year lease on the property, but since there had been some questionable insurance dealings, it made more financial sense for them to take the money and run rather than reinvest in a dying property located in a well-past-dead area.

Now it was a wasteland, a rough circle of rubble five blocks in radius and 80 feet high, homeland to bums and stray cats and anyone on the lam. The glass was still there, too, heavy shards of it underfoot, most pieces already trampled into a fine powder. I got the feeling that for all of the *Off Limits* and *Do Not Enter* signs posted around the site, they generally sat unviewed, unused.

Rain had fallen hard on the city two days earlier, so it wasn't difficult to locate a jumble of footprints in the muddy ground. A definite trail ran between the two gargantuan piles of debris, then split into a fork: One led to the rubble on the left, one to the rubble on the right. I stayed in the middle, scanner by my side, the green glow of the screen lighting my way.

For a while, there was nothing. I increased the range, searching out into the wilds of the city, and began to ping some 'forgs, but not the ones I was looking for. I was about to go back to the beginning and start all over again when I heard a *thunk* behind me. Hand firm on my hip, midway between my gun and a garrote, I turned, trying to stay in the shadows.

A bent, wizened old man, one leg a good six inches shorter than the other, picked his way through the debris, lifting rocks with a dexterity belying his age. I scanned him, but the old fella came up clean. Surprising, considering that over 90 percent of folks his age had some artificial part; the remaining 10 percent were either health freaks or too close to death for an artiforg to matter.

But as I stood there in the shadows, I found myself mesmerized by his strength. Heavy chunks of rock and mortar flew to the side as he lifted and tossed, exposing a small, dark cave within the plaza rubble. Gathering the rocks around him, he backed into the hole and began pulling the pieces into place, covering up his entranceway until it was indistinguishable from the mess surrounding it.

I aimed my scanner right where the hole used to be. Flicked it on with my right thumb. Ping. Two kidneys, right where I wanted 'em.

Bending at the knee (never at the waist), I squatted down to move one of those heavy slabs of rock. Tucked my fingers beneath the cragged edges, set my feet, and lifted. The stone flew into the air, landing fifteen feet behind me, the lack of anticipated counterweight nearly throwing me off balance. I tried another stone, and another, soon finding that the majority of rubble in this area was of the costume-prop variety, no heavier than a hunk of Styrofoam. Chuckling to myself—after twenty years on the job, this was a first for me—I opened up an entrance large enough to accommodate my frame and picked my way down into the remains of the Oceanic Plaza.

———

There were others down there with me. I could feel them shuffling by, hear them scurrying through the tight, cramped corridors. There were murmurs and gasps, and somewhere in the distance, a woman was singing. High, sweet, the echo drifting through the chaotic air. This was negative space, crude passageways hewn from within, rooms bare millimeters from collapse.

As I walked the underground city, the scanner's glow kept me company, scaring off anyone else who might have thought of following me deep into the belly. Digits flew onto my screen from all sides, the scanner pinging back organ after organ, many with manufacture dates well over a decade ago. This was a hideout, to be sure, a nest of deadbeats unlike any I'd seen in the decades of my life's work. I'd have to make out a full report upon returning to the Union offices.

The passageways grew smaller as I made my way farther inside, the bricks scratching at my arms, tearing at my clothes. Soon I was bent over, tucking my shoulders into my body, trying to become as small a package as possible. I've never been claustrophobic; it's an undesirable trait in a Bio-Repo man, and one that can get you killed. But being down there, beneath thousands of tons of rubble I knew could collapse on me at any second, was as close as I ever came to worrying about my own death by suffocation. I realigned my mind to the task at hand and kept shuffling.

The scanner led me down a number of false corridors; though it was able to send its rays through most materials, I was still flesh and bone. So even if the kidneys I was looking for were just beyond the next wall, it didn't help unless I could find an unfettered passageway. I had no urge to go breaking through bricks with my laser.

My shuffle became a hop, which soon became a crawl as the ceiling overhead lowered to a three-foot height. Now I was slinking through the corridors on my hands and knees, scanner tight in my right hand, Taser firm in my left, pack wrapped around my leg and dragging behind me, the ether canisters clanging against the rock beneath. I thought for a brief moment about turning back, about staking out the perimeter of the plaza, hoping that the deadbeat might make a run into the real world, but I knew that any client holed up this tight wouldn't be emerging for a long time. I needed this job; I needed the commission. If I lost this one, the whole financial pile of cards would come down on my head harder than the pile of rubble above me.

Eventually, after my pants had worn through and I was crawling on bare, skinned knees, my palms raw and sore from the brick below, I got what I'd been looking for. Righteous pings from my scanner, dead shot ahead. Two kidneys, ready and waiting for me. Already thinking about the ride back home, the cash I would receive, the bills I could pay off, I picked up speed, fingering my Taser all the way.

Soon, I began to make out sounds. A conversation? No, there was only one voice. The closer I got, the more it coalesced, and suddenly, I wanted to slow down and speed up all at the same time. Wanted to get there to see if I was hearing it correctly, wanted to stay away in case I was right. And there it was, a low murmur trickling down the passageway ahead of me, coming from that cavern a hundred yards away. One voice, high, lilting, falling and rising. Singing.

I want to swim in the sea with the bears and the hummingbirds. . .

————

Melinda was on her back, splayed out flat against the rocks, staring up at the cavernous ceiling above her. I'd entered into what had once been the lobby of the western wing of the Oceanic Plaza, much of it still intact despite crashed support beams and crumbling walls. It was still extant, I guessed, due to the combined pressure of the destruction on all other sides, staying up like a giant teepee. I had no illusions about its safety, though; at any moment, this thing could collapse.

But that wasn't foremost on my mind. Melinda, still singing, unaware that I'd entered the room 50 feet away, was all I could think about. It was her, no doubt. Fifteen years since I'd last seen her, but she'd aged at least thirty. The once-taut skin on her full, wide face sagged beneath her atrophied cheeks, pulling down the thick, caterpillar pouches beneath her sunken eyes. Her hair, once full and rich, swirling about her head in a corona that made shampoo models jealous, was limp and dead, chopped off in a ragged pageboy, the ends uneven, splitting even at their short length. Old, worn jeans, frayed at the edges, enveloped her legs, and I barely recognized the pink blouse as the one she used to wear around the house when she was feeling randy. The buttons had all but fallen off, and great holes had been torn in the side, her sickly yellow flesh poking through.

. . . swim with the dogs and the monkeys and the kangaroos. . .

I took a step into the lobby, the great windows crushed and poked through with stone and brick, my footsteps echoing in the dark, cold cavern. I didn't need to realign my scanner, but I held it up to get that final ping, and sure enough, it was Melinda's kidneys coming back to me, the ones Peter had slipped and told me about years and years ago. Without conscious thought, my hands went to the dossier, opening it to the first page, the page I should have looked at way back in my supervisor's office at the Credit Union.

Melinda Rasmussen. Bold, black, definite. Her maiden name, but I couldn't convince myself that there were two of them. Certainly not two who knew the song with which we sang our son to sleep.

. . . and I want them to a-swim with me. . .

She didn't look up as I approached, just kept staring at the ceiling, humming and singing, starting the song over again once the final lines were sung, pausing only for a moment to catch her breath and then launching into the first line again. Like someone had come along and pressed the replay button.

I knelt down by my third ex-wife, snapping my fingers in front of her eyes. Nothing. "Melinda," I called, my low tones bouncing around the expansive cavern. "Melinda, come out of it."

Unresponsive. This didn't seem like the usual dementia I'd seen in nursing-home patients or those with frazzled-out Ghost systems; this was something else entirely. She was caught up in some other place, some other time, and as soon as I came in close enough to see the trickle of red powder lining her lips, I knew Melinda had gotten herself hooked on the Q.

"Melinda," I said again, this time louder, taking hold of her thin, bony shoulders and shaking hard, her head flopping about on that pipe cleaner of a neck. The drug had sapped up all her fat, soaking whatever energy it could out of her once-robust body. She was a skeleton draped with skin, nothing more, and I was surprised that her kidneys were the only implanted artiforgs. The rest of her body, though natural, must have been failing or already dead.

A few slaps across the face, and she was finally trying to focus in, bringing her vision back from whatever fantasy world she'd been visiting. I could see the pupils contracting as they hit the glow of my scanner screen, and I knew that for the moment, at least, she hadn't gone away. "Come up," I said to her. "Melinda, come up."

Blinking. Coughing. The shoulders shuddering, arms dancing uncontrollably, a full-body tremor that precipitated a mess of vomit deposited on my shoes. I stood back as she fell to the ground, barely supporting herself on her hands and knees, head bent deep beneath her chest. Slivers of red in that vomit, streams of blood shooting through the meager bits of undigested food.

I backed away, letting her sick herself to a state of consciousness. Eventually, her coughs settled down into dry heaves, and soon she was lying back against the rock, sweaty, panting, but alive and in the here and now.

"You don't look so good," I said, coming into her line of sight.

Her eyes fluttered up toward my face, falling across my features, taking them in. Somewhere, a recognition center was clicking to life. "Knucklehead?" she asked wearily, a thin grin forming on her lips. Her teeth were stained red, the gums beneath barren of flesh, nerves decayed from the action of the Q.

"Yeah," I replied, "it's Knucklehead." I cleared away some of the rubble and sat down next to her, taking one of her frail hands in mine. It trembled between my palms like a dying bird, fluttering against my skin.

Melinda's breath came hard, straining out of her lungs. "We were going to the park, Knucklehead. What happened at the park?"

I didn't know what she was talking about. Probably lost in some memory of an ancient excursion, some trip we took years ago. Or her addled mind was making it up, reality and fantasy merging as one. "We loved that park," I answered. "It's beautiful there. We can go whenever you want."

Melinda coughed again and pulled her hand away from mine. She reached into her blouse, down between the breasts that were no longer there, just hanging bags of skin, and pulled out a small, crimson pouch. Before I realized what she was doing, Melinda had her finger stuck in a vial, scooping up a thick wad of Q.

I snatched her hand on the way to her gums and knocked the vile sand from her fingertip, wiping it clean with my shirt. She pulled away for a second, anger flashing across her face, but soon it was gone, forgotten, her short-term memory unable to keep up with current events. "Peter needs to sleep," she whispered, "Baby needs to sleep."

I tried to tell her that she was hallucinating, tried to reason that we were inside the remains of the Oceanic Plaza, far from our home in the suburbs in both time and distance. But she was having none of it.

"Sing that song with me, Knucklehead," she whispered. "Sing the song for Peter." And like everything else that came out of Melinda, it wasn't a question.

She opened her mouth, the corners of her lips cracked, coated with dried blood and Q particles, and began to sing. Her voice was still clear, resonant, just as it was all those years ago.

I want to swim in the sea with the bears and the hummingbirds. . .

On the second go-round, I joined in.

After a half hour of song and incoherent babbling, it all came to a head. She was weak, she was tired, and she didn't seem to understand why I'd come. "You've got to have some money," I pleaded with her. "Tell me where to find it, and we can make this right."

But all she could do was talk about the Q. How to get it, where to get it, what it cost. Every few minutes, she'd reach for another vial; whatever toll it had taken on her mind had not dampened her ability to find the hidden stashes on her own body. I knocked away dose after dose, trying to keep her with me and in the moment.

"Melinda," I said sternly, not worrying anymore that the echo of my loud voice would bring down the roof, "you have to pay back the Union. If you can't find the money, I—they . . . Is there someone I can call? Someone who has money?"

She opened her lips to speak, and I pulled in closer. "Call my husband," she whispered.

"Your husband?" I hadn't spoken to Peter for a few months, but I was sure he would have mentioned a new development like this.

"My husband," she repeated, and then gave my name.

Just like that, it all broke. A flood of reason spilling over the dam I'd erected, and I knew instantly that Melinda was lost somewhere and was never coming back. All of the money earmarked to pay off her artiforgs had been spent on Q, her bills and mortgage as well, most likely. It had eaten her pocketbook, it had eaten her investments, it had eaten her savings, and, when there was nothing else and still the Q was not sated, it had gone after her brain. Melinda, my fiscally responsible, morally upright, thoughtful and kind and beautiful Melinda, had left the building.

And I still had a job to do.

I let go of her hand, kissed her forehead gently, and pulled out a canister of ether.

I don't remember the actual extraction; for that, I'm thankful. Maybe some of the residual Q worked its way onto my gums, maybe my mind is walling it off good and tight, making it easier on me, but my memory of that half hour tapers off as soon as I stick the ether tube into her mouth and turn the knob, and doesn't click back on again until I find myself crawling back down the corridor, pack and kidneys in tow.

I do remember going back for her, realizing that it wasn't right to let her body rot inside that heap of rubble, where no one but the other bums would ever find it. Grasping her body beneath the arms, dragging her backward, out of the west tower lobby, into that dark passageway. Pulling her through halls and passageways, squirming along on my back, trying to stay in control, making wrong turns, my eyes blinded by salty liquid, by what must have been sweat, bumping into dead ends and having to back up, hauling Melinda around and about for another go at finding the exit.

It was hours of that, but somehow, I found my way out, and somehow, I was able to drag her body up and into the cold night air. The area was still deserted, and it was perfectly still and quiet as I hefted her up and over my shoulder in a fireman's carry, her arms draped over my chest, dangling down to my stomach, looking to all the world like I was just transporting my drunk girlfriend home for the night. She'd had one too many and was feeling no pain.

———

We sat in the car, me and Melinda, or whatever it was Melinda had become, for a long time. Hours, I'm sure, though I can't really remember. After some time, I drove to a local Snack Shack, mostly because it was the first place I saw, but partially because I was unnaturally thirsty. I couldn't do this with a dry throat. I went inside, bought a

64-ounce soda, and sucked it down in a few hard, fast gulps. Before I could stop myself, I grabbed the nearest pay phone and dialed.

Peter's roommate said he was out at the student union. I gave him the number of the phone, told him it was urgent, and asked him to have my son call me back.

Two hours passed, and I waited by the phone, Melinda propped in the passenger seat of my car five feet away. No one paid any attention to her. I watched people come and go, finding myself commenting to my ex-wife as we waited.

At some point, the phone rang. I reached out to answer, knowing I would much rather have been far, far away.

"Peter," I said, "it's Dad."

"Hey," he said, and I could hear the good cheer in his voice. It made me want to hang up the phone, to tell him I only called to say hi, to run to that pit of rubble and put Melinda's kidneys back inside, stitch her up, and call everything off. "I got my grades today—guess what I got in chemistry?"

I guessed an A, and I was right. The rest of his grades were A's, too, except for a C in modern English lit, because, as he put it, "the professor said my midterm essay had a male-centric point of view. I mean, come on, Dad, what am I supposed to do about that? Get an artiforg vulva? I should probably drop the course, but—"

"I found Mom, Peter. She's dead." I let it out just like that, like ripping off a Band-Aid, hoping it would be so quick he'd brush by it and continue telling me about his schoolwork.

Silence on the other end of the line, dead space. I tried to fill it. "She's . . . it's going to be all right, now," I said, trying to remember what consolation was supposed to sound like. "Better place and all that."

Nothing. He was there; I could hear the breathing,

the sobbing, his throat closing up, choking off his voice. "Where . . . where is she?" he asked.

"Here in town," I said.

"Where?" he repeated. "I want to see her."

"That's not a good—"

"Where?" He had his mother's tone, asking questions that were really statements, forcing you to answer just to keep up the flow of conversation.

"With me," I told him. "At the Snack Shack." Then, figuring I would have to tell him about it all sometime, I gave him the address and directions and the number of a few mortuaries I knew off the top of my head, and promised I'd stay with her until he arrived.

———

That morning, as the sun rose over the Snack Shack, was the last time I saw my son. He hit me, slammed away with his fists, whacking me on the head, in my body, trying to bring me down. Alternating between hugging his mother's corpse and coming at me again, resisting my attempts to grab him, hold him, try to calm him. But he was a whirlwind of fury and futility, beating at my chest like he did when he was six and didn't want to go to bed.

"Peter," I said, trying to evade the blows, "Peter, it's for the best—"

"You—you could have—could have helped her," he cried. "You could have done something."

"I couldn't," I swore, truthfully. "She was addicted, she was past due. I don't have any money, I don't have—"

"You have clout."

"I don't," I said. "I don't. I'm a hired scalpel, that's all. They don't listen to me, they don't care about me, they just need me to do a job. So I do it. I just do my job."

He stopped then, mid-breath, catching himself from throwing another punch. He stooped into the car, bent over his mother and lifted her up, struggling under her light-weight frame. But once up, he held here there, high, proud, smoothing back her limp brown hair with one hand as he straightened out her blouse with the other.

"You're always doing your job," he said. "And that's always been the problem."

On the way home, I stopped off at a pond where Melinda and I used to visit when we were both alive. I liked the sound of the ducks beating their wings; she liked the sounds of sex amongst the reeds. It worked out fine for the both of us.

I stood on a small footbridge overlooking the still, blue-green water, and dropped both her kidneys into the pond. They immediately sunk to the bottom, disappearing from view. Melinda might not get to keep what she couldn't pay for, but I'd be damned if the Union was going to chalk this one up as a win.

CHAPTER 18

Bonnie was quiet after I finished telling my story, and I let her sit and think. She leaned back against a pile of generic heart replacements, her eyes closed. I didn't know if she was planning on running out of the warehouse or if she was just formulating the right words to tell me how low I'd sunk, but I sat there and waited for it. Watched her lips part, the tongue come out and wet them with artificial saliva, disappear back into her mouth.

In time, she sat upright again. "Afterward . . . ? You didn't take any more jobs?"

She wanted me to go on with the tale. I was glad to oblige, relieved to be momentarily free of reprisal. "I tried, I guess. Lied about Melinda, said I couldn't find her, and Frank kept handing the clients down to me, but as soon as I left the office, my finger would start shaking. Once I got in my car, the hand would get going, and soon it was my whole body. By the time I got to the client's house, I was a walking earthquake, vibrating up and down my spine. No way I could go inside. As soon as I drove away, got off the block, it got better, smoothed out, and I could move and breathe and talk again. Whiskey helped. For that first month, I ended up taking the jobs and outsourcing them to Jake or another Bio-Repo, just to cover up my problem, but I wasn't getting much of a commission that way. Ten percent, tops, for the finder's fee. I wasn't making ends meet.

"The final straw came when I decided I was going to go through with a repo, just to get me over the hump. Shrink talk, right? Carol's therapist would have loved it. If I could get through one simple repossession, I figured, the rest would fall into place and the shakes would stop. It was an easy case, a factory owner who'd been known for mistreating his workers all throughout his professional life, and I guessed it wouldn't be too hard to repo a liver from a guy brimming over with evil.

"Got to his workshop around four, and by four fifteen, I'd only made it up to the door. My pack was rumbling around on my shoulders, the ether canisters slamming into each other, and I was barely able to hold the scanner in place long enough to get a good ping. By four thirty, I'd managed to bore a hole in the window for the ether tube, and by five—thirty minutes longer than it ever took me before—I was standing over the client, ready to do what I had always, always done.

"I didn't black out until I dug in with my scalpel, but by then, it was much too late."

————

They threw me a going-away party. Jake and Frank and the rest of the crew gathered around, lit candles, and gave me artiforg credits to put toward my Jarvik or, should I ever need it, another implantation. If any more grand mals came my way, it was a likely scenario. "Better than a watch," I joked.

Jake took me out for drinks afterward, hauling me down to the same bar where we'd first gotten a glimpse of that

Union employment flyer. It hadn't changed a wink in the intervening years, except for the owner and bartender. The old man had been replaced by his son, who didn't know us or care about our makeshift reunion. He still overcharged and watered down the drinks.

"You need anything?" Jake asked.

"I'm all right," I lied. "I've got investments."

"Sure," he nodded. "Don't we all." Bio-Repo men are not known to be fiscally shrewd. "If you ever do need anything, you give me a call. Day or night." And he gave me a card. Just like that, I was on his *give a call* list. I'd known his number by heart for ten years, and there he was handing me a business card.

Dumbfounded, I took it, thanked him. We drank in silence. There wasn't much to say, us two. We'd been through school, through the war together, the training program; he'd been part of my life for nearly all my life, and though I knew that, while on the surface, we were still as close as we would ever be, something had fundamentally changed between us.

"Well," he burped after our second, wordless beer together, "I've got clients to get to."

"Gas, grab, and go," I said, trying to sound chipper.

Jake laughed, a little sadly I like to think, and slapped me on the back. We pressed thumbs and hugged, friends who knew it would be a long time before we saw each other again, and he threw some bills on the counter and walked out of the bar.

I still have his business card in my pocket.

Another day gone, the typing regimen slowed to a crawl. The Underwood doesn't react well in the midst of all this high technology. Ashamed, perhaps, of its hammer and ink, clicking and clacking. And the tight confines that were once so comforting to me have become stifling. Cramped.

Bonnie and I have fallen into a comfortable pattern, an easy way of living our attempt at life. We talk, we eat, we drink, we make love. Late at night, after everything is closed up and the automatic timer turns out the warehouse lights, I lie down on our shelf with my head pressed against her abdomen, and I fall asleep to the tune of her artiforgs whooshing and clicking in beautiful, sonorous symphony.

———

Tomorrow, we are going back to see the Outsider; by now, Asbury should have found another place for us to hole up. After that, we've decided, it will be up to us to find a way out of the city, out of the country if possible. Airport personnel won't be looking for us unless the Union's initiated one of their biweekly hunts for the Big Hundred, and we should be able to make it safe and sound if we can get our hands on a scanning jammer and some forged documents. Asbury can help on that end, I'm sure; Outsiders have friends in all the darker walks of life.

And then, we're off. To . . . I don't know. South America? Myanmar? Does it matter?

They talk about an island somewhere in the South Seas that hasn't found the modern age yet, a primitive land where they still practice open-heart surgery and put people on gargantuan dialysis machines. If it is true, we'll find it soon enough. Change our names, our faces, settle down, start a family, run a shop selling trinkets to tourists on the beach. Live hard until the rest of us dies, happy and whole.

I know full well that this is the kind of thinking that gets you killed. Then on with it, already, I say. On with it.

———

Wendy and I had dreams, once upon a healthier time. We had hopes and aspirations, and despite my age, plans for children of our own. Peter was nearly grown by the year I married my fifth ex-wife, and it was time to bring some more rug rats into the fold.

We met at a funeral, just after the casket was lowered into the ground. I was there as the dead man's former employee; Wendy was there as his daughter. Her father had been my boss's boss at the Union, and though Wendy and I had never met, I'd heard stories of her youth, beauty, and brains countless times from the old man.

I was going left, she was going right, and we collided beneath an overgrown banyan tree, dripping with moisture from that morning's rain. I apologized, she apologized, and we ended up sipping coffee and eating Danish together at the gathering afterward before either of us realized our relationship to the deceased.

She treated Peter like a special gift, a beautiful young man whom she could shower with love and affection, and it hurt her almost as bad as it hurt me when he stopped coming around, stopped calling, stopped having any contact with his father. It wasn't much longer after then that I went on the run, signing my divorce papers from within the confines of the same seedy Midwestern motel in which I'd found the Flying Moellering Brothers. It was comfortable for some reason, fitting, and I hunkered down there for a week before leaving to search out new digs.

I could call Wendy now, I suppose, and she'd take me back. She'd hole me up, if I asked, penalties notwithstanding. And when they came to take my heart away, she'd throw herself in front of the Bio-Repo man's scalpel in order to save my life. She'd sacrifice herself for me, and I don't think I could do the same for her. I don't think I could do the same for any of them.

They all sacrificed for me, in a way:

   Beth: Her career, certainly. Her freedom.
   Mary-Ellen: Her ethics. Her moral tent-pole.
   Melinda: Best left unstated.
   Carol: Her lifestyle.
   Wendy: Her hopes for a future.

I see it now, a bit of a smudge on what had once been a clear picture of my ex-wives. I'd had it all figured out, had all five of them drawn so nicely in long, broad caricature, and now this realization has come along and filled in the lines for me, forcing me to see color in a world that used to be so perfectly black-and-white. The more I think about it, the sleepier I get. I should stop thinking. I should stop typing.

We've moved. Too tired to explain. Bonnie is alive. I am, too. For now, this is enough. It's more than I could hope for.

Two hours from now, I expect to be dead. This will be a voluntary decision on my part, a decision made after a long day's thought, and one which I will embrace willingly. This will not involve anyone else, and should go a long way toward righting what has been wrong. Two hours from now, I will walk into the Credit Union offices, approach my best and oldest friend Jake Freivald, and bare my chest for his talented scalpel. What happens after that is none of my business.

CHAPTER 19

This will be my typing regimen: Two hours straight. I will try to get out the events of yesterday before my time is up, banging away at the Underwood as hard as I can without waking Bonnie. She is sleeping two cots over. It is good to have a real bed again.

We're in a hospital, St. Anne's, I think, holed up on a floor usually reserved for supplies and medications. This is a broom closet, though there are no brooms inside, and despite the relatively cramped interior, it's a palace compared to the Gabelman shelf and the Tyler Street Hotel. Such opulence for my final days, such grandeur.

Top of the world, Ma. Top of the world.

———

It was time to ditch the warehouse and take our chances in the outside world. Asbury had said he'd be able to scratch up some new accommodations for us, and we had to take the run out to his flat in order to make the switch. Bonnie and I were anxious about leaving the safety of the shelf, which had essentially become our de-facto home. But the security guard was getting antsy with the two of us holed up there for so long, and I was beginning to doubt the safety of the whole complex. I'd begun to hear noises at night, footsteps in the darkness, a familiar hum shaking the walls. Best to leave. Best to relocate, again.

Heads down, walking quickly, avoiding eye contact with all other pedestrians, we hustled through the city streets, making our way quickly underground. It was morning rush hour by the time we reached the subway, and we were pressed in against a throng of passengers, buffeted by their coats and their briefcases and their stink. I hadn't bathed in over two weeks, so I can only imagine the Guinness-record lengths those folks had gone without a dip.

The train rumbled through the city, bearing us to Asbury's part of town. We were three stations away from our stop when I felt the tap on my shoulder, heard my name called out. I pretended to pay no attention, to be lost in reading the subway map, but another tap came, and another call of my name. The woman moved into my line of sight.

"Is it—oh my God, it's you!" shrieked Mary-Ellen. She embraced me for a brief moment, then pulled back quickly. I could see her nose wrinkling at the tip, face pulling into a sour-lemon grimace. She'd gotten a whiff.

"Sorry, lady," I mumbled, trying to turn away from my second ex-wife. "Got the wrong guy." The wonders of living in the big city: It's so large, you never have to see anyone you don't want to, unless you don't want to, in which case they're right in front of your nose.

She slipped back in front of me, drawing my face up to hers. "Funny, funny, always a funny guy. You still ripping out organs for a living?" She had that grin on her face, the one she always wore whenever we got into arguments. It was nice to see that she was starting it up again where we left off, not missing a beat after almost fifteen years. Consistency is what I treasure in a woman.

Now the other passengers were beginning to clear away, pressing up against each other in an effort to let us perform our melodrama on an empty stage. To make matters worse, not twenty feet away, two transit cops started to take notice. They don't have scanners or the power to repossess arti-forgs, but they sure as hell know how to make phone calls. I had twenty or thirty transit cops on my own personal payroll back in the day; their info came in damned handy.

"Look, ma'am," I said, trying to sound pissed off, "I don't know you. Go away."

"You don't know me?" she said, volume rising with each word. "We were married, you sonofoabitch. Don't pretend you don't know who I am."

The silence of our audience turned to murmurs as the transit cops moved closer. No matter their intentions, I didn't want them any more involved in this than necessary. "Look," I muttered to Mary-Ellen, dropping my voice to a whisper. "It's good to see you and all, but I'd appreciate it if you'd just go away."

She shook her head. "Go away?" she practically yelled, keeping her voice at a distressingly high level. "Isn't that what you'd like—for all your problems to just go away? That's how you deal with everything. Rip it out and toss it to the side. Well, not today. I've got to know—what's a big, bad Bio-Repo man like you doing with his life these days, other than not sending any of the alimony I was promised. Still hanging out with that no-good friend of yours? Got a new wife, yet? Got a new—"

That's when Mary-Ellen fell to the ground, shaking, tongue waggling to the filthy tiled floor, eyes rolled back in her head, that caterwaul of a voice blissfully silenced. I looked up to find Bonnie standing in her place, my Taser in her hand, the metal knobs sparkling with the residual energy of a job well done.

"And you let that one get away?" Bonnie mused. "I'd hate to meet the one you killed."

I let them all get away, in a sense. Carol even gave me a chance to win her back. Once it was clear that our two-year marriage wasn't working out, that I was spending less time at home than I was in the Union offices, she decided to kick me out of the house. This was the first experience of that kind for me; my other wives had gone off on their own, leaving me to the big, empty domicile. But Carol, who was never one to give up any of her material goods, was most insistent that I be the one to vanish from her life.

My first step was to get as far away as I could from Alabama, so I moved back here, transferring back to the main Union offices. Jake was the only one who seemed particularly thrilled about seeing me again, but the others were good-natured enough about stepping aside to get me back into the flow of high-level gigs. I found an apartment in a mid-rise building and set about readjusting my life for the thousandth time.

As soon as everything had settled down and I'd all but forgotten that I was anything but a merry bachelor, Carol called. "I'm giving you another chance," she said. "I'm thinking that if you learn how to change, if you can compute a way to work with me instead of against me, we can figure out this marriage."

So I put in for another transfer, moved back to Alabama, hauled my ass and meager furniture back into her wide plantation homestead, and gave married life another shot.

A week later, it was over, and she was suing me for divorce based on trumped-up charges of adultery. So much for second chances.

The rest of the trip to Asbury's was a cakewalk in comparison. A few close brushes with the local cops, a slip or two down some side alleys, but we arrived at his building physically unscathed and took the elevator up to the fifteenth floor.

It felt wrong as soon as we stepped out of the elevator. Not quiet so much as empty. When we'd come the last time, there was music drifting down the hallways, kids scampering past our feet. Energy. Life. This time, it was like we'd been dropped into a soundproofed chamber; even the floorboards refused to creak.

"It's a weekday," I said out loud, reminding myself that the last time we came had been a Saturday. "Everyone's at work."

"Or at school," Bonnie chimed in. She was feeling it, too. We moved on.

The door to Asbury's apartment was unlocked. We knocked a few times, banging on the metal frame; it swung open in response to our pounding, and, with no other options, we stepped inside.

The Chinese screens were still set up, though it seemed to me that their positions had been changed. Instead of creating sections throughout the otherwise large living room, they had been arranged so as to create a single corridor twisting into the apartment, like the entrance to a hedge maze. "Asbury?" Bonnie called out, the mechanical twinge of her voice steady and even. "Are you home?"

The only answer we got was a whisper from the breeze, snaking in through an unseen open window. I tried to call out again, but my throat seized up. There was no point. Bonnie took my hand, and together, we stepped into the apartment.

Rather than enter the makeshift corridor of Chinese screens, I lashed out with my leg, kicking the nearest one to the ground. Halfway down, it bumped against another, and another, and soon we had a domino effect rumbling through the flat, sunlight strobing through thin sheets of paper as it all fell into a heap on the floor.

The Outsider was on the sofa. Reclining. Comfortable. A tray of uneaten food by his side. Head lolled back against the cushions, the very beginnings of a grin plastered on his face. By the time we reached him, both Bonnie and I knew he was dead.

There was a yellow receipt on his lap.

———

"We should go," I insisted. "He can't help us anymore."

Bonnie was shaking; anger, fear, I didn't know. "They killed him."

"Someone did," I agreed. "That's what they do. I've told you the stories, I've —"

"There's a receipt. They took something."

They did indeed. Despite his Outsider status, Asbury had obviously obtained a loan quite some time ago from a small supply house in St. Louis, an independent boutique which made, of all things, artificial gall bladders. A wholly useless organ, transplanted into individuals who want it only for the status, the artiforg gall bladder is the pinnacle of mechanical hubris.

"That's Asbury," Bonnie sniffed. "Always wanted to be on top."

His midsection was open, a flap of skin dangling down, intestines protruding slightly from the incision. A modicum of blood had seeped into the couch, but for the most part, I noticed that the gall bladder extraction had been done with expert, surgical precision. This was no hack job; it was Level Four, at least. Level Five, most likely.

My suspicions were confirmed a moment later. A very familiar signature rode the bottom of the receipt, scrawled

there in wide John Hancock letters, more of a message than
an autograph.

Jake Freivald had come for lunch.

———————

Bonnie has just woken up, asked for the time. I told her to
go back to sleep, that it was early yet, that she needed her
rest. She doesn't know that I'm going to turn myself in. She
doesn't know that I'll be dead long before she even knows
I'm gone. She doesn't know that when I kiss her on the lips
one hour from now, it will be the last time. I tell the truth,
but I don't need to divulge everything.

———————

We decided to pimp him out. Bonnie and I both wanted to
leave the apartment, knew we should get out of there, but
our fate was inexorably tangled up with Asbury's, and no
matter what had happened to him, we had to be privy to
it. Fortunately, his Ghost system was intact, modern, and
extensive; whatever experiences he'd had right before his
demise would have been fully recorded in this artificial
memory bank. The gleaming silver nodes sticking out of his
neck and skull were still in place, begging to be plugged in
and turned on.

"One sense at a time," I reminded Bonnie. "Which do
you want?"

"Audio," she said emphatically. "I don't want to see it."

I don't know if I expected Asbury to move as we approached him, wires in our hands, ready to invade what
used to be his brain, but he sat there motionless through
the procedure, never losing that embryonic grin. It took
me a few minutes to work back to my Ghost training
sessions, trying to remember which nodes attached to
which portions of the artificial brain. I didn't want to plug
the goggles into the taste center, or the headphones into the
eye socket; the day had been strange enough without me

trying to visualize the taste of radishes or Bonnie listening to the color red.

It was relatively simple to pop the contact lenses into my eyes this time around. I watched as Bonnie ripped the headset off its wire, pinned back a section of her ear, and plugged the frayed cord into her own input socket. We were attached, the three of us, an electric triumvirate waiting for show and tell.

It took a little digging with the scalpel, but I was able to find the Ghost system control box buried in a shallow groove beneath the Outsider's chin. There was no counter, no control code, but I figured that a quick rewind would get us to where we wanted to go. Grabbing Bonnie's hand in mine—"It's just like a movie," I told her. "Just like going to the pictures"—I found the replay switch and hit it hard.

———

A tray of food in front of me. Held in a pair of hands, also in front of me. The room telescoping past me, streaming by on all sides as Asbury walked to the sofa. I noticed that the Chinese paper screens were set up as they usually were, delineating workspace as opposed to the creepy corridor; that must have been done later.

Soon I was sitting on the sofa, prepping for the meal. The wall across the living room slid to one side, exposing an older television. It flipped on, the screen huge, curved at the edges, shows flipping by at incredible rates of speed.

"He's humming," Bonnie said, the voice seemingly coming out of the TV.

"Sitting down to eat," I relayed to her. "Nothing yet."

The food, lifted on a fork, headed for where the mouth would be. I marveled for a moment at how different Asbury's vision was from mine. He must have scored some high-definition eyeball artiforgs to go along with the

Ghost system, because every morsel of egg and toast was clear down to the crumbs, perfect resolution even at two, three feet.

"A noise," Bonnie told me. "There's a bump, a crash."

Concurrent with this, the picture swung rapidly to the left, and I staggered a bit, trying to keep my balance. It was like going to one of those full-body movies at the carnival, where they make you stand in the middle of the footage and see how long you can take it. The flat was empty, same as it was before, and so Asbury turned his attention back to the television.

For five minutes, we watched the tube, me and the dead Outsider, Bonnie keeping us updated on the audio portion of the program. I was reluctant to fast-forward the replay, worried that we'd miss something crucial.

"Another bump," Bonnie said suddenly, and the view twisted and spun as Asbury flipped to one side; I caught a glimpse of sofa, of his hands—my hands—pulling out a suitcase from beneath, popping open the latches, reaching for the pistol sandwiched inside, fingers about to grab metal—

And then stopping. The picture in front of me held still, Asbury's swarthy arms reaching out toward the gun, holding steadily in place. "What happened?" I asked, trying to feel Bonnie's hand in mine. "What's going on?"

"Click of a gun," she said morosely. "He's in the room."

———

Jake hadn't changed much since I'd seen him last. His stubble had given way to a scraggly beard, his wiry hair clipped hard against his head. A black leather jacket, similar to mine, covered the standard-issue black tank top, and the gun in his hand, holding Asbury in place, was the same he'd been using for years: .9 mm Mauser, the Bio-Repo man's favorite.

He started talking, his mouth moving at great speeds, and Bonnie, though quick to keep up with the audio, was still a few seconds late coming in with the dialogue. It was like watching a film that'd been knocked off track.

"He's talking about the gall bladder," she said, trying to keep pace. "He's saying that they know about his implant, and they know he stole the merchandise, and that the Union doesn't appreciate Outsiders."

"Give it to me like he's saying it," I suggested. "Word for word."

Bonnie tried, her Vocom Expressor dropping an octave as she spoke. "Now, there are situations in which we can be friends, ways we can be friendly about this. I'm not a monster, I'm not here to get you. Sit down. Back on the couch, like you were, sit down. Let's talk."

And Asbury's motions followed the orders. Worried about my balance, I took a seat on the sofa, as well, my leg brushing up against the dead Outsider's. The movie continued.

"I know you've been seeing some friends of mine," Jake was saying, his voice Bonnie's but the words all his. "One man, one woman. They were seen entering your building."

Silence, as Asbury spoke; though residual sound should clearly be picked up on any Ghost audio system, the device weeded out the client's own voice to avoid feedback loops. That rock-concert whine of a microphone and amp could permanently deafen if localized within the eardrum. But I could see hand gestures out of the corners of my eyes, and I knew that the Outsider was trying to talk his way out of it.

Jake cut him off. "I know you know where they are," he said. "And I've spent too much time and energy looking for them." Bonnie's voice cut out again as I watched Jake spin and walk to the far side of the room. He brought back a Union pack.

The lips moved again, Jake was talking, but Bonnie wasn't dictating. "What's he saying?" I asked. "What's he doing?"

I felt her presence next to me, and scootched over so she could join me on the couch. Jake was still standing over me—over Asbury—sharpening his scalpel, jabbering on and on.

"He's talking to you," she said. "He knows you're watching."

———

He wasn't, of course, but the assumption was not far off. The things Jake said to Asbury hit me closer to home much more, I'm sure, than they affected the Outsider. I held my breath, watched those lips, and listened to Bonnie channel my old friend:

"Can you see me? Can you? Are you listening?" He was leaning into Asbury's field of vision, Jake's face filling the room. I imagine that the Outsider had shut himself off in anticipation of what was to come. Turned out the lights. Jake knew the trick. "It's no use, my friend. I've had men pass out on me, rip out their own tongues, and I still got what I wanted. And you're next on the list."

The room was shaking, vibrating; Asbury must have been terrified. I watched as Jake knelt down next to the sofa, taking the Outsider's hand in his own, stroking it gently. "This is the man," he said, holding up my Credit Union mug shot, "and I'm sure you know the woman he's traveling with. He's an old friend of mine, and it's killing me to do this—but I don't have much of a choice. It's what I do. You understand that, right?

"The thing is, I want to apologize to him. That's all. An apology, and I'll be on my way."

Bonnie was silent for a moment, and Jake's lips stopped moving. Asbury must have been asking a question.

"Oh, I apologize when it's warranted," Jake said. "See, this friend of mine was a Bio-Repo man, one of the best, and I made a mistake. I tried to help him, tried to make him see what I could see—that he wasn't meant to be a regular Joe like everyone else. That he was repo, through and through. We're cogs in a machine, yeah, but we're the most important cogs there are. He wanted out, but I found a way to keep him in. At least, I thought I did.

"And I just want to say I'm sorry before I have to rip out his heart."

———

Watershed days in my life:

> When I realized that my parents probably had sex for
>   more than just procreation.
> When I saw that my own son was going to look like
>   me when he got older.
> When I decided I was in love with each of my wives.
> When I found out that each of my marriages had
>   come to a close.

And the new one, learned this afternoon from Jake Freivald's own lips:

> When it became clear to me that my best friend had
>   hacked my defib unit and set me up to die.

CHAPTER 20

It came in flashes, sudden bursts of realization entering my brain, like data downloading in huge, unwieldy chunks. He'd been trying to keep me from sales since Wendy brought up the idea, knew that I could make a go of it on the sales floor so long as I didn't have too many expenses. The only way to keep me around, keep me by his side and doing the things we'd done together for decades, was to get me in deep to the same system for which we worked.

Jake Freivald, witness to my weddings, godfather to my child, friend for life, might have tried to have me killed, but I can't knock the guy on his long-range planning.

———

They've called out two code blues here in the hospital during the last thirty minutes; it must be the right day to die. It's amazing to me how they announce it like that, blasting a cardiac arrest over the hospital loudspeaker. For all of their problems, hospitals have evolved over the rest of us to a point where they don't see death as something to be feared. With their amplified call of Code Blue, it's as much a part of everyday life as birthday announcements, bingo calls, and annoying Christmas music.

————

The contacts popped out of their own accord, falling to the stained carpet by my feet. The apartment swam back into focus, left much the same as it was when the Outsider's Ghost system got the signal from his dying brain to finish up with the recording process. Bonnie plucked the wire from her ear and sat next to me on the couch, hands curled around her head.

"We can't go back," I pointed out. "He'll be looking at the Gabelman."

"That's okay," she said, lifting her head and smoothing out the tears that had rained down those cheeks. The time for crying was over; Asbury was gone, and Bonnie was all business. "My husband's friends can still help us out if we need it. They've come through when I needed them to, doctors in the private sector who —"

I cut her off. "Wait. Wait." I didn't need an artiforg audio system to hear the elevator door pinging open, footsteps coming down the hall.

"A resident," said Bonnie. "There are fifty flats on this floor—"

Between the footsteps, the even clunk of heavy-soled shoes, there was a hum, steady and sure. A hum and a ping, to be precise, followed by a single, rumbling laugh that I'd known for years.

————

One morning when Peter was in his early teens and I was between my marriages to Carol and Wendy, Jake drove up to the house I was renting on the edge of town in a brand-new Italian convertible. We tumbled out of the house in our pajamas, gasping over the wheels and the engine and the sticker price. It was a two-seater, so I let Jake take Peter out for a spin around the block; he screeched out of the driveway and around the corner, and was back before I'd grabbed the morning paper from the front walk.

Later that afternoon, after Jake had taken his plaything to show off to others, Peter asked me why his godfather had a car like that, and his father didn't.

"Jake makes a lot of money," I explained.

"So do you," said my son. "You do the same job."

"That's true. We just have different ways of getting it done. I like to take my time."

"So is Uncle Jake better than you?" he asked.

And I gave it a moment's thought, despite my immediate inclination to laugh it off. I didn't want to lie to the boy; perhaps Jake was, indeed, a better repo man. Was he better with the gas? With the extractions? With the necessary weapons?

The answer I eventually gave Peter was, as far as I could tell, the correct one, and it's the same answer I'm holding out for today:

"No," I told him. "I'd say we're about equal."

————

We met in the hallway, just beyond Asbury's door. Jake was laughing, mid-chuckle when we appeared, and it took him a moment to sober up as Bonnie and I shuffled out of the apartment.

"Halfway there," Jake began, talking as if we were three friends casually meeting at a bar, "I realized you'd probably flown the coop already. The Outsider told me it had been three days, and I guess I figured . . . Hell, it doesn't matter. We're all here and cozy, now."

"You set me up," I said. It was all that would come out of my mouth. "You fucked with my defib unit."

Jake shrugged. "Had I known you were going to be such a pussy about the whole thing . . ."

"You tried to kill me."

"I tried to *save* you!" yelled Jake, taking a decisive step in our direction. "You're not a goddamned salesman, and you never were. You think that's living? You think that's life? That's the walking dead, brother, and I'm sorry it ended up like this, I really am, but you ain't much worse off now than you would have been then."

"How sweet of you," said Bonnie, her own anger rising. I wanted to shield her, to tell her to run and get out, block her exit with my body, but I knew she'd never go.

There was nowhere to run. It would be him or us, one way or the other. Jake said, "I wish you would have done a better job of running."

"That makes two of us," I replied.

Jake nodded and picked at his ear, pulling out a gob of wax. "So. I guess we should get this over with."

———

It should all be a blur, considering the speed at which everything happened, but I can pinpoint this afternoon's activities perfectly, close my eyes and see it go down, as if I were still plugged into the Outsider's brain, watching from afar:

Jake moved first, dropping to one knee as his right hand dove into his jacket. I was on the ground two tics later, hitting hard with my shoulder as my other arm flipped to the gun in my heel. I caught a glimpse of Bonnie diving to the side, impossibly fast, slamming into the door of a nearby apartment, breaking it in with incredible strength.

The first shot from Jake's Mauser zinged over my head, the bullet racing down the hallway and crashing through the window at the far end. By then, my finger was a rapid-fire blur, unleashing the clip in Jake's direction, plaster flying off the walls, shots lodging in the walls. I kept rolling as I fired, mindful of the trail of gunfire following me across the wide hallway.

We must have run out of ammo at the same time, because as Jake was reaching for his next pistol and I was reaching for my scalpel, Bonnie burst out of the apartment with my Taser in her hand, aiming to bring Jake down like she did Mary-Ellen. The prongs flew out of the base, trailing wire following behind, clipping him on the knee. His body buckled for a second, legs falling out beneath him, and I watched the look of surprise and anguish stretch his face into putty.

But the shot was slightly off-kilter, and the prongs, instead of digging in, bounced off Jake's leg, the electrical stimulation cut short. He staggered to his knees.

I was up, backing away, pulling Bonnie with me. We ran through the living room, put our heads down low, and crashed through the sliding-glass doors at the far end, aiming for the balcony beyond.

No fire escape. No ladder. The drop was fifteen stories down. Free fall. We'd never survive.

"That's breaking the rules," came a panting voice from behind us. We turned slowly to find Jake, two-fisting it, a .45 aimed at me, a .38 at Bonnie. "That Taser is Union property, and you're not licensed."

"It's honorary," said Bonnie. "I'm learning from the best."

"The fox isn't a hound," Jake replied, "no matter how much he hangs out in the backyard. Seeing as you've got no place to go, let me do my job correctly. I'll do you both at once, if you don't mind. Time crunch." He cleared his throat, making a big show of the cough, shaking his head, getting into character:

"You have both exceeded the time limits given to you in payment on your debts for artificial organs, loans which were granted with full faith and trust. Do either one of you have your payments in full?"

"Jake," I said, trying to stall, "let's figure something out."

"I'll take that as a no. Ma'am?"

Bonnie didn't even try. "No," she said, head high, keeping eye contact. "I do not." Out of the corner of my eye, I noticed her hand dropping slowly toward her hip; I hoped Jake did not.

"Excellent," he said. "Then it's my duty to let you know that once you are immobilized, I will begin the repossession procedure. If there are any questions or problems, your next of kin may call a toll-free number listed at the bottom of the receipt I will leave on your bodies.

"Good-bye, brother," Jake said. "It was a pretty fun ride, huh?"

———

The voice came from inside the apartment, from just behind Jake's back, loud and insistent. "What's going on in there?"

In that moment, three things happened: Jake whirled around. Bonnie went for his legs, I went for the arms. We all fell down in a six-legged heap.

Surprise was on our side, anger fueling the fire; within seconds, I had my hands around his head, smashing it into the ground to stun him as Bonnie bound his arms and legs with a few strands of artificial ligaments we found inside one of Asbury's miscellaneous boxes. At my urging, Bonnie dragged Jake's pack over to me, and we extracted a sizable can of ether from the depths. I shoved the tube into his mouth, keeping it there until the ether release had lulled him to sleep.

We sat on the floor, catching our breaths over Jake's unconscious form. "That voice," I said, "the one that turned him around . . ."

Bonnie grinned and pulled out the remote control for her Vocom Expressor; a yellow light flashed on and off. "Ventriloquism mode," she said, the sound popping out of the air behind my head. "Ten-thousand-dollar option, but I figured it might come in handy someday."

We didn't kill him. It would have been an option, to let the ether stream into his lungs, slowly choking off the oxygen until his brain collapsed from starvation, but neither Bonnie nor I was interested in such an ending. Those days were behind me; besides, it wouldn't help our situation. Another Bio-Repo man would be assigned to our cases in his stead, and this one might not give us the chance to get the drop on him. We left Jake tied up, certainly, and unconscious, but it wouldn't be long before he came back up and figured a way out of the bind.

And then he'd be looking for us again. That much was clear. It still is.

A friend of Bonnie's, more precisely, a friend of her ex-husband's, found this broom closet at his hospital for us, said it would provide a modicum of security while we figured out what to do next.

I've done that already. I have fifteen minutes left.

I have loved seven women. I could have loved more. I have loved some men. I could have loved more. I have watched my friends and my family die and be killed around me, watched their spirits shrivel into raisins because of my actions, watched them fall off the edge of their own psyches trying to save mine, and I have never done a thing to stop it, never helped bring them back to safety, never shed a tear.

I have been sacrificed for and sacrificed for and sacrificed for, and not once have I stepped under the hammer myself. And if it has taken me a lifetime of doing and a month of typing to learn one thing, it's that there's no hope for someone who doesn't even know what hope is.

When I called Jake two hours ago, he didn't care about my explanation. Didn't want to reopen old wounds or relive old memories. "If you're turning yourself in," he said, his voice still drugged, groggy from the ether, "then come down to the Union in two hours. I'll meet you at the Pink Door."

———————

The deal we made, the one he'll have ready for me in writing, is that if I willingly turn myself in, hand over my Jarvik–13 and relinquish all rights to the rest of my body, the Union will take Bonnie off the Hundred Most Wanted list. Despite the fact that she's still in possession of millions of dollars of Union-financed equipment, they want me more. I'm number twelve, she's number one, but because I was once on the team, I'm more of an embarrassment to management.

So that's the deal. I give it up, they give her up. They'll drop her into the regular pool of non-pays; hunted, certainly, but not with ferocity. It will give her extra time, years, perhaps, and hopefully a chance to get out of the country, out to that island we talked about, where they don't know from mechanical parts.

I will leave this manuscript behind, not so that Bonnie can know what I've done, but so that perhaps she can one day pass it on to Peter. I don't look for forgiveness; I don't deserve it. I don't look for understanding; there is none. But if these pages can help my son in any way, even if they teach him to run his life 180 degrees different from his pop, then I owe it to him not to burn these sheets.

Or scatter them if you want, Peter. Scatter them along with my ashes. Find me a place on the bad side of town, an empty lot, a darkened alley, an abandoned hotel. Find me a place and toss me around. Coat me good and hard on the walls. Let me hide out for all eternity. It will be good to know I'm safe, for once.

My watch says I'm right on time. The taxi I called should be waiting downstairs. Bonnie is sleeping next to me, curled up on the sterile hospital cot, her breath strong and even, her soft skin begging for my touch. I think I'll kiss her once, on the forehead, wrap my hand in hers for a heartbeat, and whisper good-bye.

A Lifetime Can Be Yours!

CHAPTER 21

They're letting me type again, which is good of them. The doctors have told me that I should remain lying down for most of the day, but during those periods when I feel well enough to sit upright, I can type for as long as I wish. Fortunately, I don't want to do much; just get this last little bit out.

It's been two months since the last time my fingers touched a keyboard, and even though the soft keyboard doesn't match the feel of the old Underwood, it feels good to be banging away again. My weapons are gone, sold for scrap, my canisters and my scalpel destroyed in the hospital trash rounds. So the typing is all I have left, really. It's what sustains me. That, and the crappy hospital food.

I went to kiss Bonnie good-bye. That was the plan, and that was what I did. I pulled the last sheet of my manuscript from the Underwood, placed it atop the others, and bound them with a rubber band inside a faded yellow file folder which I left in the middle of my cot. Knelt by Bonnie's side, watching her sleep, listening to her breathe, marveling at the steady, even tones of her artificial respiratory system.

I leaned in to give her that kiss, my lips touching the cool sweat beading on her forehead, and suddenly, I realized that my hands were caught, held. I looked down to find my arms in Bonnie's tight grasp, her eyes wide open, a soft smile on her face.

"This is for the best," she whispered to me, letting her lips come up to touch mine before retreating again. "You'll understand in time."

And that's when I felt the arms behind me, grabbing me, slipping the mask over my head, around my mouth, my struggling only bringing in deeper breaths, deeper gasps, sucking down the ether that I'd evaded for so long. The last time I saw Bonnie, she was fading into the darkness, disappearing behind a creeping black fog that spiraled in and finally obscured the only woman I loved who never divorced me.

I awoke in terrible pain, my chest burning from the inside, as if someone had replaced my heart with a pile of smoldering coals. Tried to lift my arms to check it out, to inspect, but I was too weak. Barely able to turn my head. Sitting up was not on the menu, either.

After a time, a doctor entered the room. Tall, assured. It was the surgeon who had found us the broom closet at the hospital, the friend of Bonnie's ex-husband, and he put a hand on my arm as I tried to speak.

"Shhh," he said. "It's better not to talk right now. You've been through a lot."

I wanted to ask what had happened, how it happened, where I was, when Bonnie was coming to see me, but the doctor had it all mapped out. He nodded as I tried to work the words out of my throat, nothing but gurgles emerging, and pulled a chair up beside my bed.

"I know you've got questions, and I'll do my best to

answer them," he said, and launched into a detailed explanation of what had happened.

But I'm too tired to give a blow-by-blow analysis, so I'll stick to the bottom line. It's sustained me in the past, and it will sustain me now.

Bonnie gave me her heart. Our jigsaw puzzle was complete.

She left me a note, a short message on one of my scraps of paper explaining everything and nothing all at the same time. I've got it tucked away in the folds of my hospital gown; I read it once every few hours.

I'm not going to reprint it here; it would be pointless to do so. But it explains why she instructed the doctors to take out her organic, perfectly beating heart and replace it with my Jarvik–13, why she chose to make herself completely biomechanical while leaving me fully natural.

And it didn't have anything to do with keeping me safe from the Union—though I am safe, now, according to official Union doctrine; they can't touch me any more, though I doubt they'll reinstate my pension—or with the fact that an extra artiforg in her own body is just one more legume in an artificial hill of beans. As I've said before, they can't leave you any more dead.

No, Bonnie said that her gift was all about proving me wrong.

People can change, she wrote, in part. *And people can sacrifice, even if they never have before. But they shouldn't have to. You, of all people, shouldn't have to.*

Jake came by the hospital to say hello. Pay his respects. I must have been sleeping when he came into the room, because when I awoke in the middle of a dream about a ladder climbing up a field of white irises, he was hovering over me, his soft grin inches from my face.

"Hey," he said, placing a bouquet of irises on my bedside table. The smell of them must have infected my dreams.

"Hey," I replied.

Jake took a look around the room. "Back in the hospital again. Getting to be a habit."

"Yeah. Hopefully, it's the last time."

"Sure."

He sat down on a chair next to my bed, and we didn't say much. The television in the corner was playing a repeat of an old, famous football game, and we watched the score rise to the numbers we knew it would eventually reach.

After about thirty minutes, a nurse came in to give me lunch, and as she bent over my table to adjust the height, Jake raised an eyebrow at me. Without another word, he took the plastic straw from my tray and loaded it with a saliva-soaked piece of napkin. As the nurse headed out of the room, he placed the straw in his mouth and blew hard, launching a spitball fifteen feet away. It landed in the nurse's hair and stuck there.

"Same old Jake," I said.

"Damn right."

I couldn't help but grin as I took the straw from his hands. "Double or nothing I make the next shot."

———

As for Bonnie, I don't know where she is. They won't tell me. They probably don't know, themselves. The doctors said she saw me through the operation, ensured that her organic heart wouldn't be rejected by my body, and, once her own short recovery time had been reached, checked herself out of the hospital and disappeared into the city streets.

I do know that the Underwood was missing from the broom closet, along with a ream of blank paper, and the thought of it is the only thing that makes me smile. Wherever she is, she's typing, taking up the recording duties where I left off. That's one manuscript I would love to read one day, preferably with the author by my side.

————

The night before I shipped off to San Diego for basic training, my father called me into his den and sat me down on the wide-backed chair. The party guests had all gone home for the evening; Sharon Cosgrove had rebuttoned her dress and kissed me good-ye. Mother was in the kitchen, washing dishes and cleaning up.

"Son," he said, "you're going to work in this life, and you're going to play. And when the last days come, you'll look back and find that that's all there was, an endless stream of days going back to today. But if you can find the thing you should be doing, the thing that makes you *you*, and if you can make that thing yours, then you've beaten the game. I haven't. Most men don't. You probably won't, either, but the point is to try, and to never give up, even when you think it's over. Do you get me, son?"

I said that I did. I said that I did and then I left and I didn't see him again until he was gone. But I didn't understand, not a wink.

Today, right now, I might. I know I haven't found that thing yet. I don't know if I ever will. But I'm young, in a relative sense. I'm young, and I've got my health.

Yet every once in a while, I miss the old ticking of my Jarvik–13, the feel of the remote welded onto my hip, the reassuring beeps that told me the device was still on top of its game. I miss the comforting assurances that high technology brought to the complex machinery of my body. It's a reassuring feeling to know that your involuntary processes are being taken care of by a force higher than yourself, by a time-tested technology honed to a fine art.

But it's even better to lie back in my hospital bed, place my hand over the long, wide scar rippling across my chest, and feel Bonnie thumping away in there, like she's just dropped by and is knocking on the door to say hello.

ACKNOWLEDGMENTS

I have come to accept, at the age of thirty-five, that I am a bit odd. I write stories about talking dinosaurs, OCD- afflicted con men, women who tie up men for their own edification, and artificial-organ repossessions. Strangely enough, I've still got a lot of friends and business associates who choose to speak with me on a regular basis. This is my chance to thank them for sticking around.

The Repossession Mambo, as a whole, wouldn't be what it is without my very good friend and co-screenwriter Garrett Lerner. Similarly, I don't know if or when this book would have made its way into your grubby little hands without the continual support of Miguel Sapochnik, our tireless and talented film director. I could go on about Garrett and Miguel—and I will, if you'll just flip ahead and check out the essay titled "The Taming of the Mambo" following these pages. Go on, we'll wait for you.

As always, eternal love and gratitude to my wife, Sabrina. We'll have been together for eighteen years and married for more than thirteen by the time this book comes out, and the sheer fact that she still thinks I'm funny proves we're meant to be together. I literally couldn't tie my shoes without her (especially on days when my back is acting up), and I honestly can't remember what life was like without her. In a good way.

One day, when they're much, much, *much* older, I'll let my amazing, beautiful, and currently innocent girls Bailey (age eight) and Chloe (age two) read this book. It's not that I'm worried they'll try and reenact any of the scenes within; I simply don't want to be responsible for any more years of future therapy than I already am. So far as they know, Daddy is the silly man who sings songs, tells stories, and loves them more than anything. They don't yet need to know he's also the guy who writes gleefully about liver extractions. Someone's bound to tell 'em soon enough. Playground chatter and all that.

Mad props to my parents, Manny and Judi, and I expect they're now running to the urban dictionary to find out what "mad props" means and learning that I'm at least five years behind the times in my slang. Their support has been constant since the very beginning of my career (and long before said career took off). If I could fault them for anything, it's for raising me in an overly functional manner; writers are supposed to be much more neurotic than I am. It's a bit of a problem. Perhaps I could be neurotic about my lack of neuroses. I'll have to look into that.

Thanks to my editor, Jennifer Brehl, who's clearly as weird as the rest of us for getting involved with this in the first place. When it came time to find someone who would understand the book as a *book*, and not just as an ancillary product to a film already in production, Jennifer was the one who stepped up and stood out. I'm honored to be working with her, and hope to do so again in the future.

Shout-out to all my agents at Endeavor—Brian Lipson (novel-to-film rights), Richard Abate (book),

Phil D'Amecourt (film), Becka Oliver (foreign), and Hugh Fitzpatrick (TV). A lot of agents, I know, but they're all wonderful, and they all work so nicely together. It's like a well-oiled machine wearing a very expensive suit.

Further on the film front, thanks to Valerie Dean, who had faith in the project when it was just a messy script making the rounds. She's got impeccable taste, and I know that when Val's interested in something, there's a damned good reason for it. Thanks to Scott Stuber, uber-producer of the film, who took a risk with an odd, odd project and shepherded it through the Byzantine processes of a giant corporate-owned studio, and to Jon Mone, our co-producer, who believed in the project from day one and was on set every day in Toronto, pinky-toe frostbite or no.

Finally, thanks to my other collaborators, close friends all, who have put up with my roller-coaster life during the *Mambo* craziness and understood while I put our joint projects on hold during this process. Dan Ewen, Brian Feinstein, Ian Goldberg, and Jordan Roter are all incredibly creative and talented people who keep me on my toes, and I can't wait to get back to work with all of them. Just give me another couple of months, guys, I swear . . .

AUTHOR'S NOTE
The Taming
of the Mambo

A film version of *The Repossession Mambo* was released under the title *Repo Men*.

This is the story of how *The Repossession Mambo* was wrangled from short story to novel to film and back to novel again over the course of approximately twelve years. It should be interesting to anyone curious about the adaptation process or looking to make a career in writing, and though it's short on tabloid-style gossip, I'll be sure to throw in a little Hollywood intrigue.

There are three main methods via which a book (or article or comic) is adapted into a motion picture, and I've now been involved in all three.

Method #1: Author writes a book, author sells a book to a publishing house, the book is published, the rights are optioned and/or purchased by a film company, a script is commissioned, a crew is hired, the film is produced, distributed, and everyone's happy, or sad, or litigious, but in any case, done. This is how it worked with my Rex series, a comedy/sci-fi series exploring the lives of dinosaurs hiding as humans in modern-day society. Turning it into a two-hour TV movie was a process that took approximately five years from publication of the first book to its eventual appearance on the SciFi Channel.

Method #2: Author writes a book, author sells a book to a publishing house, the manuscript is "leaked" to the film companies, who decide to option/purchase the rights before the book is even out, and the rest pretty much picks up right along with Method #1. The book usually comes out long before the movie does, because print production schedules, though lengthy, take a fraction of the time that it takes to get a film up and running. This is more or less how it worked with *Matchstick Men*, a book I wrote in 2000 about a con artist with obsessive-compulsive disorder. The book was published in 2002, and Warner Brothers released the feature film in 2003.

And then there's Method #3, which I shall describe, in excruciating detail, below. Method #3 is, as far as I'm aware, relatively rare, and my personal experience with it goes like so:

Sometime in 1997, while visiting my family in South Florida, I was driving along a street near my old high school and passed by a pawn shop I'd never noticed before. It must have been around Valentine's Day, because in the window was a big cartoon heart, poorly drawn in marker, and I found myself wondering: *Are they suggesting you pawn something you own to buy your sweetie a present for Valentine's Day, or are they actually looking to buy used hearts?* By the time I got back to my parents' house, I had an idea brewing.

The result, a thirteen-page short story called "The Telltale Pancreas," told the tale of an unnamed "bio-mechanical claims and collections" specialist who'd had an unfortunate accident with a defibrillator, received a new artificial heart that he couldn't pay for, and was now holed up in the basement of his house, waiting for his former employers to try and come take back what was fiscally theirs. Sound familiar?

Now, keep in mind that in 1997, I was twenty-five years old, relatively fresh out of college, and teaching SAT and GRE test-prep to supplement the income my wife, Sabrina, was making as an elementary-school teacher. I had written but not yet sold *Anonymous Rex*, and it's not like the short-story market was the booming, multibillion-dollar business that it is today. I didn't expect much out of my little yarn, and with low expectations come low results. (That's an important lesson to remember, kids.)

I do remember a few people being interested in the story, one of whom was Bob Kurtzman, a director, special-effects wizard, and friend who'd given me my first screenwriting gig ever. He felt like there was a potential film lurking in the tale, but I wasn't ready to let the story go just yet. I found that I wanted to know more about my main character, and about the world he lived in. It was one of those ideas that held on and wouldn't let go, and usually the only way to pry off the claws is to just write the damned thing. I decided to turn it into a book.

By this point, a year had passed, and in December 1998 (according to my computer) I started in on the novel. I'd recently sold *Anonymous Rex*, and I imagine that I was flush with dreams of literary stardom, anticipating that every word I'd write would receive accolades from critics and millions of sales orders from adoring fans.

It's good to be young.

I worked on the novel over the course of the next year or so, interrupted here and there by publicity duties for *Anonymous Rex* (published in the fall of 1999) and the beginnings of *Casual Rex*. *Mambo* wasn't the quickest book I've ever written, or the easiest. Its main difficulties, writing-wise, lay in the structure that I'd chosen for the piece. In order to portray a man whose job and worldview had taken away his ability to interact with and perceive humanity as anything other than a dysfunctional collection of its representative parts, I created a book that had a constantly looping internal structure and populated it with a bunch of characters who were independently related to the protagonist, like spokes of a wheel. Twenty years, five wives, ten soldiers, a score of co-workers, a hundred different clients, all in bits and bursts of sentences and paragraphs—not the most straightforward narrative.

Keep in mind, meanwhile, that the first draft of *The Repossession Mambo* was not the tome you now hold in your hands, but a rough-hewn ancestor, unruly and wild. Naturally, you'd think I'd dive into a rewrite and polish up those edges, *tout de suite*.

You'd think.

Instead, I did what I seem to do with certain books (and yet not with others)—I passed it around to friends. Surprisingly, few of them were frightened of me afterward, and most were excited by the potential. Special mention here to Brian Carter, who, over the last nine years or so, has never stopped asking me what's going on with "that organ book." Well, Brian, here it is. Ta da.

Then, a crucial turning point:

In May 2001, my daughter Bailey was a year old, and my wife did what many new mothers are conditioned to do: She joined a playgroup. It's a good way for babies to get a chance to meet (and pull and pinch and occasionally smile at) their peers, and for moms to speak to other adults once in a while. One of the babies in that group was an adorable little boy named Zeke, and his mom was a friendly blonde named Kim.

Kim and Sabrina became fast friends, and, as will happen, they wanted to force their husbands to get along so we could all hang out together. It helped that Kim's husband Garrett was a television writer, and we had all grown up within twenty miles of each other in South Florida, even though we now lived in California.

Garrett and I quickly formed a friendship. Though we had a lot in common, we never really talked about working together, mainly because I don't have the stamina to write for television, and Garrett didn't have a lot of interest in writing novels. What's more, Garrett already had a longtime writing partner, a good egg named Russel Friend, and that's not the kind of relationship you mess with lightly.

As will happen, I eventually forced *The Repossession Mambo* on Garrett, just to gauge his reaction and potentially alienate a newfound friend. Lo and behold, Garrett not only liked the book, but enjoyed it enough to suggest that we write a screenplay adaptation of it together.

Of course I'd considered the idea prior to this, but only in a far-off, one-of-these-days way. I'd never given thought to writing a script adaptation of one of my novels before even placing the book with a publisher. It simply wasn't done. But as soon as Garrett said it, it made sense. No reason I couldn't write the script at the same time as I was revising the book, right? As soon as Garrett ran it past Russel and got the okay—opening up their marriage, so to speak—we were off.

It was May 2002 when we began; Garrett was on hiatus from the TV season, and we worked diligently through the summer to wrestle the story lines in the book into something resembling a linear tale. We knew we'd need to give the main character a name, if only to be able to refer to him in the action of the script, and Garrett came up with Remy (ReMy—RM—Repo Man). We worked with note cards, a different color for each story thread, hopping back and forth in time and space, hoping that the visual nature of film would ground what was otherwise a tangled web of a narrative. Green note cards represented the main character's present story line; yellow note cards were his past, slowly coming up to meet the present halfway through the film. Purple cards were designated as "pops"—quick bits of introduction to help ground the viewer in the world we'd created. The walls of my office slowly but surely filled up with this shifting, multicolored pattern.

On July 29, 2002, we had a draft. That first screenplay, while a definite adaptation, more or less presented the story as it was in the book you just (presumably) read. It starred our Bio-Repo man, his five wives, a sixth love interest and partner-on-the-run named Bonnie, a lifelong best friend named Jake, and their employers, the Credit Union.

It began in a rotted-out hotel room, with Remy at a typewriter, pounding out his life story, and ended with him in a hospital room, finishing up his tale, Bonnie's heart beating away inside his chest. There were scenes of repossessions, of triumphs and arguments with his wives, of good times and bad times and scary times with Jake, and a lot of dark comedy that made Garrett and me laugh every time we read it. Many of those scenes would eventually make it into the shooting script and final film; many would not.

That fall, Garrett and I sent the script to our respective agents. We're each fortunate to be represented by some of the largest talent agencies in the world, with immeasurable contacts in the industry. Naturally, we were excited when our script went out to select producers, and—

Crickets.

It was too strange. Too dark. Not action-y enough. Not for kids. Not for adults. Too expensive. Not big enough. Name the reason, and we had a pass for it. This is generally par for the course in Hollywood—there's way too much product for too few buyers, and the law of supply and demand holds true everywhere—but doubly so for a script that actively tries to flaunt the rules. Our hero killed five "innocent" people within the first ten pages (and they said it like that was a *bad* thing).

Yet there was one lone voice of encouragement, calling out to us in the wilderness: Valerie Dean.

Valerie is a producer with fantastic taste, who's got a knack for tearing off messy wrapping paper to uncover the perfect present within. She's also got a wickedly dark sense of humor, which matched the *Mambo* sensibility perfectly. Over the course of the next half-decade, we'd find similar folk who would immediately spark to the script and invariably they'd be people we'd end up liking quite a bit. There's a definite type that finds this sort of thing entertaining, I guess, and I'm proud to count many of them among my friends.

Val loved the script, and really seemed to get what we were going for. If anything, her suggestions were to make the script even darker in tone, and I couldn't argue with that. My trusty computer lists 10 different drafts between April of 2003 and February of 2004, as Garrett and I refined the script based on our own ideas and excellent notes from Valerie.

At least two of the wives disappeared during this phase, a necessary cutback to allow us more time with the central characters. Furthermore, Val had the inspired idea to fuse the Bonnie character with the Beth character, allowing Remy not only to find love in the middle of the chase, but to re-find it, as well. We adjusted the ending to make it bigger in scale and concept, introducing the idea that there might be a way for Remy to free not only himself from the clutches of the Credit Union, but others, too.

The script, no doubt about it, was getting better.

Things move very slowly in Hollywood, and just when you think they can't get any slower—boom—they all but moonwalk backward. But every once in a while, there's a small shift that indicates progress. Just as we'd found Valerie a year or so before, we soon came upon the next piece of the puzzle.

Through Val, we were introduced to a young film director named Miguel Sapochnik. A British Argentinian—or is it Argentinian Brit? I still don't know—he'd directed some music videos and commercials, but had really hit the mark with a short film called *The Dreamer*, which I'd recommend to anyone interested in cinema. (Notice how I used the word 'cinema' to make it sound all fancy? Hell, it's just a great short film.)

As soon as Garrett and I saw *The Dreamer*, which is a visual mix of Ridley Scott, Terry Gilliam, and Stanley Kubrick (I know, big shoes), we knew Miguel would be a perfect fit for *Mambo*. Meeting Miguel in person only cemented our feelings; his wit was dry, he was incredibly easy to get along with, and, as we'd soon learn, he had a nonstop motor.

Miguel had only one concern: The ending. It was a bit too pat, a bit too easy, and didn't follow through on the promise of the first two acts. Fortunately, it didn't take long before we all figured out exactly what we wanted to do: a finish to the film that truly reflected the themes we'd worked so hard to infuse throughout the movie, and one that seemed to actually follow, logically, from the story that was already there. We went through a process of honing the screenplay even further.

More wives got lost along the way, and suddenly our main character was down from five wives plus a current love interest to two wives total. Peter was introduced as a character in his own right, rather than just someone who got mentioned here and there. Sergeant Tyrell Ignakowski disappeared, reappeared for a brief but glorious moment, then disappeared again. The war scenes got trimmed back; war training got lost entirely. In a screenplay, space is limited. You've got 120 pages, max, to tell your story, translated to 120 minutes up on that screen. Each moment so precious and difficult to pull off it costs hundreds of thousands of dollars—if not millions—to create. Every scene, every action, every bit of dialogue, has to drive the story either through narrative, character, or theme, or it goes bye-bye. There's no space for fun but nonessential flourishes.

We lost scenes that I loved, but created more that I loved just as intensely. *The Repossession Mambo*, the film, was becoming quite different from *The Repossession Mambo*, the novel, yet still somehow retained the same feel, tone, and story. It's what I imagine might happen if you were to clone someone at birth and raise the original and the clone in different households—their core makeups would be the same, but no doubt the environments would play a huge factor in the people they'd eventually become, and when they'd meet at the family reunion BBQ, they'd remark on how their hair and teeth and smile were the same, but one loves potato salad and it makes the other want to hurl. And so forth. We'd created both Mambo versions with the same DNA, but cultured one in a petri dish of words and the other in a petri dish of images. Neither was superior or inferior to the other; they were simply different creatures of the same lineage.

On November 7, 2004, we had a draft that we all adored. From that point on, everything should be smooth sailing, right? Great script, great director, what could possibly get in our way?

Lots and lots of nothing. Okay, perhaps it's not fair to say "nothing," because we had a fair number of nibbles along the way. Overtures from one company, "firm" commitments from another. We always believed that *Mambo* would find its best traction with an independent film company, one will-

·ing to put up a small-to-medium budget. Such companies are, theoretically, usually more willing to take chances with material than are the studios, yet as a result of said chances, most indies don't have the funds or power to throw around, so things tend to take even longer. I started to believe that I'd be well into my sixties by the time the film ever got made.

Another year and a half went by, during which time Miguel was a tireless advocate for the movie. He went to more *Mambo* meetings than I've had hot meals, and each one looked promising before it, too, fell apart.

By this time, I'd already written and published *Hot & Sweaty Rex*; written, published, and seen the film version of *Matchstick Men*; written and published *Cassandra French's Finishing School for Boys*. It wasn't looking good.

Hey, that's okay, I figured. I'd been meaning to get back to the book, anyway. . .

Then we got lucky.

Hollywood studios release about 150 movies a year, in aggregate. For every film that gets released, there are at least twenty-five in "development," most of which will never see the glow of a projector. Much of the time, scripts languish not for lack of creativity—the writers and producers who put them together are talented people who, Hollywood tales of debauchery aside, work hard and believe deeply in their stories. Yet there are only so many release dates to go around, and only so much money that a studio, even a giant conglomerate, is willing to shell out. They want assurances that audiences will come to see the film, and there's one sure-fire way to convince them of that:

If a movie star is willing to "attach" himself to the project, to essentially promise that he'll act in it, then it gives the script a major boost in the eyes of the studio. Most films these days are set up only once they've got at least one attachment, and very few films, if any, are given the green light to start production unless the primary acting corps is in place.

In mid-2006, Jude Law read the *Mambo* script, and loved it. Even better, he loved the character of Remy, and wanted to play the part. I'm not going to start name-dropping (even though I just did), but I can't say enough about Jude. He's not only a fantastic, committed actor, but he has a knowledge and passion for the character that really helped to shape who Remy was and how he functioned in the world we created. Jude's notes were on target, throughout the process. He's bright, literate, and, okay, ridiculously handsome, and if he weren't so damned nice I'd have to hate him just for that.

Now things really got moving. By the end of 2006, we'd hooked up with Scott Stuber, a producer who'd only recently given up running Universal and had a deal at the studio to produce films for them. At first blush, we were concerned that a place like Universal, home to blockbusters and broad comedies, might not be interested or the right place for our movie, but after conversations with Scott and our awesome executive, Jeff Kirschenbaum, we came to believe that they had the same vision for the movie that we did.

So: More revisions were suggested, and more revisions were implemented. Everything started to move quickly as the film began to come together. As we were rewriting throughout the first half of 2007, Miguel was meeting with actors and actresses to play the other parts, even before we'd officially made a deal with Universal. Word was out: We were going to make a movie.

Of course, there were still some minor things to settle, like filling out the cast, finding a location to shoot, hiring a giant crew, and getting the studio to sign off. Fortunately, all Garrett and I had to worry about was making the script the best it could be.

Finally, in late spring 2007, we made the deal and began working throughout the summer on further rewrites as we geared up for an October 2007 beginning of production. Soon, Forest Whitaker signed on to play Jake, Remy's best friend and partner, and Liev Schreiber took the role of Frank. We couldn't have asked for a stronger cast, or better actors to bring these characters to life. Remy, Jake, Frank— the people who'd lived inside my head for a decade—were finally becoming flesh and blood.

On October 15, 2007, we went before the cameras in Toronto, Canada, and with that, *The Repossession Mambo* was officially in production. I won't bore you (much further) with the details, but from the day we finished the very first adaptation of *The Repossession Mambo* in summer 2002 to the day we finally began production, more than five years later, we'd written thirty-nine drafts. It had been seven years since I began the book, and nearly ten years since I wrote the short story. By the time you're reading this in 2009, a full twelve years will have passed from inception to distribution.

An overnight sensation!

The upswing in the project's film fortunes got me excited once again about the novel, and in early 2007, I dove into my own rewrite, tackling the book even as I worked on the screenplay.

Look, I love writing scripts. It's fun, it's a challenge, and I am, quite simply, a fan of the medium. I've spent many a wonderful hour in a darkened theater, and I can rant and rave about my favorites along with the geekiest film buff out there.

There's something about writing prose, though, about really digging into the characters and story, shaping it in the manner that I want to shape it, that brings me unparalleled joy. Revising *The Repossession Mambo,* the novel, was like

Dorothy returning to Kansas. I'd seen all my friends over there in Oz, and had a great time, but still and all, there's no place like home.

So I kept the unruly structure, the five wives, the soldiers, the clients, the bits and bursts and all of that, but now with nearly seven years of distance, I was able to find the parts that weren't working and either make them sing or cut them completely. I was able to see what had been missing before and find a way to fill in the gaps. Soon we sold it to William Morrow, and I got to work with my fantastic editor, Jennifer Brehl, in continuing to refine the story, world, and characters.

In short, it became the book I wanted, the way I wanted it. As a novelist, I couldn't ask for more.

As I write this in the summer of 2008, *The Repossession Mambo*, as a novel, is finished, edited, and more or less out of my hands. *The Repossession Mambo*, the film, is still in post-production, but every cut I've seen indicates that we've made a movie that I'd adore even if I'd had nothing to do with it.

If there's a take-away lesson for other writers (and there's always a take-away lesson), it's simply this: Write the things you want to write. If they're weird or strange or don't fit into some mold that the rest of the world seems to conform to, don't stress over it. Don't change what you're doing one iota, so long as you still believe in it. That sounds all hippie-dippie and Up-with-People, I know, but I strongly believe that if I'm not absolutely in love with what I'm writing, then all I'm doing is typing. And there are lots of people out there who type a hell of a lot better than I do.